RIDGECREST BRANCH LIBRARY
131 E. LAS FLORES AVE.
RIDGECREST, CA 93555

FROM THE PAGES OF *WARD NO. 6 AND OTHER STORIES*

The storm still raged without. Something wailed in the stove, in the chimney, outside the walls, and it seemed to Savély that the wailing was within him, in his ears. This evening had completely confirmed him in his suspicions about his wife. (from "The Witch," page 22)

"Faith is a faculty of the spirit. It is just the same as a talent, one must be born with it." (from "On the Road," page 47)

"There are ever so many more good people than bad in this world." (from "On the Road," page 53)

A heavy nightmarish lethargy gradually gained possession of him and fettered his limbs. (from "Typhus," page 94)

"Things happen so queerly in this world that it is simply laughable and nothing else." (from "The Pipe," page 101)

"A person who does not feel the difference between a human being and a lap-dog ought not to go in for philanthropy." (from "The Princess," page 116)

"Starving oneself is no help in sorrow." (from "Neighbours," page 124)

She did not think now of the moonlight evening on the Volga, nor the words of love, nor their poetical life in the peasant's hut. She thought only that from an idle whim, from self-indulgence, she had sullied herself all over from head to foot in something filthy, sticky, which one could never wash off.

(from "T

"Even in Siberia there is happiness." (from "In Exile," page 171)

"Superstition and all the nastiness and abominations of daily life were necessary, since in process of time they worked out to something sensible, just as manure turns into black earth. There was nothing on earth so good that it had not something nasty about its first origin." (from "Ward No. 6," page 189)

"So long as prisons and madhouses exist someone must be shut up in them." (from "Ward No. 6," page 201)

"A man's peace and contentment do not lie outside a man, but in himself." (from "Ward No. 6," page 205)

Why did people in general hinder each other from living? What losses were due to it! What terrible losses! If it were not for hatred and malice people would get immense benefit from one another.
(from "Rothschild's Fiddle," page 240)

"A change in life for the better, and being well-fed and idle develop in a Russian the most insolent self-conceit."
(from "Gooseberries," page 279)

"The happy man only feels at ease because the unhappy bear their burdens in silence, and without that silence happiness would be impossible." (from "Gooseberries," page 281)

He always seemed to women different from what he was, and they loved in him not himself, but the man created by their imagination, whom they had been eagerly seeking all their lives; and afterwards, when they noticed their mistake, they loved him all the same. And not one of them had been happy with him.
(from "The Lady with the Dog," page 301)

WARD NO. 6 AND OTHER STORIES

ANTON CHEKHOV

With an Introduction and Notes by David Plante

Translated by Constance Garnett

George Stade
Consulting Editorial Director

BARNES & NOBLE CLASSICS
NEW YORK

BARNES & NOBLE CLASSICS

NEW YORK

Published by Barnes & Noble Books
122 Fifth Avenue
New York, NY 10011

www.barnesandnoble.com/classics

Footnotes created with the help of notes by Ronald Hingley in *Stories,* by Anton Chekhov, 9 vols., translated and edited by Ronald Hingley, London: Oxford University Press, 1975, and *The Penguin Encyclopedia of Places,* New York: Viking Press, 1971.

Introduction, Notes, and For Further Reading
Copyright © 2003 by David Plante.

Constance Garnett's translations of Chekhov's stories were first published by Chatto & Windus in thirteen volumes, between 1916 and 1922.

Note on Anton Chekhov, The World of Anton Chekhov, Inspired by Anton Chekhov, and Comments & Questions
Copyright © 2003 by Barnes & Noble, Inc.

All rights reserved. No part of this publication may be reproduced or transmitted in any form or by any means, electronic or mechanical, including photocopy, recording, or any information storage and retrieval system, without the prior written permission of the publisher.

Barnes & Noble Classics and the Barnes & Noble Classics colophon are trademarks of Barnes & Noble, Inc.

Ward No. 6 and Other Stories
ISBN 1-59308-003-4
LC Control Number 2003102750

Produced and published in conjunction with:
Fine Creative Media, Inc.
322 Eighth Avenue
New York, NY 10001

Michael J. Fine, President and Publisher

Printed in the United States of America

QM

5 7 9 10 8 6 4

ANTON CHEKHOV

Anton Pavlovich Chekhov was born, the third of six children, on January 17, 1860, in the Russian port town of Taganrog. His parents earned a modest living from a shop and sent their children to the state school. Construction of a house plunged his father into debt, and he was declared bankrupt and was forced to relocate to Moscow, where his two oldest sons were at the University. The rest of the family, except for Anton, joined them some months later. At age sixteen, Anton was left to complete his schooling in Taganrog, where he supported himself as a tutor.

After receiving his diploma, Chekhov joined his family in Moscow and began his study of medicine at the University. Using the alias Antosha Chekhonte, he wrote humorous sketches and tales for various weekly journals in Moscow and St. Petersburg to help support his family and fund his education. The turning point in his literary career came in 1886 when the important literary figure D. V. Grigorovich wrote to him, urging him to turn his talents to more serious writing. The young writer took this advice to heart.

Chekhov once said that while medicine was his "lawful wife," literature was his "mistress." During his writing career of more than twenty years, he alternated between creating short stories and plays. Although he made his mark as a playwright, Chekhov was more prolific as a writer of prose. His stories and sketches focus on the interior lives of his characters in a style characterized by a deft use of objective detail. A hallmark of his stories is that they accurately portray the characters' experience without the intrusion of preaching or explicit judgments from the author. Chekhov's stories are subtle and achieve their effect through oblique revelations and understated climaxes.

When early theatrical productions of his plays were unsuccessful, Chekhov vowed to give up dramatic writing. However, his reputation as a playwright began to build when Konstantin Stanislavski's productions of *The Seagull* and *Uncle Vanya* earned great acclaim at the Moscow Art Theatre. Despite the popular and critical success of his plays, Chekhov disagreed with Stanislavski's approach of understating the comedic elements and emphasizing the tragedy in his plays.

Chekhov stood aside from the violent and angry literary temper of his time. His good humor and his gentle, ineffectual aristocratic characters stand in contrast to the charged ambience of, for example, Dostoyevsky's novels. However, Chekhov's subtlety of style did not mean that he lacked personal conviction: He renounced his membership in the Academy of Sciences over its exclusion of Maxim Gorki because of the czar's disapproval of Gorki's political stance.

In 1902 the tuberculosis that had plagued Chekhov since his youth worsened dramatically. After overseeing preparations for the production of his new play *The Cherry Orchard,* he went to a spa in Germany to try to regain his health, but after suffering two heart attacks, he died on July 2, 1904.

TABLE OF CONTENTS

The World of Anton Chekhov ix

Introduction by David Plante xiii

WARD NO. 6 AND OTHER STORIES 1

Inspired by Chekhov's Stories 359

Comments & Questions 361

For Further Reading 369

THE WORLD OF ANTON CHEKHOV

1854 Pavel Egorovich Chekhov and Evgenia Jacovlevna marry. Pavel is the son of a serf who bought his family's freedom before the emancipation of the Russian serfs, which Czar Alexander II would grant in 1861.

1855–1863 The Chekhov children are born—from oldest to youngest: Alexander, Nikolai, Anton, Ivan, Maria, and Michael—in Taganrog, a Russian seaport on the Sea of Azov, a northern arm of the Black Sea. Anton Pavlovich is born on January 17, 1860.

1870–1873 Anton's father, Pavel, opens a store that his three oldest sons manage. Anton attends the Taganrog State School, where he meets F. P. Pokrovsky, a religion instructor. Seeing Anton's potential, Pokrovsky encourages him to read Molière, Jonathan Swift, and the Russian satirist M. Y. Saltykov, and gives him the nickname Antosha Chekhonte, which Chekhov would use to sign his early published writings. Anton attends his first theatrical performance, Jacques Offenbach's operetta *La Belle Helene.* Chekhov and a schoolmate put together a homemade theater, where Anton stages his first dramatic sketches and plays.

1874 The Chekhovs move into a house built by Pavel, who spends the family's entire assets on the construction. In June Anton contracts his first serious illness, acute peritonitis, and is sick for a long time.

1876–1879 Unable to repay money he had borrowed to help build the family house, Pavel is declared bankrupt, and the house is repossessed. Threatened with imprisonment for debt, Pavel moves to Moscow, where Alexander and Nikolai are studying; some months later, his wife joins him with the younger children. Anton remains alone in Taganrog; he is given a bed in his former home in exchange for tutoring the landlord's nephew for military school entrance exams. Anton supports himself by tutoring other pupils as well and spends his free time reading at the municipal library. He occasionally visits his family in Moscow.

1879 After receiving his diploma in the fall, Anton joins his family in Moscow and enrolls at the University to study medicine. To support his family and pay his educational expenses, he begins to contribute humorous sketches and tales to minor magazines under the pen name Antosha Chekhonte.

1880 His first published story, "Letter of a Landowner in the Don District to His Learned Neighbor," appears in *The Dragonfly,* a weekly humor magazine published in St. Petersburg.

1882 Chekhov contributes short stories regularly to *Fragments,* a St. Petersburg humor journal.

1884 In June he completes his medical studies and begins his practice. He funds the publication of his first short-story collection in Moscow. His health begins to deteriorate; between 1884 and 1889 he has several hemorrhages.

1886 Impressed by "A. Chekhonte's" stories in the *St. Petersburg Gazette,* the important literary figure D. V. Grigorovich writes Chekhov asking him to forego journalism in order to devote himself to the production of "excellent, really artistic" works of literature; the letter marks a turning point in the writer's career; Chekhov states that the letter "left a profound impression on my soul" and that he "shall still have time to achieve something." He starts to write more serious stories that reflect the interior lives of his characters; his style becomes characterized by a deft use of objective detail and an accurate portrayal of experience rendered without judgment.

The Chekhov family moves to Kudrino, a remote suburb of Moscow, where Anton spends the four most peaceful years of his life. A second, larger collection of his short stories, *Motley Stories,* is published. Chekhov befriends Alexis Suvorin, an outcast from St. Petersburg literary circles because of his conservatism and anti-Semitism, who invites Chekhov to contribute to his journal *New Times.* The two men continue an intellectual friendship until 1898.

1887 Chekhov's first play, *Ivanov,* is a critical success. His story collection *In the Twilight* is published.

1888 His collection *Stories* is published; it includes "The Steppe," a nostalgic "poem in prose," which earns him the prestigious Pushkin Prize.

1889 Chekhov's second play, *The Wood Demon,* opens but is not successful; it will later serve as the basis for his play *Uncle Vanya.* Chekhov's favorite brother, Nikolai, an aspiring painter, dies of tuberculosis at age thirty-one.

1890 Chekhov travels across Siberia to visit the penal colony on Sakhalin Island and writes a report, *The Island of Sakhalin,* which will be published in installments in 1893 and 1894.

1892 In order to be closer to nature and improve his health, Chekhov moves to an estate in rural Melikhovo, outside Moscow.

1894 The Moscow education department appoints Chekhov administrator of the primary schools at Talezh, a village near Melikhovo; two years later, Chekhov personally will fund the construction of a new school.

1895 Chekhov writes *The Seagull.*

1896 *The Seagull* opens at the Alexandrinski Theatre in St. Petersburg but survives only five performances; discouraged, Chekhov vows never to write another play.

1897 Chekhov is put in charge of the first national census for the Melikhov district. He lives among peasants and gains an understanding of their social conditions. He suffers another serious hemorrhage; while he is hospitalized, the great Russian writer Leo Tolstoy pays him a visit.

1898 Chekhov donates an inscribed copy of Tolstoy's *The Power of Darkness* to the Taganrog library, of which he is curator. Over the next few years, he gives the library a large number of books, including 319 volumes of French classic literature. He befriends Vladimir Nemirovich-Danchenko and Konstantin Stanislavski, who founded the Moscow Art Theatre in 1895. Stanislavski directs a new production of a revised version of *The Seagull,* which opens to great success. However, Chekhov is dissatisfied with what he sees as the director's misinterpretation of his play.

1899 *Uncle Vanya* opens at the Moscow Art Theatre and receives accolades.

1900 Chekhov begins to write *The Three Sisters.* He is elected to the Academy of Sciences.

1901 *The Three Sisters* is produced to poor reviews. Chekhov marries Olga Knipper, an actress with the Moscow Art Theatre. He writes his last play, *The Cherry Orchard.*

1902 Chekhov resigns from the Academy of Sciences when it expels his pupil Maxim Gorki because the czar disapproves of Gorki's political ideas.

1903 Despite his losing battle with tuberculosis, Chekhov visits Moscow to supervise the production of his new play.

1904 In January *The Cherry Orchard* is produced at the Moscow Art Theatre and is an immediate success. In May Chekhov travels to a spa at Badenweiler, Germany. Though his health seems to improve, in late June he suffers two heart attacks. On July 2 Anton Chekhov dies.

1954 In *The Unknown Chekhov* Avrahm Yarmolinsky publishes several obscure works by Chekhov.

1998 Thirty-eight stories by Chekhov previously unavailable in English are published in *The Undiscovered Chekhov,* translated by Peter Constantine.

INTRODUCTION

"Has it ever happened to you to experience a feeling as though some unseen force were drawing you out longer and longer? You are drawn out and turn into the finest wire. Subjectively this finds expression in a curious voluptuous feeling which is impossible to compare with anything."

—Chekhov, from "A Woman's Kingdom"

In an interesting turnabout, Chekhov's publisher, Alexis Suvorin, sent the fiction he himself wrote to Chekhov for criticism. Chekhov was always stone-cold honest, and in his comments to Suvorin about his work he revealed fundamentals of his own work. In an 1888 letter, he admonished his publisher: ". . . you confuse two things: *solving a problem and stating a problem correctly.* It is only the second that is obligatory for the artist" (*Letters on the Short Story, the Drama, and Other Literary Topics by Anton Chekhov,* edited by Louis S. Friedland, p. 60; see "For Further Reading").

In Chekhov's writing, everything, absolutely everything, is seen as a problem that has no solution; everything, absolutely everything, is questioned by why? why? why? though no answer to the question is ever proposed. In his story "Rothschild's Fiddle" (1894), the all-pervasive questions are asked: "Why was it a man could not live so as to avoid . . . losses and misfortunes? One wondered why they had cut down the birch copse and the pine forest. . . . Why do people always do what isn't needful? Why had Yakov all his life scolded, bellowed, shaken his fists, ill-treated his wife, and, one might ask, what necessity was there for him to frighten and insult the Jew that day? Why did people in general hinder each other from living?" (p. 240). At times in his stories, the unanswerable questions seem to be asked with the perplexed wonder of a child, as in "The Darling" (1898): "One sees a bottle . . . , or the rain, or a peasant driving his cart, but what the bottle is for, or the rain, or the peasant, and what is the meaning of it, one can't say" (p. 255). And from a short story called

"Terror" (1892): "We Russians of the educated class have a partiality for those questions that remain unanswered."

Chekhov denied there was anything of himself in his work. He wrote to Suvorin: "When I offer you a professor's ideas, trust me, and do not search in them for Chekhov's ideas. . . . For me as a writer all these ideas are, in themselves, of no value. . . . One must regard them as material things, as symptoms, entirely from an objective standpoint, trying not to agree or disagree with them" (*Letters on the Short Story,* p. 17). I take Chekhov at his word about his ideas, but I'm sure that his life occurs in his fiction, for it often happens that his characters describe their lives in ways that are clearly parallel to Chekhov's own. So, in his long story "Three Years," he has the main character, Laptev, say to his wife:

> "You're surprised that such a stalwart, broad-shouldered father should have such stunted, narrow-chested sons as Fyodor and me. Yes; but it's easy to explain! . . . Fyodor and I were begotten and born after mother had been worn out by terror. I can remember my father correcting me—or, to speak plainly, beating me—before I was five years old. He used to thrash me with a birch, pull my ears, hit me on the head, and every morning when I woke up my first thought was whether he would beat me that day. Play and childish mischief was forbidden us. We had to go to morning service and to early mass. When we met priests or monks we had to kiss their hands; at home we had to sing hymns. Here you are religious and love all that, but I'm afraid of religion, and when I pass a church I remember my childhood, and am overcome with horror. I was taken to the warehouse as soon as I was eight years old. I worked like a working boy, and it was bad for my health, for I used to be beaten there every day" (*The Tales of Chekhov,* Vol. 1, translated by Constance Garnett, p. 229).

Turn that warehouse into the shop his father owned, and you have a pretty accurate account of the youth of Anton. His father, Pavel, brought up his family of four sons and a daughter very strictly, with daily beatings and in the fear of God. The boys were obliged to observe all the fasts and attend long church services, during which they were made to sing. Anton often said to friends, "I had no childhood" (*The Life and Letters of Anton Chekhov,* edited by S. S. Koteliansky and Philip Tomlinson, p. 2).

In the story "Three Years" Laptev says to his brother Fyodor: "The landowners beat our grandfather and every low little government clerk punched him in the face. Our grandfather thrashed our father, and our father thrashed us." In fact, Anton's grandfather Egor was a serf who bought his own and his family's freedom in 1841. Anton's father Pavel Egorovich was sixteen. With the same ruthless willfulness as his father, he managed to open a grocery in the town of Taganrog on the Sea of Azov and rise into a class above his by marrying the daughter of a cloth merchant.

Later in the story "Three Years," Laptev asks a friend, Yartsev, if he loves life, and when Yartsev answers he does, Laptev says:

> "Do you know, I can never understand myself about that. I'm always in a gloomy mood or else indifferent. I'm timid, without self-confidence; I have a cowardly conscience; I never can adapt myself to life, or become its master. Some people talk nonsense or cheat, and even so enjoy life, while I consciously do good, and feel nothing but uneasiness or complete indifference. I explain all that . . . by my being a slave, the grandson of a serf" (*The Tales of Chekhov,* Vol. 1, p. 286).

Anton Pavlovich Chekhov was born in 1860, and from his earliest childhood his father was, I believe, the greatest influence on him as a man and as a writer. As brutal as his father was, he was not stupid, and he insisted on the education of his children, assuming as a matter of course that his sons would somehow go on to university. And, dogmatic in his religious beliefs, he had a substantial collection of religious books that indicate his faith was informed by study. But Pavel Egorovich had bad luck. Circumstances beyond his control—a newly built railroad shifted the entire economy of the town to his drastic disadvantage—led to his having to close the grocery shop and to his escaping to Moscow, where his two elder sons were already studying, to avoid debtors' prison. There, he was only able to find work as a clerk in a warehouse (how interesting that Laptev in "Three Years" remembers working in a warehouse!), and his will was broken. It was at this point that his son Anton took over the responsibility of the family.

Anton was sixteen, the same age as his father when he was freed from being a serf. Still a student in Tanganrog, he sold family furniture to pay for the fare of his mother and a younger brother and sister to Moscow, and, though not a very brilliant student himself, he tutored other students to earn money to send to his family. He seemed, too, to take on the moral as well as the financial guidance of his family.

From Taganrog, he wrote to his younger brother Mishka, rather condescendingly: "You write well, and in the whole letter I have not found a single mistake in spelling," then, with moral authority, he lectured: "But there is one thing I do not like: why do you call yourself 'your worthless and insignificant brother?' . . . Recognize it before God; perhaps, too, in the presence of beauty, wisdom, nature, but not before men. Among men you must be conscious of your dignity and worth" (*Letters on the Short Story,* p. 291).

Later, when he was himself living with his family in Moscow in a half basement apartment and attending the faculty of medicine at the University, he continued to help support the family: He added to the insufficient earnings of his father by writing what he called "stories, tales, vaudevilles, any sort of rubbish" (*Life and Letters,* p. 4) for periodicals. He had been introduced to editors by his older brother Alexander, who himself wrote for the periodicals, but Alexander and the next older brother Nikolai, a painter, had already taken to the drink that destroyed them.

If, in becoming the financial and moral force of the family, Anton had taken on the tenacity of his father's will, he also became essentially different from him—in reaction, I'm tempted to say, to free himself from his father's dogmatic will. Anton had developed into a light-spirited, witty fellow who amused others with "all sorts of pranks and inventions" (*Life and Letters,* p. 3); he had become liberal; and he no longer believed in the religion that had been inculcated in him. And, unlike his father, Anton never imposed his will on anyone.

In a sense, his was a negative will, for, absolute as it was, it kept him from imposing himself not only on others but on the characters of his fiction—he refused, in the name of what he believed to be absolute freedom from tyranny, to judge. He was as strict as his father was, though not in insisting on a dominating ideology; on the contrary, he insisted on freedom from any such ideology.

When in 1888 he admitted in a letter to Suvorin that he had been hemorrhaging from his lungs, he would not admit he had tuberculosis. (I believe that his hard life in Taganrog, where he often walked from student to student in the freezing snow with leaking galoshes, to support the family his father could not, resulted in his fatal illness.) It was as though, experienced doctor that he now was, he wanted to remain detached from—even indifferent to—the disease as an answer to the question of why he was so ill, or, even more generally, why he should have to die. The question why should one die has absolutely no answer.

He became, with his stories and his plays, famous, though never rich. Already in the advanced stages of tuberculosis, in 1899 he and the actress Olga Knipper became lovers, though he was very often separated from her, as he was then living in the warm climate of Yalta for his health and she acting in Moscow. His Russian writer-friend Evgenii Zamyatin wrote of him: "Acquaintances he had many, but friends, friends he would let into his soul, he had none" (*Life and Letters,* p. 15). This might be said, too, about his relationship with Olga Knipper, whom he married but to whom he wrote letters that for their very charm hide, as Zamyatin wrote, "assiduously everything that agitated him profoundly." He died at the age of forty-four, in 1904, at a German spa, where he had gone with Olga for an attempted cure. Because he hid so much—because, as Zamyatin speculated, of "a sort of chastity within"—it is "difficult to establish the time of his inner development, the biography of his spirit."

In his youth, as a writer of little more than light-spirited, comic anecdotes, based on types derived in large part from Nikolay Gogol and written for money, Chekhov seemed genuinely surprised when a letter to him came from the most established of Russian writers at the time, D. V. Grigorovich, admonishing him: "Respect your talent, for it is a rare gift; . . . save your impressions for careful, thoughtful work, not written at one sitting . . . you will at once attract the attention of responsive souls, and before long of the entire reading public" (*Letters on the Short Story,* p. 70). Chekhov, twenty-six years of age, wrote back: "If I have a gift that ought to be respected, then I confess before the purity of your heart that hitherto I have not respected it. I feel that I possess it, but I am accustomed to consider it insignificant. . . . Hitherto, my attitude toward my literary work was sufficiently light-minded, negligent, superficial. I can recall but a single story on which I worked more than a day; and 'Iegor,' which you liked, was written in a bath house! . . . All my hope is in the future" (*Letters on the Short Story*, pp. 56–57).

In this future, Chekhov gave in to the "gloomy moods" Laptev in "Three Years" reproaches himself for, as the stories become increasingly dark and, in the end, are expressions of stark, startling, and, in their way, deeply stirring tragedy. Why this happened can only be explained by that hidden biography of Chekhov's spirit.

And it is only our speculation about Chekhov's spirit or, perhaps, his personal disposition, that places him in the great tradition of modernist writers. Some of his early stories were influenced not only by Gogol but by Guy de Maupassant, who himself was influenced by Gustave Flaubert, the writer who made it the most outspoken and uncompromising condition of his art that the artist must never express his or her opinions or even ideas in his work (what Chekhov called "subjective" writing), but must remain outside the world he or she creates and simply describe it, as objectively and as vividly as possible. This is in fact the very condition that was adhered to by Henry James, Joseph Conrad, James Joyce, Katherine Mansfield, Ernest Hemingway, Eudora Welty—right down to Raymond Carver. In a letter to his brother Alexander, Anton was severe: "To describe . . . you need . . . to free yourself from the personal expression. . . . Subjectivity is a terrible thing" (*Letters on the Short Story*, p. 69). Again, in a letter to Suvorin that restates his belief that fiction does not offer answers: "It seems to me that the writer of fiction should not try to solve such questions as those of God, pessimism, etc. His business is but to describe those who have been speaking or thinking about God and pessimism, how, and under what circumstances. The artist should be, not the judge of his characters and their conversations, but only an unbiased witness" (*Letters on the Short Story*, p. 58). And in a letter to a woman who had sent him one of her stories to criticize, he wrote: "When you depict sad or unlucky people, and want to touch the reader's heart, try to be cold—it gives their grief as it were a background against which it stands out in greater relief. As it is, your heroes weep and you sigh. Yes, you must be cold" (*Letters on the Short Story*, p. 97).

Chekhov was for this very reason criticized for not taking on moral or social or religious responsibility. Even his publisher Suvorin evidently accused him, for he defended himself by replying, "You abuse me for objectivity, calling it indifference to good and evil, lack of ideals and ideas, and so on" (*Letters on the Short Story*, p. 64). In fact, Chekhov's acts of generosity—his devotion to his patients, from whom he rarely took any money; his offering his services as a medical doctor for free during an epidemic; his building schools for the children of peasants; and not least his going a long way across Russia to the penal island of Sakhalin to write a report of the living conditions of the prisoners and their families there—were greater than any other writer I can think of, as stressed as he always was about money. He seemed to be as detached from these acts of generosity *as* acts of moral value as he seemed to be detached from any stated or even stateable moral value in his writing.

Of course, when he felt he must take a stand against injustice, which he loathed, he did. He rebuked his publisher when Suvorin, anti-Semitic, took the side of the French anti-Dreyfusades, Chekhov seeing that Alfred Dreyfus had obviously been falsely accused. He resigned his membership in the Russian Academy when Gorky's election to the Academy was annulled for ideological reasons. And at a time when the weekend entertainment of men in every provincial town was to go to the red light district, he even wrote a story, "A Nervous Breakdown" (1889), about a student who has a breakdown after visiting a house of prostitution and seeing how badly the women are treated, a story, he described in a letter to Suvorin as speaking "at length about prostitution" but settling "nothing." This disclaimer seems meant to restate his principle of making no judgments in his fiction, but I see the principle as disingenuous, for in the same letter he asks Suvorin, "Why do they write nothing about prostitution in your paper? It is the most fearful evil, you know. Our Sobolev street is a regular slave-market" (*Letters on the Short Story*, pp. 27–28). And yet, some time later, he wrote to a friend who disapproved of the same street, "I love people who go there, although I go as rarely as you do. One mustn't disdain life" (Donald Rayfield,

Anton Chekhov: A Life, p. 181). Chekhov, I believe, would have disapproved of any attempt to justify his contradictions, but this approval of Sobolev Street *may* have been in reaction to his friend's righteous moral stand, for Chekhov hated any *talk* about morality—whether sexual, political, or spiritual—as if any individual expression of it could only be foolish. In his memoir of Chekhov, Maxim Gorky recounts a visit to him by a number of ladies who put questions to him about the war between the Turks and the Greeks and which side he likes, to which he answers, with a meek smile, "I love candied fruit . . . don't you?" (Maxim Gorky, Alexander Kuprin, and I. A. Bunin, *Reminiscences of Anton Chekhov,* p. 11).

But the more one reads Chekhov's letters and stories and, as it were, crosses over from one to the other, the more disingenuous some of his disclaimers seem. The most obvious is his insistence that a work of fiction have no obvious moral, but his short story "The Bet" (1889) has an embarrassingly obvious moral. It is about a man who bets with a millionaire that he will be able to live totally isolated from the world for ten years as long as he has all the books he wants, but he gives up the money owed him by the now impoverished millionaire by walking out of his isolation just short of the ten years because of the wisdom he has gained from the books. The story seems to have been inspired by Tolstoy's "How Much Land Does a Man Need?" (1886). It is a good idea to keep in mind that Chekhov did contradict himself, for contradiction—or his reaction to unresolvable contradiction—is, I believe, an essential impulse to his writing.

Chekhov wrote to his friend Pleshcheyev what he wanted to do in his writing:

> My goal is to kill two birds with one stone: to paint life in its true aspects, and to show how far this life falls short of the ideal life. I don't know what this ideal life is, just as it is unknown to all of us. We all know what a dishonest deed is, but who has looked upon the face of honor? I shall keep to the truth nearest my heart and which has been tested by men stronger and wiser than I am. The truth is the absolute freedom of man, freedom from oppression, from prejudices, ignorance, passions, etc. (*Letters on the Short Story,* p. 15).

And later in that same year he wrote, as if to define his morality as forcefully for himself as for Pleshcheyev:

> I am afraid of those who look for a tendency between the lines, and who are determined to regard me either as a liberal or as a conservative. I am not a liberal, not a conservative, not a believer in gradual progress, not a monk, not an indifferentist. I should like to be a free artist and nothing more, and I regret that God has not given me the power to be one. I hate lying and violence in all their forms. . . . Pharisaism, stupidity, and despotism reign not in merchants' houses and prisons alone. I see them in science, in literature, in the younger generation. . . . That is why I have no preference either for gendarmes, or for butchers, or for scientists, or for writers, or for the younger generation. I regard trade-marks and labels as a superstition. My holy of holies is the human body, health, intelligence, talent, inspiration, love, and the most absolute freedom—freedom from violence and lying, whatever forms they may take. This is the program I would follow if I were a great artist (*Letters on the Short Story,* p. 63).

Surely, the awareness of his father is somewhere behind this.

He would object to any critic making limiting statements about his work, and he would be right. Knowing this, I will take the great risk and say observations can be made about Chekhov's work as a whole so long as they go deeper than that he was a liberal or a conservative, etc.; observations that not only allow him his total freedom, but are a result—the highest moral, even spiritual, result—of freedom from all lower levels of the moral and spiritual, freedom not only from any belief but from any sensibility that can be stated.

Those "stories, tales, vaudevilles, any sort of rubbish" he wrote for money and signed with pseudonyms—for the most part A. Chekhonte, a nickname from when he was a school boy—would not be given the attention they are now if Chekhov had not gone on to write the great later stories he acknowledged by using his own name. And yet, even when he was writing quickly for rubles in the way he informed Grigorovich he did, he was, as he also informed the older, famous writer, aware of something to which he might eventually devote himself. "I tried by all means not to lavish on the stories those images and pictures that were dear to me, and which, God knows why, I was treasuring and carefully hiding" (*Letters on the Short Story,* p. 56). In a letter to his publisher, Suvorin, he lamented: "Literary society, students, . . . young ladies, etc., were enthusiastic in their praise of my 'Nervous Breakdown,' but Grigorovich is the only one who has noticed the description of the first snow" (*Letters on the Short Story,* p. 61). And again to Suvorin he reiterated the importance he gave to the image: "What do I call good? The images which seem best to me, which I love and jealously guard lest I spend and spoil them for the sake of some [story] written against time" (*Letters on the Short Story,* p. 16). There is a paucity of such images in the early stories, but from time to time an image will flash and reveal a dimension beyond the flatness, however incidental—and perhaps even because incidental—this detailed image is. So, in a story called "Mutual Superiority" (1884)—which is little more than an idea of a newly married man who worries that his relatives are far below the social standing of his wife's but who finds that her relatives, though titled, are poorer than his—the husband is in one small moment made vividly individual with just this: "Screwing up his eyes and wheezing so that it could be heard all over the house, he was taking orange peel out of the vodka decanter with a piece of wire." Such details—as unexpected as they are vivid—occur to greater and greater effect in later stories, though they by no means dominate. In those early stories, types, rather like received ideas taken in large part from Gogol and Maupassant—petty functionaries, pretentious bourgeois, hypocritical officials, adulterous husbands caught by their wives—can suddenly come alive in a detail. An image from the story "A Marriageable Girl" (1903) is as evocative as it is simple: "On the table, next to a cold samovar, lay a broken plate and a sheet of dark paper."

> These images flash with what? Not with ideas, if one takes as an "idea" a concept or a proposition as basic as: All men are mortal. Chekhov might have asked: Why are all men mortal? The question explodes the idea, and "Why?" becomes a state of—sometimes anguish-making, sometimes marvelous-wonder. In Chekhov's works, the wonder is most effectively concentrated in sights, smells,

> sounds, tastes, the sense of touch, all in their most amazing—and yet their most commonplace—particularity. How does he do this?

There is in Russian a word for it: *ostranenie.* This means: *making it strange.* Thomas Winner, in his book *Chekhov and His Prose,* describes this effect as "a peculiar semantic shift which transfers a depicted object to a different plane of reality. The habitual is 'made strange' by a distortion causing the perceiver to see the object in a fresh light, as though for the first time" (p. 26). So, the image of the samovar on the table is made strange by (a) its being cold, (b) the plate being cracked, and (c) the sheet of paper being dark, for what writing would show up on a dark sheet of paper? Thomas Winner points to the story "Grisha" (1886), included in this collection, as an outstanding example of making the familiar strange. Though this idea was proposed after Chekhov's death by Russian formalists, the fact is that the very subject of "Grisha" can be read as the awakening of a boy's consciousness to the strangeness of the commonplace, which so upsets him his mother has to give him castor oil.

The strange and the commonplace in one! Isn't that a contradiction? Yes, and this is one example of the contradiction at the very center of Chekhov's accomplishment.

There are other elements in the early stories that are developed in the later and become uniquely Chekhovian. To continue with images, which were so important to Chekhov: He will break the narrative with an apparently incongruous image, revealing by doing so a world beyond the immediate world he is describing. Here is a sound described in the story "Happiness" (1887): "A sound suddenly broke on the still air, and floated in all directions over the steppe. . . . 'It's a bucket broken away at the pits,' said the young shepherd after a moment's thought." This sound also appears in "A Marriageable Girl" and then, most famously, in the play *The Cherry Orchard* (1904), when a picnic is interrupted by this sound, which seems to resonate from an altogether other and perhaps unknowable world.

Also, Chekhov's early stories often have endings that in his later stories become so associated with him that any writer trying to do the same would immediately be thought to be derivative. The early story "Anyuta" (1886) ends with an incongruous interjection similar to those images that occur within his narratives; but coming at the end of a story that it has nothing at all to do with, the effect is to open up the story to an entirely other world that takes over the world in which the story occurs, so the events of the story become incidental to the larger, outside world. In "Anyuta," the last line is someone entirely outside the story shouting to someone else outside the story, "Griogry! The samovar!"

There is a more extended use of endings found in the lesser stories that is entirely Chekhov's at his most mature. These endings, usually a paragraph long, state the final realization of one of the main characters. The story "A Misfortune" (1885) ends with: "She was breathless, hot with shame, did not feel her legs under her, but what drove her on was stronger than shame, reason, or fear." This realization implies a continuation that is greater, more complex than the story itself, as occurs in the famous last lines of "The Lady with the Dog" (1899): "And it seemed as though in a little while the solution would be found, and then a new and splendid life would begin; and it was clear to both of them that they had still a long, long way to go, and that the most complicated and difficult part of it was only just beginning."

If Chekhov denied that he was expressing any of his own ideas in his stories, he gives his characters, from some of the early stories, ideas enough to disgust them, for very often they turn on their own or others' ideas with: "Damn all this philosophy" ("A Happy Man," 1886). And as his characters do, so does Chekhov. In a letter to Suvorin: "The devil take the philosophy of the great ones of this world! All the great sages are as despotic as generals, and as ignorant and as indelicate as generals, because they feel secure" (*Letters on the Short Story*, p. 207). The fact is, his characters are (as I believe Chekhov was) obsessed with general ideas, possessed (as Chekhov was) by them, but they (unlike Chekhov) are capable of summing up their entire lives, at the end of a story, in a generalization that seems to be a summation of their fate. The end of "Neighbours" (1892) is not untypical:

> From Koltovitch's copse and garden there came a strong fragrant scent of lilies of the valley and honey-laden flowers. Pyotr Mihalitch rode along the bank of the pond and looked mournfully into the

> water. And thinking about his life, he came to the conclusion he had never said or acted upon what he really thought, and other people had repaid him in the same way. And so the whole of life seemed to him as dark as this water in which the night sky was reflected and water-weeds grew in a tangle. And it seemed to him that nothing could ever set it right (p. 139).

Ideas are often of the essence to the conflict in the stories, Chekhov assigning conflicting ideas to two conflicting characters, as in "Ward No. 6" (1892). He engages his characters in arguments about the individual and society, about morality and immorality, art and the realities of life, the possibility of change and the impossibility of change. Of course ideas are a deep preoccupation of Chekhov's characters; their ideas, however, finally cannot be made to hold together as a coherent philosophy. In the very dramatizing of the ideas, the ideas are destroyed by the contradictions the characters are helpless to resolve among themselves. (It could be said that it was because Chekhov was aware that a coherent view of the world was impossible that he himself abandoned any attempt at one, and, unable to see the world under the aspect of a generalization, saw it in its particulars, and therefore his attention to the most vivid—and in their vividness the strangest—details.)

But there is something in the stories far beyond ideas, something that survives the destruction of all ideas by contradiction—some "awareness" that cannot be contradicted because it rises so above any idea at all. In an attempt to identify it, this "awareness" is sometimes seen by critics as a Chekhovian "mood." As though to give the "mood" an image that was itself as evocative as one that Chekhov himself might have used, the subtitle to an early collection in Russian edited by Nina Toumanova was *The Voice of Twilight Russia,* a title the critic Rufus W. Mathewson (Afterword, "Ward Six and Other Stories," translated by Ann Dunnigan) condemns for being sentimental and not accounting for the "tough and skeptical, even ruthless" sensibility Chekhov reveals in his work. That he must be read "as a poet of murder and terror whose vision of the pain of existence is heightened by the controlled understanding voice in which he tells it" is vitally true, but Mathewson may not have known that Chekhov himself called his second collection of stories

In the Twilight (1887), indicating, I think, that he too was aware of something in his work that has the effect of a "mood."

It is interesting to note, to add to the evidence of Chekhov's own sense of something going on in his work that is greater than what can be stated, a posthumously published fragment called "A Letter," written a year before he died, in which a critic of literature confesses: "I'm no artist: . . . it's only words, not images and moods, which engross my mind" (Chekhov, *Stories,* vol. 9, p. 259). The critic makes a distinction between "words," which try to explain, and "images and moods," which don't. "Mood," evoked by the most vivid and at the same time most incidental of images, may be a poor word to attempt to account for the *something* that is so powerfully present in Chekhov's stories, but it has its reasons, seen by Chekhov himself.

Another revealing fragment of 1903, posthumously published, is "Poor Compensation," in which the main character, after leaving, with loathing for it, the final religious service at the bedside of a dying friend, goes to the train station to be among a crowd, and there: "He wanted to glimpse a different world, to be caught up in something unconnected with himself" (*Stories,* vol. 9, p. 259).*

It is, perhaps, a presumption to extrapolate from a fragment, but this one merely centers what I believe to be of the essence of the "mood" that dominates Chekhov's work, and that is a great, unrealizable longing impelling the cry "Why? why?" while the one crying out knows that there are no answers. Chekhov might have said this longing was what made a Russian Russian (his grand subject is Russia—Russia and Little Russia, or the Ukraine—with which he identified himself totally, so that when he did, rarely, place scenes outside Russia, they are not convincing). He had suffered the forced inculcation of religion as a boy by his father, and I sense he suffered this inculcation all the more when religion ceased to answer his

*I'm reminded of Dr. Dorn, in Chekhov's play *The Seagull* (1898), talking about a trip he took to Italy, where, in Genoa, he found the life in the streets wonderful. "You wander aimlessly zigzagging about among the crowd, backwards and forwards; you live with it, are psychologically at one with it and begin almost to believe that a world soul is really possible" (Constance Garnett, *The Cherry Orchard and Other Plays,* p. 214).

questions. Not in fragments, but throughout his work, Chekhov is engaged with a God he does not believe in.

Chekhov freed himself of the intellectual and emotional constrains imposed by ideas, and especially by dogma, by questioning everything, but the longing for something greater (to some critics, a longing for death, though he has the main character of "Gooseberries" [1898] exclaim, ". . . one wants to live!") is expressed, not by him, but by his characters.

In the distance Chekhov kept from his characters, he seemed to take no responsibility for their lives even when they suffer unbearably. (I find "In the Ravine" [1900] a story of unbearable suffering.) He wrote to an admirer: "You complain that my heroes are gloomy,—alas! that's not my fault. This happens apart from my will" (*Letters on the Short Story,* p. 65). It is as though Chekhov allowed his characters the greatest possible freedom to be themselves, even especially when they despair. But it was in the distance he kept that there occurs the something other that makes the stories, even "In the Ravine," transcend a stark account of the deepest suffering and fills them with what I can only call universal compassion. And Chekhov allows that something other to occur of itself, beyond his intentions. It is as though in writing his clearly delineated stories, Chekhov's only intention was to create a space in which something happens that he did not make happen, something he in himself was indifferent toward, but in which he nevertheless knew was the highest meaning his stories could possibly have.

The longing for something that can only ever be longed for is the tragic force of Chekhov's work. It is also the work's moral and spiritual force. To repeat his own hope as a writer: "My goal is to kill two birds with one stone: to paint life in its true aspects, and to show how far this life falls short of the ideal life. I don't know what this ideal life is, just as it is unknown to all of us. We all know what a dishonest deed is, but who has looked upon the face of honor?" No one, especially an ardent Russian Orthodox believer, would ever presume to be able to look upon the face of God, who is utterly unknowable. And yet, the longing to be united with God, beyond understanding, must awaken the vastest possible awareness, itself beyond understanding. In Chekhov, that vast awareness is inspired by such incidentals as a cold samovar and a cracked plate and a sheet of dark paper, of a twanging guitar string, of a lark singing in a dark bush ("The Kiss"; 1887), of a slice of watermelon ("The Lady with the Dog"), of a coat with bright buttons ("Grisha"). Not that, in a story by Chekhov, the reader is left contemplating the infinite. That vast awareness becomes the high overview from which the world is seen with profound compassion for being a finite world suffering through its contradictions. That vast awareness is holy.

David Plante is Professor of Writing at Columbia University. He is the author of many novels; they include *The Ghost of Henry James, The Family* (nominated for the National Book Award), *The Woods, The Country, The Foreigner, The Native, The Accident, Annunciation,* and *The Age of Terror.* He has been a contributor to *The New Yorker, Esquire,* and *Vogue,* and a reviewer and features writer for the *New York Times Book Review.* He is a recipient of awards from the American Academy and Institute of Arts and Letters, The Guggenheim Foundation, and a British Arts Council Bursary. He has been writer in residence at the Gorki Institute of Literature in Moscow, l'Universite de Quebec a Montreal, King's College, Cambridge, the University of Tulsa Oklahoma, and the University of East Anglia in England. He has recently been elected a Fellow of the Royal Society of Literature in England. He makes his home in both New York and London.

WARD NO. 6
AND OTHER STORIES

CONTENTS

The Cook's Wedding (1885) 5

The Witch (1886) 11

A Dead Body (1886) 23

Easter Eve (1886) 29

On the Road (1886) 41

The Dependents (1886) 59

Grisha (1886) 67

The Kiss (1887) 71

Typhus (1887) 91

The Pipe (1887) 99

The Princess (1889) 109

Neighbours (1892) 121

The Grasshopper (1892) 141

In Exile (1892) 167

Ward No. 6 (1892) 177

Rothschild's Fiddle (1894) 233

The Student (1894) 243

The Darling (1898) 247

A Doctor's Visit (1898) 261

Gooseberries (1898) 273

The Lady with the Dog (1899) 285

In the Ravine (1900) 303

The Bishop (1902) 343

THE COOK'S WEDDING

Grisha, a fat, solemn little person of seven, was standing by the kitchen door listening and peeping through the keyhole. In the kitchen something extraordinary, and in his opinion never seen before, was taking place. A big, thick-set, red-haired peasant, with a beard, and a drop of perspiration on his nose, wearing a cabman's full coat, was sitting at the kitchen table on which they chopped the meat and sliced the onions. He was balancing a saucer on the five fingers of his right hand and drinking tea out of it, and crunching sugar so loudly that it sent a shiver down Grisha's back. Aksinya Stepanovna, the old nurse, was sitting on the dirty stool facing him, and she, too, was drinking tea. Her face was grave, though at the same time it beamed with a kind of triumph. Pelageya, the cook, was busy at the stove, and was apparently trying to hide her face. And on her face Grisha saw a regular illumination: it was burning and shifting through every shade of colour, beginning with a crimson purple and ending with a deathly white. She was continually catching hold of knives, forks, bits of wood, and rags with trembling hands, moving, grumbling to herself, making a clatter, but in reality doing nothing. She did not once glance at the table at which they were drinking tea, and to the questions put to her by the nurse she gave jerky, sullen answers without turning her face.

"Help yourself, Danilo Semyonitch," the nurse urged him hospitably. "Why do you keep on with tea and nothing but tea? You should have a drop of vodka!"

And nurse put before the visitor a bottle of vodka and a wineglass, while her face wore a very wily expression.

"I never touch it. . . . No . . ." said the cabman, declining. "Don't press me, Aksinya Stepanovna."

"What a man! . . . A cabman and not drink! . . . A bachelor can't get on without drinking. Help yourself!"

The cabman looked askance at the bottle, then at nurse's wily face, and his own face assumed an expression no less cunning, as much as to say, "You won't catch me, you old witch!"

"I don't drink; please excuse me. Such a weakness does not do in our calling. A man who works at a trade may drink, for he sits at home, but we cabmen are always in view of the public. Aren't we? If one goes into a pothouse one finds one's horse gone; if one takes a drop too much it is worse still; before you know where you are you will fall asleep or slip off the box. That's where it is."

"And how much do you make a day, Danilo Semyonitch?"

"That's according. One day you will have a fare for three roubles, and another day you will come back to the yard without a farthing. The days are very different. Nowadays our business is no good. There are lots and lots of cabmen as you know, hay is dear, and folks are paltry nowadays and always contriving to go by tram. And yet, thank God, I have nothing to complain of. I have plenty to eat and good clothes to wear, and . . . we could even provide well for another . . ." (the cabman stole a glance at Pelageya) "if it were to their liking. . . ."

Grisha did not hear what was said further. His mamma came to the door and sent him to the nursery to learn his lessons.

"Go and learn your lesson. It's not your business to listen here!"

When Grisha reached the nursery, he put "My Own Book" in front of him, but he did not get on with his reading. All that he had just seen and heard aroused a multitude of questions in his mind.

"The cook's going to be married," he thought. "Strange—I don't understand what people get married for. Mamma was married to papa, Cousin Verotchka to Pavel Andreyitch. But one might be married to papa and Pavel Andreyitch after all: they have gold watch-chains and nice suits, their boots are always polished; but to marry that dreadful cabman with a red nose and felt boots. . . . Fi! And why is it nurse wants poor Pelageya to be married?"

When the visitor had gone out of the kitchen, Pelageya appeared and began clearing away. Her agitation still persisted. Her face was red and looked scared. She scarcely touched the floor with the broom, and swept every corner five times over. She lingered for a long time in the room where mamma was sitting. She was evidently oppressed by her isolation, and she was longing to express herself, to share her impressions with some one, to open her heart.

"He's gone," she muttered, seeing that mamma would not begin the conversation.

"One can see he is a good man," said mamma, not taking her eyes off her sewing. "Sober and steady."

"I declare I won't marry him, mistress!" Pelageya cried suddenly, flushing crimson. "I declare I won't!"

"Don't be silly; you are not a child. It's a serious step; you must think it over thoroughly, it's no use talking nonsense. Do you like him?"

"What an idea mistress!" cried Pelageya, abashed. "They say such things that . . . my goodness. . . ."

"She should say she doesn't like him!" thought Grisha.

"What an affected creature you are. . . . Do you like him?"

"But he is old, mistress!"

"Think of something else," nurse flew out at her from the next room. "He has not reached his fortieth year; and what do you want a young man for? Handsome is as handsome does. . . . Marry him and that's all about it!"

"I swear I won't," squealed Pelageya.

"You are talking nonsense. What sort of rascal do you want? Anyone else would have bowed down to his feet, and you declare you won't marry him. You want to be always winking at the postmen and tutors. That tutor that used to come to Grishenka, mistress . . . she was never tired of making eyes at him. O—o, the shameless hussy!"

"Have you seen this Danilo before?" mamma asked Pelageya.

"How could I have seen him? I set eyes on him to-day for the first time. Aksinya picked him up and brought him along . . . the accursed devil. . . . And where has he come from for my undoing!"

At dinner, when Pelageya was handing the dishes, everyone looked into her face and teased her about the cabman. She turned fearfully red, and went off into a forced giggle.

"It must be shameful to get married," thought Grisha. "Terribly shameful."

All the dishes were too salty, and blood oozed from the half-raw chickens, and, to cap it all, plates and knives kept dropping out of Pelageya's hands during dinner, as though from a shelf that had given way; but no one said a word of blame to her, as they all understood the state of her feelings. Only once papa flicked his table-napkin angrily and said to mamma:

"What do you want to be getting them all married for? What business is it of yours? Let them get married of themselves if they want to."

After dinner, neighbouring cooks and maidservants kept flitting into the kitchen, and there was the sound of whispering till late evening. How they had scented out the matchmaking, God knows. When Grisha woke in the night he heard his nurse and the cook whispering together in the nursery. Nurse was talking persuasively, while the cook alternately sobbed and giggled. When he fell asleep after this, Grisha dreamed of Pelageya being carried off by Tchernomor and a witch.

Next day there was a calm. The life of the kitchen went on its accustomed way as though the cabman did not exist. Only from time to time nurse put on her new shawl, assumed a solemn and austere air, and went off somewhere for an hour or two, obviously to conduct negotiations. . . . Pelageya did not see the cabman, and when his name was mentioned she flushed up and cried:

"May he be thrice damned! As though I should be thinking of him! Tfoo!"

In the evening mamma went into the kitchen, while nurse and Pelageya were zealously mincing something, and said:

"You can marry him, of course—that's your business—but I must tell you, Pelageya, that he cannot live here. . . . You know I don't like to have anyone sitting in the kitchen. Mind now, remember. . . . And I can't let you sleep out."

"Goodness knows! What an idea, mistress!" shrieked the cook. "Why do you keep throwing him up at me? Plague take him! He's a regular curse, confound him! . . ."

Glancing one Sunday morning into the kitchen, Grisha was struck dumb with amazement. The kitchen was crammed full of people. Here were cooks from the whole courtyard, the porter, two policemen, a non-commissioned officer with good-conduct stripes, and the boy Filka. . . . This Filka was generally hanging about the laundry playing with the dogs; now he was combed and washed, and was holding an ikon in a tinfoil setting. Pelageya was standing in the middle of the kitchen in a new cotton dress, with a flower on her head. Beside her stood the cabman. The happy pair were red in the face and perspiring and blinking with embarrassment.

"Well . . . I fancy it is time," said the non-commissioned officer, after a prolonged silence.

Pelageya's face worked all over and she began blubbering. . . .

The soldier took a big loaf from the table, stood beside nurse, and began blessing the couple. The cabman went up to the soldier, flopped down on his knees, and gave a smacking kiss on his hand. He did the same before nurse. Pelageya followed him mechanically, and she too bowed down to the ground. At last the outer door was opened, there was a whiff of white mist, and the whole party flocked noisily out of the kitchen into the yard.

"Poor thing, poor thing," thought Grisha, hearing the sobs of the cook. "Where have they taken her? Why don't papa and mamma protect her?"

After the wedding there was singing and concertina-playing in the laundry till late evening. Mamma was cross all the evening because nurse smelt of vodka, and owing to the wedding there was no one to heat the samovar. Pelageya had not come back by the time Grisha went to bed.

"The poor thing is crying somewhere in the dark!" he thought. "While the cabman is saying to her 'shut up!' "

Next morning the cook was in the kitchen again. The cabman came in for a minute. He thanked mamma, and glancing sternly at Pelageya, said:

"Will you look after her, madam? Be a father and a mother to her. And you, too, Aksinya Stepanovna, do not forsake her, see that everything is as it should be . . . without any nonsense. . . . And also, madam, if you would kindly advance me five roubles of her wages. I have got to buy a new horse-collar."

Again a problem for Grisha: Pelageya was living in freedom, doing as she liked, and not having to account to anyone for her actions, and all at once, for no sort of reason, a stranger turns up, who has somehow acquired rights over her conduct and her property! Grisha was distressed. He longed passionately, almost to tears, to comfort this victim, as he supposed, of man's injustice. Picking out the very biggest apple in the storeroom he stole into the kitchen, slipped it into Pelageya's hand, and darted headlong away.

THE WITCH

It was approaching nightfall. The sexton, Savély Gykin, was lying in his huge bed in the hut adjoining the church. He was not asleep, though it was his habit to go to sleep at the same time as the hens. His coarse red hair peeped from under one end of the greasy patchwork quilt, made up of coloured rags, while his big unwashed feet stuck out from the other. He was listening. His hut adjoined the wall that encircled the church and the solitary window in it looked out upon the open country. And out there a regular battle was going on. It was hard to say who was being wiped off the face of the earth, and for the sake of whose destruction nature was being churned up into such a ferment; but, judging from the unceasing malignant roar, someone was getting it very hot. A victorious force was in full chase over the fields, storming in the forest and on the church roof, battering spitefully with its fists upon the windows, raging and tearing, while something vanquished was howling and wailing. . . . A plaintive lament sobbed at the window, on the roof, or in the stove. It sounded not like a call for help, but like a cry of misery, a consciousness that it was too late, that there was no salvation. The snow-drifts were covered with a thin coating of ice; tears quivered on them and on the trees; a dark slush of mud and melting snow flowed along the roads and paths. In short, it was thawing, but through the dark night the heavens failed to see it, and flung flakes of fresh snow upon the melting earth at a terrific rate. And the wind staggered like a drunkard. It would not let the snow settle on the ground, and whirled it round in the darkness at random.

Savély listened to all this din and frowned. The fact was that he knew, or at any rate suspected, what all this racket outside the window was tending to and whose handiwork it was.

"I know!" he muttered, shaking his finger menacingly under the bedclothes; "I know all about it."

On a stool by the window sat the sexton's wife, Raïssa Nilovna. A tin lamp standing on another stool, as though timid and distrustful of its powers, shed a dim and flickering light on her broad shoulders, on the handsome, tempting-looking contours of her person, and on her thick plait, which reached to the floor. She was making sacks out of coarse hempen stuff. Her hands moved nimbly, while her whole body, her eyes, her eyebrows, her full lips, her white neck were as still as though they were asleep, absorbed in the monotonous, mechanical toil. Only from time to time she raised her head to rest her weary neck, glanced for a moment towards the window, beyond which the snow-storm was raging, and bent again over her sacking. No desire, no joy, no grief, nothing was expressed by her handsome face with its turned-up nose and its dimples. So a beautiful fountain expresses nothing when it is not playing.

But at last she had finished a sack. She flung it aside, and, stretching luxuriously, rested her motionless, lack-lustre eyes on the window. The panes were swimming with drops like tears, and white with short-lived snow-flakes which fell on the window, glanced at Raïssa, and melted. . . .

"Come to bed!" growled the sexton. Raïssa remained mute. But suddenly her eyelashes flickered and there was a gleam of attention in her eye. Savély, all the time watching her expression from under the quilt, put out his head and asked:

"What is it?"

"Nothing. . . . I fancy someone's coming," she answered quietly.

The sexton flung the quilt off with his arms and legs, knelt up in bed, and looked blankly at his wife. The timid light of the lamp illuminated his hirsute, pock-marked countenance and glided over his rough matted hair.

"Do you hear?" asked his wife.

Through the monotonous roar of the storm he caught a scarcely audible thin and jingling monotone like the shrill note of a gnat when it wants to settle on one's cheek and is angry at being prevented.

"It's the post," muttered Savély, squatting on his heels.

Two miles from the church ran the posting road. In windy weather, when the wind was blowing from the road to the church, the inmates of the hut caught the sound of bells.

"Lord! fancy people wanting to drive about in such weather," sighed Raïssa.

"It's government work. You've to go whether you like or not."

The murmur hung in the air and died away.

"It has driven by," said Savély, getting into bed.

But before he had time to cover himself up with the bedclothes he heard a distinct sound of the bell. The sexton looked anxiously at his wife, leapt out of bed and walked, waddling, to and fro by the stove. The bell went on ringing for a little, then died away again as though it had ceased.

"I don't hear it," said the sexton, stopping, and looking at his wife with his eyes screwed up.

But at that moment the wind rapped on the window and with it floated a shrill jingling note. Savély turned pale, cleared his throat, and flopped about the floor with his bare feet again.

"The postman is lost in the storm," he wheezed out, glancing malignantly at his wife. "Do you hear? The postman has lost his way! . . . I . . . I know! Do you suppose I . . . don't understand?" he muttered. "I know all about it, curse you!"

"What do you know?" Raïssa asked quietly, keeping her eyes fixed on the window.

"I know that it's all your doing, you she-devil! Your doing, damn you! This snow-storm and the post going wrong, you've done it all—you!"

"You're mad, you silly," his wife answered calmly.

"I've been watching you for a long time past and I've seen it. From the first day I married you I noticed that you'd bitch's blood in you!"

"Tfoo!" said Raïssa, surprised, shrugging her shoulders and crossing herself. "Cross yourself, you fool!"

"A witch is a witch," Savély pronounced in a hollow, tearful voice, hurriedly blowing his nose on the hem of his shirt; "though you are my wife, though you are of a clerical family, I'd say what you are even at confession. . . . Why, God have mercy upon us! Last year on the Eve of the Prophet Daniel and the Three Young Men there was a snow-storm, and what happened then? The mechanic came in to warm himself. Then on St. Alexey's Day the ice broke on the river and the district policeman turned up, and he was chatting with you all night . . . the damned brute! And when he came out in the morning and I looked at him, he had rings under his eyes and his cheeks were hollow! Eh? During the August fast there were two storms and each time the huntsman turned up. I saw it all, damn him! Oh, she is redder than a crab now, aha!"

"You didn't see anything."

"Didn't I! And this winter before Christmas on the Day of the Ten Martyrs of Crete, when the storm lasted for a whole day and night—do you remember?—the marshal's clerk was lost, and turned up here, the hound. . . . Tfoo! To be tempted by the clerk! It was worth upsetting God's weather for him! A drivelling scribbler not a foot from the ground, pimples all over his mug and his neck awry! If he were good-looking, anyway—but he, tfoo! he is as ugly as Satan!"

The sexton took breath, wiped his lips and listened. The bell was not to be heard, but the wind banged on the roof, and again there came a tinkle in the darkness.

And it's the same thing now!" Savély went on. "It's not for nothing the postman is lost! Blast my eyes if the postman isn't looking for you! Oh, the devil is a good hand at his work; he is a fine one to help! He will turn him round and round and bring him here. I know, I see! You can't conceal it, you devil's bauble, you heathen wanton! As soon as the storm began I knew what you were up to."

"Here's a fool!" smiled his wife. "Why, do you suppose, you thick-head, that I make the storm?"

"H'm! . . . Grin away! Whether it's your doing or not, I only know that when your blood's on fire there's sure to be bad weather, and when there's bad weather there's bound to be some crazy fellow turning up here. It happens so every time! So it must be you!"

To be more impressive the sexton put his finger to his forehead, closed his left eye, and said in a sing-song voice:

"Oh, the madness! oh, the unclean Judas! If you really are a human being and not a witch, you ought to think what if he is not the mechanic, or the clerk, or the huntsman, but the devil in their form! Ah! You'd better think of that!"

"Why, you are stupid, Savély," said his wife, looking at him compassionately. "When father was alive and living here, all sorts of people used to come to him to be cured of the ague: from the village, and the hamlets, and the Armenian settlement. They came almost every day, and no one called them devils. But if anyone once a year comes in bad weather to warm himself, you wonder at it, you silly, and take all sorts of notions into your head at once."

His wife's logic touched Savély. He stood with his bare feet wide apart, bent his head, and pondered. He was not firmly convinced yet of the truth of his suspicions, and his wife's genuine and unconcerned tone quite disconcerted him. Yet after a moment's thought he wagged his head and said:

"It's not as though they were old men or bandy-legged cripples; it's always young men who want to come for the night. . . . Why is that? And if they only wanted to warm themselves—— But they are up to mischief. No, woman; there's no creature in this world as cunning as your female sort! Of real brains you've not an ounce, less than a starling, but for devilish slyness—oo-oo-oo! The Queen of Heaven protect us! There is the postman's bell! When the storm was only beginning I knew all that was in your mind. That's your witchery, you spider!"

"Why do you keep on at me, you heathen?" His wife lost her patience at last. "Why do you keep sticking to it like pitch?"

"I stick to it because if anything—God forbid—happens tonight . . . do you hear? . . . if anything happens to-night, I'll go straight off to-morrow morning to Father Nikodim and tell him all about it. 'Father Nikodim,' I shall say, 'graciously excuse me, but she is a witch.' 'Why so?' 'H'm! do you want to know why? Certainly . . .' And I shall tell him. And woe to you, woman! Not only at the dread Seat of Judgment, but in your earthly life you'll be punished, too! It's not for nothing there are prayers in the breviary against your kind!"

Suddenly there was a knock at the window, so loud and unusual that Savély turned pale and almost dropped backwards with fright. His wife jumped up, and she, too, turned pale.

"For God's sake, let us come in and get warm!" they heard in a trembling deep bass. "Who lives here? For mercy's sake! We've lost our way."

"Who are you?" asked Raïssa, afraid to look at the window.

"The post," answered a second voice.

"You've succeeded with your devil's tricks," said Savély with a wave of his hand. "No mistake; I am right! Well, you'd better look out!"

The sexton jumped on to the bed in two skips, stretched himself on the feather mattress, and sniffing angrily, turned with his face to the wall. Soon he felt a draught of cold air on his back. The door creaked and the tall figure of a man, plastered over with snow from head to foot, appeared in the doorway. Behind him could be seen a second figure as white.

"Am I to bring in the bags?" asked the second in a hoarse bass voice.

"You can't leave them there." Saying this, the first figure began untying his hood, but gave it up, and pulling it off impatiently with his cap, angrily flung it near the stove. Then taking off his great-coat, he threw that down beside it, and without saying good-evening, began pacing up and down the hut.

He was a fair-haired, young postman wearing a shabby uniform and black rusty-looking high boots. After warming himself by walking to and fro, he sat down at the table, stretched out his muddy feet towards the sacks and leaned his chin on his fist. His pale face, reddened in places by the cold, still bore vivid traces of the pain and terror he had just been through. Though distorted by anger and bearing traces of recent suffering, physical and moral, it was handsome in spite of the melting snow on the eyebrows, moustaches, and short beard.

"It's a dog's life!" muttered the postman, looking round the walls and seeming hardly able to believe that he was in the warmth. "We were nearly lost! If it had not been for your light, I don't know what would have happened. Goodness only knows when it will all be over! There's no end to this dog's life! Where have we come?" he asked, dropping his voice and raising his eyes to the sexton's wife.

"To the Gulyaevsky Hill on General Kalinovsky's estate," she answered, startled and blushing.

"Do you hear, Stepan?" The postman turned to the driver, who was wedged in the doorway with a huge mail-bag on his shoulders. "We've got to Gulyaevsky Hill."

"Yes . . . we're a long way out." Jerking out these words like a hoarse sigh, the driver went out and soon after returned with another bag, then went out once more and this time brought the postman's sword on a big belt, of the pattern of that long flat blade with which Judith is portrayed by the bedside of Holofernes in cheap woodcuts. Laying the bags along the wall, he went out into the outer room, sat down there and lighted his pipe.

"Perhaps you'd like some tea after your journey?" Raïssa inquired.

"How can we sit drinking tea?" said the postman, frowning. "We must make haste and get warm, and then set off, or we shall be late for the mail train. We'll stay ten minutes and then get on our way. Only be so good as to show us the way."

"What an infliction it is, this weather!" sighed Raïssa.

"H'm, yes. . . . Who may you be?"

"We? We live here, by the church. . . . We belong to the clergy. . . . There lies my husband. Savély, get up and say good-evening! This used to be a separate parish till eighteen months ago. Of course, when the gentry lived here there were more people, and it was worth while to have the services. But now the gentry have gone, and I need not tell you there's nothing for the clergy to live on. The nearest village is Markovka, and that's over three miles away. Savély is on the retired list now, and has got the watchman's job; he has to look after the church. . . ."

And the postman was immediately informed that if Savély were to go to the General's lady and ask her for a letter to the bishop, he would be given a good berth. "But he doesn't go to the General's lady because he is lazy and afraid of people. We belong to the clergy all the same . . ." added Raïssa.

"What do you live on?" asked the postman.

"There's a kitchen garden and a meadow belonging to the church. Only we don't get much from that," sighed Raïssa. "The old skinflint, Father Nikodim, from the next village celebrates here on St. Nicolas' Day in the winter and on St. Nicolas' Day in the summer, and for that he takes almost all the crops for himself. There's no one to stick up for us!"

"You are lying," Savély growled hoarsely. "Father Nikodim is a saintly soul, a luminary of the Church; and if he does take it, it's the regulation!"

"You've a cross one!" said the postman, with a grin. "Have you been married long?"

"It was three years ago the last Sunday before Lent. My father was sexton here in the old days, and when the time came for him to die, he went to the Consistory and asked them to send some unmarried man to marry me that I might keep the place. So I married him."

"Aha, so you killed two birds with one stone!" said the postman, looking at Savély's back. "Got wife and job together."

Savély wriggled his leg impatiently and moved closer to the wall. The postman moved away from the table, stretched, and sat down on the mail-bag. After a moment's thought he squeezed the bags with his hands, shifted his sword to the other side, and lay down with one foot touching the floor.

"It's a dog's life," he muttered, putting his hands behind his head and closing his eyes. "I wouldn't wish a wild Tatar such a life."

Soon everything was still. Nothing was audible except the sniffing of Savély and the slow, even breathing of the sleeping postman, who uttered a deep prolonged "h-h-h" at every breath. From time to time there was a sound like a creaking wheel in his throat, and his twitching foot rustled against the bag.

Savély fidgeted under the quilt and looked round slowly. His wife was sitting on the stool, and with her hands pressed against her cheeks was gazing at the postman's face. Her face was immovable, like the face of someone frightened and astonished.

"Well, what are you gaping at?" Savély whispered angrily.

"What is it to you? Lie down!" answered his wife without taking her eyes off the flaxen head.

Savély angrily puffed all the air out of his chest and turned abruptly to the wall. Three minutes later he turned over restlessly again, knelt up on the bed, and with his hands on the pillow looked askance at his wife. She was still sitting motionless, staring at the visitor. Her cheeks were pale and her eyes were glowing with a strange fire. The sexton cleared his throat, crawled on his stomach off the bed, and going up to the postman, put a handkerchief over his face.

"What's that for?" asked his wife.

"To keep the light out of his eyes."

"Then put out the light!"

Savély looked distrustfully at his wife, put out his lips towards the lamp, but at once thought better of it and clasped his hands.

"Isn't that devilish cunning?" he exclaimed. "Ah! Is there any creature slyer than women-kind?"

"Ah, you long-skirted devil!" hissed his wife, frowning with vexation. "You wait a bit!"

And settling herself more comfortably, she stared at the postman again.

It did not matter to her that his face was covered. She was not so much interested in his face as in his whole appearance, in the novelty of this man. His chest was broad and powerful, his hands were slender and well formed, and his graceful, muscular legs were much comelier than Savély's stumps. There could be no comparison, in fact.

"Though I am a long-skirted devil," Savély said after a brief interval, "they've no business to sleep here. . . . It's government work; we shall have to answer for keeping them. If you carry the letters, carry them, you can't go to sleep. . . . Hey! you!" Savély shouted into the outer room. "You, driver. . . . What's your name? Shall I show you the way? Get up; postmen mustn't sleep!"

And Savély, thoroughly roused, ran up to the postman and tugged him by the sleeve.

"Hey, your honour, if you must go, go; and if you don't, it's not the thing. . . . Sleeping won't do."

The postman jumped up, sat down, looked with blank eyes round the hut, and lay down again.

"But when are you going?" Savély pattered away. "That's what the post is for—to get there in good time, do you hear? I'll take you."

The postman opened his eyes. Warmed and relaxed by his first sweet sleep, and not yet quite awake, he saw as through a mist the white neck and the immovable, alluring eyes of the sexton's wife. He closed his eyes and smiled as though he had been dreaming it all.

"Come, how can you go in such weather!" he heard a soft feminine voice; "you ought to have a sound sleep and it would do you good!"

"And what about the post?" said Savély anxiously. "Who's going to take the post? Are you going to take it, pray, you?"

The postman opened his eyes again, looked at the play of the dimples on Raïssa's face, remembered where he was, and understood

Savély. The thought that he had to go out into the cold darkness sent a chill shudder all down him, and he winced.

"I might sleep another five minutes," he said, yawning. "I shall be late, anyway. . . ."

"We might be just in time," came a voice from the outer room. "All days are not alike; the train may be late for a bit of luck."

The postman got up, and stretching lazily began putting on his coat.

Savély positively neighed with delight when he saw his visitors were getting ready to go.

"Give us a hand," the driver shouted to him as he lifted up a mail-bag.

The sexton ran out and helped him drag the post-bags into the yard. The postman began undoing the knot in his hood. The sexton's wife gazed into his eyes, and seemed trying to look right into his soul.

"You ought to have a cup of tea . . ." she said.

"I wouldn't say no . . . but, you see, they're getting ready," he assented. "We are late, anyway."

"Do stay," she whispered, dropping her eyes and touching him by the sleeve.

The postman got the knot undone at last and flung the hood over his elbow, hesitating. He felt it comfortable standing by Raïssa.

"What a . . . neck you've got! . . ." And he touched her neck with two fingers. Seeing that she did not resist, he stroked her neck and shoulders.

"I say, you are . . ."

"You'd better stay . . . have some tea."

"Where are you putting it?" The driver's voice could be heard outside. "Lay it crossways."

"You'd better stay. . . . Hark how the wind howls."

And the postman, not yet quite awake, not yet quite able to shake off the intoxicating sleep of youth and fatigue, was suddenly overwhelmed by a desire for the sake of which mail-bags, postal trains . . . and all things in the world, are forgotten. He glanced at the door in a frightened way, as though he wanted to escape or hide himself, seized Raïssa round the waist, and was just bending over the lamp to put out the light, when he heard the tramp of boots in the outer room, and the driver appeared in the doorway. Savély peeped in over his shoulder. The postman dropped his hands quickly and stood still as though irresolute.

"It's all ready," said the driver. The postman stood still for a moment, resolutely threw up his head as though waking up completely, and followed the driver out. Raïssa was left alone.

"Come, get in and show us the way!" she heard.

One bell sounded languidly, then another, and the jingling notes in a long delicate chain floated away from the hut.

When little by little they had died away, Raïssa got up and nervously paced to and fro. At first she was pale, then she flushed all over. Her face was contorted with hate, her breathing was tremulous, her eyes gleamed with wild, savage anger, and, pacing up and down as in a cage, she looked like a tigress menaced with red-hot iron. For a moment she stood still and looked at her abode. Almost half of the room was filled up by the bed, which stretched the length of the whole wall and consisted of a dirty feather-bed, coarse grey pillows, a quilt, and nameless rags of various sorts. The bed was a shapeless ugly mass which suggested the shock of hair that always stood up on Savély's head whenever it occurred to him to oil it. From the bed to the door that led into the cold outer room stretched the dark stove surrounded by pots and hanging clouts. Everything, including the absent Savély himself, was dirty, greasy, and smutty to the last degree, so that it was strange to see a woman's white neck and delicate skin in such surroundings.

Raïssa ran up to the bed, stretched out her hands as though she wanted to fling it all about, stamp it underfoot, and tear it to shreds. But then, as though frightened by contact with the dirt, she leapt back and began pacing up and down again.

When Savély returned two hours later, worn out and covered with snow, she was undressed and in bed. Her eyes were closed, but from the slight tremor that ran over her face he guessed that she was not asleep. On his way home he had vowed inwardly to wait till next day and not to touch her, but he could not resist a biting taunt at her.

"Your witchery was all in vain: he's gone off," he said, grinning with malignant joy.

His wife remained mute, but her chin quivered. Savély undressed slowly, clambered over his wife, and lay down next to the wall.

"To-morrow I'll let Father Nikodim know what sort of wife you are!" he muttered, curling himself up.

Raïssa turned her face to him and her eyes gleamed.

"The job's enough for you, and you can look for a wife in the forest, blast you!" she said. "I am no wife for you, a clumsy lout, a slug-a-bed, God forgive me!"

"Come, come . . . go to sleep!"

"How miserable I am!" sobbed his wife. "If it weren't for you, I might have married a merchant or some gentleman! If it weren't for you, I should love my husband now! And you haven't been buried in the snow, you haven't been frozen on the high-road, you Herod!"*

Raïssa cried for a long time. At last she drew a deep sigh and was still. The storm still raged without. Something wailed in the stove, in the chimney, outside the walls, and it seemed to Savély that the wailing was within him, in his ears. This evening had completely confirmed him in his suspicions about his wife. He no longer doubted that his wife, with the aid of the Evil One, controlled the winds and the post sledges. But to add to his grief, this mysteriousness, this supernatural, weird power gave the woman beside him a peculiar, incomprehensible charm of which he had not been conscious before. The fact that in his stupidity he unconsciously threw a poetic glamour over her made her seem, as it were, whiter, sleeker, more unapproachable.

"Witch!" he muttered indignantly. "Tfoo, horrid creature!"

Yet, waiting till she was quiet and began breathing evenly, he touched her head with his finger . . . held her thick plait in his hand for a minute. She did not feel it. Then he grew bolder and stroked her neck.

"Leave off!" she shouted, and prodded him on the nose with her elbow with such violence that he saw stars before his eyes.

The pain in his nose was soon over, but the torture in his heart remained.

---

*King of Judaea who ruled from 38 B.C. until his death in 4 B.C.; he commanded the massacre of the Innocents (see the Bible, Matthew 2).

A DEAD BODY

A still August night. A mist is rising slowly from the fields and casting an opaque veil over everything within eyesight. Lighted up by the moon, the mist gives the impression at one moment of a calm, boundless sea, at the next of an immense white wall. The air is damp and chilly. Morning is still far off. A step from the bye-road which runs along the edge of the forest a little fire is gleaming. A dead body, covered from head to foot with new white linen, is lying under a young oak-tree. A wooden ikon is lying on its breast. Beside the corpse almost on the road sits the "watch"—two peasants performing one of the most disagreeable and uninviting of peasants' duties. One, a tall young fellow with a scarcely perceptible moustache and thick black eyebrows, in a tattered sheepskin and bark shoes, is sitting on the wet grass, his feet stuck out straight in front of him, and is trying to while away the time with work. He bends his long neck, and breathing loudly through his nose, makes a spoon out of a big crooked bit of wood; the other—a little scraggy, pock-marked peasant with an aged face, a scanty moustache, and a little goat's beard—sits with his hands dangling loose on his knees, and without moving gazes listlessly at the light. A small camp-fire is lazily burning down between them, throwing a red glow on their faces. There is perfect stillness. The only sounds are the scrape of the knife on the wood and the crackling of damp sticks in the fire.

"Don't you go to sleep, Syoma . . ." says the young man.

"I . . . I am not asleep . . ." stammers the goat-beard.

"That's all right. . . . It would be dreadful to sit here alone, one would be frightened. You might tell me something, Syoma."

"I . . . I can't. . . ."

"You are a queer fellow, Syomushka! Other people will laugh and tell a story and sing a song, but you—there is no making you out. You sit like a scarecrow in the garden and roll your eyes at the fire. You can't say anything properly . . . when you speak you seem frightened. I dare say you are fifty, but you have less sense than a child. . . . Aren't you sorry that you are a simpleton?"

"I am sorry," the goat-beard answers gloomily.

"And we are sorry to see your foolishness, you may be sure. You are a good-natured, sober peasant, and the only trouble is that you have no sense in your head. You should have picked up some sense for yourself if the Lord has afflicted you and given you no understanding. You must make an effort, Syoma. . . . You should listen hard when anything good's being said, note it well and keep thinking and thinking. . . . If there is any word you don't understand, you should make an effort and think over in your head in what meaning the word is used. Do you see? Make an effort! If you don't gain some sense for yourself you'll be a simpleton and of no account at all to your dying day."

All at once a long-drawn-out, moaning sound is heard in the forest. Something rustles in the leaves as though torn from the very top of the tree and falls to the ground. All this is faintly repeated by the echo. The young man shudders and looks enquiringly at his companion.

"It's an owl at the little birds," says Syoma, gloomily.

"Why, Syoma, it's time for the birds to fly to the warm countries!"

"To be sure, it is time."

"It is chilly at dawn now. It is co-old. The crane is a chilly creature, it is tender. Such cold is death to it. I am not a crane, but I am frozen. . . . Put some more wood on!"

Syoma gets up and disappears in the dark undergrowth. While he is busy among the bushes, breaking dry twigs, his companion puts his hand over his eyes and starts at every sound. Syoma brings an armful of wood and lays it on the fire. The flame irresolutely licks the black twigs with its little tongues, then suddenly, as though at the word of command, catches them and throws a crimson light on the faces, the road, the white linen with its prominences where the hands and feet of the corpse raise it, the ikon. The "watch" is silent. The young man bends his neck still lower and sets to work with still more nervous haste. The goat-beard sits motionless as before and keeps his eyes fixed on the fire. . . .

"Ye that love not Zion . . . shall be put to shame by the Lord." A falsetto voice is suddenly heard singing in the stillness of the night, then slow footsteps are audible, and the dark figure of a man in a short monkish cassock and a broad-brimmed hat, with a wallet on his shoulders, comes into sight on the road in the crimson firelight.

"Thy will be done, O Lord! Holy Mother!" the figure says in a husky falsetto. "I saw the fire in the outer darkness and my soul leapt for joy. . . . At first I thought it was men grazing a drove of horses, then I thought it can't be that, since no horses were to be seen. 'Aren't they thieves,' I wondered, 'aren't they robbers lying in wait for a rich Lazarus?* Aren't they the gypsy people offering sacrifices to idols?' And my soul leapt for joy. 'Go, Feodosy, servant of God,' I said to myself, 'and win a martyr's crown!' And I flew to the fire like a light-winged moth. Now I stand before you, and from your outer aspect I judge of your souls: you are not thieves and you are not heathens. Peace be to you!"

"Good-evening."

"Good orthodox people, do you know how to reach the Makuhinsky Brickyards from here?"

"It's close here. You go straight along the road; when you have gone a mile and a half there will be Ananova, our village. From the village, father, you turn to the right by the river-bank, and so you will get to the brickyards. It's two miles from Ananova."

"God give you health. And why are you sitting here?"

"We are sitting here watching. You see, there is a dead body. . . ."

"What? what body? Holy Mother!"

The pilgrim sees the white linen with the ikon on it, and starts so violently that his legs give a little skip. This unexpected sight has an overpowering effect upon him. He huddles together and stands as though rooted to the spot, with wide-open mouth and staring eyes. For three minutes he is silent as though he could not believe his eyes, then begins muttering:

---

*Raised from the dead by Christ.

"O Lord! Holy Mother! I was going along not meddling with anyone, and all at once such an affliction."

"What may you be?" enquires the young man. "Of the clergy?"

"No . . . no. . . . I go from one monastery to another. . . . Do you know Mi . . . Mihail Polikarpitch, the foreman of the brickyard? Well, I am his nephew. . . . Thy will be done, O Lord! Why are you here?"

"We are watching . . . we are told to."

"Yes, yes . . ." mutters the man in the cassock, passing his hand over his eyes. "And where did the deceased come from?"

"He was a stranger."

"Such is life! But I'll . . . er . . . be getting on, brothers. . . . I feel flustered. I am more afraid of the dead than of anything, my dear souls! And only fancy! while this man was alive he wasn't noticed, while now when he is dead and given over to corruption we tremble before him as before some famous general or a bishop. . . . Such is life; was he murdered, or what?"

"The Lord knows! Maybe he was murdered, or maybe he died of himself."

"Yes, yes. . . . Who knows, brothers? Maybe his soul is now tasting the joys of Paradise."

"His soul is still hovering here, near his body," says the young man. "It does not depart from the body for three days."

"H'm, yes! . . . How chilly the nights are now! It sets one's teeth chattering. . . . So then I am to go straight on and on? . . ."

"Till you get to the village, and then you turn to the right by the river-bank."

"By the river-bank. . . . To be sure. . . . Why am I standing still? I must go on. Farewell, brothers."

The man in the cassock takes five steps along the road and stops.

"I've forgotten to put a kopeck for the burying," he says. "Good orthodox friends, can I give the money?"

"You ought to know best, you go the round of the monasteries. If he died a natural death it would go for the good of his soul; if it's a suicide it's a sin."

"That's true. . . . And maybe it really was a suicide! So I had better keep my money. Oh, sins, sins! Give me a thousand roubles and I would not consent to sit here. . . . Farewell, brothers."

The cassock slowly moves away and stops again.

"I can't make up my mind what I am to do," he mutters. "To stay here by the fire and wait till daybreak. . . . I am frightened; to go on is dreadful, too. The dead man will haunt me all the way in the darkness. . . . The Lord has chastised me indeed! Over three hundred miles I have come on foot and nothing happened, and now I am near home and there's trouble. I can't go on. . . ."

"It is dreadful, that is true."

"I am not afraid of wolves, of thieves, or of darkness, but I am afraid of the dead. I am afraid of them, and that is all about it. Good orthodox brothers, I entreat you on my knees, see me to the village."

"We've been told not to go away from the body."

"No one will see, brothers. Upon my soul, no one will see! The Lord will reward you a hundredfold! Old man, come with me, I beg! Old man! Why are you silent?"

"He is a bit simple," says the young man.

"You come with me, friend; I will give you five kopecks."

"For five kopecks I might," says the young man, scratching his head, "but I was told not to. If Syoma here, our simpleton, will stay alone, I will take you. Syoma, will you stay here alone?"

"I'll stay," the simpleton consents.

"Well, that's all right, then. Come along!"

The young man gets up, and goes with the cassock. A minute later the sound of their steps and their talk dies away. Syoma shuts his eyes and gently dozes. The fire begins to grow dim, and a big black shadow falls on the dead body.

EASTER EVE

I was standing on the bank of the river Goltva, waiting for the ferry-boat from the other side. At ordinary times the Goltva is a humble stream of moderate size, silent and pensive, gently glimmering from behind thick reeds; but now a regular lake lay stretched out before me. The waters of spring, running riot, had overflowed both banks and flooded both sides of the river for a long distance, submerging vegetable gardens, hayfields and marshes, so that it was no unusual thing to meet poplars and bushes sticking out above the surface of the water and looking in the darkness like grim solitary crags.

The weather seemed to me magnificent. It was dark, yet I could see the trees, the water and the people. . . . The world was lighted by the stars, which were scattered thickly all over the sky. I don't remember ever seeing so many stars. Literally one could not have put a finger in between them. There were some as big as a goose's egg, others tiny as hempseed. . . . They had come out for the festival procession, every one of them, little and big, washed, renewed and joyful, and every one of them was softly twinkling its beams. The sky was reflected in the water; the stars were bathing in its dark depths and trembling with the quivering eddies. The air was warm and still. . . . Here and there, far away on the further bank in the impenetrable darkness, several bright red lights were gleaming. . . .

A couple of paces from me I saw the dark silhouette of a peasant in a high hat, with a thick knotted stick in his hand.

"How long the ferry-boat is in coming!" I said.

"It is time it was here," the silhouette answered.

"You are waiting for the ferry-boat, too?"

"No, I am not," yawned the peasant—"I am waiting for the illumination. I should have gone, but, to tell you the truth, I haven't the five kopecks for the ferry."

"I'll give you the five kopecks."

"No; I humbly thank you. . . . With that five kopecks put up a candle for me over there in the monastery. . . . That will be more interesting, and I will stand here. What can it mean, no ferry-boat, as though it had sunk in the water!"

The peasant went up to the water's edge, took the rope in his hands, and shouted: "Ieronim! Ieron—im!"

As though in answer to his shout, the slow peal of a great bell floated across from the further bank. The note was deep and low, as from the thickest string of a double bass; it seemed as though the darkness itself had hoarsely uttered it. At once there was the sound of a cannon shot. It rolled away in the darkness and ended somewhere in the far distance behind me. The peasant took off his hat and crossed himself.

"Christ is risen," he said.

Before the vibrations of the first peal of the bell had time to die away in the air a second sounded, after it at once a third, and the darkness was filled with an unbroken quivering clamour. Near the red lights fresh lights flashed, and all began moving together and twinkling restlessly.

"Ieron—im!" we heard a hollow prolonged shout.

"They are shouting from the other bank," said the peasant, "so there is no ferry there either. Our Ieronim has gone to sleep."

The lights and the velvety chimes of the bell drew one towards them. . . . I was already beginning to lose patience and grow anxious, but behold at last, staring into the dark distance, I saw the outline of something very much like a gibbet. It was the long-expected ferry. It moved towards us with such deliberation that if it had not been that its lines grew gradually more definite, one might have supposed that it was standing still or moving to the other bank.

"Make haste! Ieronim!" shouted my peasant. "The gentleman's tired of waiting!"

The ferry crawled to the bank, gave a lurch and stopped with a creak. A tall man in a monk's cassock and a conical cap stood on it, holding the rope.

"Why have you been so long?" I asked, jumping upon the ferry.

"Forgive me, for Christ's sake," Ieronim answered gently. "Is there no one else?"

"No one. . . ."

Ieronim took hold of the rope in both hands, bent himself to the figure of a mark of interrogation, and gasped. The ferryboat creaked and gave a lurch. The outline of the peasant in the high hat began slowly retreating from me—so the ferry was moving off. Ieronim soon drew himself up and began working with one hand only. We were silent, gazing towards the bank to which we were floating. There the illumination for which the peasant was waiting had begun. At the water's edge barrels of tar were flaring like huge camp fires. Their reflections, crimson as the rising moon, crept to meet us in long broad streaks. The burning barrels lighted up their own smoke and the long shadows of men flitting about the fire; but further to one side and behind them from where the velvety chime floated there was still the same unbroken black gloom. All at once, cleaving the darkness, a rocket zigzagged in a golden ribbon up the sky; it described an arc and, as though broken to pieces against the sky, was scattered crackling into sparks. There was a roar from the bank like a far-away hurrah.

"How beautiful!" I said.

"Beautiful beyond words!" sighed Ieronim. "Such a night, sir! Another time one would pay no attention to the fireworks, but to-day one rejoices in every vanity. Where do you come from?"

I told him where I came from.

"To be sure . . . a joyful day to-day. . . ." Ieronim went on in a weak sighing tenor like the voice of a convalescent. "The sky is rejoicing and the earth and what is under the earth. All the creatures are keeping holiday. Only tell me, kind sir, why, even in the time of great rejoicing, a man cannot forget his sorrows?"

I fancied that this unexpected question was to draw me into one of those endless religious conversations which bored and idle monks are so fond of. I was not disposed to talk much, and so I only asked:

"What sorrows have you, father?"

"As a rule only the same as all men, kind sir, but to-day a special sorrow has happened in the monastery: at mass, during the reading of the Bible, the monk and deacon Nikolay died."

"Well, it's God's will!" I said, falling into the monastic tone. "We must all die. To my mind, you ought to rejoice indeed. . . . They say if anyone dies at Easter he goes straight to the kingdom of heaven."

"That's true."

We sank into silence. The figure of the peasant in the high hat melted into the lines of the bank. The tar barrels were flaring up more and more.

"The Holy Scripture points clearly to the vanity of sorrow, and so does reflection," said Ieronim, breaking the silence; "but why does the heart grieve and refuse to listen to reason? Why does one want to weep bitterly?"

Ieronim shrugged his shoulders, turned to me and said quickly:

"If I died, or anyone else, it would not be worth notice, perhaps; but, you see, Nikolay is dead! No one else but Nikolay! Indeed, it's hard to believe that he is no more! I stand here on my ferry-boat and every minute I keep fancying that he will lift up his voice from the bank. He always used to come to the bank and call to me that I might not be afraid on the ferry. He used to get up from his bed at night on purpose for that. He was a kind soul. My God! how kindly and gracious! Many a mother is not so good to her child as Nikolay was to me! Lord, save his soul!"

Ieronim took hold of the rope, but turned to me again at once.

"And such a lofty intelligence, your honour," he said in a vibrating voice. "Such a sweet and harmonious tongue! Just as they will sing immediately at early matins: 'Oh lovely! oh sweet is Thy Voice!' Besides all other human qualities, he had, too, an extraordinary gift!"

"What gift?" I asked.

The monk scrutinized me, and as though he had convinced himself that he could trust me with a secret, he laughed good-humouredly.

"He had a gift for writing hymns of praise," he said. "It was a marvel, sir; you couldn't call it anything else! You will be amazed if I tell you about it. Our Father Archimandrite comes from Moscow, the Father Sub-Prior studied at the Kazan academy, we have wise monks and elders, but, would you believe it, no one could write them; while Nikolay, a simple monk, a deacon, had not studied anywhere, and had not even any outer appearance of it, but he wrote them! A marvel! a real marvel!" Ieronim clasped his hands and, completely forgetting the rope, went on eagerly:

"The Father Sub-Prior has great difficulty in composing sermons; when he wrote the history of the monastery he worried all the brotherhood and drove a dozen times to town, while Nikolay wrote canticles! Hymns of praise! That's a very different thing from a sermon or a history!"

"Is it difficult to write them?" I asked.

"There's great difficulty!" Ieronim wagged his head. "You can do nothing by wisdom and holiness if God has not given you the gift. The monks who don't understand argue that you only need to know the life of the saint for whom you are writing the hymn, and to make it harmonize with the other hymns of praise. But that's a mistake, sir. Of course, anyone who writes canticles must know the life of the saint to perfection, to the least trivial detail. To be sure, one must make them harmonize with the other canticles and know where to begin and what to write about. To give you an instance, the first response begins everywhere with 'the chosen' or 'the elect.' . . . The first line must always begin with the 'angel.' In the canticle of praise to Jesus the Most Sweet, if you are interested in the subject, it begins like this: 'Of angels Creator and Lord of all powers!' In the canticle to the Holy Mother of God: 'Of angels the foremost sent down from on high'; to Nikolay, the Wonder-worker—'An angel in semblance, though in substance a man,' and so on. Everywhere you begin with the angel. Of course, it would be impossible without making them harmonize, but the lives of the saints and conformity with the others is not what matters; what matters is the beauty and sweetness of it. Everything must be harmonious, brief and complete. There must be in every line softness, graciousness and tenderness; not one word should be harsh or rough or unsuitable. It must be written so that the worshipper may rejoice at heart and weep, while his mind is stirred and he is thrown into a tremor. In the canticle to the Holy Mother are the words: 'Rejoice, O Thou too high for human thought to reach! Rejoice, O Thou too deep for angels' eyes to fathom!' In another place in the same canticle: 'Rejoice, O tree that bearest the fair fruit of light that is the food of the faithful! Rejoice, O tree of gracious spreading shade, under which there is shelter for multitudes!' "

Ieronim hid his face in his hands, as though frightened at something or overcome with shame, and shook his head.

"Tree that bearest the fair fruit of light . . . tree of gracious spreading shade . . ." he muttered. "To think that a man should find words like those! Such a power is a gift from God! For brevity he packs many thoughts into one phrase, and how smooth and complete it all is! 'Light-radiating torch to all that be . . .' comes in the canticle to Jesus the Most Sweet. 'Light-radiating!' There is no such word in conversation or in books, but you see he invented it, he found it in his mind! Apart from the smoothness and grandeur of language, sir, every line must be beautified in every way; there must be flowers and lightning and wind and sun and all the objects of the visible world. And every exclamation ought to be put so as to be smooth and easy for the ear. 'Rejoice, thou flower of heavenly growth!' comes in the hymn to Nikolay the Wonder-worker. It's not simply 'heavenly flower,' but 'flower of heavenly growth.' It's smoother so and sweet to the ear. That was just as Nikolay wrote it! exactly like that! I can't tell you how he used to write!"

"Well, in that case it is a pity he is dead," I said; "but let us get on, father, or we shall be late."

Ieronim started and ran to the rope; they were beginning to peal all the bells. Probably the procession was already going on near the monastery, for all the dark space behind the tar barrels was now dotted with moving lights.

"Did Nikolay print his hymns?" I asked Ieronim.

"How could he print them?" he sighed. "And, indeed, it would be strange to print them. What would be the object? No one in the monastery takes any interest in them. They don't like them. They knew Nikolay wrote them, but they let it pass unnoticed. No one esteems new writings nowadays, sir!"

"Were they prejudiced against him?"

"Yes, indeed. If Nikolay had been an elder perhaps the brethren would have been interested, but he wasn't forty, you know. There were some who laughed and even thought his writing a sin."

"What did he write them for?"

"Chiefly for his own comfort. Of all the brotherhood, I was the only one who read his hymns. I used to go to him in secret, that no one else might know of it, and he was glad that I took an interest in them. He would embrace me, stroke my head, speak to me in caressing words as to a little child. He would shut his cell, make me sit down beside him, and begin to read. . . ."

Ieronim left the rope and came up to me.

"We were dear friends in a way," he whispered, looking at me with shining eyes. "Where he went I would go. If I were not there he would miss me. And he cared more for me than for anyone, and all because I used to weep over his hymns. It makes me sad to remember. Now I feel just like an orphan or a widow. You know, in our monastery they are all good people, kind and pious, but . . . there is no one with softness and refinement, they are just like peasants. They all speak loudly, and tramp heavily when they walk; they are noisy, they clear their throats, but Nikolay always talked softly, caressingly, and if he noticed that anyone was asleep or praying he would slip by like a fly or a gnat. His face was tender, compassionate. . . ."

Ieronim heaved a deep sigh and took hold of the rope again. We were by now approaching the bank. We floated straight out of the darkness and stillness of the river into an enchanted realm, full of stifling smoke, crackling lights and uproar. By now one could distinctly see people moving near the tar barrels. The flickering of the lights gave a strange, almost fantastic, expression to their figures and red faces. From time to time one caught among the heads and faces a glimpse of a horse's head motionless as though cast in copper.

"They'll begin singing the Easter hymn directly, . . ." said Ieronim, "and Nikolay is gone; there is no one to appreciate it. . . . There was nothing written dearer to him than that hymn. He used to take in every word! You'll be there, sir, so notice what is sung; it takes your breath away!"

"Won't you be in church, then?"

"I can't; . . . I have to work the ferry. . . ."

"But won't they relieve you?"

"I don't know. . . . I ought to have been relieved at eight; but, as you see, they don't come! . . . And I must own I should have liked to be in the church. . . ."

"Are you a monk?"

"Yes . . . that is, I am a lay brother."

The ferry ran into the bank and stopped. I thrust a five-kopeck piece into Ieronim's hand for taking me across, and jumped on land. Immediately a cart with a boy and a sleeping woman in it drove creaking on to the ferry. Ieronim, with a faint glow from the lights on his figure, pressed on the rope, bent down to it, and started the ferry back. . . .

I took a few steps through mud, but a little further walked on a soft freshly trodden path. This path led to the dark monastery gates, that looked like a cavern through a cloud of smoke, through a disorderly crowd of people, unharnessed horses, carts and chaises. All this crowd was rattling, snorting, laughing, and the crimson light and wavering shadows from the smoke flickered over it all. . . . A perfect chaos! And in this hubbub the people yet found room to load a little cannon and to sell cakes. There was no less commotion on the other side of the wall in the monastery precincts, but there was more regard for decorum and order. Here there was a smell of juniper and incense. They talked loudly, but there was no sound of laughter or snorting. Near the tombstones and crosses people pressed close to one another with Easter cakes and bundles in their arms. Apparently many had come from a long distance for their cakes to be blessed and now were exhausted. Young lay brothers, making a metallic sound with their boots, ran busily along the iron slabs that paved the way from the monastery gates to the church door. They were busy and shouting on the belfry, too.

"What a restless night!" I thought. "How nice!"

One was tempted to see the same unrest and sleeplessness in all nature, from the night darkness to the iron slabs, the crosses on the tombs and the trees under which the people were moving to and fro. But nowhere was the excitement and restlessness so marked as in the church. An unceasing struggle was going on in the entrance between the inflowing stream and the outflowing stream. Some were going in, others going out and soon coming back again to stand still for a little and begin moving again. People were scurrying from place to place, lounging about as though they were looking for something. The stream flowed from the entrance all round the church, disturbing even the front rows, where persons of weight and dignity were standing. There could be no thought of concentrated prayer. There were no prayers at all, but a sort of continuous, childishly irresponsible joy, seeking a pretext to break out and vent itself in some movement, even in senseless jostling and shoving.

The same unaccustomed movement is striking in the Easter service itself. The altar gates are flung wide open, thick clouds of incense float in the air near the candelabra; wherever one looks there are lights, the gleam and splutter of candles. . . . There is no reading; restless and light-hearted singing goes on to the end without ceasing. After each hymn the clergy change their vestments and come out to burn incense, which is repeated every ten minutes.

I had no sooner taken a place, when a wave rushed from in front and forced me back. A tall thick-set deacon walked before me with a long red candle; the grey-headed archimandrite in his golden mitre hurried after him with the censer. When they had vanished from sight the crowd squeezed me back to my former position. But ten minutes had not passed before a new wave burst on me, and again the deacon appeared. This time he was followed by the Father Sub-Prior, the man who, as Ieronim had told me, was writing the history of the monastery.

As I mingled with the crowd and caught the infection of the universal joyful excitement, I felt unbearably sore on Ieronim's account. Why did they not send someone to relieve him? Why could not someone of less feeling and less susceptibility go on the ferry? "Lift up thine eyes, O Sion, and look around," they sang in the choir, "for thy children have come to thee as to a beacon of divine light from north and south, and from east and from the sea. . . ."

I looked at the faces; they all had a lively expression of triumph, but no one was listening to what was being sung and taking it in, and not one was "holding his breath." Why was not Ieronim released? I could fancy Ieronim standing meekly somewhere by the wall, bending forward and hungrily drinking in the beauty of the holy phrase. All this that glided by the ears of people standing by me he would have eagerly drunk in with his delicately sensitive soul, and would have been spell-bound to ecstasy, to holding his breath, and there would not have been a man happier than he in all the church. Now he was plying to and fro over the dark river and grieving for his dead friend and brother.

The wave surged back. A stout smiling monk, playing with his rosary and looking round behind him, squeezed sideways by me, making way for a lady in a hat and velvet cloak. A monastery servant hurried after the lady, holding a chair over our heads.

I came out of the church. I wanted to have a look at the dead Nikolay, the unknown canticle writer. I walked about the monastery wall, where there was a row of cells, peeped into several windows, and, seeing nothing, came back again. I do not regret now that I did not see Nikolay; God knows, perhaps if I had seen him I should have lost the picture my imagination paints for me now. I imagine that lovable poetical figure, solitary and not understood, who went out at nights to call to Ieronim over the water, and filled his hymns with flowers, stars and sunbeams, as a pale timid man with soft, mild, melancholy features. His eyes must have shone, not only with intelligence, but with kindly tenderness and that hardly restrained child-like enthusiasm which I could hear in Ieronim's voice when he quoted to me passages from the hymns.

When we came out of church after mass it was no longer night. The morning was beginning. The stars had gone out and the sky was a morose greyish blue. The iron slabs, the tombstones and the buds on the trees were covered with dew. There was a sharp freshness in the air. Outside the precincts I did not find the same animated scene as I had beheld in the night. Horses and men looked exhausted, drowsy, scarcely moved, while nothing was left of the tar barrels but heaps of black ash. When anyone is exhausted and sleepy he fancies that nature, too, is in the same condition. It seemed to me that the trees and the young grass were asleep. It seemed as though even the bells were not pealing so loudly and gaily as at night. The restlessness was over, and of the excitement nothing was left but a pleasant weariness, a longing for sleep and warmth.

Now I could see both banks of the river; a faint mist hovered over it in shifting masses. There was a harsh cold breath from the water. When I jumped on to the ferry, a chaise and some two dozen men and women were standing on it already. The rope, wet and as I fancied drowsy, stretched far away across the broad river and in places disappeared in the white mist.

"Christ is risen! Is there no one else?" asked a soft voice.

I recognized the voice of Ieronim. There was no darkness now to hinder me from seeing the monk. He was a tall narrow-shouldered man of five-and-thirty, with large rounded features, with half-closed listless-looking eyes and an unkempt wedge-shaped beard. He had an extraordinarily sad and exhausted look.

"They have not relieved you yet?" I asked in surprise.

"Me?" he answered, turning to me his chilled and dewy face with a smile. "There is no one to take my place now till morning. They'll all be going to the Father Archimandrite's to break the fast directly."

With the help of a little peasant in a hat of reddish fur that looked like the little wooden tubs in which honey is sold, he threw his weight on the rope; they gasped simultaneously, and the ferry started.

We floated across, disturbing on the way the lazily rising mist. Everyone was silent. Ieronim worked mechanically with one hand. He slowly passed his mild lustreless eyes over us; then his glance rested on the rosy face of a young merchant's wife with black eyebrows, who was standing on the ferry beside me silently shrinking from the mist that wrapped her about. He did not take his eyes off her face all the way.

There was little that was masculine in that prolonged gaze. It seemed to me that Ieronim was looking in the woman's face for the soft and tender features of his dead friend.

ON THE ROAD

"Upon the breast of a gigantic crag,
A golden cloudlet rested for one night."
LERMONTOV.*

In the room which the tavern keeper, the Cossack Semyon Tchistopluy, called the "travellers' room," that is kept exclusively for travellers, a tall, broad-shouldered man of forty was sitting at the big unpainted table. He was asleep with his elbows on the table and his head leaning on his fist. An end of tallow candle, stuck into an old pomatum pot, lighted up his light brown beard, his thick, broad nose, his sunburnt cheeks, and the thick, black eyebrows overhanging his closed eyes. . . . The nose and the cheeks and the eyebrows, all the features, each taken separately, were coarse and heavy, like the furniture and the stove in the "travellers' room," but taken all together they gave the effect of something harmonious and even beautiful. Such is the lucky star, as it is called, of the Russian face: the coarser and harsher its features the softer and more good-natured it looks. The man was dressed in a gentleman's reefer jacket, shabby, but bound with wide new braid, a plush waistcoat, and full black trousers thrust into big high boots.

On one of the benches, which stood in a continuous row along the wall, a girl of eight, in a brown dress and long black stockings, lay asleep on a coat lined with fox. Her face was pale, her hair was flaxen, her shoulders were narrow, her whole body was thin and frail, but her nose stood out as thick and ugly a lump as the man's. She was sound asleep, and unconscious that her semi-circular comb had fallen off her head and was cutting her cheek.

The "travelers' room" had a festive appearance. The air was full of the smell of freshly scrubbed floors, there were no rags hanging as usual on the line that ran diagonally across the room, and a little

*Mikhail Yurevich Lermontov (1814–1841) wrote lyrical and narrative poetry.

lamp was burning in the corner over the table, casting a patch of red light on the ikon of St. George the Victorious. From the ikon stretched on each side of the corner a row of cheap oleographs, which maintained a strict and careful gradation in the transition from the sacred to the profane. In the dim light of the candle end and the red ikon lamp the pictures looked like one continuous stripe, covered with blurs of black. When the tiled stove, trying to sing in unison with the weather, drew in the air with a howl, while the logs, as though waking up, burst into bright flame and hissed angrily, red patches began dancing on the log walls, and over the head of the sleeping man could be seen first the Elder Seraphim,* then the Shah Nasir-ed-Din, then a fat, brown baby with goggle eyes, whispering in the ear of a young girl with an extraordinarily blank, and indifferent face. . . .

Outside a storm was raging. Something frantic and wrathful, but profoundly unhappy, seemed to be flinging itself about the tavern with the ferocity of a wild beast and trying to break in. Banging at the doors, knocking at the windows and on the roof, scratching at the walls, it alternately threatened and besought, then subsided for a brief interval, and then with a gleeful, treacherous howl burst into the chimney, but the wood flared up, and the fire, like a chained dog, flew wrathfully to meet its foe, a battle began, and after it—sobs, shrieks, howls of wrath. In all of this there was the sound of angry misery and unsatisfied hate, and the mortified impatience of something accustomed to triumph.

Bewitched by this wild, inhuman music the "travellers' room" seemed spellbound for ever, but all at once the door creaked and the potboy, in a new print shirt, came in. Limping on one leg, and blinking his sleepy eyes, he snuffed the candle with his fingers, put some more wood on the fire and went out. At once from the church, which was three hundred paces from the tavern, the clock struck midnight. The wind played with the chimes as with the snowflakes; chasing the sounds of the clock it whirled them round and round over a vast space, so that some strokes were cut short or drawn out in long, vibrating notes, while others were completely lost in the

---

*The highest of the nine orders of angels.

general uproar. One stroke sounded as distinctly in the room as though it had chimed just under the window. The child, sleeping on the fox-skin, started and raised her head. For a minute she stared blankly at the dark window, at Nasir-ed-Din over whom a crimson glow from the fire flickered at that moment, then she turned her eyes upon the sleeping man.

"Daddy," she said.

But the man did not move. The little girl knitted her brow angrily, lay down, and curled up her legs. Someone in the tavern gave a loud, prolonged yawn. Soon afterwards there was the squeak of the swing door and the sound of indistinct voices. Someone came in, shaking the snow off, and stamping in felt boots which made a muffled thud.

"What is it?" a woman's voice asked languidly.

"Mademoiselle Ilovaisky has come, . . ." answered a bass voice.

Again there was the squeak of the swing door. Then came the roar of the wind rushing in. Someone, probably the lame boy, ran to the door leading to the "travelers' room," coughed deferentially, and lifted the latch.

"This way, lady, please," said a woman's voice in dulcet tones. "It's clean in here, my beauty. . . ."

The door was opened wide and a peasant with a beard appeared in the doorway, in the long coat of a coachman, plastered all over with snow from head to foot, and carrying a big trunk on his shoulder. He was followed into the room by a feminine figure, scarcely half his height, with no face and no arms, muffled and wrapped up like a bundle and also covered with snow. A damp chill, as from a cellar, seemed to come to the child from the coachman and the bundle, and the fire and the candles flickered.

"What nonsense!" said the bundle angrily, "We could go perfectly well. We have only nine more miles to go, mostly by the forest, and we should not get lost. . . ."

"As for getting lost, we shouldn't, but the horses can't go on, lady!" answered the coachman. "And it is Thy Will, O Lord! As though I had done it on purpose!"

"God knows where you have brought me. . . . Well, be quiet. . . . There are people asleep here, it seems. You can go. . . ."

The coachman put the portmanteau on the floor, and as he did so, a great lump of snow fell off his shoulders. He gave a sniff and went out.

Then the little girl saw two little hands come out from the middle of the bundle, stretch upwards and begin angrily disentangling the network of shawls, kerchiefs, and scarves. First a big shawl fell on the ground, then a hood, then a white knitted kerchief. After freeing her head, the traveller took off her pelisse and at once shrank to half the size. Now she was in a long, grey coat with big buttons and bulging pockets. From one pocket she pulled out a paper parcel, from the other a bunch of big, heavy keys, which she put down so carelessly that the sleeping man started and opened his eyes. For some time he looked blankly round him as though he didn't know where he was, then he shook his head, went to the corner and sat down. . . . The newcomer took off her great coat, which made her shrink to half her size again, she took off her big felt boots, and sat down, too.

By now she no longer resembled a bundle: she was a thin little brunette of twenty, as slim as a snake, with a long white face and curly hair. Her nose was long and sharp, her chin, too, was long and sharp, her eyelashes were long, the corners of her mouth were sharp, and, thanks to this general sharpness, the expression of her face was biting. Swathed in a closely fitting black dress with a mass of lace at her neck and sleeves, with sharp elbows and long pink fingers, she recalled the portraits of mediæval English ladies. The grave concentration of her face increased this likeness.

The lady looked round at the room, glanced sideways at the man and the little girl, shrugged her shoulders, and moved to the window. The dark windows were shaking from the damp west wind. Big flakes of snow glistening in their whiteness, lay on the window frame, but at once disappeared, borne away by the wind. The savage music grew louder and louder. . . .

After a long silence the little girl suddenly turned over, and said angrily, emphasizing each word:

"Oh, goodness, goodness, how unhappy I am! Unhappier than anyone!"

The man got up and moved with little steps to the child with a guilty air, which was utterly out of keeping with his huge figure and big beard.

"You are not asleep, dearie?" he said, in an apologetic voice. "What do you want?"

"I don't want anything, my shoulder aches! You are a wicked man, Daddy, and God will punish you! You'll see He will punish you."

"My darling, I know your shoulder aches, but what can I do, dearie?" said the man, in the tone in which men who have been drinking excuse themselves to their stern spouses. "It's the journey has made your shoulder ache, Sasha. To-morrow we shall get there and rest, and the pain will go away. . . ."

"To-morrow, to-morrow. . . . Every day you say to-morrow. We shall be going on another twenty days."

"But we shall arrive to-morrow, dearie, on your father's word of honour. I never tell a lie, but if we are detained by the snowstorm it is not my fault."

"I can't bear any more, I can't, I can't!"

Sasha jerked her leg abruptly and filled the room with an unpleasant wailing. Her father made a despairing gesture, and looked hopelessly towards the young lady. The latter shrugged her shoulders, and hesitatingly went up to Sasha.

"Listen, my dear," she said, "it is no use crying. It's really naughty; if your shoulder aches it can't be helped."

"You see, Madam," said the man quickly, as though defending himself, "we have not slept for two nights, and have been travelling in a revolting conveyance. Well, of course, it is natural she should be ill and miserable, . . . and then, you know, we had a drunken driver, our portmanteau has been stolen . . . the snowstorm all the time, but what's the use of crying Madam? I am exhausted, though, by sleeping in a sitting position, and I feel as though I were drunk. Oh, dear! Sasha, and I feel sick as it is, and then you cry!"

The man shook his head, and with a gesture of despair sat down.

"Of course you mustn't cry," said the young lady. "It's only little babies cry. If you are ill, dear, you must undress and go to sleep. . . . Let us take off your things!"

When the child had been undressed and pacified a silence reigned again. The young lady seated herself at the window, and looked round wonderingly at the room of the inn, at the ikon, at the stove. . . . Apparently the room and the little girl with the thick nose, in her short boy's nightgown, and the child's father, all seemed strange to her. This strange man was sitting in a corner; he kept looking about him helplessly, as though he were drunk, and rubbing his face with the palm of his hand. He sat silent, blinking, and judging from his guilty-looking figure it was difficult to imagine that he would soon begin to speak. Yet he was the first to begin. Stroking his knees, he gave a cough, laughed, and said:

"It's a comedy, it really is. . . . I look and I cannot believe my eyes: for what devilry has destiny driven us to this accursed inn? What did she want to show by it? Life sometimes performs such '*salto mortale*,'* one can only stare and blink in amazement. Have you come from far, Madam?"

"No, not from far," answered the young lady. "I am going from our estate, fifteen miles from here, to our farm, to my father and brother. My name is Ilovaisky, and the farm is called Ilovaiskoe. It's nine miles away. What unpleasant weather!"

"It couldn't be worse."

The lame boy came in and stuck a new candle in the pomatum pot.

"You might bring us the samovar, boy," said the man, addressing him.

"Who drinks tea now?" laughed the boy. "It is a sin to drink tea before mass. . . ."

"Never mind boy, you won't burn in hell if we do. . . ."

Over the tea the new acquaintances got into conversation.

Mlle. Ilovaisky learned that her companion was called Grigory Petrovitch Liharev, that he was the brother of the Liharev who was Marshal of Nobility in one of the neighbouring districts, and he himself had once been a landowner, but had "run through everything in his time." Liharev learned that her name was Marya Mihailovna, that her father had a huge estate, but that she was the only one to look after it as her father and brother looked at life through their fingers, were irresponsible, and were too fond of harriers.

"My father and brother are all alone at the farm," she told him, brandishing her fingers (she had the habit of moving her fingers be-

---

*Mortal leap (Italian).

fore her pointed face as she talked, and after every sentence moistened her lips with her sharp little tongue). "They, I mean men, are an irresponsible lot, and don't stir a finger for themselves. I can fancy there will be no one to give them a meal after the fast! We have no mother, and we have such servants that they can't lay the tablecloth properly when I am away. You can imagine their condition now! They will be left with nothing to break their fast, while I have to stay here all night. How strange it all is."

She shrugged her shoulders, took a sip from her cup, and said:

"There are festivals that have a special fragrance: at Easter, Trinity and Christmas there is a peculiar scent in the air. Even unbelievers are fond of those festivals. My brother, for instance, argues that there is no God, but he is the first to hurry to Matins at Easter."

Liharev raised his eyes to Mlle. Ilovaisky and laughed.

"They argue that there is no God," she went on, laughing too, "but why is it, tell me, all the celebrated writers, the learned men, clever people generally, in fact, believe towards the end of their life?"

"If a man does not know how to believe when he is young, Madam, he won't believe in his old age if he is ever so much of a writer."

Judging from Liharev's cough he had a bass voice, but, probably from being afraid to speak aloud, or from exaggerated shyness, he spoke in a tenor. After a brief pause he heaved a sign and said:

"The way I look at it is that faith is a faculty of the spirit. It is just the same as a talent, one must be born with it. So far as I can judge by myself, by the people I have seen in my time, and by all that is done around us, this faculty is present in Russians in its highest degree. Russian life presents us with an uninterrupted succession of convictions and aspirations, and if you care to know, it has not yet the faintest notion of lack of faith or scepticism. If a Russian does not believe in God, it means he believes in something else."

Liharev took a cup of tea from Mlle. Ilovaisky, drank off half in one gulp, and went on:

"I will tell you about myself. Nature has implanted in my breast an extraordinary faculty for belief. Whisper it not to the night, but half my life I was in the ranks of the Atheists and Nihilists, but there was not one hour in my life in which I ceased to believe. All talents, as a rule, show themselves in early childhood, and so my faculty showed itself when I could still walk upright under the table. My mother liked her children to eat a great deal, and when she gave me food she used to say: 'Eat! Soup is the great thing in life!' I believed, and ate the soup ten times a day, ate like a shark, ate till I was disgusted and stupefied. My nurse used to tell me fairy tales, and I believed in house-spirits, in wood-elves, and in goblins of all kinds. I used sometimes to steal corrosive sublimate from my father, sprinkle it on cakes, and carry them up to the attic that the house-spirits, you see, might eat them and be killed. And when I was taught to read and understand what I read, then there was a fine to-do. I ran away to America and went off to join the brigands, and wanted to go into a monastery, and hired boys to torture me for being a Christian. And note that my faith was always active, never dead. If I was running away to America I was not alone, but seduced someone else, as great a fool as I was, to go with me, and was delighted when I was nearly frozen outside the town gates and when I was thrashed; if I went to join the brigands I always came back with my face battered. A most restless childhood, I assure you! And when they sent me to the high school and pelted me with all sorts of truths—that is, that the earth goes round the sun, or that white light is not white, but is made up of seven colours—my poor little head began to go round! Everything was thrown into a whirl in me: Navin who made the sun stand still, and my mother who in the name of the Prophet Elijah* disapproved of lightning conductors, and my father who was indifferent to the truths I had learned. My enlightenment inspired me. I wandered about the house and stables like one possessed, preaching my truths, was horrified by ignorance, glowed with hatred for anyone who saw in white light nothing but white light. . . . But all that's nonsense and childishness. Serious, so to speak, manly enthusiasms began only at the university. You have, no doubt, Madam, taken your degree somewhere?"

"I studied at Novotcherkask† at the Don Institute."

"Then you have not been to a university? So you don't know what science means. All the sciences in the world have the same passport,

---

*Biblical prophet of the Old Testament whose mission was to end the worship of foreign gods and to safeguard justice.

†Industrial town in Russia, on the River Don, founded in 1805 as the capital and cultural center of the Don Cossacks.

without which they regard themselves as meaningless . . . the striving towards truth! Every one of them, even pharmacology, has for its aim not utility, not the alleviation of life, but truth. It's remarkable! When you set to work to study any science, what strikes you first of all is its beginning. I assure you there is nothing more attractive and grander, nothing is so staggering, nothing takes a man's breath away like the beginning of any science. From the first five or six lectures you are soaring on wings of the brightest hopes, you already seem to yourself to be welcoming truth with open arms. And I gave myself up to science, heart and soul, passionately, as to the woman one loves. I was its slave; I found it the sun of my existence, and asked for no other. I studied day and night without rest, ruined myself over books, wept when before my eyes men exploited science for their own personal ends. But my enthusiasm did not last long. The trouble is that every science has a beginning but not an end, like a recurring decimal. Zoology has discovered 35,000 kinds of insects, chemistry reckons 60 elements. If in time tens of noughts can be written after these figures, Zoology and chemistry will be just as far from their end as now, and all contemporary scientific work consists in increasing these numbers. I saw through this trick when I discovered the 35,001-st and felt no satisfaction. Well, I had no time to suffer from disillusionment, as I was soon possessed by a new faith. I plunged into Nihilism,* with its manifestoes, its 'black divisions,' and all the rest of it. I 'went to the people,' worked in factories, worked as an oiler, as a barge hauler. Afterwards, when wandering over Russia, I had a taste of Russian life, I turned into a fervent devotee of that life. I loved the Russian people with poignant intensity; I loved their God and believed in Him, and in their language, their creative genius. . . . And so on, and so on. . . . I have been a Slavophile in my time, I used to pester Aksakov† with letters, and I was a Ukrainophile,‡ and an

*Philosophical and literary movement in Russia that stressed the need to destroy existing economic and social institutions; popularized by Ivan Turgenev's novel *Father and Sons* (1862).

†Sergei Timofeyevich Aksakov (1791–1859) wrote nostalgic descriptions of Russian rural life in the days of serfdom.

‡A Slavophile admires Slavic people and ideals; a Ukrainophile feels similarly about things Ukrainian.

archæologist, and a collector of specimens of peasant art. . . . I was enthusiastic over ideas, people, events, places . . . my enthusiasm was endless! Five years ago I was working for the abolition of private property; my last creed was non-resistance to evil."

Sasha gave an abrupt sigh and began moving. Liharev got up and went to her.

"Won't you have some tea, dearie?" he asked tenderly.

"Drink it yourself," the child answered rudely.

Liharev was disconcerted, and went back to the table with a guilty step.

"Then you have had a lively time," said Mlle. Ilovaisky; "you have something to remember."

"Well, yes, it's all very lively when one sits over tea and chatters to a kind listener, but you should ask what that liveliness has cost me! What price have I paid for the variety of my life? You see, Madam, I have not held my convictions like a German doctor of philosophy, *zierlichmännerlich*, I have not lived in solitude, but every conviction I have had has bound my back to the yoke, has torn my body to pieces. Judge, for yourself. I was wealthy like my brothers, but now I am a beggar. In the delirium of my enthusiasm I smashed up my own fortune and my wife's—a heap of other people's money. Now I am forty-two, old age is close upon me, and I am homeless, like a dog that has dropped behind its waggon at night. All my life I have not known what peace meant, my soul has been in continual agitation, distressed even by its hopes . . . I have been wearied out with heavy irregular work, have endured privation, have five times been in prison, have dragged myself across the provinces of Archangel and of Tobolsk* . . . it's painful to think of it! I have lived, but in my fever I have not even been conscious of the process of life itself. Would you believe it, I don't remember a single spring, I never noticed how my wife loved me, how my children were born. What more can I tell you? I have been a misfortune to all who have loved me. . . . My mother has worn mourning for me all these fif-

---

*Archangel is a far-northern Russian seaport, founded in the mid-sixteenth century, that is ice-bound in winter. Tobolsk is a remote Siberian city, founded in 1587, that trades in fish and furs.

teen years, while my proud brothers, who have had to wince, to blush, to bow their heads, to waste their money on my account, have come in the end to hate me like poison."

Liharev got up and sat down again.

"If I were simply unhappy I should thank God," he went on without looking at his listener. "My personal unhappiness sinks into the background when I remember how often in my enthusiasms I have been absurd, far from the truth, unjust, cruel, dangerous! How often I have hated and despised those whom I ought to have loved, and *vice versa*, I have changed a thousand times. One day I believe, fall down and worship, the next I flee like a coward from the gods and friends of yesterday, and swallow in silence the 'scoundrel!' they hurl after me. God alone has seen how often I have wept and bitten my pillow in shame for my enthusiasms. Never once in my life have I intentionally lied or done evil, but my conscience is not clear! I cannot even boast, Madam, that I have no one's life upon my conscience, for my wife died before my eyes, worn out by my reckless activity. Yes, my wife! I tell you they have two ways of treating women nowadays. Some measure women's skulls to prove woman is inferior to man, pick out her defects to mock at her, to look original in her eyes, and to justify their sensuality. Others do their utmost to raise women to their level, that is, force them to learn by heart the 35,000 species, to speak and write the same foolish things as they speak and write themselves."

Liharev's face darkened.

"I tell you that woman has been and always will be the slave of man," he said in a bass voice, striking his fist on the table. "She is the soft, tender wax which a man always moulds into anything he likes. . . . My God! for the sake of some trumpery masculine enthusiasm she will cut off her hair, abandon her family, die among strangers! . . . among the ideas for which she has sacrificed herself there is not a single feminine one. . . . An unquestioning, devoted slave! I have not measured skulls, but I say this from hard, bitter experience: the proudest, most independent women, if I have succeeded in communicating to them my enthusiasm, have followed me without criticism, without question, and done anything I chose; I have turned a nun into a Nihilist who, as I heard afterwards, shot a gendarme; my wife never left me for a minute in my wanderings, and like a weathercock changed her faith in step with my changing enthusiasms.

Liharev jumped up and walked up and down the room.

"A noble, sublime slavery!" he said, clasping his hands. "It is just in it that the highest meaning of woman's life lies! Of all the fearful medley of thoughts and impressions accumulated in my brain from my association with women my memory, like a filter, has retained no ideas, no clever saying, no philosophy, nothing but that extraordinary, resignation to fate, that wonderful mercifulness, forgiveness of everything."

Liharev clenched his fists, stared at a fixed point, and with a sort of passionate intensity, as though he were savouring each word as he uttered it, hissed through his clenched teeth:

"That . . . that great-hearted fortitude, faithfulness unto death, poetry of the heart. . . . The meaning of life lies in just that unrepining martyrdom, in the tears which would soften a stone, in the boundless, all-forgiving love which brings light and warmth into the chaos of life. . . ."

Mlle. Ilovaisky got up slowly, took a step towards Liharev, and fixed her eyes upon his face. From the tears that glittered on his eyelashes, from his quivering, passionate voice, from the flush on his cheeks, it was clear to her that women were not a chance, not a simple subject of conversation. They were the object of his new enthusiasm, or, as he said himself, his new faith! For the first time in her life she saw a man carried away, fervently believing. With his gesticulations, with his flashing eyes he seemed to her mad, frantic, but there was a feeling of such beauty in the fire of his eyes, in his words, in all the movements of his huge body, that without noticing what she was doing she stood facing him as though rooted to the spot, and gazed into his face with delight.

"Take my mother," he said, stretching out his hand to her with an imploring expression on his face, "I poisoned her existence, according to her ideas disgraced the name of Liharev, did her as much harm as the most malignant enemy, and what do you think? My brothers give her little sums for holy bread and church services, and outraging her religious feelings, she saves that money and sends it in secret to her erring Grigory. This trifle alone elevates and ennobles the soul far more than all the theories, all the clever sayings and the 35,000 species. I can give you thousands of instances. Take you, even, for instance! With tempest and darkness outside you are going to your father and your brother to cheer them with your affection in the holiday, though very likely they have forgotten and are not thinking of you. And, wait a bit, and you will love a man and follow him to the North Pole. You would, wouldn't you?"

"Yes, if I loved him."

"There, you see," cried Liharev delighted, and he even stamped with his foot. "Oh dear! How glad I am that I have met you! Fate is kind to me, I am always meeting splendid people. Not a day passes but one makes acquaintance with somebody one would give one's soul for. There are ever so many more good people than bad in this world. Here, see, for instance, how openly and from our hearts we have been talking as though we had known each other a hundred years. Sometimes, I assure you, one restrains oneself for ten years and holds one's tongue, is reserved with one's friends and one's wife, and meets some cadet in a train and babbles one's whole soul out to him. It is the first time I have the honour of seeing you, and yet I have confessed to you as I have never confessed in my life. Why is it?"

Rubbing his hands and smiling good-humouredly Liharev walked up and down the room, and fell to talking about women again. Meanwhile they began ringing for matins.

"Goodness," wailed Sasha. "He won't let me sleep with his talking!"

"Oh, yes!" said Liharev, startled. "I am sorry, darling, sleep, sleep. . . . I have two boys besides her," he whispered. "They are living with their uncle, Madam, but this one can't exist a day without her father. She's wretched, she complains, but she sticks to me like a fly to honey. I have been chattering too much, Madam, and it would do you no harm to sleep. Wouldn't you like me to make up a bed for you?"

Without waiting for permission he shook the wet pelisse, stretched it on a bench, fur side upwards, collected various shawls and scarves, put the overcoat folded up into a roll for a pillow, and all this he did in silence with a look of devout reverence, as though he were not handling a woman's rags, but the fragments of holy vessels. There was something apologetic, embarrassed about his whole figure, as though in the presence of a weak creature he felt ashamed of his height and strength. . . .

When Mlle. Ilovaisky had lain down, he put out the candle and sat down on a stool by the stove.

"So, Madam," he whispered, lighting a fat cigarette and puffing the smoke into the stove. "Nature has put into the Russian an extraordinary faculty for belief, a searching intelligence, and the gift of speculation, but all that is reduced to ashes by irresponsibility, laziness, and dreamy frivolity. . . . Yes. . . ."

She gazed wonderingly into the darkness, and saw only a spot of red on the ikon and the flicker of the light of the stove on Liharev's face. The darkness, the chime of the bells, the roar of the storm, the lame boy, Sasha with her fretfulness, unhappy Liharev and his sayings—all this was mingled together, and seemed to grow into one huge impression, and God's world seemed to her fantastic, full of marvels and magical forces. All that she had heard was ringing in her ears, and human life presented itself to her as a beautiful poetic fairy-tale without an end.

The immense impression grew and grew, clouded consciousness, and turned into a sweet dream. She was asleep, though she saw the little ikon lamp and a big nose with the light playing on it.

She heard the sound of weeping.

"Daddy, darling," a child's voice was tenderly entreating, "let's go back to uncle! There is a Christmas-tree there! Styopa and Kolya are there!"

"My darling, what can I do?" a man's bass persuaded softly. "Understand me! Come, understand!"

And the man's weeping blended with the child's. This voice of human sorrow, in the midst of the howling of the storm, touched the girl's ear with such sweet human music that she could not bear the delight of it, and wept too. She was conscious afterwards of a big, black shadow coming softly up to her, picking up a shawl that had dropped on to the floor and carefully wrapping it round her feet.

Mlle. Ilovaisky was awakened by a strange uproar. She jumped up and looked about her in astonishment. The deep blue dawn was looking in at the window half-covered with snow. In the room there was a grey twilight, through which the stove and the sleeping child and Nasir-ed-Din stood out distinctly. The stove and the lamp were both out. Through the wide-open door she could see the big tavern room with a counter and chairs. A man, with a stupid, gipsy face and astonished eyes, was standing in the middle of the room in a puddle of melting snow, holding a big red star on a stick. He was surrounded by a group of boys, motionless as statues, and plastered over with snow. The light shone through the red paper of the star, throwing a glow of red on their wet faces. The crowd was shouting in disorder, and from its uproar Mlle. Ilovaisky could make out only one couplet:

> "Hi, you Little Russian lad,
> Bring your sharp knife,
> We will kill the Jew, we will kill him,
> The son of tribulation. . . ."

Liharev was standing near the counter, looking feelingly at the singers and tapping his feet in time. Seeing Mlle. Ilovaisky, he smiled all over his face and came up to her. She smiled too.

"A happy Christmas!" he said. "I saw you slept well."

She looked at him, said nothing, and went on smiling.

After the conversation in the night he seemed to her not tall and broad shouldered, but little, just as the biggest steamer seems to us a little thing when we hear that it has crossed the ocean.

"Well, it is time for me to set off," she said. "I must put on my things. Tell me where you are going now?"

"I? To the station of Klinushki, from there to Sergievo, and from Sergievo, with horses, thirty miles to the coal mines that belong to a horrid man, a general called Shashkovsky. My brothers have got me the post of superintendent there. . . . I am going to be a coal miner."

"Stay, I know those mines. Shashkovsky is my uncle, you know. But . . . what are you going there for?" asked Mlle. Ilovaisky, looking at Liharev in surprise.

"As superintendent. To superintend the coal mines."

"I don't understand!" she shrugged her shoulders. "You are going to the mines. But you know, it's the bare steppe, a desert, so dreary that you couldn't exist a day there! It's horrible coal, no one will buy it, and my uncle's a maniac, a despot, a bankrupt. . . . You won't get your salary!"

"No matter," said Liharev, unconcernedly, "I am thankful even for coal mines."

She shrugged her shoulders, and walked about the room in agitation.

"I don't understand, I don't understand," she said, moving her fingers before her face. "It's impossible, and . . . and irrational! You must understand that it's . . . it's worse than exile. It is a living tomb! O Heavens!" she said hotly, going up to Liharev and moving her fingers before his smiling face; her upper lip was quivering, and her sharp face turned pale, "Come, picture it, the bare steppe, solitude. There is no one to say a word to there, and you . . . are enthusiastic over women! Coal mines . . . and women!"

Mlle. Ilovaisky was suddenly ashamed of her heat and, turning away from Liharev, walked to the window.

"No, no, you can't go there," she said, moving her fingers rapidly over the pane.

Not only in her heart, but even in her spine she felt that behind her stood an infinitely unhappy man, lost and outcast, while he, as though he were unaware of his unhappiness, as though he had not shed tears in the night, was looking at her with a kindly smile. Better he should go on weeping! She walked up and down the room several times in agitation, then stopped short in a corner and sank into thought. Liharev was saying something, but she did not hear him. Turning her back on him she took out of her purse a money note, stood for a long time crumpling it in her hand, and looking round at Liharev, blushed and put it in her pocket.

The coachman's voice was heard through the door. With a stern, concentrated face she began putting on her things in silence. Liharev wrapped her up, chatting gaily, but every word he said lay on her heart like a weight. It is not cheering to hear the unhappy or the dying jest.

When the transformation of a live person into a shapeless bundle had been completed, Mlle. Ilovaisky looked for the last time round the "travellers' room," stood a moment in silence, and slowly walked out. Liharev went to see her off. . . .

Outside, God alone knows why, the winter was raging still.

Whole clouds of big soft snowflakes were whirling restlessly over the earth, unable to find a resting-place. The horses, the sledge, the trees, a bull tied to a post, all were white and seemed soft and fluffy.

"Well, God help you," muttered Liharev, tucking her into the sledge. "Don't remember evil against me. . . ."

She was silent. When the sledge started, and had to go round a huge snowdrift, she looked back at Liharev with an expression as though she wanted to say something to him. He ran up to her, but she did not say a word to him, she only looked at him through her long eyelashes with little specks of snow on them.

Whether his finely intuitive soul were really able to read that look, or whether his imagination deceived him, it suddenly began to seem to him that with another touch or two that girl would have forgiven him his failures, his age, his desolate position, and would have followed him without question or reasonings. He stood a long while as though rooted to the spot, gazing at the tracks left by the sledge runners. The snowflakes greedily settled on his hair, his beard, his shoulders. . . . Soon the track of the runners had vanished, and he himself covered with snow, began to look like a white rock, but still his eyes kept seeking something in the clouds of snow.

THE DEPENDENTS

Mihail Petrovitch Zotov, a decrepit and solitary old man of seventy, belonging to the artisan class, was awakened by the cold and the aching in his old limbs. It was dark in his room, but the little lamp before the ikon was no longer burning. Zotov raised the curtain and looked out of the window. The clouds that shrouded the sky were beginning to show white here and there, and the air was becoming transparent, so it must have been nearly five, not more.

Zotov cleared his throat, coughed, and shrinking from the cold, got out of bed. In accordance with years of habit, he stood for a long time before the ikon, saying his prayers. He repeated "Our Father," "Hail Mary," the Creed, and mentioned a long string of names. To whom those names belonged he had forgotten years ago, and he only repeated them from habit. From habit, too, he swept his room and entry, and set his fat little four-legged copper samovar. If Zotov had not had these habits he would not have known how to occupy his old age.

The little samovar slowly began to get hot, and all at once, unexpectedly, broke into a tremulous bass hum.

"Oh, you've started humming!" grumbled Zotov. "Hum away then, and bad luck to you!"

At that point the old man appropriately recalled that, in the preceding night, he had dreamed of a stove, and to dream of a stove is a sign of sorrow.

Dreams and omens were the only things left that could rouse him to reflection; and on this occasion he plunged with a special zest into the considerations of the questions: What the samovar was humming for? and what sorrow was foretold by the stove? The dream seemed to come true from the first. Zotov rinsed out his teapot and was about to make his tea, when he found there was not one teaspoonful left in the box.

"What an existence!" he grumbled, rolling crumbs of black bread round in his mouth. "It's a dog's life. No tea! And it isn't as though I were a simple peasant: I'm an artisan and a house-owner. The disgrace!"

Grumbling and talking to himself, Zotov put on his overcoat, which was like a crinoline, and, thrusting his feet into huge clumsy golosh-boots (made in the year 1867 by a bootmaker called Prohoritch), went out into the yard. The air was grey, cold, and sullenly still. The big yard, full of tufts of burdock and strewn with yellow leaves, was faintly silvered with autumn frost. Not a breath of wind nor a sound. The old man sat down on the steps of his slanting porch, and at once there happened what happened regularly every morning: his dog Lyska, a big, mangy, decrepit-looking, white yard-dog, with black patches, came up to him with its right eye shut. Lyska came up timidly, wriggling in a frightened way, as though her paws were not touching the earth but a hot stove, and the whole of her wretched figure was expressive of abjectness. Zotov pretended not to notice her, but when she faintly wagged her tail, and, wriggling as before, licked his golosh, he stamped his foot angrily.

"Be off! The plague take you!" he cried. "Con-found-ed bea-east!"

Lyska moved aside, sat down, and fixed her solitary eye upon her master.

"You devils!" he went on. "You are the last straw on my back, you Herods."

And he looked with hatred at his shed with its crooked, overgrown roof; there from the door of the shed a big horse's head was looking out at him. Probably flattered by its master's attention, the head moved, pushed forward, and there emerged from the shed the whole horse, as decrepit as Lyska, as timid and as crushed, with spindly legs, grey hair, a pinched stomach, and a bony spine. He came out of the shed and stood still, hesitating as though overcome with embarrassment.

"Plague take you," Zotov went on. "Shall I ever see the last of you, you jail-bird Pharaohs! . . . I wager you want your breakfast!" he jeered, twisting his angry face into a contemptuous smile. "By all means, this minute! A priceless steed like you must have your fill of the best oats! Pray begin! This minute! And I have something to give to the magnificent, valuable dog! If a precious dog like you does not care for bread, you can have meat."

Zotov grumbled for half an hour, growing more and more irritated. In the end, unable to control the anger that boiled up in him, he jumped up, stamped with his goloshes, and growled out to be heard all over the yard:

"I am not obliged to feed you, you loafers! I am not some millionaire for you to eat me out of house and home! I have nothing to eat myself, you cursed carcasses, the cholera take you! I get no pleasure or profit out of you; nothing but trouble and ruin. Why don't you give up the ghost? Are you such personages that even death won't take you? You can live, damn you! but I don't want to feed you! I have had enough of you! I don't want to!"

Zotov grew wrathful and indignant, and the horse and dog listened. Whether these two dependents understood that they were being reproached for living at his expense, I don't know, but their stomachs looked more pinched than ever, and their whole figures shrivelled up, grew gloomier and more abject than before. . . . Their submissive air exasperated Zotov more than ever.

"Get away!" he shouted, overcome by a sort of inspiration. "Out of my house! Don't let me set eyes on you again! I am not obliged to keep all sorts of rubbish in my yard! Get away!"

The old man moved with little hurried steps to the gate, opened it, and picking up a stick from the ground, began driving out his dependents. The horse shook its head, moved its shoulder-blades, and limped to the gate; the dog followed him. Both of them went out into the street, and, after walking some twenty paces, stopped at the fence.

"I'll give it you!" Zotov threatened them.

When he had driven out his dependents he felt calmer, and began sweeping the yard. From time to time he peeped out into the street: the horse and the dog were standing like posts by the fence, looking dejectedly towards the gate.

"Try how you can do without me," muttered the old man, feeling as though a weight of anger were being lifted from his heart. "Let somebody else look after you now! I am stingy and ill-tempered. . . . It's nasty living with me, so you try living with other people. . . . Yes. . . ."

After enjoying the crushed expression of his dependents, and grumbling to his heart's content, Zotov went out of the yard, and, assuming a ferocious air, shouted:

"Well, why are you standing there? Whom are you waiting for? Standing right across the middle of the road and preventing the public from passing! Go into the yard!"

The horse and the dog with drooping heads and a guilty air turned towards the gate. Lyska, probably feeling she did not deserve forgiveness, whined piteously.

"Stay you can, but as for food, you'll get nothing from me! You may die, for all I care!"

Meanwhile the sun began to break through the morning mist; its slanting rays glided over the autumn frost. There was a sound of steps and voices. Zotov put back the broom in its place, and went out of the yard to see his crony and neighbour, Mark Ivanitch, who kept a little general shop. On reaching his friend's shop, he sat down on a folding-stool, sighed sedately, stroked his beard, and began about the weather. From the weather the friends passed to the new deacon, from the deacon to the choristers; and the conversation lengthened out. They did not notice as they talked how time was passing, and when the shop-boy brought in a big teapot of boiling water, and the friends proceeded to drink tea, the time flew as quickly as a bird. Zotov got warm and felt more cheerful.

"I have a favour to ask of you, Mark Ivanitch," he began, after the sixth glass, drumming on the counter with his fingers. "If you would just . . . be so kind as to give me a gallon of oats again to-day. . . ."

From behind the big tea-chest behind which Mark Ivanitch was sitting came the sound of a deep sigh.

"Do be so good," Zotov went on; "never mind tea—don't give it me to-day, but let me have some oats. . . . I am ashamed to ask you, I have wearied you with my poverty, but the horse is hungry."

"I can give it you," sighed the friend—"why not? But why the devil do you keep those carcases? Tell me that, please. It would be all right if it were a useful horse, but—tfoo!—one is ashamed to look at it. . . . And the dog's nothing but a skeleton! Why the devil do you keep them?"

"What am I to do with them?"

"You know. Take them to Ignat the slaughterer—that is all there is to do. They ought to have been there long ago. It's the proper place for them."

"To be sure, that is so! . . . I dare say! . . ."

"You live like a beggar and keep animals," the friend went on. "I don't grudge the oats. . . . God bless you. But as to the future, brother . . . I can't afford to give regularly every day! There is no end to your poverty! One gives and gives, and one doesn't know when there will be an end to it all."

The friend sighed and stroked his red face.

"If you were dead that would settle it," he said. "You go on living, and you don't know what for. . . . Yes, indeed! But if it is not the Lord's will for you to die, you had better go somewhere into an almshouse or a refuge."

"What for? I have relations. I have a great-niece. . . ."

And Zotov began telling at great length of his great-niece Glasha, daughter of his niece Katerina, who lived somewhere on a farm.

"She is bound to keep me!" he said. "My house will be left to her, so let her keep me; I'll go to her. It's Glasha, you know . . . Katya's daughter; and Katya, you know, was my brother Panteley's step-daughter. . . . You understand? The house will come to her. . . . Let her keep me!"

"To be sure; rather than live, as you do, a beggar, I should have gone to her long ago."

"I will go! As God's above, I will go. It's her duty."

When an hour later the old friends were drinking a glass of vodka, Zotov stood in the middle of the shop and said with enthusiasm:

"I have been meaning to go to her for a long time; I will go this very day."

"To be sure; rather than hanging about and dying of hunger, you ought to have gone to the farm long ago."

"I'll go at once! When I get there, I shall say: Take my house, but keep me and treat me with respect. It's your duty! If you don't care to, then there is neither my house, nor my blessing for you! Good-bye, Ivanitch!"

Zotov drank another glass, and, inspired by the new idea, hurried home. The vodka had upset him and his head was reeling, but instead of lying down, he put all his clothes together in a bundle, said a prayer, took his stick, and went out. Muttering and tapping on the stones with his stick, he walked the whole length of the street without looking back, and found himself in the open country. It was eight or nine miles to the farm. He walked along the dry road, looked at the town herd lazily munching the yellow grass, and pondered on the abrupt change in his life which he had only just brought about so resolutely. He thought, too, about his dependents. When he went out of the house, he had not locked the gate, and so had left them free to go whither they would.

He had not gone a mile into the country when he heard steps behind him. He looked round and angrily clasped his hands. The horse and Lyska, with their heads drooping and their tails between their legs, were quietly walking after him.

"Go back!" he waved to them.

They stopped, looked at one another, looked at him. He went on, they followed him. Then he stopped and began ruminating. It was impossible to go to his great-niece Glasha, whom he hardly knew, with these creatures; he did not want to go back and shut them up, and, indeed, he could not shut them up, because the gate was no use.

"To die of hunger in the shed," thought Zotov. "Hadn't I really better take them to Ignat?"

Ignat's hut stood on the town pasture-ground, a hundred paces from the flagstaff. Though he had not quite made up his mind, and did not know what to do, he turned towards it. His head was giddy and there was a darkness before his eyes. . . .

He remembers little of what happened in the slaughterer's yard. He has a memory of a sickening, heavy smell of hides and the savoury steam of the cabbage-soup Ignat was sipping when he went in to him. As in a dream he saw Ignat, who made him wait two hours, slowly preparing something, changing his clothes, talking to some women about corrosive sublimate; he remembered the horse was put into a stand, after which there was the sound of two dull thuds, one of a blow on the skull, the other the fall of a heavy body. When Lyska, seeing the death of her friend, flew at Ignat, barking shrilly, there was the sound of a third blow that cut short the bark abruptly. Further, Zotov remembers that in his drunken foolishness, seeing the two corpses, he went up to the stand, and put his own forehead ready for a blow.

And all that day his eyes were dimmed by a haze, and he could not even see his own fingers.

GRISHA

Grisha, a chubby little boy, born two years and eight months ago, is walking on the boulevard with his nurse. He is wearing a long, wadded pelisse, a scarf, a big cap with a fluffy pom-pom, and warm over-boots. He feels hot and stifled, and now, too, the rollicking April sunshine is beating straight in his face, and making his eyelids tingle.

The whole of his clumsy, timidly and uncertainly stepping little figure expresses the utmost bewilderment.

Hitherto Grisha has known only a rectangular world, where in one corner stands his bed, in the other nurse's trunk, in the third a chair, while in the fourth there is a little lamp burning. If one looks under the bed, one sees a doll with a broken arm and a drum; and behind nurse's trunk, there are a great many things of all sorts: cotton reels, boxes without lids, and a broken Jack-a-dandy. In that world, besides nurse and Grisha, there are often mamma and the cat. Mamma is like a doll, and puss is like papa's fur-coat, only the coat hasn't got eyes and a tail. From the world which is called the nursery a door leads to a great expanse where they have dinner and tea. There stands Grisha's chair on high legs, and on the wall hangs a clock which exists to swing its pendulum and chime. From the dining-room, one can go into a room where there are red armchairs. Here, there is a dark patch on the carpet, concerning which fingers are still shaken at Grisha. Beyond that room is still another, to which one is not admitted, and where one sees glimpses of papa—an extremely enigmatical person! Nurse and mamma are comprehensible: they dress Grisha, feed him, and put him to bed, but what papa exists for is unknown. There is another enigmatical person, auntie, who presented Grisha with a drum. She appears and disappears. Where does she disappear to? Grisha has more than once looked under the bed, behind the trunk, and under the sofa, but she was not there. . . .

In this new world, where the sun hurts one's eyes, there are so many papas and mammas and aunties, that there is no knowing to whom to run. But what is stranger and more absurd than anything is the horses. Grisha gazes at their moving legs, and can make nothing of it. He looks at his nurse for her to solve the mystery, but she does not speak.

All at once he hears a fearful tramping. . . . A crowd of soldiers, with red faces and bath brooms under their arms, move in step along the boulevard straight upon him. Grisha turns cold all over with terror, and looks inquiringly at nurse to know whether it is dangerous. But nurse neither weeps nor runs away, so there is no danger. Grisha looks after the soldiers, and begins to move his feet in step with them himself.

Two big cats with long faces run after each other across the boulevard, with their tongues out, and their tails in the air. Grisha thinks that he must run too, and runs after the cats.

"Stop!" cries nurse, seizing him roughly by the shoulder. "Where are you off to? Haven't you been told not to be naughty?"

Here there is a nurse sitting holding a tray of oranges. Grisha passes by her, and, without saying anything, takes an orange.

"What are you doing that for?" cries the companion of his travels, slapping his hand and snatching away the orange. "Silly!"

Now Grisha would have liked to pick up a bit of glass that was lying at his feet and gleaming like a lamp, but he is afraid that his hand will be slapped again.

"My respects to you!" Grisha hears suddenly, almost above his ear a loud thick voice, and he sees a tall man with bright buttons.

To his great delight, this man gives nurse his hand, stops, and begins talking to her. The brightness of the sun, the noise of the carriages, the horses, the bright buttons are all so impressively new and not dreadful, that Grisha's soul is filled with a feeling of enjoyment and he begins to laugh.

"Come along! Come along!" he cries to the man with the bright buttons, tugging at his coat-tails.

"Come along where?" asks the man.

"Come along!" Grisha insists.

He wants to say that it would be just as well to take with them papa, mamma, and the cat, but his tongue does not say what he wants to.

A little later, nurse turns out of the boulevard, and leads Grisha into a big courtyard where there is still snow; and the man with the bright buttons comes with them too. They carefully avoid the lumps of snow and the puddles, then, by a dark and dirty staircase, they go into a room. Here there is a great deal of smoke, there is a smell of roast meat, and a woman is standing by the stove frying cutlets. The cook and the nurse kiss each other, and sit down on the bench together with the man, and begin talking in a low voice. Grisha, wrapped up as he is, feels insufferably hot and stifled.

"Why is this?" he wonders, looking about him.

He sees the dark ceiling, the oven fork with two horns, the stove which looks like a great black hole.

"Mam-ma," he drawls.

"Come, come, come!" cries the nurse. "Wait a bit!"

The cook puts a bottle on the table, two wineglasses, and a pie. The two women and the man with the bright buttons clink glasses and empty them several times, and the man puts his arm round first the cook and then the nurse. And then all three begin singing in an undertone.

Grisha stretches out his hand towards the pie, and they give him a piece of it. He eats it and watches nurse drinking. . . . He wants to drink too.

"Give me some, nurse!" he begs.

The cook gives him a sip out of her glass. He rolls his eyes, blinks, coughs, and waves his hands for a long time afterwards, while the cook looks at him and laughs.

When he gets home Grisha begins to tell mamma, the walls, and the bed where he has been, and what he has seen. He talks not so much with his tongue, as with his face and his hands. He shows how the sun shines, how the horses run, how the terrible stove looks, and how the cook drinks. . . .

In the evening he cannot get to sleep. The soldiers with the brooms, the big cats, the horses, the bit of glass, the tray of oranges, the bright buttons, all gathered together, weigh on his brain. He tosses from side to side, babbles, and, at last, unable to endure his excitement, begins crying.

"You are feverish," says mamma, putting her open hand on his forehead. "What can have caused it?"

"Stove!" wails Grisha. "Go away, stove!"

"He must have eaten too much . . ." mamma decides.

And Grisha, shattered by the impressions of the new life he has just experienced, receives a spoonful of castor-oil from mamma.

THE KISS

At eight o'clock on the evening of the twentieth of May all the six batteries of the N—— Reserve Artillery Brigade halted for the night in the village of Myestetchki on their way to camp. When the general commotion was at its height, while some officers were busily occupied around the guns, while others, gathered together in the square near the church enclosure, were listening to the quartermasters, a man in civilian dress, riding a strange horse, came into sight round the church. The little dun-coloured horse with a good neck and a short tail came, moving not straight forward, but as it were sideways, with a sort of dance step, as though it were being lashed about the legs. When he reached the officers the man on the horse took off his hat and said:

"His Excellency Lieutenant-General von Rabbek invites the gentlemen to drink tea with him this minute. . . ."

The horse turned, danced, and retired sideways; the messenger raised his hat once more, and in an instant disappeared with his strange horse behind the church.

"What the devil does it mean?" grumbled some of the officers, dispersing to their quarters. "One is sleepy, and here this Von Rabbek with his tea! We know what tea means."

The officers of all the six batteries remembered vividly an incident of the previous year, when during manœuvres they, together with the officers of a Cossack regiment, were in the same way invited to tea by a count who had an estate in the neighbourhood and was a retired army officer: the hospitable and genial count made much of them, fed them, and gave them drink, refused to let them go to their quarters in the village and made them stay the night. All that, of course, was very nice—nothing better could be desired, but the worst of it was, the old army officer was so carried away by the pleasure of the young men's company that till sunrise he was telling the officers anecdotes of his glorious past, taking them over the house, showing them expensive pictures, old engravings, rare guns, reading them autograph letters from great people, while the weary and exhausted officers looked and listened, longing for their beds and yawning in their sleeves; when at last their host let them go, it was too late for sleep.

Might not this Von Rabbek be just such another? Whether he were or not, there was no help for it. The officers changed their uniforms, brushed themselves, and went all together in search of the gentleman's house. In the square by the church they were told they could get to His Excellency's by the lower path—going down behind the church to the river, going along the bank to the garden, and there an avenue would take them to the house; or by the upper way—straight from the church by the road which, half a mile from the village, led right up to His Excellency's granaries. The officers decided to go by the upper way.

"What Von Rabbek is it?" they wondered on the way. "Surely not the one who was in command of the N—— cavalry division at Plevna?"

"No, that was not Von Rabbek, but simply Rabbe and no 'von.'"

"What lovely weather!"

At the first of the granaries the road divided in two: one branch went straight on and vanished in the evening darkness, the other led to the owner's house on the right. The officers turned to the right and began to speak more softly. . . . On both sides of the road stretched stone granaries with red roofs, heavy and sullen-looking, very much like barracks of a district town. Ahead of them gleamed the windows of the manor-house.

"A good omen, gentlemen," said one of the officers. "Our setter is the foremost of all; no doubt he scents game ahead of us! . . ."

Lieutenant Lobytko, who was walking in front, a tall and stalwart fellow, though entirely without moustache (he was over five-and-twenty, yet for some reason there was no sign of hair on his round, well-fed face), renowned in the brigade for his peculiar faculty for divining the presence of women at a distance, turned round and said:

"Yes, there must be women here; I feel that by instinct."

On the threshold the officers were met by Von Rabbek himself, a comely-looking man of sixty in civilian dress. Shaking hands with his guests, he said that he was very glad and happy to see them, but begged them earnestly for God's sake to excuse him for not asking them to stay the night; two sisters with their children, some brothers, and some neighbours, had come on a visit to him, so that he had not one spare room left.

The General shook hands with every one, made his apologies, and smiled, but it was evident by his face that he was by no means so delighted as their last year's count, and that he had invited the officers simply because, in his opinion, it was a social obligation to do so. And the officers themselves, as they walked up the softly carpeted stairs, as they listened to him, felt that they had been invited to this house simply because it would have been awkward not to invite them; and at the sight of the footmen, who hastened to light the lamps in the entrance below and in the anteroom above, they began to feel as though they had brought uneasiness and discomfort into the house with them. In a house in which two sisters and their children, brothers, and neighbours were gathered together, probably on account of some family festivity, or event, how could the presence of nineteen unknown officers possibly be welcome?

At the entrance to the drawing-room the officers were met by a tall, graceful old lady with black eyebrows and a long face, very much like the Empress Eugénie. Smiling graciously and majestically, she said she was glad and happy to see her guests, and apologized that her husband and she were on this occasion unable to invite *messieurs les officiers* to stay the night. From her beautiful majestic smile, which instantly vanished from her face every time she turned away from her guests, it was evident that she had seen numbers of officers in her day, that she was in no humour for them now, and if she invited them to her house and apologized for not doing more, it was only because her breeding and position in society required it of her.

When the officers went into the big dining-room, there were about a dozen people, men and ladies, young and old, sitting at tea at the end of a long table. A group of men was dimly visible behind their chairs, wrapped in a haze of cigar smoke; and in the midst of them stood a lanky young man with red whiskers, talking loudly, with a lisp, in English. Through a door beyond the group could be seen a light room with pale blue furniture.

"Gentlemen, there are so many of you that it is impossible to introduce you all!" said the General in a loud voice, trying to sound very cheerful. "Make each other's acquaintance, gentlemen, without any ceremony!"

The officers—some with very serious and even stern faces, others with forced smiles, and all feeling extremely awkward—somehow made their bows and sat down to tea.

The most ill at ease of them all was Ryabovitch—a little officer in spectacles, with sloping shoulders, and whiskers like a lynx's. While some of his comrades assumed a serious expression, while others wore forced smiles, his face, his lynx-like whiskers, and spectacles seemed to say: "I am the shyest, most modest, and most undistinguished officer in the whole brigade!" At first, on going into the room and sitting down to the table, he could not fix his attention on any one face or object. The faces, the dresses, the cut-glass decanters of brandy, the steam from the glasses, the moulded cornices—all blended in one general impression that inspired in Ryabovitch alarm and a desire to hide his head. Like a lecturer making his first appearance before the public, he saw everything that was before his eyes, but apparently only had a dim understanding of it (among physiologists this condition, when the subject sees but does not understand, is called psychical blindness). After a little while, growing accustomed to his surroundings, Ryabovitch saw clearly and began to observe. As a shy man, unused to society, what struck him first was that in which he had always been deficient—namely, the extraordinary boldness of his new acquaintances. Von Rabbek, his wife, two elderly ladies, a young lady in a lilac dress, and the young man with the red whiskers, who was, it appeared, a younger son of Von Rabbek, very cleverly, as though they had rehearsed it beforehand, took seats between the officers, and at once got up a heated discussion in which the visitors could not help taking part. The lilac young lady hotly asserted that the artillery had a much better time than the cavalry and the infantry, while Von

Rabbek and the elderly ladies maintained the opposite. A brisk interchange of talk followed. Ryabovitch watched the lilac young lady who argued so hotly about what was unfamiliar and utterly uninteresting to her, and watched artificial smiles come and go on her face.

Von Rabbek and his family skilfully drew the officers into the discussion, and meanwhile kept a sharp lookout over their glasses and mouths, to see whether all of them were drinking, whether all had enough sugar, why some one was not eating cakes or not drinking brandy. And the longer Ryabovitch watched and listened, the more he was attracted by this insincere but splendidly disciplined family.

After tea the officers went into the drawing-room. Lieutenant Lobytko's instinct had not deceived him. There were a great number of girls and young married ladies. The "setter" lieutenant was soon standing by a very young, fair girl in a black dress, and, bending down to her jauntily, as though leaning on an unseen sword, smiled and shrugged his shoulders coquettishly. He probably talked very interesting nonsense, for the fair girl looked at his well-fed face condescendingly and asked indifferently, "Really?" And from that uninterested "Really?" the setter, had he been intelligent, might have concluded that she would never call him to heel.

The piano struck up; the melancholy strains of a valse floated out of the wide open windows, and every one, for some reason, remembered that it was spring, a May evening. Every one was conscious of the fragrance of roses, of lilac, and of the young leaves of the poplar. Ryabovitch, in whom the brandy he had drunk made itself felt, under the influence of the music stole a glance towards the window, smiled, and began watching the movements of the women, and it seemed to him that the smell of roses, of poplars, and lilac came not from the garden, but from the ladies' faces and dresses.

Von Rabbek's son invited a scraggy-looking young lady to dance, and waltzed round the room twice with her. Lobytko, gliding over the parquet floor, flew up to the lilac young lady and whirled her away. Dancing began. . . . Ryabovitch stood near the door among those who were not dancing and looked on. He had never once danced in his whole life, and he had never once in his life put his arm round the waist of a respectable woman. He was highly delighted that a man should in the sight of all take a girl he did not know round the waist and offer her his shoulder to put her hand on, but he could not imagine himself in the position of such a man. There were times when he envied the boldness and swagger of his companions and was inwardly wretched; the consciousness that he was timid, that he was round-shouldered and uninteresting, that he had a long waist and lynx-like whiskers, had deeply mortified him, but with years he had grown used to this feeling, and now, looking at his comrades dancing or loudly talking, he no longer envied them, but only felt touched and mournful.

When the quadrille began, young Von Rabbek came up to those who were not dancing and invited two officers to have a game at billiards. The officers accepted and went with him out of the drawing-room. Ryabovitch, having nothing to do and wishing to take part in the general movement, slouched after them. From the big drawing-room they went into the little drawing-room, then into a narrow corridor with a glass roof, and thence into a room in which on their entrance three sleepy-looking footmen jumped up quickly from the sofa. At last, after passing through a long succession of rooms, young Von Rabbek and the officers came into a small room where there was a billiard-table. They began to play.

Ryabovitch, who had never played any game but cards, stood near the billiard-table and looked indifferently at the players, while they in unbuttoned coats, with cues in their hands, stepped about, made puns, and kept shouting out unintelligible words.

The players took no notice of him, and only now and then one of them, shoving him with his elbow or accidentally touching him with the end of his cue, would turn round and say "Pardon!" Before the first game was over he was weary of it, and began to feel he was not wanted and in the way. . . . He felt disposed to return to the drawing-room, and he went out.

On his way back he met with a little adventure. When he had gone half-way he noticed he had taken a wrong turning. He distinctly remembered that he ought to meet three sleepy footmen on his way, but he had passed five or six rooms, and those sleepy figures seemed to have vanished into the earth. Noticing his mistake, he walked back a little way and turned to the right; he found himself in a little dark room which he had not seen on his way to the billiard-room. After standing there a little while, he resolutely opened the first door that met his eyes and walked into an absolutely dark room. Straight in front could be seen the crack in the doorway through which there was a gleam of vivid light; from the other side of the door came the muffled sound of a melancholy mazurka. Here, too, as in the drawing-room, the windows were wide open and there was a smell of poplars, lilac and roses. . . .

Ryabovitch stood still in hesitation. . . . At that moment, to his surprise, he heard hurried footsteps and the rustling of a dress, a breathless feminine voice whispered "At last!" And two soft, fragrant, unmistakably feminine arms were clasped about his neck; a warm cheek was pressed to his cheek, and simultaneously there was the sound of a kiss. But at once the bestower of the kiss uttered a faint shriek and skipped back from him, as it seemed to Ryabovitch, with aversion. He, too, almost shrieked and rushed towards the gleam of light at the door. . . .

When he went back into the drawing-room his heart was beating and his hands were trembling so noticeably that he made haste to hide them behind his back. At first he was tormented by shame and dread that the whole drawing-room knew that he had just been kissed and embraced by a woman. He shrank into himself and looked uneasily about him, but as he became convinced that people were dancing and talking as calmly as ever, he gave himself up entirely to the new sensation which he had never experienced before in his life. Something strange was happening to him. . . . His neck, round which soft, fragrant arms had so lately been clasped, seemed to him to be anointed with oil; on his left cheek near his moustache where the unknown had kissed him there was a faint chilly tingling sensation as from peppermint drops, and the more he rubbed the place the more distinct was the chilly sensation; all over, from head to foot, he was full of a strange new feeling which grew stronger and stronger. . . . He wanted to dance, to talk, to run into the garden, to laugh aloud. . . . He quite forgot that he was round-shouldered and uninteresting, that he had lynx-like whiskers and an "undistinguished appearance" (that was how his appearance had been described by some ladies whose conversation he had accidentally overheard). When Von Rabbek's wife happened to pass by him, he gave her such a broad and friendly smile that she stood still and looked at him inquiringly.

"I like your house immensely!" he said, setting his spectacles straight.

The General's wife smiled and said that the house had belonged to her father; then she asked whether his parents were living, whether he had long been in the army, why he was so thin, and so on. . . . After receiving answers to her questions, she went on, and after his conversation with her his smiles were more friendly than ever, and he thought he was surrounded by splendid people. . . .

At supper Ryabovitch ate mechanically everything offered him, drank, and without listening to anything, tried to understand what had just happened to him. . . . The adventure was of a mysterious and romantic character, but it was not difficult to explain it. No doubt some girl or young married lady had arranged a tryst with some one in the dark room; had waited a long time, and being nervous and excited had taken Ryabovitch for her hero; this was the more probable as Ryabovitch had stood still hesitating in the dark room, so that he, too, had seemed like a person expecting something. . . . This was how Ryabovitch explained to himself the kiss he had received.

"And who is she?" he wondered, looking round at the women's faces. "She must be young, for elderly ladies don't give rendezvous. That she was a lady, one could tell by the rustle of her dress, her perfume, her voice. . . ."

His eyes rested on the lilac young lady, and he thought her very attractive; she had beautiful shoulders and arms, a clever face, and a delightful voice. Ryabovitch, looking at her, hoped that she and no one else was his unknown. . . . But she laughed somehow artificially and wrinkled up her long nose, which seemed to him to make her look old. Then he turned his eyes upon the fair girl in a black dress. She was younger, simpler, and more genuine, had a charming brow, and drank very daintily out of her wineglass. Ryabovitch now hoped that it was she. But soon he began to think her face flat, and fixed his eyes upon the one next her.

"It's difficult to guess," he thought, musing. "If one takes the shoulders and arms of the lilac one only, adds the brow of the fair one and the eyes of the one on the left of Lobytko, then . . ."

He made a combination of these things in his mind and so

formed the image of the girl who had kissed him, the image that he wanted her to have, but could not find at the table. . . .

After supper, replete and exhilarated, the officers began to take leave and say thank you. Von Rabbek and his wife began again apologizing that they could not ask them to stay the night.

"Very, very glad to have met you, gentlemen," said Von Rabbek, and this time sincerely (probably because people are far more sincere and good-humoured at speeding their parting guests than on meeting them). "Delighted. I hope you will come on your way back! Don't stand on ceremony! Where are you going? Do you want to go by the upper way? No, go across the garden; it's nearer here by the lower way."

The officers went out into the garden. After the bright light and the noise the garden seemed very dark and quiet. They walked in silence all the way to the gate. They were a little drunk, pleased, and in good spirits, but the darkness and silence made them thoughtful for a minute. Probably the same idea occurred to each one of them as to Ryabovitch: would there ever come a time for them when, like Von Rabbek, they would have a large house, a family, a garden—when they, too, would be able to welcome people, even though insincerely, feed them, make them drunk and contented?

Going out of the garden gate, they all began talking at once and laughing loudly about nothing. They were walking now along the little path that led down to the river, and then ran along the water's edge, winding round the bushes on the bank, the pools, and the willows that overhung the water. The bank and the path were scarcely visible, and the other bank was entirely plunged in darkness. Stars were reflected here and there on the dark water; they quivered and were broken up on the surface—and from that alone it could be seen that the river was flowing rapidly. It was still. Drowsy curlews cried plaintively on the further bank, and in one of the bushes on the nearest side a nightingale was trilling loudly, taking no notice of the crowd of officers. The officers stood round the bush, touched it, but the nightingale went on singing.

"What a fellow!" they exclaimed approvingly. "We stand beside him and he takes not a bit of notice! What a rascal!"

At the end of the way the path went uphill, and, skirting the church enclosure, turned into the road. Here the officers, tired with walking uphill, sat down and lighted their cigarettes. On the other side of the river a murky red fire came into sight, and having nothing better to do, they spent a long time in discussing whether it was a camp fire or a light in a window, or something else. . . . Ryabovitch, too, looked at the light, and he fancied that the light looked and winked at him, as though it knew about the kiss.

On reaching his quarters, Ryabovitch undressed as quickly as possible and got into bed. Lobytko and Lieutenant Merzlyakov—a peaceable, silent fellow, who was considered in his own circle a highly educated officer, and was always, whenever it was possible, reading the "Vyestnik Evropi,"* which he carried about with him everywhere—were quartered in the same hut with Ryabovitch. Lobytko undressed, walked up and down the room for a long while with the air of a man who has not been satisfied, and sent his orderly for beer. Merzlyakov got into bed, put a candle by his pillow and plunged into reading the "Vyestnik Evropi."

"Who was she?" Ryabovitch wondered, looking at the smoky ceiling.

His neck still felt as though he had been anointed with oil, and there was still the chilly sensation near his mouth as though from peppermint drops. The shoulders and arms of the young lady in lilac, the brow and the truthful eyes of the fair girl in black, waists, dresses, and brooches, floated through his imagination. He tried to fix his attention on these images, but they danced about, broke up and flickered. When these images vanished altogether from the broad dark background, which every man sees when he closes his eyes, he began to hear hurried footsteps, the rustle of skirts, the sound of a kiss and—an intense groundless joy took possession of him. . . . Abandoning himself to this joy, he heard the orderly return and announce that there was no beer. Lobytko was terribly indignant, and began pacing up and down again.

"Well, isn't he an idiot?" he kept saying, stopping first before Ryabovitch and then before Merzlyakov. "What a fool and a dummy a man must be not to get hold of any beer! Eh? Isn't he a scoundrel?"

---

*A journal of European news.

"Of course you can't get beer here," said Merzlyakov, not removing his eyes from the "Vyestnik Evropi."

"Oh! Is that your opinion?" Lobytko persisted. "Lord have mercy upon us, if you dropped me on the moon I'd find you beer and women directly! I'll go and find some at once. . . . You may call me an impostor if I don't!"

He spent a long time in dressing and pulling on his high boots, then finished smoking his cigarette in silence and went out.

"Rabbek, Grabbek, Labbek," he muttered, stopping in the outer room. "I don't care to go alone, damn it all! Ryabovitch, wouldn't you like to go for a walk? Eh?"

Receiving no answer, he returned, slowly undressed and got into bed. Merzlyakov sighed, put the "Vyestnik Evropi" away, and put out the light.

"H'm! . . ." muttered Lobytko, lighting a cigarette in the dark.

Ryabovitch pulled the bed-clothes over his head, curled himself up in bed, and tried to gather together the floating images in his mind and to combine them into one whole. But nothing came of it. He soon fell asleep, and his last thought was that some one had caressed him and made him happy—that something extraordinary, foolish, but joyful and delightful, had come into his life. The thought did not leave him even in his sleep.

When he woke up the sensations of oil on his neck and the chill of peppermint about his lips had gone, but joy flooded his heart just as the day before. He looked enthusiastically at the window-frames, gilded by the light of the rising sun, and listened to the movement of the passers-by in the street. People were talking loudly close to the window. Lebedetsky, the commander of Ryabovitch's battery, who had only just overtaken the brigade, was talking to his sergeant at the top of his voice, being always accustomed to shout.

"What else?" shouted the commander.

"When they were shoeing yesterday, your high nobility, they drove a nail into Pigeon's hoof. The vet put on clay and vinegar; they are leading him apart now. And also, your honour, Artemyev got drunk yesterday, and the lieutenant ordered him to be put in the limber of a spare gun-carriage."

The sergeant reported that Karpov had forgotten the new cords for the trumpets and the rings for the tents, and that their honours, the officers, had spent the previous evening visiting General Von Rabbek. In the middle of this conversation the red-bearded face of Lebedetsky appeared in the window. He screwed up his short-sighted eyes, looking at the sleepy faces of the officers, and said good-morning to them.

"Is everything all right?" he asked.

"One of the horses has a sore neck from the new collar," answered Lobytko, yawning.

The commander sighed, thought a moment, and said in a loud voice:

"I am thinking of going to see Alexandra Yevgrafovna. I must call on her. Well, good-bye. I shall catch you up in the evening."

A quarter of an hour later the brigade set off on its way. When it was moving along the road by the granaries, Ryabovitch looked at the house on the right. The blinds were down in all the windows. Evidently the household was still asleep. The one who had kissed Ryabovitch the day before was asleep, too. He tried to imagine her asleep. The wide-open windows of the bedroom, the green branches peeping in, the morning freshness, the scent of the poplars, lilac, and roses, the bed, a chair, and on it the skirts that had rustled the day before, the little slippers, the little watch on the table—all this he pictured to himself clearly and distinctly, but the features of the face, the sweet sleepy smile, just what was characteristic and important, slipped through his imagination like quicksilver through the fingers. When he had ridden on half a mile, he looked back: the yellow church, the house, and the river, were all bathed in light; the river with its bright green banks, with the blue sky reflected in it and glints of silver in the sunshine here and there, was very beautiful. Ryabovitch gazed for the last time at Myestetchki, and he felt as sad as though he were parting with something very near and dear to him.

And before him on the road lay nothing but long familiar, uninteresting pictures. . . . To right and to left, fields of young rye and buckwheat with rooks hopping about in them. If one looked ahead, one saw dust and the backs of men's heads; if one looked back, one saw the same dust and faces. . . . Foremost of all marched four men with sabres—this was the vanguard. Next, behind, the crowd of singers, and behind them the trumpeters on horseback. The vanguard and the chorus of singers, like torch-bearers in a funeral procession, often forgot to keep the regulation distance and pushed a long way ahead. . . . Ryabovitch was with the first cannon of the fifth battery. He could see all the four batteries moving in front of him. For any one not a military man this long tedious procession of a moving brigade seems an intricate and unintelligible muddle; one cannot understand why there are so many people round one cannon, and why it is drawn by so many horses in such a strange network of harness, as though it really were so terrible and heavy. To Ryabovitch it was all perfectly comprehensible and therefore uninteresting. He had known for ever so long why at the head of each battery there rode a stalwart bombardier, and why he was called a bombardier; immediately behind this bombardier could be seen the horsemen of the first and then of the middle units. Ryabovitch knew that the horses on which they rode, those on the left, were called one name, while those on the right were called another—it was extremely uninteresting. Behind the horsemen came two shaft-horses. On one of them sat a rider with the dust of yesterday on his back and a clumsy and funny-looking piece of wood on his leg. Ryabovitch knew the object of this piece of wood, and did not think it funny. All the riders waved their whips mechanically and shouted from time to time. The cannon itself was ugly. On the fore part lay sacks of oats covered with canvas, and the cannon itself was hung all over with kettles, soldiers' knapsacks, bags, and looked like some small harmless animal surrounded for some unknown reason by men and horses. To the leeward of it marched six men, the gunners, swinging their arms. After the cannon there came again more bombardiers, riders, shaft-horses, and behind them another cannon, as ugly and unimpressive as the first. After the second followed a third, a fourth; near the fourth an officer, and so on. There were six batteries in all in the brigade, and four cannons in each battery. The procession covered half a mile; it ended in a string of wagons near which an extremely attractive creature—the ass, Magar, brought by a battery commander from Turkey—paced pensively with his long-eared head drooping.

Ryabovitch looked indifferently before and behind, at the backs of heads and at faces; at any other time he would have been half asleep, but now he was entirely absorbed in his new agreeable thoughts. At first when the brigade was setting off on the march he tried to persuade himself that the incident of the kiss could only be interesting as a mysterious little adventure, that it was in reality trivial, and to think of it seriously, to say the least of it, was stupid; but now he bade farewell to logic and gave himself up to dreams. . . . At one moment he imagined himself in Von Rabbek's drawing-room beside a girl who was like the young lady in lilac and the fair girl in black; then he would close his eyes and see himself with another, entirely unknown girl, whose features were very vague. In his imagination he talked, caressed her, leaned on her shoulder, pictured war, separation, then meeting again, supper with his wife, children. . . .

"Brakes on!" the word of command rang out every time they went downhill.

He, too, shouted "Brakes on!" and was afraid this shout would disturb his reverie and bring him back to reality. . . .

As they passed by some landowner's estate Ryabovitch looked over the fence into the garden. A long avenue, straight as a ruler, strewn with yellow sand and bordered with young birch-trees, met his eyes. . . . With the eagerness of a man given up to dreaming, he pictured to himself little feminine feet tripping along yellow sand, and quite unexpectedly had a clear vision in his imagination of the girl who had kissed him and whom he had succeeded in picturing to himself the evening before at supper. This image remained in his brain and did not desert him again.

At midday there was a shout in the rear near the string of wagons:

"Easy! Eyes to the left! Officers!"

The general of the brigade drove by in a carriage with a pair of white horses. He stopped near the second battery, and shouted something which no one understood. Several officers, among them Ryabovitch, galloped up to them.

"Well?" asked the general, blinking his red eyes. "Are there any sick?"

Receiving an answer, the general, a little skinny man, chewed, thought for a moment and said, addressing one of the officers:

"One of your drivers of the third cannon has taken off his leg-guard and hung it on the fore part of the cannon, the rascal. Reprimand him."

He raised his eyes to Ryabovitch and went on:

"It seems to me your front strap is too long."

Making a few other tedious remarks, the general looked at Lobytko and grinned.

"You look very melancholy today, Lieutenant Lobytko," he said. "Are you pining for Madame Lopuhov? Eh? Gentlemen, he is pining for Madame Lopuhov."

The lady in question was a very stout and tall person who had long passed her fortieth year. The general, who had a predilection for solid ladies, whatever their ages, suspected a similar taste in his officers. The officers smiled respectfully. The general, delighted at having said something very amusing and biting, laughed loudly, touched his coachman's back, and saluted. The carriage rolled on. . . .

"All I am dreaming about now which seems to me so impossible and unearthly is really quite an ordinary thing," thought Ryabovitch, looking at the clouds of dust racing after the general's carriage. "It's all very ordinary, and every one goes through it. . . . That general, for instance, has once been in love; now he is married and has children. Captain Vahter, too, is married and beloved, though the nape of his neck is very red and ugly and he has no waist. . . . Salmanov is coarse and very Tatar, but he has had a love affair that has ended in marriage. . . . I am the same as every one else, and I, too, shall have the same experience as every one else, sooner or later. . . ."

And the thought that he was an ordinary person, and that his life was ordinary, delighted him and gave him courage. He pictured *her* and his happiness as he pleased, and put no rein on his imagination. . . .

When the brigade reached their halting-place in the evening, and the officers were resting in their tents, Ryabovitch, Merzlyakov, and Lobytko were sitting round a box having supper. Merzlyakov ate without haste, and, as he munched deliberately, read the "Vyestnik Evropi," which he held on his knees. Lobytko talked incessantly and kept filling up his glass with beer, and Ryabovitch, whose head was confused from dreaming all day long, drank and said nothing. After three glasses he got a little drunk, felt weak, and had an irresistible desire to impart his new sensations to his comrades.

"A strange thing happened to me at those Von Rabbeks'," he began, trying to put an indifferent and ironical tone into his voice. "You know I went into the billiard-room. . . ."

He began describing very minutely the incident of the kiss, and a moment later relapsed into silence. . . . In the course of that moment he had told everything, and it surprised him dreadfully to find how short a time it took him to tell it. He had imagined that he could have been telling the story of the kiss till next morning. Listening to him, Lobytko, who was a great liar and consequently believed no one, looked at him sceptically and laughed. Merzlyakov twitched his eyebrows and, without removing his eyes from the "Vyestnik Evropi," said:

"That's an odd thing! How strange! . . . throws herself on a man's neck, without addressing him by name. . . . She must be some sort of hysterical neurotic."

"Yes, she must," Ryabovitch agreed.

"A similar thing once happened to me," said Lobytko, assuming a scared expression. "I was going last year to Kovno. . . . I took a second-class ticket. The train was crammed, and it was impossible to sleep. I gave the guard half a rouble; he took my luggage and led me to another compartment. . . . I lay down and covered myself with a rug. . . . It was dark, you understand. Suddenly I felt some one touch me on the shoulder and breathe in my face. I made a movement with my hand and felt somebody's elbow. . . . I opened my eyes and only imagine—a woman. Black eyes, lips red as a prime salmon, nostrils breathing passionately—a bosom like a buffer. . . ."

"Excuse me," Merzlyakov interrupted calmly, "I understand about the bosom, but how could you see the lips if it was dark?"

Lobytko began trying to put himself right and laughing at Merzlyakov's unimaginativeness. It made Ryabovitch wince. He walked away from the box, got into bed, and vowed never to confide again.

Camp life began. . . . The days flowed by, one very much like another. All those days Ryabovitch felt, thought, and behaved as though he were in love. Every morning when his orderly handed him water to wash with, and he sluiced his head with cold water, he thought there was something warm and delightful in his life.

In the evenings when his comrades began talking of love and women, he would listen, and draw up closer; and he wore the expression of a soldier when he hears the description of a battle in which he has taken part. And on the evenings when the officers, out on the spree with the setter—Lobytko—at their head, made Don Juan excursions to the "suburb," and Ryabovitch took part in such excursions, he always was sad, felt profoundly guilty, and inwardly begged *her* forgiveness. . . . In hours of leisure or on sleepless nights, when he felt moved to recall his childhood, his father and mother—everything near and dear, in fact, he invariably thought of Myestetchki, the strange horse, Von Rabbek, his wife who was like the Empress Eugénie, the dark room, the crack of light at the door. . . .

On the thirty-first of August he went back from the camp, not with the whole brigade, but with only two batteries of it. He was dreaming and excited all the way, as though he were going back to his native place. He had an intense longing to see again the strange horse, the church, the insincere family of the Von Rabbeks, the dark room. The "inner voice," which so often deceives lovers, whispered to him for some reason that he would be sure to see her . . . and he was tortured by the questions, How he should meet her? What he would talk to her about? Whether she had forgotten the kiss? If the worst came to the worst, he thought, even if he did not meet her, it would be a pleasure to him merely to go through the dark room and recall the past. . . .

Towards evening there appeared on the horizon the familiar church and white granaries. Ryabovitch's heart beat. . . . He did not hear the officer who was riding beside him and saying something to him, he forgot everything, and looked eagerly at the river shining in the distance, at the roof of the house, at the dovecote round which the pigeons were circling in the light of the setting sun.

When they reached the church and were listening to the billeting orders, he expected every second that a man on horseback would come round the church enclosure and invite the officers to tea, but . . . the billeting orders were read, the officers were in haste to go on to the village, and the man on horseback did not appear.

"Von Rabbek will hear at once from the peasants that we have come and will send for us," thought Ryabovitch, as he went into the hut, unable to understand why a comrade was lighting a candle and why the orderlies were hurriedly setting samovars. . . .

A painful uneasiness took possession of him. He lay down, then got up and looked out of the window to see whether the messenger were coming. But there was no sign of him.

He lay down again, but half an hour later he got up, and, unable to restrain his uneasiness, went into the street and strode towards the church. It was dark and deserted in the square near the church. . . . Three soldiers were standing silent in a row where the road began to go downhill. Seeing Ryabovitch, they roused themselves and saluted. He returned the salute and began to go down the familiar path.

On the further side of the river the whole sky was flooded with crimson: the moon was rising; two peasant women, talking loudly, were picking cabbage in the kitchen garden; behind the kitchen garden there were some dark huts. . . . And everything on the near side of the river was just as it had been in May: the path, the bushes, the willows overhanging the water . . . but there was no sound of the brave nightingale, and no scent of poplar and fresh grass.

Reaching the garden, Ryabovitch looked in at the gate. The garden was dark and still. . . . He could see nothing but the white stems of the nearest birch-trees and a little bit of the avenue; all the rest melted together into a dark blur. Ryabovitch looked and listened eagerly, but after waiting for a quarter of an hour without hearing a sound or catching a glimpse of a light, he trudged back. . . .

He went down to the river. The General's bath-house and the bath-sheets on the rail of the little bridge showed white before him. . . . He went on to the bridge, stood a little, and, quite unnecessarily, touched the sheets. They felt rough and cold. He looked down at the water. . . . The river ran rapidly and with a faintly audible gurgle round the piles of the bath-house. The red moon was reflected near the left bank; little ripples ran over the reflection, stretching it out, breaking it into bits, and seemed trying to carry it away. . . .

"How stupid, how stupid!" thought Ryabovitch, looking at the running water. "How unintelligent it all is!"

Now that he expected nothing, the incident of the kiss, his impatience, his vague hopes and disappointment, presented themselves in a clear light. It no longer seemed to him strange that he had not seen the General's messenger, and that he would never see the girl who had accidentally kissed him instead of some one else; on the contrary, it would have been strange if he had seen her. . . .

The water was running, he knew not where or why, just as it did in May. In May it had flowed into the great river, from the great river into the sea; then it had risen in vapour, turned into rain, and perhaps the very same water was running now before Ryabovitch's eyes again. . . . What for? Why?

And the whole world, the whole of life, seemed to Ryabovitch an unintelligible, aimless jest. . . . And turning his eyes from the water and looking at the sky, he remembered again how fate in the person of an unknown woman had by chance caressed him, he remembered his summer dreams and fancies, and his life struck him as extraordinarily meagre, poverty-stricken, and colourless. . . .

When he went back to his hut he did not find one of his comrades. The orderly informed him that they had all gone to "General von Rabbek's, who had sent a messenger on horseback to invite them. . . ."

For an instant there was a flash of joy in Ryabovitch's heart, but he quenched it at once, got into bed, and in his wrath with his fate, as though to spite it, did not go to the General's.

TYPHUS

A young lieutenant called Klimov was travelling from Petersburg to Moscow in a smoking carriage of the mail train. Opposite him was sitting an elderly man with a shaven face like a sea captain's, by all appearances a well-to-do Finn or Swede. He pulled at his pipe the whole journey and kept talking about the same subject:

"Ha, you are an officer! I have a brother an officer too, only he is a naval officer. . . . He is a naval officer, and he is stationed at Kronstadt. Why are you going to Moscow?"

"I am serving there."

"Ha! And are you a family man?"

"No, I live with my sister and aunt."

"My brother's an officer, only he is a naval officer; he has a wife and three children. Ha!"

The Finn seemed continually surprised at something, and gave a broad idiotic grin when he exclaimed "Ha!" and continually puffed at his stinking pipe. Klimov, who for some reason did not feel well, and found it burdensome to answer questions, hated him with all his heart. He dreamed of how nice it would be to snatch the wheezing pipe out of his hand and fling it under the seat, and drive the Finn himself into another compartment.

"Detestable people these Finns and . . . Greeks," he thought. "Absolutely superfluous, useless, detestable people. They simply fill up space on the earthly globe. What are they for?"

And the thought of Finns and Greeks produced a feeling akin to sickness all over his body. For the sake of comparison he tried to think of the French, of the Italians, but his efforts to think of these people evoked in his mind, for some reason, nothing but images of organ-grinders, naked women, and the foreign oleographs which hung over the chest of drawers at home, at his aunt's.

Altogether the officer felt in an abnormal state. He could not arrange his arms and legs comfortably on the seat, though he had the whole seat to himself. His mouth felt dry and sticky; there was a heavy fog in his brain; his thoughts seemed to be straying, not only within his head, but outside his skull, among the seats and the people that were shrouded in the darkness of night. Through the mist in his brain, as through a dream, he heard the murmur of voices, the rumble of wheels, the slamming of doors. The sounds of the bells, the whistles, the guards, the running to and fro of passengers on the platforms, seemed more frequent than usual. The time flew by rapidly, imperceptibly, and so it seemed as though the train were stopping at stations every minute, and metallic voices crying continually:

"Is the mail ready?"

"Yes!" was repeatedly coming from outside.

It seemed as though the man in charge of the heating came in too often to look at the thermometer, that the noise of trains going in the opposite direction and the rumble of the wheels over the bridges was incessant. The noise, the whistles, the Finn, the tobacco smoke—all this mingling with the menace and flickering of the misty images in his brain, the shape and character of which a man in health can never recall, weighed upon Klimov like an unbearable nightmare. In horrible misery he lifted his heavy head, looked at the lamp in the rays of which shadows and misty blurs seemed to be dancing. He wanted to ask for water, but his parched tongue would hardly move, and he scarcely had strength to answer the Finn's questions. He tried to lie down more comfortably and go to sleep, but he could not succeed. The Finn several times fell asleep, woke up again, lighted his pipe, addressed him with his "Ha!" and went to sleep again; and still the lieutenant's legs could not get into a comfortable position, and still the menacing images stood facing him.

At Spirovo he went out into the station for a drink of water. He saw people sitting at the table and hurriedly eating.

"And how can they eat!" he thought, trying not to sniff the air, that smelt of roast meat, and not to look at the munching mouths—they both seemed to him sickeningly disgusting.

A good-looking lady was conversing loudly with a military man in a red cap, and showing magnificent white teeth as she smiled; and the smile, and the teeth, and the lady herself made on Klimov the same revolting impression as the ham and the rissoles. He could not understand how it was the military man in the red cap was not ill at ease, sitting beside her and looking at her healthy, smiling face.

When after drinking some water he went back to his carriage, the Finn was sitting smoking; his pipe was wheezing and squelching like a golosh with holes in it in wet weather.

"Ha!" he said, surprised; "what station is this?"

"I don't know," answered Klimov, lying down and shutting his mouth that he might not breathe the acrid tobacco smoke.

"And when shall we reach Tver?"*

"I don't know. Excuse me, I . . . I can't answer. I am ill. I caught cold today."

The Finn knocked his pipe against the windowframe and began talking of his brother, the naval officer. Klimov no longer heard him; he was thinking miserably of his soft, comfortable bed, of a bottle of cold water, of his sister Katya, who was so good at making one comfortable, soothing, giving one water. He even smiled when the vision of his orderly Pavel, taking off his heavy stifling boots and putting water on the little table, flitted through his imagination. He fancied that if he could only get into his bed, have a drink of water, his nightmare would give place to sound healthy sleep.

"Is the mail ready?" a hollow voice reached him from the distance.

"Yes," answered a bass voice almost at the window.

It was already the second or third station from Spirovo.

The time was flying rapidly in leaps and bounds, and it seemed as though the bells, whistles, and stoppings would never end. In despair Klimov buried his face in the corner of the seat, clutched his head in his hands, and began again thinking of his sister Katya and his orderly Pavel, but his sister and his orderly were mixed up with

---

*Old city 100 miles northwest of Moscow, on the Volga River; in 1932 renamed Kalinin.

the misty images in his brain, whirled round, and disappeared. His burning breath, reflected from the back of the seat, seemed to scald his face; his legs were uncomfortable; there was a draught from the window on his back; but, however wretched he was, he did not want to change his position. . . . A heavy nightmarish lethargy gradually gained possession of him and fettered his limbs.

When he brought himself to raise his head, it was already light in the carriage. The passengers were putting on their fur coats and moving about. The train was stopping. Porters in white aprons and with discs on their breasts were bustling among the passengers and snatching up their boxes. Klimov put on his great-coat, mechanically followed the other passengers out of the carriage, and it seemed to him that not he, but some one else was moving, and he felt that his fever, his thirst, and the menacing images which had not let him sleep all night, came out of the carriage with him. Mechanically he took his luggage and engaged a sledge-driver. The man asked him for a rouble and a quarter to drive to Povarsky Street, but he did not haggle, and without protest got submissively into the sledge. He still understood the difference of numbers, but money had ceased to have any value to him.

At home Klimov was met by his aunt and his sister Katya, a girl of eighteen. When Katya greeted him she had a pencil and exercise book in her hand, and he remembered that she was preparing for an examination as a teacher. Gasping with fever, he walked aimlessly through all the rooms without answering their questions or greetings, and when he reached his bed he sank down on the pillow. The Finn, the red cap, the lady with the white teeth, the smell of roast meat, the flickering blurs, filled his consciousness, and by now he did not know where he was and did not hear the agitated voices.

When he recovered consciousness he found himself in bed, undressed, saw a bottle of water and Pavel, but it was no cooler, nor softer, nor more comfortable for that. His arms and legs, as before, refused to lie comfortably; his tongue stuck to the roof of his mouth, and he heard the wheezing of the Finn's pipe. . . . A stalwart, black-bearded doctor was busy doing something beside the bed, brushing against Pavel with his broad back.

"It's all right, it's all right, young man," he muttered. "Excellent, excellent . . . goo-od, goo-od . . . !"

The doctor called Klimov "young man," said "goo-od" instead of "good" and "so-o" instead of "so."

"So-o . . . so-o . . . so-o," he murmured. "Goo-od, goo-od . . . ! Excellent, young man. . . . You mustn't lose heart!"

The doctor's rapid, careless talk, his well-fed countenance, and condescending "young man," irritated Klimov.

"Why do you call me 'young man'?" he moaned. "What familiarity! Damn it all!"

And he was frightened by his own voice. The voice was so dried up, so weak and peevish, that he would not have known it.

"Excellent, excellent!" muttered the doctor, not in the least offended. . . . "You mustn't get angry, so-o, so-o, so-o. . . ."

And the time flew by at home with the same startling swiftness as in the railway carriage. . . . The daylight was continually being replaced by the dusk of evening. The doctor seemed never to leave his bedside, and he heard at every moment his "so-o, so-o, so-o." A continual succession of people was incessantly crossing the bedroom. Among them were: Pavel, the Finn, Captain Yaroshevitch, Lance-Corporal Maximenko, the red cap, the lady with the white teeth, the doctor. They were all talking and waving their arms, smoking and eating. Once by daylight Klimov saw the chaplain of the regiment, Father Alexandr, who was standing before the bed, wearing a stole and with a prayer-book in his hand. He was muttering something with a grave face such as Klimov had never seen in him before. The lieutenant remembered that Father Alexandr used in a friendly way to call all the Catholic officers "Poles," and wanting to amuse him, he cried:

"Father, Yaroshevitch the Pole has climbed up a pole!"

But Father Alexandr, a light-hearted man who loved a joke, did not smile, but became graver than ever, and made the sign of the cross over Klimov. At night-time by turn two shadows came noiselessly in and out; they were his aunt and sister. His sister's shadow knelt down and prayed; she bowed down to the ikon, and her grey shadow on the wall bowed down too, so that two shadows were praying. The whole time there was a smell of roast meat and the Finn's pipe, but once Klimov smelt the strong smell of incense. He felt so sick he could not lie still, and began shouting:

"The incense! Take away the incense!"

There was no answer. He could only hear the subdued singing of the priest somewhere and some one running upstairs.

When Klimov came to himself there was not a soul in his bedroom. The morning sun was streaming in at the window through the lower blind, and a quivering sunbeam, bright and keen as the sword's edge, was flashing on the glass bottle. He heard the rattle of wheels—so there was no snow now in the street. The lieutenant looked at the ray, at the familiar furniture, at the door, and the first thing he did was to laugh. His chest and stomach heaved with delicious, happy, tickling laughter. His whole body from head to foot was overcome by a sensation of infinite happiness and joy in life, such as the first man must have felt when he was created and first saw the world. Klimov felt a passionate desire for movement, people, talk. His body lay a motionless block; only his hands stirred, but that he hardly noticed, and his whole attention was concentrated on trifles. He rejoiced in his breathing, in his laughter, rejoiced in the existence of the water-bottle, the ceiling, the sunshine, the tape on the curtains. God's world, even in the narrow space of his bedroom, seemed beautiful, varied, grand. When the doctor made his appearance, the lieutenant was thinking what a delicious thing medicine was, how charming and pleasant the doctor was, and how nice and interesting people were in general.

"So-o, so, so. . . . Excellent, excellent! . . . Now we are well again. . . . Goo-od, goo-od!" the doctor pattered.

The lieutenant listened and laughed joyously; he remembered the Finn, the lady with the white teeth, the train, and he longed to smoke, to eat.

"Doctor," he said, "tell them to give me a crust of rye bread and salt, and . . . and sardines."

The doctor refused; Pavel did not obey the order, and did not go for the bread. The lieutenant could not bear this and began crying like a naughty child.

"Baby!" laughed the doctor. "Mammy, bye-bye!"

Klimov laughed, too, and when the doctor went away he fell into a sound sleep. He woke up with the same joyfulness and sensation of happiness. His aunt was sitting near the bed.

"Well, aunt," he said joyfully. "What has been the matter?"

"Spotted typhus."

"Really. But now I am well, quite well! Where is Katya?"

"She is not at home. I suppose she has gone somewhere from her examination."

The old lady said this and looked at her stocking; her lips began quivering, she turned away, and suddenly broke into sobs. Forgetting the doctor's prohibition in her despair, she said:

"Ah, Katya, Katya! Our angel is gone! Is gone!"

She dropped her stocking and bent down to it, and as she did so her cap fell off her head. Looking at her grey head and understanding nothing, Klimov was frightened for Katya, and asked:

"Where is she, aunt?"

The old woman, who had forgotten Klimov and was thinking only of her sorrow, said:

"She caught typhus from you, and is dead. She was buried the day before yesterday."

This terrible, unexpected news was fully grasped by Klimov's consciousness; but terrible and startling as it was, it could not overcome the animal joy that filled the convalescent. He cried and laughed, and soon began scolding because they would not let him eat.

Only a week later when, leaning on Pavel, he went in his dressing-gown to the window, looked at the overcast spring sky and listened to the unpleasant clang of the old iron rails which were being carted by, his heart ached, he burst into tears, and leaned his forehead against the window-frame.

"How miserable I am!" he muttered. "My God, how miserable!"

And joy gave way to the boredom of everyday life and the feeling of his irrevocable loss.

THE PIPE

Meliton Shishkin, a bailiff from the Dementyev farm, exhausted by the sultry heat of the fir-wood and covered with spiders' webs and pine-needles, made his way with his gun to the edge of the wood. His Damka—a mongrel between a yard dog and a setter—an extremely thin bitch heavy with young, trailed after her master with her wet tail between her legs, doing all she could to avoid pricking her nose. It was a dull, overcast morning. Big drops dripped from the bracken and from the trees that were wrapped in a light mist; there was a pungent smell of decay from the dampness of the wood.

There were birch-trees ahead of him where the wood ended, and between their stems and branches he could see the misty distance. Beyond the birch-trees someone was playing on a shepherd's rustic pipe. The player produced no more than five or six notes, dragged them out languidly with no attempt at forming a tune, and yet there was something harsh and extremely dreary in the sound of the piping.

As the copse became sparser, and the pines were interspersed with young birch-trees, Meliton saw a herd. Hobbled horses, cows, and sheep were wandering among the bushes and, snapping the dry branches, sniffed at the herbage of the copse. A lean old shepherd, bareheaded, in a torn grey smock, stood leaning against the wet trunk of a birch-tree. He stared at the ground, pondering something, and played his pipe, it seemed, mechanically.

"Good-day, grandfather! God help you!" Meliton greeted him in a thin, husky voice which seemed incongruous with his huge stature and big, fleshy face. "How cleverly you are playing your pipe! Whose herd are you minding?"

"The Artamonovs'," the shepherd answered reluctantly, and he thrust the pipe into his bosom.

"So I suppose the wood is the Artamonovs' too?" Meliton inquired, looking about him. "Yes, it is the Artamonovs'; only fancy . . . I had completely lost myself. I got my face scratched all over in the thicket."

He sat down on the wet earth and began rolling up a bit of newspaper into a cigarette.

Like his voice, everything about the man was small and out of keeping with his height, his breadth, and his fleshy face: his smiles, his eyes, his buttons, his tiny cap, which would hardly keep on his big, closely-cropped head. When he talked and smiled there was something womanish, timid, and meek about his puffy, shaven face and his whole figure.

"What weather! God help us!" he said, and he turned his head from side to side. "Folk have not carried the oats yet, and the rain seems as though it had been taken on for good, God bless it."

The shepherd looked at the sky, from which a drizzling rain was falling, at the wood, at the bailiff's wet clothes, pondered, and said nothing.

"The whole summer has been the same," sighed Meliton. "A bad business for the peasants and no pleasure for the gentry."

The shepherd looked at the sky again, thought a moment, and said deliberately, as though chewing each word:

"It's all going the same way. . . . There is nothing good to be looked for."

"How are things with you here?" Meliton inquired, lighting his cigarette. "Haven't you seen any coveys of grouse in the Artamonovs' clearing?"

The shepherd did not answer at once. He looked again at the sky and to right and left, thought a little, blinked. . . . Apparently he attached no little significance to his words, and to increase their value tried to pronounce them with deliberation and a certain solemnity. The expression of his face had the sharpness and staidness of old age, and the fact that his nose had a saddle-shaped depression across the middle and his nostrils turned upwards gave him a sly and sarcastic look.

"No, I believe I haven't," he said. "Our huntsman Eryomka was saying that on Elijah's Day he started one covey near Pustoshye, but I dare say he was lying. There are very few birds."

"Yes, brother, very few. . . . Very few everywhere! The shooting here, if one is to look at it with common sense, is good for nothing and not worth having. There is no game at all, and what there is is not worth dirtying your hands over—it is not full-grown. It is such poor stuff that one is ashamed to look at it."

Meliton gave a laugh and waved his hands.

"Things happen so queerly in this world that it is simply laughable and nothing else. Birds nowadays have become so unaccountable: they sit late on their eggs, and there are some, I declare, that have not hatched them by St. Peter's Day!"

"It's all going the same way," said the shepherd, turning his face upwards. "There was little game last year, this year there are fewer birds still, and in another five years, mark my words, there will be none at all. As far as I can see there will soon be not only no game, but no birds at all."

"Yes," Meliton assented, after a moment's thought. "That's true."

The shepherd gave a bitter smile and shook his head.

"It's a wonder," he said, "what has become of them all! I remember twenty years ago there used to be geese here, and cranes and ducks and grouse—clouds and clouds of them! The gentry used to meet together for shooting, and one heard nothing but pouf-pouf-pouf! pouf-pouf-pouf! There was no end to the woodcocks, the snipe, and the little teals, and the water-snipe were as common as starlings, or let us say sparrows—lots and lots of them! And what has become of them all? We don't even see the birds of prey. The eagles, the hawks, and the owls have all gone. . . . There are fewer of every sort of wild beast, too. Nowadays, brother, even the wolf and the fox have grown rare, let alone the bear or the otter. And you know in old days there were even elks! For forty years I have been observing the works of God from year to year, and it is my opinion that everything is going the same way."

"What way?"

"To the bad, young man. To ruin, we must suppose. . . . The time has come for God's world to perish."

The old man put on his cap and began gazing at the sky.

"It's a pity," he sighed, after a brief silence. "O God, what a pity! Of course it is God's will; the world was not created by us, but yet it is a pity, brother. If a single tree withers away, or let us say a single cow dies, it makes one sorry, but what will it be, good man, if the whole world crumbles into dust? Such blessings, Lord Jesus! The sun, and the sky, and the forest, and the rivers, and the creatures—all these have been created, adapted, and adjusted to one another. Each has been put to its appointed task and knows its place. And all that must perish."

A mournful smile gleamed on the shepherd's face, and his eyelids quivered.

"You say—the world is perishing," said Meliton, pondering. "It may be that the end of the world is near at hand, but you can't judge by the birds. I don't think the birds can be taken as a sign."

"Not the birds only," said the shepherd. "It's the wild beasts, too, and the cattle, and the bees, and the fish. . . . If you don't believe me ask the old people; every old man will tell you that the fish are not at all what they used to be. In the seas, in the lakes, and in the rivers, there are fewer fish from year to year. In our Pestchanka, I remember, pike used to be caught a yard long, and there were eel-pouts, and roach, and bream, and every fish had a presentable appearance; while nowadays, if you catch a wretched little pikelet or perch six inches long you have to be thankful. There are not any gudgeon even worth talking about. Every year it is worse and worse, and in a little while there will be no fish at all. And take the rivers now . . . the rivers are drying up, for sure."

"It is true; they are drying up."

"To be sure, that's what I say. Every year they are shallower and shallower, and there are not the deep holes there used to be. And do you see the bushes yonder?" the old man asked, pointing to one side. "Beyond them is an old river-bed; it's called a backwater. In my father's time the Pestchanka flowed there, but now look; where have the evil spirits taken it to? It changes its course, and, mind you, it will go on changing till such time as it has dried up altogether. There used to be marshes and ponds beyond Kurgasovo, and where are they now? And what has become of the streams? Here in this very wood we used to have a stream flowing, and such a stream that the peasants used to set creels in it and caught pike; wild ducks used to spend the winter by it, and nowadays there is no water in it worth speaking of, even at the spring floods. Yes, brother, look where you will, things are bad everywhere. Everywhere!"

A silence followed. Meliton sank into thought, with his eyes fixed on one spot. He wanted to think of some one part of nature as yet untouched by the all-embracing ruin. Spots of light glistened on the mist and the slanting streaks of rain as though on opaque glass, and immediately died away again—it was the rising sun trying to break through the clouds and peep at the earth.

"Yes, the forests, too . . ." Meliton muttered.

"The forests, too," the shepherd repeated. "They cut them down, and they catch fire, and they wither away, and no new ones are growing. Whatever does grow up is cut down at once; one day it shoots up and the next it has been cut down—and so on without end till nothing's left. I have kept the herds of the commune ever since the time of Freedom,* good man; before the time of Freedom I was shepherd of the master's herds. I have watched them in this very spot, and I can't remember a summer day in all my life that I have not been here. And all the time I have been observing the works of God. I have looked at them in my time till I know them, and it is my opinion that all things growing are on the decline. Whether you take the rye, or the vegetables, or flowers or any sort, they are all going the same way."

"But people have grown better," observed the bailiff.

"In what way better?"

"Cleverer."

"Cleverer, maybe, that's true, young man; but what's the use of that? What earthly good is cleverness to people on the brink of ruin? One can perish without cleverness. What's the good of cleverness to a huntsman if there is no game? What I think is that God has given men brains and taken away their strength. People have grown weak, exceedingly weak. Take me, for instance . . . I am not

---

*Czar Alexander II freed the serfs in 1861.

worth a halfpenny, I am the humblest peasant in the whole village, and yet, young man, I have strength. Mind you, I am in my seventies, and I tend my herd day in and day out, and keep the night watch, too, for twenty kopecks, and I don't sleep, and I don't feel the cold; my son is cleverer than I am, but put him in my place and he would ask for a rise next day, or would be going to the doctors. There it is. I eat nothing but bread, for 'Give us this day our daily bread,' and my father ate nothing but bread, and my grandfather; but the peasant nowadays must have tea and vodka and white loaves, and must sleep from sunset to dawn, and he goes to the doctor and pampers himself in all sorts of ways. And why is it? He has grown weak; he has not the strength to endure. If he wants to stay awake, his eyes close—there is no doing anything."

"That's true," Meliton agreed; "the peasant is good for nothing nowadays."

"It's no good hiding what is wrong; we get worse from year to year. And if you take the gentry into consideration, they've grown feebler even more than the peasants have. The gentleman nowadays has mastered everything; he knows what he ought not to know, and what is the sense of it? It makes you feel pitiful to look at him. . . . He is a thin, puny little fellow, like some Hungarian or Frenchman; there is no dignity nor air about him; it's only in name he is a gentleman. There is no place for him, poor dear, and nothing for him to do, and there is no making out what he wants. Either he sits with a hook catching fish, or he lolls on his back reading, or trots about among the peasants saying all sorts of things to them, and those that are hungry go in for being clerks. So he spends his life in vain. And he has no notion of doing something real and useful. The gentry in old days were half of them generals, but nowadays they are—a poor lot."

"They are badly off nowadays," said Meliton.

"They are poorer because God has taken away their strength. You can't go against God."

Meliton stared at a fixed point again. After thinking a little he heaved a sigh as staid, reasonable people do sigh, shook his head, and said:

"And all because of what? We have sinned greatly, we have forgotten God . . . and it seems that the time has come for all to end.

And, after all, the world can't last for ever—it's time to know when to take leave."

The shepherd sighed and, as though wishing to cut short an unpleasant conversation, he walked away from the birch-tree and began silently reckoning over the cows.

"Hey-hey-hey!" he shouted. "Hey-hey-hey! Bother you, the plague take you! The devil has taken you into the thicket. Tu-lu-lu!"

With an angry face he went into the bushes to collect his herd. Meliton got up and sauntered slowly along the edge of the wood. He looked at the ground at his feet and pondered; he still wanted to think of something which had not yet been touched by death. Patches of light crept upon the slanting streaks of rain again; they danced on the tops of the trees and died away among the wet leaves. Damka found a hedgehog under a bush, and wanting to attract her master's attention to it, barked and howled.

"Did you have an eclipse or not?" the shepherd called from the bushes.

"Yes, we had," answered Meliton.

"Ah! Folks are complaining all about that there was one. It shows there is disorder even in the heavens! It's not for nothing. . . . Hey-hey-hey! Hey!"

Driving his herd together to the edge of the wood, the shepherd leaned against the birch-tree, looked up at the sky, without haste took his pipe from his bosom and began playing. As before, he played mechanically and took no more than five or six notes; as though the pipe had come into his hands for the first time, the sounds floated from it uncertainly, with no regularity, not blending into a tune, but to Meliton, brooding on the destruction of the world, there was a sound in it of something very depressing and revolting which he would much rather not have heard. The highest, shrillest notes, which quivered and broke, seemed to be weeping disconsolately, as though the pipe were sick and frightened, while the lowest notes for some reason reminded him of the mist, the dejected trees, the grey sky. Such music seemed in keeping with the weather, the old man and his sayings.

Meliton wanted to complain. He went up to the old man and, looking at his mournful, mocking face and at the pipe, muttered:

"And life has grown worse, grandfather. It is utterly impossible to live. Bad crops, want. . . . Cattle plague continually, diseases of all sorts. . . . We are crushed by poverty."

The bailiff's puffy face turned crimson and took a dejected, womanish expression. He twirled his fingers as though seeking words to convey his vague feeling and went on:

"Eight children, a wife . . . and my mother still living, and my whole salary ten roubles a month and to board myself. My wife has become a Satan from poverty. . . . I go off drinking myself. I am a sensible, steady man; I have education. I ought to sit at home in peace, but I stray about all day with my gun like a dog because it is more than I can stand; my home is hateful to me!"

Feeling that his tongue was uttering something quite different from what he wanted to say, the bailiff waved his hand and said bitterly:

"If the world's going to end I wish it would make haste about it. There's no need to drag it out and make folks miserable for nothing. . . ."

The old man took the pipe from his lips and, screwing up one eye, looked into its little opening. His face was sad and covered with thick drops like tears. He smiled and said:

"It's a pity, my friend! My goodness, what a pity! The earth, the forest, the sky, the beasts of all sorts—all this has been created, you know, adapted; they all have their intelligence. It is all going to ruin. And most of all I am sorry for people."

There was the sound in the wood of heavy rain coming nearer. Meliton looked in the direction of the sound, did up all his buttons, and said:

"I am going to the village. Good-bye, grandfather. What is your name?"

"Luka the Poor."

"Well, good-bye, Luka! Thank you for your good words. Damka, ici!"

After parting from the shepherd Meliton made his way along the edge of the wood, and then down hill to a meadow which by degrees turned into a marsh. There was a squelch of water under his feet, and the rusty marsh sedge, still green and juicy, drooped down to the earth as though afraid of being trampled underfoot. Beyond the marsh, on the bank of the Pestchanka, of which the old man had spoken, stood a row of willows, and beyond the willows a barn looked dark blue in the mist. One could feel the approach of that miserable, utterly inevitable season, when the fields grow dark and the earth is muddy and cold, when the weeping willow seems still more mournful and tears trickle down its stem, and only the cranes fly away from the general misery, and even they, as though afraid of insulting dispirited nature by the expression of their happiness, fill the air with their mournful, dreary notes.

Meliton plodded along to the river, and heard the sounds of the pipe gradually dying away behind him. He still wanted to complain. He looked dejectedly about him, and he felt insufferably sorry for the sky and the earth and the sun and the woods and his Damka, and when the highest drawn-out note of the pipe floated quivering in the air, like a voice weeping, he felt extremely bitter and resentful of the impropriety in the conduct of nature.

The high note quivered, broke off, and the pipe was silent.

THE PRINCESS

A carriage with four fine sleek horses drove in at the big so-called Red Gate of the N—— Monastery. While it was still at a distance, the priests and monks who were standing in a group round the part of the hostel allotted to the gentry, recognised by the coachman and horses that the lady in the carriage was Princess Vera Gavrilovna, whom they knew very well.

An old man in livery jumped off the box and helped the princess to get out of the carriage. She raised her dark veil and moved in a leisurely way up to the priests to receive their blessing; then she nodded pleasantly to the rest of the monks and went into the hostel.

"Well, have you missed your princess?" she said to the monk who brought in her things. "It's a whole month since I've been to see you. But here I am; behold your princess. And where is the Father Superior? My goodness, I am burning with impatience! Wonderful, wonderful old man! You must be proud of having such a Superior."

When the Father Superior came in, the princess uttered a shriek of delight, crossed her arms over her bosom, and went up to receive his blessing.

"No, no, let me kiss your hand," she said, snatching it and eagerly kissing it three times. "How glad I am to see you at last, holy Father! I'm sure you've forgotten your princess, but my thoughts have been in your dear monastery every moment. How delightful it is here! This living for God far from the busy, giddy world has a special charm of its own, holy Father, which I feel with my whole soul although I cannot express it!"

The princess's cheeks glowed and tears came into her eyes. She talked incessantly, fervently, while the Father Superior, a grave, plain, shy old man of seventy, remained mute or uttered abruptly, like a soldier on duty, phrases such as:

"Certainly, Your Excellency. . . . Quite so. I understand."

"Has Your Excellency come for a long stay?" he inquired.

"I shall stay the night here, and to-morrow I'm going on to Klavida Nikolaevna's—it's a long time since I've seen her—and the day after to-morrow I'll come back to you and stay three or four days. I want to rest my soul here among you, holy Father. . . ."

The princess liked being at the monastery at N——. For the last two years it had been a favourite resort of hers; she used to go there almost every month in the summer and stay two or three days, even sometimes a week. The shy novices, the stillness, the low ceilings, the smell of cypress, the modest fare, the cheap curtains on the windows—all this touched her, softened her, and disposed her to contemplation and good thoughts. It was enough for her to be half an hour in the hostel for her to feel that she, too, was timid and modest, and that she, too, smelt of cypress-wood. The past retreated into the background, lost its significance, and the princess began to imagine that in spite of her twenty-nine years she was very much like the old Father Superior, and that, like him, she was created not for wealth, not for earthly grandeur and love, but for a peaceful life secluded from the world, a life in twilight like the hostel.

It happens that a ray of light gleams in the dark cell of the anchorite absorbed in prayer, or a bird alights on the window and sings its song; the stern anchorite will smile in spite of himself, and a gentle, sinless joy will pierce through the load of grief over his sins, like water flowing from under a stone. The princess fancied she brought from the outside world just such comfort as the ray of light or the bird. Her gay, friendly smile, her gentle eyes, her voice, her jests, her whole personality in fact, her little graceful figure always dressed in simple black, must arouse in simple, austere people a feeling of tenderness and joy. Every one, looking at her, must think: "God has sent us an angel. . . ." And feeling that no one could help thinking this, she smiled still more cordially, and tried to look like a bird.

After drinking tea and resting, she went for a walk. The sun was already setting. From the monastery garden came a moist fragrance of freshly watered mignonette, and from the church floated the soft singing of men's voices, which seemed very pleasant and mournful in the distance. It was the evening service. In the dark windows where the little lamps glowed gently, in the shadows, in the figure of the old monk sitting at the church door with a collecting-box, there was such unruffled peace that the princess felt moved to tears.

Outside the gate, in the walk between the wall and the birch-trees where there were benches, it was quite evening. The air grew rapidly darker and darker. The princess went along the walk, sat on a seat, and sank into thought.

She thought how good it would be to settle down for her whole life in this monastery where life was as still and unruffled as a summer evening; how good it would be to forget the ungrateful, dissipated prince; to forget her immense estates, the creditors who worried her every day, her misfortunes, her maid Dasha, who had looked at her impertinently that morning. It would be nice to sit here on the bench all her life and watch through the trunks of the birch-trees the evening mist gathering in wreaths in the valley below; the rooks flying home in a black cloud like a veil far, far away above the forest; two novices, one astride a piebald horse, another on foot driving out the horses for the night and rejoicing in their freedom, playing pranks like little children; their youthful voices rang out musically in the still air, and she could distinguish every word. It is nice to sit and listen to the silence: at one moment the wind blows and stirs the tops of the birch-trees, then a frog rustles in last year's leaves, then the clock on the belfry strikes the quarter. . . . One might sit without moving, listen and think, and think. . . .

An old woman passed by with a wallet on her back. The princess thought that it would be nice to stop the old woman and to say something friendly and cordial to her, to help her. . . . But the old woman turned the corner without once looking round.

Not long afterwards a tall man with a grey beard and a straw hat came along the walk. When he came up to the princess, he took off his hat and bowed. From the bald patch on his head and his sharp, hooked nose the princess recognised him as the doctor, Mihail Ivanovitch, who had been in her service at Dubovki. She remembered that some one had told her that his wife had died the year before, and she wanted to sympathise with him, to console him.

"Doctor, I expect you don't recognise me?" she said with an affable smile.

"Yes, Princess, I recognised you," said the doctor, taking off his hat again.

"Oh, thank you; I was afraid that you, too, had forgotten your princess. People only remember their enemies, but they forget their friends. Have you, too, come to pray?"

"I am the doctor here, and I have to spend the night at the monastery every Saturday."

"Well, how are you?" said the princess, sighing. "I hear that you have lost your wife. What a calamity!"

"Yes, Princess, for me it is a great calamity."

"There's nothing for it! We must bear our troubles with resignation. Not one hair of a man's head is lost without the Divine Will."

"Yes, Princess."

To the princess's friendly, gentle smile and her sighs the doctor responded coldly and dryly: "Yes, Princess." And the expression of his face was cold and dry.

"What else can I say to him?" she wondered.

"How long it is since we met!" she said. "Five years! How much water has flowed under the bridge, how many changes in that time; it quite frightens one to think of it! You know, I am married. . . . I am not a countess now, but a princess. And by now I am separated from my husband too."

"Yes, I heard so."

"God has sent me many trials. No doubt you have heard, too, that I am almost ruined. My Dubovki, Sofyino, and Kiryakovo have all been sold for my unhappy husband's debts. And I have only Baranovo and Milhaltsevo left. It's terrible to look back: how many changes and misfortunes of all kinds, how many mistakes!"

"Yes, Princess, many mistakes."

The princess was a little disconcerted. She knew her mistakes; they were all of such a private character that no one but she could think or speak of them. She could not resist asking:

"What mistakes are you thinking about?"

"You referred to them, so you know them . . ." answered the doctor, and he smiled. "Why talk about them!"

"No; tell me, doctor. I shall be very grateful to you. And please don't stand on ceremony with me. I love to hear the truth."

"I am not your judge, Princess."

"Not my judge! What a tone you take! You must know something about me. Tell me!"

"If you really wish it, very well. Only I regret to say I'm not clever at talking, and people can't always understand me."

The doctor thought a moment and began:

"A lot of mistakes; but the most important of them, in my opinion, was the general spirit that prevailed on all your estates. You see, I don't know how to express myself. I mean chiefly the lack of love, the aversion for people that was felt in absolutely everything. Your whole system of life was built upon that aversion. Aversion for the human voice, for faces, for heads, steps . . . in fact, for everything that makes up a human being. At all the doors and on the stairs there stand sleek, rude, and lazy grooms in livery to prevent badly dressed persons from entering the house; in the hall there are chairs with high backs so that the footmen waiting there, during balls and receptions, may not soil the walls with their heads; in every room there are thick carpets that no human step may be heard; every one who comes in is infallibly warned to speak as softly and as little as possible, and to say nothing that might have a disagreeable effect on the nerves or the imagination. And in your room you don't shake hands with any one or ask him to sit down—just as you didn't shake hands with me or ask me to sit down. . . ."

"By all means, if you like," said the princess, smiling and holding out her hand. "Really, to be cross about such trifles. . . ."

"But I am not cross," laughed the doctor, but at once he flushed, took off his hat, and waving it about, began hotly: "To be candid, I've long wanted an opportunity to tell you all I think. . . . That is, I want to tell you that you look upon the mass of mankind from the Napoleonic standpoint as food for the cannon. But Napoleon had at least some idea; you have nothing except aversion."

"I have an aversion for people?" smiled the princess, shrugging her shoulders in astonishment. "I have!"

"Yes, you! You want facts? By all means. In Mihaltsevo three former cooks of yours, who have gone blind in your kitchens from the heat of the stove, are living upon charity. All the health and strength and good looks that is found on your hundreds of thousands of acres is taken by you and your parasites for your grooms, your footmen, and your coachmen. All these two-legged cattle are trained to be flunkeys, overeat themselves, grow coarse, lose the 'image and likeness,' in fact. . . . Young doctors, agricultural experts, teachers, intellectual workers generally—think of it!—are torn away from their honest work and forced for a crust of bread to take part in all sorts of mummeries which make every decent man feel ashamed! Some young men cannot be in your service for three years without becoming hypocrites, toadies, sneaks. . . . Is that a good thing? Your Polish superintendents, those abject spies, all those Kazimers and Kaetans, go hunting about on your hundreds of thousands of acres from morning to night, and to please you try to get three skins off one ox. Excuse me, I speak disconnectedly, but that doesn't matter. You don't look upon the simple people as human beings. And even the princes, counts, and bishops who used to come and see you, you looked upon simply as decorative figures, not as living beings. But the worst of all, the thing that most revolts me, is having a fortune of over a million and doing nothing for other people, nothing!"

The princess sat amazed, aghast, offended, not knowing what to say or how to behave. She had never before been spoken to in such a tone. The doctor's unpleasant, angry voice and his clumsy, faltering phrases made a harsh clattering noise in her ears and her head. Then she began to feel as though the gesticulating doctor was hitting her on the head with his hat.

"It's not true!" she articulated softly, in an imploring voice. "I've done a great deal of good for other people; you know it yourself!"

"Nonsense!" cried the doctor. "Can you possibly go on thinking of your philanthropic work as something genuine and useful, and not a mere mummery? It was a farce from beginning to end; it was playing at loving your neighbour, the most open farce which even children and stupid peasant women saw through! Take for instance your—what was it called?—house for homeless old women without relations, of which you made me something like a head doctor, and of which you were the patroness. Mercy on us! What a charming institution it was! A house was built with parquet floors and a weathercock on the roof; a dozen old women were collected from the villages and made to sleep under blanket and sheets of Dutch linen, and given toffee to eat."

The doctor gave a malignant chuckle into his hat, and went on speaking rapidly and stammering:

"It was a farce! The attendants kept the sheets and the blankets under lock and key, for fear the old women should soil them—'Let the old devil's pepper-pots sleep on the floor.' The old women did not dare to sit down on the beds, to put on their jackets, to walk over the polished floors. Everything was kept for show and hidden away from the old women as though they were thieves, and the old women were clothed and fed on the sly by other people's charity, and prayed to God night and day to be released from their prison and from the canting exhortations of the sleek rascals to whose care you committed them. And what did the managers do? It was simply charming! About twice a week there would be thirty-five thousand messages to say that the princess—that is, you—were coming to the home next day. That meant that next day I had to abandon my patients, dress up and be on parade. Very good; I arrive. The old women, in everything clean and new, are already drawn up in a row, waiting. Near them struts the old garrison rat—the superintendent with his mawkish, sneaking smile. The old women yawn and exchange glances, but are afraid to complain. We wait. The junior steward gallops up. Half an hour later the senior steward; then the superintendent of the accounts' office, then another, and then another of them . . . they keep arriving endlessly. They all have mysterious, solemn faces. We wait and wait, shift from one leg to another, look at the clock—all this in monumental silence because we all hate each other like poison. One hour passes, then a second, and then at last the carriage is seen in the distance, and . . . and . . ."

The doctor went off into a shrill laugh and brought out in a shrill voice:

"You get out of the carriage, and the old hags, at the word of command from the old garrison rat, begin chanting: 'The Glory of our Lord in Zion the tongue of man cannot express. . . .' A pretty scene, wasn't it?"

The doctor went off into a bass chuckle, and waved his hand as though to signify that he could not utter another word for laughing. He laughed heavily, harshly, with clenched teeth, as ill-natured people laugh; and from his voice, from his face, from his glittering, rather insolent eyes it could be seen that he had a profound contempt for the princess, for the home, and for the old women. There was nothing amusing or laughable in all that he described so clumsily and coarsely, but he laughed with satisfaction, even with delight.

"And the school?" he went on, panting from laughter. "Do you remember how you wanted to teach peasant children yourself? You must have taught them very well, for very soon the children all ran away, so that they had to be thrashed and bribed to come and be taught. And you remember how you wanted to feed with your own hands the infants whose mothers were working in the fields. You went about the village crying because the infants were not at your disposal, as the mothers would take them to the fields with them. Then the village foreman ordered the mothers by turn to leave their infants behind for your entertainment. A strange thing! They all ran away from your benevolence like mice from a cat! And why was it? It's very simple. Not because our people are ignorant and ungrateful, as you always explained it to yourself, but because in all your fads, if you'll excuse the word, there wasn't a ha'p'orth of love and kindness! There was nothing but the desire to amuse yourself with living puppets, nothing else. . . . A person who does not feel the difference between a human being and a lap-dog ought not to go in for philanthropy. I assure you, there's a great difference between human beings and lap-dogs!"

The princess's heart was beating dreadfully; there was a thudding in her ears, and she still felt as though the doctor were beating her on the head with his hat. The doctor talked quickly, excitedly, and uncouthly, stammering and gesticulating unnecessarily. All she grasped was that she was spoken to by a coarse, ill-bred, spiteful, and ungrateful man; but what he wanted of her and what he was talking about, she could not understand.

"Go away!" she said in a tearful voice, putting up her hands to protect her head from the doctor's hat; "go away!"

"And how you treat your servants!" the doctor went on, indignantly. "You treat them as the lowest scoundrels, and don't look upon them as human beings. For example, allow me to ask, why did you dismiss me? For ten years I worked for your father and afterwards for you, honestly, without vacations or holidays. I gained the love of all for more than seventy miles round, and suddenly one fine day I am informed that I am no longer wanted. What for? I've no idea to this day. I, a doctor of medicine, a gentleman by birth, a student of the Moscow University, father of a family—am such a petty, insignificant insect that you can kick me out without explaining the reason! Why stand on ceremony with me! I heard afterwards that my wife went without my knowledge three times to intercede with you for me—you wouldn't receive her. I am told she cried in your hall. And I shall never forgive her for it, never!"

The doctor paused and clenched his teeth, making an intense effort to think of something more to say, very unpleasant and vindictive. He thought of something, and his cold, frowning face suddenly brightened.

"Take your attitude to this monastery!" he said with avidity. "You've never spared any one, and the holier the place, the more chance of its suffering from your loving-kindness and angelic sweetness. Why do you come here? What do you want with the monks here, allow me to ask you? What is Hecuba to you or you to Hecuba? It's another farce, another amusement for you, another sacrilege against human dignity, and nothing more. Why, you don't believe in the monks' God; you've a God of your own in your heart, whom you've evolved for yourself at spiritualist séances. You look with condescension upon the ritual of the Church; you don't go to mass or vespers; you sleep till midday. . . . Why do you come here? . . . You come with a God of your own into a monastery you have nothing to do with, and you imagine that the monks look upon it as a very great honour. To be sure they do! You'd better ask, by the way, what your visits cost the monastery. You were graciously pleased to arrive here this evening, and a messenger from your estate arrived on horseback the day before yesterday to warn them of your coming. They were the whole day yesterday getting the rooms ready and expecting you. This morning your advance-guard arrived—an insolent maid, who keeps running across the courtyard, rustling her skirts, pestering them with questions, giving orders. . . . I can't endure it! The monks have been on the lookout all day, for if you were not met with due ceremony, there would be trouble! You'd complain to the bishop! 'The monks don't like me, your holiness; I don't know what I've done to displease them. It's true I'm a great sinner, but I'm so unhappy!' Already one monastery has been in hot water over you. The Father Superior is a busy, learned man; he hasn't a free moment, and you keep sending for him to come to your rooms. Not a trace of respect for age or for rank! If at least you were a bountiful giver to the monastery, one wouldn't resent it so much, but all this time the monks have not received a hundred roubles from you!"

Whenever people worried the princess, misunderstood her, or mortified her, and when she did not know what to say or do, she usually began to cry. And on this occasion, too, she ended by hiding her face in her hands and crying aloud in a thin treble like a child. The doctor suddenly stopped and looked at her. His face darkened and grew stern.

"Forgive me, Princess," he said in a hollow voice. "I've given way to a malicious feeling and forgotten myself. It was not right."

And coughing in an embarrassed way, he walked away quickly, without remembering to put his hat on.

Stars were already twinkling in the sky. The moon must have been rising on the further side of the monastery, for the sky was clear, soft, and transparent. Bats were flitting noiselessly along the white monastery wall.

The clock slowly struck three quarters, probably a quarter to nine. The princess got up and walked slowly to the gate. She felt wounded and was crying, and she felt that the trees and the stars and even the bats were pitying her, and that the clock struck musically only to express its sympathy with her. She cried and thought how nice it would be to go into a monastery for the rest of her life. On still summer evenings she would walk alone through the avenues, insulted, injured, misunderstood by people, and only God and the starry heavens would see the martyr's tears. The evening service was still going on in the church. The princess stopped and listened to the singing; how beautiful the singing sounded in the still darkness! How sweet to weep and suffer to the sound of that singing!

Going into her rooms, she looked at her tear-stained face in the glass and powdered it, then she sat down to supper. The monks knew that she liked pickled sturgeon, little mushrooms, Malaga and plain honey-cakes that left a taste of cypress in the mouth, and every time she came they gave her all these dishes. As she ate the mushrooms and drank the Malaga, the princess dreamed of how she would be finally ruined and deserted—how all her stewards, bailiffs, clerks, and maid-servants for whom she had done so much, would be false to her, and begin to say rude things; how people all the world over would set upon her, speak ill of her, jeer at her. She would renounce her title, would renounce society and luxury, and would go into a convent without one word of reproach to any one; she would pray for her enemies—and then they would all understand her and come to beg her forgiveness, but by that time it would be too late. . . .

After supper she knelt down in the corner before the ikon and read two chapters of the Gospel. Then her maid made her bed and she got into it. Stretching herself under the white quilt, she heaved a sweet, deep sigh, as one sighs after crying, closed her eyes, and began to fall asleep.

In the morning she waked up and glanced at her watch. It was half-past nine. On the carpet near the bed was a bright, narrow streak of sunlight from a ray which came in at the window and dimly lighted up the room. Flies were buzzing behind the black curtain at the window. "It's early," thought the princess, and she closed her eyes.

Stretching and lying snug in her bed, she recalled her meeting yesterday with the doctor and all the thoughts with which she had gone to sleep the night before: she remembered she was unhappy. Then she thought of her husband living in Petersburg, her stewards, doctors, neighbours, the officials of her acquaintance . . . a long procession of familiar masculine faces passed before her imagination. She smiled and thought, if only these people could see into her heart and understand her, they would all be at her feet.

At a quarter past eleven she called her maid.

"Help me to dress, Dasha," she said languidly. "But go first and tell them to get out the horses. I must set off for Klavdia Nikolaevna's."

Going out to get into the carriage, she blinked at the glaring daylight and laughed with pleasure: it was a wonderfully fine day! As she scanned from her half-closed eyes the monks who had gathered round the steps to see her off, she nodded graciously and said:

"Good-bye, my friends! Till the day after to-morrow."

It was an agreeable surprise to her that the doctor was with the monks by the steps. His face was pale and severe.

"Princess," he said with a guilty smile, taking off his hat, "I've been waiting here a long time to see you. Forgive me, for God's sake. . . . I was carried away yesterday by an evil, vindictive feeling and I talked . . . nonsense. In short, I beg your pardon."

The princess smiled graciously, and held out her hand for him to kiss. He kissed it, turning red.

Trying to look like a bird, the princess fluttered into the carriage and nodded in all directions. There was a gay, warm, serene feeling in her heart, and she felt herself that her smile was particularly soft and friendly. As the carriage rolled towards the gates, and afterwards along the dusty road past huts and gardens, past long trains of wagons and strings of pilgrims on their way to the monastery, she still screwed up her eyes and smiled softly. She was thinking there was no higher bliss than to bring warmth, light, and joy wherever one went, to forgive injuries, to smile graciously on one's enemies. The peasants she passed bowed to her, the carriage rustled softly, clouds of dust rose from under the wheels and floated over the golden rye, and it seemed to the princess that her body was swaying not on carriage cushions but on clouds, and that she herself was like a light, transparent little cloud. . . .

"How happy I am!" she murmured, shutting her eyes. "How happy I am!"

NEIGHBOURS

Pyotr Mihalitch Ivashin was very much out of humour: his sister, a young girl, had gone away to live with Vlassitch, a married man. To shake off the despondency and depression which pursued him at home and in the fields, he called to his aid his sense of justice, his genuine and noble ideas—he had always defended free-love!—but this was of no avail, and he always came back to the same conclusion as their foolish old nurse, that his sister had acted wrongly and that Vlassitch had abducted his sister. And that was distressing.

His mother did not leave her room all day long; the old nurse kept sighing and speaking in whispers; his aunt had been on the point of taking her departure every day, and her trunks were continually being brought down to the hall and carried up again to her room. In the house, in the yard, and in the garden it was as still as though there were some one dead in the house. His aunt, the servants, and even the peasants, so it seemed to Pyotr Mihalitch, looked at him enigmatically and with perplexity, as though they wanted to say "Your sister has been seduced; why are you doing nothing?" And he reproached himself for inactivity, though he did not know precisely what action he ought to have taken.

So passed six days. On the seventh—it was Sunday afternoon—a messenger on horseback brought a letter. The address was in a familiar feminine handwriting: "Her Excy. Anna Nikolaevna Ivashin." Pyotr Mihalitch fancied that there was something defiant, provocative, in the handwriting and in the abbreviation "Excy." And advanced ideas in women are obstinate, ruthless, cruel.

"She'd rather die than make any concession to her unhappy

mother, or beg her forgiveness," thought Pyotr Mihalitch, as he went to his mother with the letter.

His mother was lying on her bed, dressed. Seeing her son, she rose impulsively, and straightening her grey hair, which had fallen from under her cap, asked quickly:

"What is it? What is it?"

"This has come . . ." said her son, giving her the letter.

Zina's name, and even the pronoun "she" was not uttered in the house. Zina was spoken of impersonally: "this has come," "Gone away," and so on. . . . The mother recognised her daughter's handwriting, and her face grew ugly and unpleasant, and her grey hair escaped again from her cap.

"No!" she said, with a motion of her hands, as though the letter scorched her fingers. "No, no, never! Nothing would induce me!"

The mother broke into hysterical sobs of grief and shame; she evidently longed to read the letter, but her pride prevented her. Pyotr Mihalitch realised that he ought to open the letter himself and read it aloud, but he was overcome by anger such as he had never felt before; he ran out into the yard and shouted to the messenger:

"Say there will be no answer! There will be no answer! Tell them that, you beast!"

And he tore up the letter; then tears came into his eyes, and feeling that he was cruel, miserable, and to blame, he went out into the fields.

He was only twenty-seven, but he was already stout. He dressed like an old man in loose, roomy clothes, and suffered from asthma. He already seemed to be developing the characteristics of an elderly country bachelor. He never fell in love, never thought of marriage, and loved no one but his mother, his sister, his old nurse, and the gardener, Vassilitch. He was fond of good fare, of his nap after dinner, and of talking about politics and exalted subjects. He had in his day taken his degree at the university, but he now looked upon his studies as though in them he had discharged a duty incumbent upon young men between the ages of eighteen and twenty-five; at any rate, the ideas which now strayed every day through his mind had nothing in common with the university or the subjects he had studied there.

In the fields it was hot and still, as though rain were coming. It was steaming in the wood, and there was a heavy fragrant scent from the pines and rotting leaves. Pyotr Mihalitch stopped several times and wiped his wet brow. He looked at his winter corn and his spring oats, walked round the clover-field, and twice drove away a partridge with its chicks which had strayed in from the wood. And all the while he was thinking that this insufferable state of things could not go on for ever, and that he must end it one way or another. End it stupidly, madly, but he must end it.

"But how? What can I do?" he asked himself, and looked imploringly at the sky and at the trees, as though begging for their help.

But the sky and the trees were mute. His noble ideas were no help, and his common sense whispered that the agonising question could have no solution but a stupid one, and that to-day's scene with the messenger was not the last one of its kind. It was terrible to think what was in store for him!

As he returned home the sun was setting. By now it seemed to him that the problem was incapable of solution. He could not accept the accomplished fact, and he could not refuse to accept it, and there was no intermediate course. When, taking off his hat and fanning himself with his handkerchief, he was walking along the road, and had only another mile and a half to go before he would reach home, he heard bells behind him. It was a very choice and successful combination of bells, which gave a clear crystal note. No one had such bells on his horses but the police captain, Medovsky, formerly an officer in the hussars, a man in broken-down health, who had been a great rake and spendthrift, and was a distant relation of Pyotr Mihalitch. He was like one of the family at the Ivashins' and had a tender, fatherly affection for Zina, as well as a great admiration for her.

"I was coming to see you," he said, overtaking Pyotr Mihalitch. "Get in; I'll give you a lift."

He was smiling and looked cheerful. Evidently he did not yet know that Zina had gone to live with Vlassitch; perhaps he had been told of it already, but did not believe it. Pyotr Mihalitch felt in a difficult position.

"You are very welcome," he muttered, blushing till the tears came into his eyes, and not knowing how to lie or what to say. "I am delighted," he went on, trying to smile, "but . . . Zina is away and mother is ill."

"How annoying!" said the police captain, looking pensively at Pyotr Mihalitch. "And I was meaning to spend the evening with you. Where has Zinaida Mihalovna gone?"

"To the Sinitsky's, and I believe she meant to go from there to the monastery. I don't quite know."

The police captain talked a little longer and then turned back. Pyotr Mihalitch walked home, and thought with horror what the police captain's feelings would be when he learned the truth. And Pyotr Mihalitch imagined his feelings, and actually experiencing them himself, went into the house.

"Lord help us," he thought, "Lord help us!"

At evening tea the only one at the table was his aunt. As usual, her face wore the expression that seemed to say that though she was a weak, defenceless woman, she would allow no one to insult her. Pyotr Mihalitch sat down at the other end of the table (he did not like his aunt) and began drinking tea in silence.

"Your mother has had no dinner again to-day," said his aunt. "You ought to do something about it, Petrusha. Starving oneself is no help in sorrow."

It struck Pyotr Mihalitch as absurd that his aunt should meddle in other people's business and should make her departure depend on Zina's having gone away. He was tempted to say something rude to her, but restrained himself. And as he restrained himself he felt the time had come for action, and that he could not bear it any longer. Either he must act at once or fall on the ground, and scream and bang his head upon the floor. He pictured Vlassitch and Zina, both of them progressive and self-satisfied, kissing each other somewhere under a maple tree, and all the anger and bitterness that had been accumulating in him for the last seven days fastened upon Vlassitch.

"One has seduced and abducted my sister," he thought, "another will come and murder my mother, a third will set fire to the house and sack the place. . . . And all this under the mask of friendship, lofty ideas, unhappiness!"

"No, it shall not be!" Pyotr Mihalitch cried suddenly, and he brought his fist down on the table.

He jumped up and ran out of the dining-room. In the stable the steward's horse was standing ready saddled. He got on it and galloped off to Vlassitch.

There was a perfect tempest within him. He felt a longing to do something extraordinary, startling, even if he had to repent of it all his life afterwards. Should he call Vlassitch a blackguard, slap him in the face, and then challenge him to a duel? But Vlassitch was not one of those men who do fight duels; being called a blackguard and slapped in the face would only make him more unhappy, and would make him shrink into himself more than ever. These unhappy, defenceless people are the most insufferable, the most tiresome creatures in the world. They can do anything with impunity. When the luckless man responds to well-deserved reproach by looking at you with eyes full of deep and guilty feeling, and with a sickly smile bends his head submissively, even justice itself could not lift its hand against him.

"No matter. I'll horsewhip him before her eyes and tell him what I think of him," Pyotr Mihalitch decided.

He was riding through his wood and waste land, and he imagined Zina would try to justify her conduct by talking about the rights of women and individual freedom, and about there being no difference between legal marriage and free union. Like a woman, she would argue about what she did not understand. And very likely at the end she would ask, "How do you come in? What right have you to interfere?"

"No, I have no right," muttered Pyotr Mihalitch. "But so much the better. . . . The harsher I am, the less right I have to interfere, the better."

It was sultry. Clouds of gnats hung over the ground and in the waste places the peewits called plaintively. Everything betokened rain, but he could not see a cloud in the sky. Pyotr Mihalitch crossed the boundary of his estate and galloped over a smooth, level field. He often went along this road and knew every bush, every hollow in it. What now in the far distance looked in the dusk like a dark cliff was a red church; he could picture it all down to the smallest detail, even the plaster on the gate and the calves that were always grazing in the church enclosure. Three-quarters of a mile to the right of the church there was a copse like a dark blur—it was Count Koltonovitch's. And beyond the church Vlassitch's estate began.

From behind the church and the count's copse a huge black storm-cloud was rising, and there were ashes of white lightning.

"Here it is!" thought Pyotr Mihalitch. "Lord help us, Lord help us!"

The horse was soon tired after its quick gallop, and Pyotr Mihalitch was tired too. The stormcloud looked at him angrily and seemed to advise him to go home. He felt a little scared.

"I will prove to them they are wrong," he tried to reassure himself. "They will say that it is freelove, individual freedom; but freedom means self-control and not subjection to passion. It's not liberty but license!"

He reached the count's big pond; it looked dark blue and frowning under the cloud, and a smell of damp and slime rose from it. Near the dam, two willows, one old and one young, drooped tenderly towards one another. Pyotr Mihalitch and Vlassitch had been walking near this very spot only a fortnight before, humming a students' song:

"'Youth is wasted, life is nought, when the heart is cold and loveless.'"

A wretched song!

It was thundering as Pyotr Mihalitch rode through the copse, and the trees were bending and rustling in the wind. He had to make haste. It was only three-quarters of a mile through a meadow from the copse to Vlassitch's house. Here there were old birch-trees on each side of the road. They had the same melancholy and unhappy air as their owner Vlassitch, and looked as tall and lanky as he. Big drops of rain pattered on the birches and on the grass; the wind had suddenly dropped, and there was a smell of wet earth and poplars. Before him he saw Vlassitch's fence with a row of yellow acacias, which were tall and lanky too; where the fence was broken he could see the neglected orchard.

Pyotr Mihalitch was not thinking now of the horsewhip or of a slap in the face, and did not know what he would do at Vlassitch's. He felt nervous. He felt frightened on his own account and on his sister's, and was terrified at the thought of seeing her. How would she behave with her brother? What would they both talk about?

And had he not better go back before it was too late? As he made these reflections, he galloped up the avenue of lime trees to the house, rode round the big clumps of lilacs, and suddenly saw Vlassitch.

Vlassitch, wearing a cotton shirt, and top-boots, bending forward, with no hat on in the rain, was coming from the corner of the house to the front door. He was followed by a workman with a hammer and a box of nails. They must have been mending a shutter which had been banging in the wind. Seeing Pyotr Mihalitch, Vlassitch stopped.

"It's you!" he said, smiling. "That's nice."

"Yes, I've come, as you see," said Pyotr Mihalitch, brushing the rain off himself with both hands.

"Well, that's capital! I'm very glad," said Vlassitch, but he did not hold out his hand: evidently he did not venture, but waited for Pyotr Mihalitch to hold out his. "It will do the oats good," he said, looking at the sky.

"Yes."

They went into the house in silence. To the right of the hall was a door leading to another hall and then to the drawing-room, and on the left was a little room which in winter was used by the steward. Pyotr Mihalitch and Vlassitch went into this little room.

"Where were you caught in the rain?"

"Not far off, quite close to the house."

Pyotr Mihalitch sat down on the bed. He was glad of the noise of the rain and the darkness of the room. It was better: it made it less dreadful, and there was no need to see his companion's face. There was no anger in his heart now, nothing but fear and vexation with himself. He felt he had made a bad beginning, and that nothing would come of this visit.

Both were silent for some time and affected to be listening to the rain.

"Thank you, Petrusha," Vlassitch began, clearing his throat. "I am very grateful to you for coming. It's generous and noble of you. I understand it, and, believe me, I appreciate it. Believe me."

He looked out of the window and went on, standing in the middle of the room:

"Everything happened so secretly, as though we were concealing it all from you. The feeling that you might be wounded and angry has been a blot on our happiness all these days. But let me justify myself. We kept it secret not because we did not trust you. To begin with, it all happened suddenly, by a kind of inspiration; there was no time to discuss it. Besides, it's such a private, delicate matter, and it was awkward to bring a third person in, even some one as intimate as you. Above all, in all this we reckoned on your generosity. You are a very noble and generous person. I am infinitely grateful to you. If you ever need my life, come and take it."

Vlassitch talked in a quiet, hollow bass, always on the same droning note; he was evidently agitated. Pyotr Mihalitch felt it was his turn to speak, and that to listen and keep silent would really mean playing the part of a generous and noble simpleton, and that had not been his idea in coming. He got up quickly and said, breathlessly in an undertone:

"Listen, Grigory. You know I liked you and could have desired no better husband for my sister; but what has happened is awful! It's terrible to think of it!"

"Why is it terrible?" asked Vlassitch, with a quiver in his voice. "It would be terrible if we had done wrong, but that isn't so."

"Listen, Grigory. You know I have no prejudices; but, excuse my frankness, to my mind you have both acted selfishly. Of course, I shan't say so to my sister—it will distress her; but you ought to know: mother is miserable beyond all description."

"Yes, that's sad," sighed Vlassitch. "We foresaw that, Petrusha, but what could we have done? Because one's actions hurt other people, it doesn't prove that they are wrong. What's to be done! Every important step one takes is bound to distress somebody. If you went to fight for freedom, that would distress your mother, too. What's to be done! Any one who puts the peace of his family before everything has to renounce the life of ideas completely."

There was a vivid flash of lightning at the window, and the lightning seemed to change the course of Vlassitch's thoughts. He sat down beside Pyotr Mihalitch and began saying what was utterly beside the point.

"I have such a reverence for your sister, Petrusha," he said. "When I used to come and see you, I felt as though I were going to a holy shrine, and I really did worship Zina. Now my reverence for her grows every day. For me she is something higher than a wife—yes, higher!" Vlassitch waved his hands. "She is my holy of holies. Since she is living with me, I enter my house as though it were a temple. She is an extraordinary, rare, most noble woman!"

"Well, he's off now!" thought Pyotr Mihalitch; he disliked the word "woman."

"Why shouldn't you be married properly?" he asked. "How much does your wife want for a divorce?"

"Seventy-five thousand."

"It's rather a lot. But if we were to negotiate with her?"

"She won't take a farthing less. She is an awful woman, brother," sighed Vlassitch. "I've never talked to you about her before—it was unpleasant to think of her; but now that the subject has come up, I'll tell you about her. I married her on the impulse of the moment—a fine, honourable impulse. An officer in command of a battalion of our regiment—if you care to hear the details—had an affair with a girl of eighteen; that is, to put it plainly, he seduced her, lived with her for two months, and abandoned her. She was in an awful position, brother. She was ashamed to go home to her parents; besides, they wouldn't have received her. Her lover had abandoned her; there was nothing left for her but to go to the barracks and sell herself. The other officers in the regiment were indignant. They were by no means saints themselves, but the baseness of it was so striking. Besides, no one in the regiment could endure the man. And to spite him, you understand, the indignant lieutenants and ensigns began getting up a subscription for the unfortunate girl. And when we subalterns met together and began to subscribe five or ten roubles each, I had a sudden inspiration. I felt it was an opportunity to do something fine. I hastened to the girl and warmly expressed my sympathy. And while I was on my way to her, and while I was talking to her, I loved her fervently as a woman insulted and injured. Yes. . . . Well, a week later I made her an offer. The colonel and my comrades thought my marriage out of keeping with the dignity of an officer. That roused me more than ever. I wrote a long letter, do you know, in which I proved that my action ought to be inscribed in the annals of the regiment in letters of gold, and so on. I sent the letter to my colonel and copies to my comrades. Well, I was excited, and, of course, I could not avoid being rude. I was asked to leave the regiment. I have a rough copy of it put away somewhere; I'll give it to you to read sometime. It was written with great feeling. You will see what lofty and noble sentiments I was experiencing. I resigned my commission and came here with my wife. My father had left a few debts, I had no money, and from the first day my wife began making acquaintances, dressing herself smartly, and playing cards, and I was obliged to mortgage the estate. She led a bad life, you understand, and you are the only one of the neighbours who hasn't been her lover. After two years I gave her all I had to set me free and she went off to town. Yes. . . . And now I pay her twelve hundred roubles a year. She is an awful woman! There is a fly, brother, which lays an egg in the back of a spider so that the spider can't shake it off: the grub fastens upon the spider and drinks its heart's blood. That was how this woman fastened upon me and sucks the blood of my heart. She hates and despises me for being so stupid; that is, for marrying a woman like her. My chivalry seems to her despicable. 'A wise man cast me off,' she says, 'and a fool picked me up.' To her thinking no one but a pitiful idiot could have behaved as I did. And that is insufferably bitter to me, brother. Altogether, I may say in parenthesis, fate has been hard upon me, very hard."

Pyotr Mihalitch listened to Vlassitch and wondered in perplexity what it was in this man that had so charmed his sister. He was not young—he was forty-one—lean and lanky, narrow-chested, with a long nose, and grey hairs in his beard. He talked in a droning voice, had a sickly smile, and waved his hands awkwardly as he talked. He had neither health, nor pleasant, manly manners, nor *savoir-faire* nor gaiety, and in all his exterior there was something colourless and indefinite. He dressed without taste, his surroundings were depressing, he did not care for poetry or painting because "they have no answer to give to the questions of the day"—that is, he did not understand them; music did not touch him. He was a poor farmer.

His estate was in a wretched condition and was mortgaged; he was paying twelve per cent on the second mortgage and owed ten thousand on personal securities as well. When the time came to pay the interest on the mortgage or to send money to his wife, he asked every one to lend him money with as much agitation as though his house were on fire, and, at the same time losing his head, he would sell the whole of his winter store of fuel for five roubles and a stack of straw for three roubles, and then have his garden fence or old cucumber-frames chopped up to heat his stoves. His meadows were ruined by pigs, the peasants' cattle strayed in the undergrowth in his woods, and every year the old trees were fewer and fewer: beehives and rusty pails lay about in his garden and kitchen-garden. He had neither talents nor abilities, nor even ordinary capacity for living like other people. In practical life he was a weak, naïve man, easy to deceive and to cheat, and the peasants with good reason called him "simple."

He was a Liberal, and in the district was regarded as a "Red," but even his progressiveness was a bore. There was no originality nor moving power about his independent views: he was revolted, indignant, and delighted always on the same note; it was always spiritless and ineffective. Even in moments of strong enthusiasm he never raised his head or stood upright. But the most tiresome thing of all was that he managed to express even his best and finest ideas so that they seemed in him commonplace and out of date. It reminded one of something old one had read long ago, when slowly and with an air of profundity he would begin discoursing of his noble, lofty moments, of his best years; or when he went into raptures over the younger generation, which has always been, and still is, in advance of society; or abused Russians for donning their dressing-gowns at thirty and forgetting the principles of their *alma mater.* If you stayed the night with him, he would put Pissarev or Darwin on your bedroom table; if you said you had read it, he would go and bring Dobrolubov.*

In the district this was called free-thinking, and many people looked upon this free-thinking as an innocent and harmless eccentricity; it made him profoundly unhappy, however. It was for him the maggot of which he had just been speaking; it had fastened upon him and was sucking his life-blood. In his past there had been the strange marriage in the style of Dostoevsky;† long letters and copies written in a bad, unintelligible hand-writing, but with great

---

*D. I. Pissarev (1840–1868) promoted nihilism, which favored the destruction of existing economic and social institutions. English naturalist Charles Darwin (1809–1882) established the theory of evolution. N. A. Dobrolubov (1836–1861) was a radical social critic.

†The influential author Fyodor Dostoevsky (1821–1881) wrote *Crime and Punishment*, *The Idiot*, and *The Brothers Karamazov*.

feeling, endless misunderstandings, explanations, disappointments, then debts, a second mortgage, the allowance to his wife, the monthly borrowing of money—and all this for no benefit to any one, either himself or others. And in the present, as in the past, he was still in a nervous flurry, on the lookout for heroic actions, and poking his nose into other people's affairs; as before, at every favourable opportunity there were long letters and copies, wearisome, stereotyped conversations about the village community, or the revival of handicrafts or the establishment of cheese factories—conversations as like one another as though he had prepared them, not in his living brain, but by some mechanical process. And finally this scandal with Zina of which one could not see the end!

And meanwhile Zina was young—she was only twenty-two—good-looking, elegant, gay; she was fond of laughing, chatter, argument, a passionate musician; she had good taste in dress, in furniture, in books, and in her own home she would not have put up with a room like this, smelling of boots and cheap vodka. She, too, had advanced ideas, but in her free-thinking one felt the overflow of energy, the vanity of a young, strong, spirited girl, passionately eager to be better and more original than others. . . . How had it happened that she had fallen in love with Vlassitch?

"He is a Quixote,* an obstinate fanatic, a maniac," thought Pyotr Mihalitch, "and she is as soft, yielding, and weak in character as I am. . . . She and I give in easily, without resistance. She loves him; but, then, I, too, love him in spite of everything."

Pyotr Mihalitch considered Vlassitch a good, straightforward man, but narrow and one-sided. In his perturbations and his sufferings, and in fact in his whole life, he saw no lofty aims, remote or immediate; he saw nothing but boredom and incapacity for life. His self-sacrifice and all that Vlassitch himself called heroic actions or noble impulses seemed to him a useless waste of force, unnecessary blank shots which consumed a great deal of powder. And Vlassitch's fanatical belief in the extraordinary loftiness and faultlessness of his own way of thinking struck him as naïve and even morbid; and the fact that Vlassitch all his life had contrived to mix the trivial with

---

*Idealistic hero of the great Spanish novel *Don Quixote* (1605, 1615), by Miguel de Cervantes Saavedra.

the exalted, that he had made a stupid marriage and looked upon it as an act of heroism, and then had affairs with other women and regarded that as a triumph of some idea or other was simply incomprehensible.

Nevertheless, Pyotr Mihalitch was fond of Vlassitch; he was conscious of a sort of power in him, and for some reason he had never had the heart to contradict him.

Vlassitch sat down quite close to him for a talk in the dark, to the accompaniment of the rain, and he had cleared his throat as a prelude to beginning on something lengthy, such as the history of his marriage. But it was intolerable for Pyotr Mihalitch to listen to him; he was tormented by the thought that he would see his sister directly.

"Yes, you've had bad luck," he said gently; "but, excuse me, we've been wandering from the point. That's not what we are talking about."

"Yes, yes, quite so. Well, let us come back to the point," said Vlassitch, and he stood up. "I tell you, Petrusha, our conscience is clear. We are not married, but there is no need for me to prove to you that our marriage is perfectly legitimate. You are as free in your ideas as I am, and, happily, there can be no disagreement between us on that point. As for our future, that ought not to alarm you. I'll work in the sweat of my brow, I'll work day and night—in fact, I will strain every nerve to make Zina happy. Her life will be a splendid one! You may ask, am I able to do it. I am, brother! When a man devotes every minute to one thought, it's not difficult for him to attain his object. But let us go to Zina; it will be a joy to her to see you."

Pyotr Mihalitch's heart began to beat. He got up and followed Vlassitch into the hall, and from there into the drawing-room. There was nothing in the huge gloomy room but a piano and a long row of old chairs ornamented with bronze, on which no one ever sat. There was a candle alight on the piano. From the drawing-room they went in silence into the dining-room. This room, too, was large and comfortless; in the middle of the room there was a round table with two leaves with six thick legs, and only one candle. A clock in a large mahogany case like an ikon stand pointed to half-past two.

Vlassitch opened the door into the next room and said:

"Zina, here is Petrusha come to see us!"

At once there was the sound of hurried footsteps and Zina came into the dining-room. She was tall, plump, and very pale, and, just as when he had seen her for the last time at home, she was wearing a black skirt and a red blouse, with a large buckle on her belt. She flung one arm round her brother and kissed him on the temple.

"What a storm!" she said. "Grigory went off somewhere and I was left quite alone in the house."

She was not embarrassed, and looked at her brother as frankly and candidly as at home; looking at her, Pyotr Mihalitch, too, lost his embarrassment.

"But you are not afraid of storms," he said, sitting down at the table.

"No," she said, "but here the rooms are so big, the house is so old, and when there is thunder it all rattles like a cupboard full of crockery. It's a charming house altogether," she went on, sitting down opposite her brother. "There's some pleasant memory in every room. In my room, only fancy, Grigory's grandfather shot himself."

"In August we shall have the money to do up the lodge in the garden," said Vlassitch.

"For some reason when it thunders I think of that grandfather," Zina went on. "And in this dining-room somebody was flogged to death."

"That's an actual fact," said Vlassitch, and he looked with wide-open eyes at Pyotr Mihalitch. "Sometime in the forties this place was let to a Frenchman called Olivier. The portrait of his daughter is lying in an attic now—a very pretty girl. This Olivier, so my father told me, despised Russians for their ignorance and treated them with cruel derision. Thus, for instance, he insisted on the priest walking without his hat for half a mile round his house, and on the church bells being rung when the Olivier family drove through the village. The serfs and altogether the humble of this world, of course, he treated with even less ceremony. Once there came along this road one of the simple-hearted sons of wandering Russia, somewhat after the style of Gogol's divinity student, Homa Brut.* He asked for a night's lodging, pleased the bailiffs, and was given a job at the

*A character in "Vy," a story in the collection *Mirgorod* (1835), by Nikolai Gogol.

office of the estate. There are many variations of the story. Some say the divinity student stirred up the peasants, others that Olivier's daughter fell in love with him. I don't know which is true, only one fine evening Olivier called him in here and cross-examined him, then ordered him to be beaten. Do you know, he sat here at this table drinking claret while the stable-boys beat the man. He must have tried to wring something out of him. Towards morning the divinity student died of the torture and his body was hidden. They say it was thrown into Koltovitch's pond. There was an inquiry, but the Frenchman paid some thousands to some one in authority and went away to Alsace. His lease was up just then, and so the matter ended."

"What scoundrels!" said Zina, shuddering.

"My father remembered Olivier and his daughter well. He used to say she was remarkably beautiful and eccentric. I imagine the divinity student had done both—stirred up the peasants and won the daughter's heart. Perhaps he wasn't a divinity student at all, but some one travelling incognito."

Zina grew thoughtful; the story of the divinity student and the beautiful French girl had evidently carried her imagination far away. It seemed to Pyotr Mihalitch that she had not changed in the least during the last week, except that she was a little paler. She looked calm and just as usual, as though she had come with her brother to visit Vlassitch. But Pyotr Mihalitch felt that some change had taken place in himself. Before, when she was living at home, he could have spoken to her about anything, and now he did not feel equal to asking her the simple question, "How do you like being here?" The question seemed awkward and unnecessary. Probably the same change had taken place in her. She was in no haste to turn the conversation to her mother, to her home, to her relations with Vlassitch; she did not defend herself, she did not say that free unions are better than marriages in the church; she was not agitated, and calmly brooded over the story of Olivier. . . . And why had they suddenly begun talking of Olivier?

"You are both of you wet with the rain," said Zina, and she smiled joyfully; she was touched by this point of resemblance between her brother and Vlassitch.

And Pyotr Mihalitch felt all the bitterness and horror of his position. He thought of his deserted home, the closed piano, and Zina's bright little room into which no one went now; he thought there were no prints of little feet on the garden-paths, and that before tea no one went off, laughing gaily, to bathe. What he had clung to more and more from his childhood upwards, what he had loved thinking about when he used to sit in the stuffy class-room or the lecture theatre—brightness, purity, and joy, everything that filled the house with life and light, had gone never to return, had vanished, and was mixed up with a coarse, clumsy story of some battalion officer, a chivalrous lieutenant, a depraved woman and a grandfather who had shot himself. . . . And to begin to talk about his mother or to think that the past could ever return would mean not understanding what was clear.

Pyotr Mihalitch's eyes filled with tears and his hand began to tremble as it lay on the table. Zina guessed what he was thinking about, and her eyes, too, glistened and looked red.

"Grigory, come here," she said to Vlassitch.

They walked away to the window and began talking of something in a whisper. From the way that Vlassitch stooped down to her and the way she looked at him, Pyotr Mihalitch realised again that everything was irreparably over, and that it was no use to talk of anything. Zina went out of the room.

"Well, brother!" Vlassitch began, after a brief silence, rubbing his hands and smiling. "I called our life happiness just now, but that was, so to speak, poetical license. In reality, there has not been a sense of happiness so far. Zina has been thinking all the time of you, of her mother, and has been worrying; looking at her, I, too, felt worried. Hers is a bold, free nature, but, you know, it's difficult when you're not used to it, and she is young, too. The servants call her 'Miss'; it seems a trifle, but it upsets her. There it is, brother."

Zina brought in a plateful of strawberries. She was followed by a little maidservant, looking crushed and humble, who set a jug of milk on the table and made a very low bow: she had something about her that was in keeping with the old furniture, something petrified and dreary.

The sound of the rain had ceased. Pyotr Mihalitch ate strawberries while Vlassitch and Zina looked at him in silence. The moment of the inevitable but useless conversation was approaching, and all three felt the burden of it. Pyotr Mihalitch's eyes filled with tears again; he pushed away his plate and said that he must be going home, or it would be getting late, and perhaps it would rain again. The time had come when common decency required Zina to speak of those at home and of her new life.

"How are things at home?" she asked rapidly, and her pale face quivered. "How is mother?"

"You know mother . . ." said Pyotr Mihalitch, not looking at her.

"Petrusha, you've thought a great deal about what has happened," she said, taking hold of her brother's sleeve, and he knew how hard it was for her to speak. "You've thought a great deal: tell me, can we reckon on mother's accepting Grigory . . . and the whole position, one day?"

She stood close to her brother, face to face with him, and he was astonished that she was so beautiful, and that he seemed not to have noticed it before. And it seemed to him utterly absurd that his sister, so like his mother, pampered, elegant, should be living with Vlassitch and in Vlassitch's house, with the petrified servant, and the table with six legs—in the house where a man had been flogged to death, and that she was not going home with him, but was staying here to sleep.

"You know mother," he said, not answering her question. "I think you ought to have . . . to do something, to ask her forgiveness or something. . . ."

"But to ask her forgiveness would mean pretending we had done wrong. I'm ready to tell a lie to comfort mother, but it won't lead anywhere. I know mother. Well, what will be, must be!" said Zina, growing more cheerful now that the most unpleasant had been said. "We'll wait for five years, ten years, and be patient, and then God's will be done."

She took her brother's arm, and when she walked through the dark hall she squeezed close to him. They went out on the steps. Pyotr Mihalitch said good-bye, got on his horse, and set off at a walk; Zina and Vlassitch walked a little way with him. It was still and warm, with a delicious smell of hay; stars were twinkling brightly between the clouds. Vlassitch's old garden, which had seen so many gloomy stories in its time, lay slumbering in the darkness, and for some reason it was mournful riding through it.

"Zina and I to-day after dinner spent some really exalted moments," said Vlassitch. "I read aloud to her an excellent article on the question of emigration. You must read it, brother! You really must. It's remarkable for its lofty tone. I could not resist writing a letter to the editor to be forwarded to the author. I wrote only a single line: 'I thank you and warmly press your noble hand.' "

Pyotr Mihalitch was tempted to say, "Don't meddle in what does not concern you," but he held his tongue.

Vlassitch walked by his right stirrup and Zina by the left; both seemed to have forgotten that they had to go home. It was damp, and they had almost reached Koltovitch's copse. Pyotr Mihalitch felt that they were expecting something from him, though they hardly knew what it was, and he felt unbearably sorry for them. Now as they walked by the horse with submissive faces, lost in thought, he had a deep conviction that they were unhappy, and could not be happy, and their love seemed to him a melancholy, irreparable mistake. Pity and the sense that he could do nothing to help them reduced him to that state of spiritual softening when he was ready to make any sacrifice to get rid of the painful feeling of sympathy.

"I'll come over sometimes for a night," he said.

But it sounded as though he were making a concession, and did not satisfy him. When they stopped near Koltovitch's copse to say good-bye, he bent down to Zina, touched her shoulder, and said:

"You are right, Zina! You have done well." To avoid saying more and bursting into tears, he lashed his horse and galloped into the wood. As he rode into the darkness, he looked round and saw Vlassitch and Zina walking home along the road—he taking long strides, while she walked with a hurried, jerky step beside him—talking eagerly about something.

"I am an old woman!" thought Pyotr Mihalitch. "I went to solve the question and I have only made it more complicated—there it is!"

He was heavy at heart. When he got out of the copse he rode at a walk and then stopped his horse near the pond. He wanted to sit and think without moving. The moon was rising and was reflected in a streak of red on the other side of the pond. There were low rumbles of thunder in the distance. Pyotr Mihalitch looked steadily at the water and imagined his sister's despair, her martyr-like pallor, the tearless eyes with which she would conceal her humiliation from others. He imagined her with child, imagined the death of their mother, her funeral, Zina's horror. . . . The proud, superstitious old woman would be sure to die of grief. Terrible pictures of the future rose before him on the background of smooth, dark water, and among pale feminine figures he saw himself, a weak, cowardly man with a guilty face.

A hundred paces off on the right bank of the pond, something dark was standing motionless: was it a man or a tall post? Pyotr Mihalitch thought of the divinity student who had been killed and thrown into the pond.

"Olivier behaved inhumanly, but one way or another he did settle the question, while I have settled nothing and have only made it worse," he thought, gazing at the dark figure that looked like a ghost. "He said and did what he thought right while I say and do what I don't think right; and I don't know really what I do think. . . ."

He rode up to the dark figure: it was an old rotten post, the relic of some shed.

From Koltovitch's copse and garden there came a strong fragrant scent of lilies of the valley and honey-laden flowers. Pyotr Mihalitch rode along the bank of the pond and looked mournfully into the water. And thinking about his life, he came to the conclusion he had never said or acted upon what he really thought, and other people had repaid him in the same way. And so the whole of life seemed to him as dark as this water in which the night sky was reflected and water-weeds grew in a tangle. And it seemed to him that nothing could ever set it right.

THE GRASSHOPPER

I

All Olga Ivanovna's friends and acquaintances were at her wedding.

"Look at him; isn't it true that there is something in him?" she said to her friends, with a nod towards her husband, as though she wanted to explain why she was marrying a simple, very ordinary, and in no way remarkable man.

Her husband, Osip Stepanitch Dymov, was a doctor, and only of the rank of a titular councillor. He was on the staff of two hospitals: in one a ward-surgeon and in the other a dissecting demonstrator. Every day from nine to twelve he saw patients and was busy in his ward, and after twelve o'clock he went by tram to the other hospital, where he dissected. His private practice was a small one, not worth more than five hundred roubles a year. That was all. What more could one say about him? Meanwhile, Olga Ivanovna and her friends and acquaintances were not quite ordinary people. Every one of them was remarkable in some way, and more or less famous; already had made a reputation and was looked upon as a celebrity; or if not yet a celebrity, gave brilliant promise of becoming one. There was an actor from the Dramatic Theatre, who was a great talent of established reputation, as well as an elegant, intelligent, and modest man, and a capital elocutionist, and who taught Olga Ivanovna to recite; there was a singer from the opera, a good-natured, fat man who assured Olga Ivanovna, with a sigh, that she was ruining herself, that if she would take herself in hand and not be lazy she might make a remarkable singer; then there were several artists, and chief among them Ryabovsky, a very handsome, fair young man of five-and-twenty who painted genre pieces, animal studies, and landscapes, was successful at exhibitions, and had sold his last picture for five hundred roubles. He touched up Olga Ivanovna's sketches, and used to say she might do something. Then a violoncellist, whose instrument used to sob, and who openly declared that of all the ladies of his acquaintance the only one who could accompany him was Olga Ivanovna; then there was a literary man, young but already well known, who had written stories, novels, and plays. Who else? Why, Vassily Vassilyitch, a landowner and amateur illustrator and vignettist, with a great feeling for the old Russian style, the old ballad and epic. On paper, on china, and on smoked plates, he produced literally marvels. In the midst of this free artistic company, spoiled by fortune, though refined and modest, who recalled the existence of doctors only in times of illness, and to whom the name of Dymov sounded in no way different from Sidorov or Tarasov—in the midst of this company Dymov seemed strange, not wanted, and small, though he was tall and broad-shouldered. He looked as though he had on somebody else's coat, and his beard was like a shopman's. Though if he had been a writer or an artist, they would have said that his beard reminded them of Zola.

An artist said to Olga Ivanovna that with her flaxen hair and in her wedding-dress she was very much like a graceful cherry-tree when it is covered all over with delicate white blossoms in spring.

"Oh, let me tell you," said Olga Ivanovna, taking his arm, "how it was it all came to pass so suddenly. Listen, listen! . . . I must tell you that my father was on the same staff at the hospital as Dymov. When my poor father was taken ill, Dymov watched for days and nights together at his bedside. Such self-sacrifice! Listen, Ryabovsky! You, my writer, listen; it is very interesting! Come nearer. Such self-sacrifice, such genuine sympathy! I sat up with my father, and did not sleep for nights, either. And all at once—the princess had won the hero's heart—my Dymov fell head over ears in love. Really, fate is so strange at times! Well, after my father's death he came to see me sometimes, met me in the street, and one fine evening, all at once he made me an offer . . . like snow upon my head. . . . I lay awake all night, crying, and fell hellishly in love myself. And here, as you see, I am his wife. There really is something strong, powerful, bearlike about him, isn't there? Now his face is turned three-quarters towards us in a bad light, but when he turns round look at his forehead. Ryabovsky, what do you say to that forehead? Dymov, we are talking about you!" she called to her husband.

"Come here; hold out your honest hand to Ryabovsky. . . . That's right, be friends."

Dymov, with a naïve and good-natured smile, held out his hand to Ryabovsky, and said:

"Very glad to meet you. There was a Ryabovsky in my year at the medical school. Was he a relation of yours?"

II

Olga Ivanovna was twenty-two, Dymov was thirty-one. They got on splendidly together when they were married. Olga Ivanovna hung all her drawing-room walls with her own and other people's sketches, in frames and without frames, and near the piano and furniture arranged picturesque corners with Japanese parasols, easels, daggers, busts, photographs, and rags of many colours. . . . In the dining-room she papered the walls with peasant wood-cuts, hung up bark shoes and sickles, stood in a corner a scythe and a rake, and so achieved a dining-room in the Russian style. In her bedroom she draped the ceiling and the walls with dark cloths to make it like a cavern, hung a Venetian lantern over the beds, and at the door set a figure with a halberd. And every one thought that the young people had a very charming little home.

When she got up at eleven o'clock every morning, Olga Ivanovna played the piano or, if it were sunny, painted something in oils. Then between twelve and one she drove to her dressmaker's. As Dymov and she had very little money, only just enough, she and her dressmaker were often put to clever shifts to enable her to appear constantly in new dresses and make a sensation with them. Very often out of an old dyed dress, out of bits of tulle, lace, plush, and silk, costing nothing, perfect marvels were created, something bewitching—not a dress, but a dream. From the dressmaker's Olga Ivanovna usually drove to some actress of her acquaintance to hear the latest theatrical gossip, and incidentally to try and get hold of tickets for the first night of some new play or for a benefit performance. From the actress's she had to go to some artist's studio or to some exhibition or to see some celebrity—either to pay a visit or to give an invitation or simply to have a chat. And everywhere she met with a gay and friendly welcome, and was assured that she was good, that she was sweet, that she was rare. . . . Those whom she called great and famous received her as one of themselves, as an equal, and predicted with one voice that, with her talents, her taste, and her intelligence, she would do great things if she concentrated herself. She sang, she played the piano, she painted in oils, she carved, she took part in amateur performances; and all this not just anyhow, but all with talent, whether she made lanterns for an illumination or dressed up or tied somebody's cravat—everything she did was exceptionally graceful, artistic, and charming. But her talents showed themselves in nothing so clearly as in her faculty for quickly becoming acquainted and on intimate terms with celebrated people. No sooner did any one become ever so little celebrated, and set people talking about him, than she made his acquaintance, got on friendly terms the same day, and invited him to her house. Every new acquaintance she made was a veritable fête for her. She adored celebrated people, was proud of them, dreamed of them every night. She craved for them, and never could satisfy her craving. The old ones departed and were forgotten, new ones came to replace them, but to these, too, she soon grew accustomed or was disappointed in them, and began eagerly seeking for fresh great men, finding them and seeking for them again. What for?

Between four and five she dined at home with her husband. His simplicity, good sense, and kindheartedness touched her and moved her up to enthusiasm. She was constantly jumping up, impulsively hugging his head and showering kisses on it.

"You are a clever, generous man, Dymov," she used to say, "but you have one very serious defect. You take absolutely no interest in art. You don't believe in music or painting."

"I don't understand them," he would say mildly. "I have spent all my life in working at natural science and medicine, and I have never had time to take an interest in the arts."

"But, you know, that's awful, Dymov!"

"Why so? Your friends don't know anything of science or medicine, but you don't reproach them with it. Every one has his own line. I don't understand landscapes and operas, but the way I look at it is that if one set of sensible people devote their whole lives to them, and other sensible people pay immense sums for them, they must be of use. I don't understand them, but not understanding does not imply disbelieving in them."

"Let me shake your honest hand!"

After dinner Olga Ivanovna would drive off to see her friends, then to a theatre or to a concert, and she returned home after midnight. So it was every day.

On Wednesdays she had "At Homes." At these "At Homes" the hostess and her guests did not play cards and did not dance, but entertained themselves with various arts. An actor from the Dramatic Theatre recited, a singer sang, artists sketched in the albums of which Olga Ivanovna had a great number, the violoncellist played, and the hostess herself sketched, carved, sang, and played accompaniments. In the intervals between the recitations, music, and singing, they talked and argued about literature, the theatre, and painting. There were no ladies, for Olga Ivanovna considered all ladies wearisome and vulgar except actresses and her dressmaker. Not one of these entertainments passed without the hostess starting at every ring at the bell, and saying, with a triumphant expression, "It is he," meaning by "he," of course, some new celebrity. Dymov was not in the drawing-room, and no one remembered his existence. But exactly at half-past eleven the door leading into the dining-room opened, and Dymov would appear with his good-natured, gentle smile and say, rubbing his hands:

"Come to supper, gentlemen."

They all went into the dining-room, and every time found on the table exactly the same things: a dish of oysters, a piece of ham or veal, sardines, cheese, caviare, mushrooms, vodka, and two decanters of wine.

"My dear *maître d' hôtel!*" Olga Ivanovna would say, clasping her hands with enthusiasm, "you are simply fascinating! My friends, look at his forehead! Dymov, turn your profile. Look! he has the face of a Bengal tiger and an expression as kind and sweet as a gazelle. Ah, the darling!"

The visitors ate, and, looking at Dymov, thought, "He really is a nice fellow"; but they soon forgot about him, and went on talking about the theatre, music, and painting.

The young people were happy, and their life flowed on without a hitch.

The third week of their honeymoon was spent, however, not quite happily—sadly, indeed. Dymov caught erysipelas in the hospital, was in bed for six days, and had to have his beautiful black hair cropped. Olga Ivanovna sat beside him and wept bitterly, but when he was better she put a white handkerchief on his shaven head and began to paint him as a Bedouin. And they were both in good spirits. Three days after he had begun to go back to the hospital he had another mischance.

"I have no luck, little mother," he said one day at dinner. "I had four dissections to do today, and I cut two of my fingers at one. And I did not notice it till I got home."

Olga Ivanovna was alarmed. He smiled, and told her that it did not matter, and that he often cut his hands when he was dissecting.

"I get absorbed, little mother, and grow careless."

Olga Ivanovna dreaded symptoms of blood-poisoning, and prayed about it every night, but all went well. And again life flowed on peaceful and happy, free from grief and anxiety. The present was happy, and to follow it spring was at hand, already smiling in the distance, and promising a thousand delights. There would be no end to their happiness. in April, May and June a summer villa a good distance out of town; walks, sketching, fishing, nightingales; and then from July right on to autumn an artist's tour on the Volga, and in this tour Olga Ivanovna would take part as an indispensable member of the society. She had already had made for her two travelling dresses of linen, had bought paints, brushes, canvases, and a new palette for the journey. Almost every day Ryabovsky visited her to see what progress she was making in her painting; when she showed him her painting, he used to thrust his hands deep into his pockets, compress his lips, sniff, and say:

"Ye—es . . . ! That cloud of yours is screaming: it's not in the evening light. The foreground is somehow chewed up, and there is something, you know, not the thing. . . . And your cottage is weighed down and whines pitifully. That corner ought to have been taken more in shadow, but on the whole it is not bad; I like it."

And the more incomprehensible he talked, the more readily Olga Ivanovna understood him.

III

After dinner on the second day of Trinity week,* Dymov bought some sweets and some savouries and went down to the villa to see his wife. He had not seen her for a fortnight, and missed her terribly. As he sat in the train and afterwards as he looked for his villa in a big wood, he felt all the while hungry and weary, and dreamed of how he would have supper in freedom with his wife, then tumble into bed and to sleep. And he was delighted as he looked at his parcel, in which there was caviare, cheese, and white salmon.

The sun was setting by the time he found his villa and recognized it. The old servant told him that her mistress was not at home, but that most likely she would soon be in. The villa, very uninviting in appearance, with low ceilings papered with writing-paper and with uneven floors full of crevices, consisted only of three rooms. In one there was a bed, in the second there were canvases, brushes, greasy papers, and men's overcoats and hats lying about on the chairs and in the windows, while in the third Dymov found three unknown men; two were dark-haired and had beards, the other was clean-shaven and fat, apparently an actor. There was a samovar boiling on the table.

"What do you want?" asked the actor in a bass voice, looking at Dymov ungraciously. "Do you want Olga Ivanovna? Wait a minute; she will be here directly."

Dymov sat down and waited. One of the dark-haired men, looking sleepily and listlessly at him, poured himself out a glass of tea, and asked:

"Perhaps you would like some tea?"

Dymov was both hungry and thirsty, but he refused tea for fear of spoiling his supper. Soon he heard footsteps and a familiar laugh; a door slammed, and Olga Ivanovna ran into the room, wearing a wide-brimmed hat and carrying a box in her hand; she was followed by Ryabovsky, rosy and good-humoured, carrying a big umbrella and a camp-stool.

"Dymov!" cried Olga Ivanovna, and she flushed crimson with

---

*Week in which Pentecost occurs.

pleasure. "Dymov!" she repeated, laying her head and both arms on his bosom. "Is that you? Why haven't you come for so long? Why? Why?"

"When could I, little mother? I am always busy, and whenever I am free it always happens somehow that the train does not fit."

"But how glad I am to see you! I have been dreaming about you the whole night, the whole night, and I was afraid you must be ill. Ah! if you only knew how sweet you are! You have come in the nick of time! You will be my salvation! You are the only person who can save me! There is to be a most original wedding here tomorrow," she went on, laughing, and tying her husband's cravat. "A young telegraph clerk at the station, called Tchikeldyeev, is going to be married. He is a handsome young man and—well, not stupid, and you know there is something strong, bearlike in his face . . . you might paint him as a young Norman. We summer visitors take a great interest in him, and have promised to be at his wedding. . . . He is a lonely, timid man, not well off, and of course it would be a shame not to be sympathetic to him. Fancy! the wedding will be after the service; then we shall all walk from the church to the bride's lodgings . . . you see the wood, the birds singing, patches of sunlight on the grass, and all of us spots of different colours against the bright green background—very original, in the style of the French impressionists. But, Dymov, what am I to go to the church in?" said Olga Ivanovna, and she looked as though she were going to cry. "I have nothing here, literally nothing! no dress, no flowers, no gloves . . . you must save me. Since you have come, fate itself bids you save me. Take the keys, my precious, go home and get my pink dress from the wardrobe. You remember it; it hangs in front. . . . Then, in the storeroom, on the floor, on the right side, you will see two cardboard boxes. When you open the top one you will see tulle, heaps of tulle and rags of all sorts, and under them flowers. Take out all the flowers carefully, try not to crush them, darling; I will choose among them later. . . . And buy me some gloves."

"Very well," said Dymov; "I will go tomorrow and send them to you."

"Tomorrow?" asked Olga Ivanovna, and she looked at him surprised. "You won't have time tomorrow. The first train goes tomorrow at nine, and the wedding's at eleven. No, darling, it must be today; it absolutely must be today. If you won't be able to come to-morrow, send them by a messenger. Come, you must run along. . . . The passenger train will be in directly; don't miss it, darling."

"Very well."

"Oh, how sorry I am to let you go!" said Olga Ivanovna, and tears came into her eyes. "And why did I promise that telegraph clerk, like a silly?"

Dymov hurriedly drank a glass of tea, took a cracknel, and, smiling gently, went to the station. And the caviare, the cheese, and the white salmon were eaten by the two dark gentlemen and the fat actor.

IV

On a still moonlight night in July Olga Ivanovna was standing on the deck of the Volga steamer and looking alternately at the water and at the picturesque banks. Beside her was standing Ryabovsky, telling her the black shadows on the water were not shadows, but a dream, that it would be sweet to sink into forgetfulness, to die, to become a memory in the sight of that enchanted water with the fantastic glimmer, in sight of the fathomless sky and the mournful, dreamy shores that told of the vanity of our life and of the existence of something higher, blessed, and eternal. The past was vulgar and uninteresting, the future was trivial, and that marvelous night, unique in a lifetime, would soon be over, would blend with eternity; then, why live?

And Olga Ivanovna listened alternately to Ryabovsky's voice and the silence of the night, and thought of her being immortal and never dying. The turquoise colour of the water, such as she had never seen before, the sky, the river-banks, the black shadows, and the unaccountable joy that flooded her soul, all told her that she would make a great artist, and that somewhere in the distance, in the infinite space beyond the moonlight, success, glory, the love of the people, lay awaiting her. . . . When she gazed steadily without blinking into the distance, she seemed to see crowds of people, lights, triumphant strains of music, cries of enthusiasm, she herself in a white dress, and flowers showered upon her from all sides. She thought, too, that beside her, leaning with his elbows on the rail of the steamer, there was standing a real great man, a genius, one of God's elect. . . . All that he had created up to the present was fine, new, and extraordinary, but what he would create in time, when with maturity his rare talent reached its full development, would be astounding, immeasurably sublime; and that could be seen by his face, by his manner of expressing himself and his attitude to nature. He talked of shadows, of the tones of evening, of the moonlight, in a special way, in a language of his own, so that one could not help feeling the fascination of his power over nature. He was very handsome, original, and his life, free, independent, aloof from all common cares, was like the life of a bird.

"It's growing cooler," said Olga Ivanovna, and she gave a shudder.

Ryabovsky wrapped her in his cloak, and said mournfully:

"I feel that I am in your power; I am a slave. Why are you so enchanting today?"

He kept staring intently at her, and his eyes were terrible. And she was afraid to look at him.

"I love you madly," he whispered, breathing on her cheek. "Say one word to me and I will not go on living; I will give up art . . ." he muttered in violent emotion. "Love me, love . . ."

"Don't talk like that," said Olga Ivanovna, covering her eyes. "It's dreadful! How about Dymov?"

"What of Dymov? Why Dymov? What have I to do with Dymov? The Volga, the moon, beauty, my love, ecstasy, and there is no such thing as Dymov. . . . Ah! I don't know . . . I don't care about the past; give me one moment, one instant!"

Olga Ivanovna's heart began to throb. She tried to think about her husband, but all her past, with her wedding, with Dymov, and with her "At Homes," seemed to her petty, trivial, dingy, unnecessary, and far, far away. . . . Yes, really, what of Dymov? Why Dymov? What had she to do with Dymov? Had he any existence in nature, or was he only a dream?

"For him, a simple and ordinary man the happiness he has had already is enough," she thought, covering her face with her hands. "Let them condemn me, let them curse me, but in spite of them all I will go to my ruin; I will go to my ruin! . . . One must experience everything in life. My God! how terrible and how glorious!"

"Well? Well?" muttered the artist, embracing her, and greedily kissing the hands with which she feebly tried to thrust him from her. "You love me? Yes? Yes? Oh, what a night! marvellous night!"

"Yes, what a night!" she whispered, looking into his eyes, which were bright with tears.

Then she looked round quickly, put her arms round him, and kissed him on the lips.

"We are nearing Kineshmo!"* said some one on the other side of the deck.

They heard heavy footsteps; it was a waiter from the refreshment-bar.

"Waiter," said Olga Ivanovna, laughing and crying with happiness, "bring us some wine."

The artist, pale with emotion, sat on the seat, looking at Olga Ivanovna with adoring, grateful eyes; then he closed his eyes, and said, smiling languidly:

"I am tired."

And he leaned his head against the rail.

V

On the second of September the day was warm and still, but overcast. In the early morning a light mist had hung over the Volga, and after nine o'clock it had begun to spout with rain. And there seemed no hope of the sky clearing. Over their morning tea Ryabovsky told Olga Ivanovna that painting was the most ungrateful and boring art, that he was not an artist, that none but fools thought that he had any talent, and all at once, for no rhyme or reason, he snatched up a knife and with it scraped over his very best sketch. After his tea he sat plunged in gloom at the window and gazed at the Volga. And now the Volga was dingy, all of one even colour without a gleam of light, cold-looking. Everything, everything recalled the approach of dreary, gloomy autumn. And it seemed as though nature had removed now from the Volga the sumptuous green covers from the banks, the brilliant reflections of the sunbeams, the transparent blue distance, and all its smart gala array, and had packed it away in boxes till the coming spring, and the crows were flying above the Volga and crying tauntingly, "Bare, bare!"

---

*Town on the Volga River some 200 miles northwest of Moscow.

Ryabovsky heard their cawing, and thought he had already gone off and lost his talent, that everything in this world was relative, conditional, and stupid, and that he ought not to have taken up with this woman. . . . In short, he was out of humour and depressed.

Olga Ivanovna sat behind the screen on the bed, and, passing her fingers through her lovely flaxen hair, pictured herself first in the drawing-room, then in the bedroom, then in her husband's study; her imagination carried her to the theatre, to the dressmaker, to her distinguished friends. Were they getting something up now? Did they think of her? The season had begun by now, and it would be time to think about her "At Homes." And Dymov? Dear Dymov! with what gentleness and childlike pathos he kept begging her in his letters to make haste and come home! Every month he sent her seventy-five roubles, and when she wrote him that she had lent the artists a hundred roubles, he sent that hundred too. What a kind, generous-hearted man! The travelling wearied Olga Ivanovna; she was bored; and she longed to get away from the peasants, from the damp smell of the river, and to cast off the feeling of physical uncleanliness of which she was conscious all the time, living in the peasants' huts and wandering from village to village. If Ryabovsky had not given his word to the artists that he would stay with them till the twentieth of September, they might have gone away that very day. And how nice that would have been!

"My God!" moaned Ryabovsky. "Will the sun ever come out? I can't go on with a sunny landscape without the sun. . . ."

"But you have a sketch with a cloudy sky," said Olga Ivanovna, coming from behind the screen. "Do you remember, in the right foreground forest trees, on the left a herd of cows and geese? You might finish it now."

"Aie!" the artist scowled. "Finish it! Can you imagine I am such a fool that I don't know what I want to do?"

"How you have changed to me!" sighed Olga Ivanovna.

"Well, a good thing too!"

Olga Ivanovna's face quivered; she moved away to the stove and began to cry.

"Well, that's the last straw—crying! Give over! I have a thousand reasons for tears, but I am not crying."

"A thousand reasons!" cried Olga Ivanovna. "The chief one is that you are weary of me. Yes!" she said, and broke into sobs. "If one is to tell the truth, you are ashamed of our love. You keep trying to prevent the artists from noticing it, though it is impossible to conceal it, and they have known all about it for ever so long."

"Olga, one thing I beg you," said the artist in an imploring voice, laying his hand on his heart—"one thing; don't worry me! I want nothing else from you!"

"But swear that you love me still!"

"This is agony!" the artist hissed through his teeth, and he jumped up. "It will end by my throwing myself in the Volga or going out of my mind! Let me alone!"

"Come, kill me, kill me!" cried Olga Ivanovna. "Kill me!"

She sobbed again, and went behind the screen. There was a swish of rain on the straw thatch of the hut. Ryabovsky clutched his head and strode up and down the hut; then with a resolute face, as though bent on proving something to somebody, put on his cap, slung his gun over his shoulder, and went out of the hut.

After he had gone, Olga Ivanovna lay a long time on the bed, crying. At first she thought it would be a good thing to poison herself, so that when Ryabovsky came back he would find her dead; then her imagination carried her to her drawing-room, to her husband's study, and she imagined herself sitting motionless beside Dymov and enjoying the physical peace and cleanliness, and in the evening sitting in the theatre, listening to Mazini.* And a yearning for civilization, for the noise and bustle of the town, for celebrated people sent a pang to her heart. A peasant woman came into the hut and began in a leisurely way lighting the stove to get the dinner. There was a smell of charcoal fumes, and the air was filled with bluish smoke. The artists came in, in muddy high boots and with faces wet with rain, examined their sketches, and comforted themselves by saying that the Volga had its charms even in bad weather. On the wall the cheap clock went "tic-tic-tic." . . . The flies, feeling chilled, crowded round the ikon in the corner, buzzing, and one could hear the cockroaches scurrying about among the thick portfolios under the seats. . . .

---

*Italian operatic tenor.

Ryabovsky came home as the sun was setting. He flung his cap on the table, and, without removing his muddy boots, sank pale and exhausted on the bench and closed his eyes.

"I am tired . . ." he said, and twitched his eyebrows, trying to raise his eyelids.

To be nice to him and to show she was not cross, Olga Ivanovna went up to him, gave him a silent kiss, and passed the comb through his fair hair. She meant to comb it for him.

"What's that?" he said, starting as though something cold had touched him, and he opened his eyes. "What is it? Please let me alone."

He thrust her off, and moved away. And it seemed to her that there was a look of aversion and annoyance on his face.

At that time the peasant woman cautiously carried him, in both hands, a plate of cabbage-soup. And Olga Ivanovna saw how she wetted her fat fingers in it. And the dirty peasant woman, standing with her body thrust forward, and the cabbage-soup which Ryabovsky began eating greedily, and the hut, and their whole way of life, which she at first had so loved for its simplicity and artistic disorder, seemed horrible to her now. She suddenly felt insulted, and said coldly:

"We must part for a time, or else from boredom we shall quarrel in earnest. I am sick of this; I am going today."

"Going how? Astride on a broomstick?"

"Today is Thursday, so the steamer will be here at half-past nine."

"Eh? Yes, yes. . . . Well, go, then . . ." Ryabovsky said softly, wiping his mouth with a towel instead of a dinner napkin. "You are dull and have nothing to do here, and one would have to be a great egoist to try and keep you. Go home, and we shall meet again after the twentieth."

Olga Ivanovna packed in good spirits. Her cheeks positively glowed with pleasure. Could it really be true, she asked herself, that she would soon be writing in her drawing-room and sleeping in her bedroom, and dining with a cloth on the table? A weight was lifted from her heart, and she no longer felt angry with the artist.

"My paints and brushes I will leave with you, Ryabovsky," she said. "You can bring what's left. . . . Mind, now, don't be lazy here when I am gone; don't mope, but work. You are such a splendid fellow, Ryabovsky!"

At ten o'clock Ryabovsky gave her a farewell kiss, in order, as she thought, to avoid kissing her on the steamer before the artists, and went with her to the landing-stage. The steamer soon came up and carried her away.

She arrived home two and a half days later. Breathless with excitement, she went, without taking off her hat or waterproof, into the drawing-room and thence into the dining-room. Dymov, with his waistcoat unbuttoned and no coat, was sitting at the table sharpening a knife on a fork; before him lay a grouse on a plate. As Olga Ivanovna went into the flat she was convinced that it was essential to hide everything from her husband, and that she would have the strength and skill to do so; but now, when she saw his broad, mild, happy smile, and shining, joyful eyes, she felt that to deceive this man was as vile, as revolting, and as impossible and out of her power as to bear false witness, to steal, or to kill, and in a flash she resolved to tell him all that had happened. Letting him kiss and embrace her, she sank down on her knees before him and hid her face.

"What is it, what is it, little mother?" he asked tenderly. "Were you homesick?"

She raised her face, red with shame, and gazed at him with a guilty and imploring look, but fear and shame prevented her from telling him the truth.

"Nothing," she said; "it's just nothing. . . ."

"Let us sit down," he said, raising her and seating her at the table. "That's right, eat the grouse. You are starving, poor darling."

She eagerly breathed in the atmosphere of home and ate the grouse, while he watched her with tenderness and laughed with delight.

VI

Apparently, by the middle of the winter Dymov began to suspect that he was being deceived. As though his conscience was not clear, he could not look his wife straight in the face, did not smile with delight when he met her, and to avoid being left alone with her, he often brought in to dinner his colleague, Korostelev, a little close-cropped man with a wrinkled face, who kept buttoning and unbuttoning his reefer jacket with embarrassment when he talked with Olga Ivanovna, and then with his right hand nipped his left moustache. At dinner the two doctors talked about the fact that a displacement of the diaphragm was sometimes accompanied by irregularities of the heart, or that a great number of neurotic complaints were met with of late, or that Dymov had the day before found a cancer of the lower abdomen while dissecting a corpse with the diagnosis of pernicious anaemia. And it seemed as though they were talking of medicine to give Olga Ivanovna a chance of being silent—that is, of not lying. After dinner Korostelev sat down to the piano, while Dymov sighed and said to him:

"Ech, brother—well, well! Play something melancholy."

Hunching up his shoulders and stretching his fingers wide apart, Korostelev played some chords and began singing in a tenor voice, "Show me the abode where the Russian peasant would not groan," while Dymov sighed once more, propped his head on his fist, and sank into thought.

Olga Ivanovna had been extremely imprudent in her conduct of late. Every morning she woke up in a very bad humour and with the thought that she no longer cared for Ryabovsky, and that, thank God, it was all over now. But as she drank her coffee she reflected that Ryabovsky had robbed her of her husband, and that now she was left with neither her husband nor Ryabovsky; then she remembered talks she had heard among her acquaintances of a picture Ryabovsky was preparing for the exhibition, something striking, a mixture of genre and landscape, in the style of Polyenov,* about which every one who had been into his studio went into raptures; and this, of course, she mused, he had created under her influence, and altogether, thanks to her influence, he had greatly changed for the better. Her influence was so beneficent and essential that if she were to leave him he might perhaps go to ruin. And she remembered, too, that the last time he had come to see her in a great-coat with flecks on it and a new tie, he had asked her languidly:

"Am I beautiful?"

And with his elegance, his long curls, and his blue eyes, he really

---

*Russian painter.

was very beautiful (or perhaps it only seemed so), and he had been affectionate to her.

Considering and remembering many things Olga Ivanovna dressed and in great agitation drove to Ryabovsky's studio. She found him in high spirits, and enchanted with his really magnificent picture. He was dancing about and playing the fool and answering serious questions with jokes. Olga Ivanovna was jealous of the picture and hated it, but from politeness she stood before the picture for five minutes in silence, and, heaving a sigh, as though before a holy shrine, said softly:

"Yes, you have never painted anything like it before. Do you know, it is positively awe-inspiring?"

And then she began beseeching him to love her and not to cast her off, to have pity on her in her misery and her wretchedness. She shed tears, kissed his hands, insisted on his swearing that he loved her, told him that without her good influence he would go astray and be ruined. And, when she had spoilt his good-humour, feeling herself humiliated, she would drive off to her dressmaker or to an actress of her acquaintance to try and get theatre tickets.

If she did not find him at his studio she left a letter in which she swore that if he did not come to see her that day she would poison herself. He was scared, came to see her, and stayed to dinner. Regardless of her husband's presence, he would say rude things to her, and she would answer him in the same way. Both felt they were a burden to each other, that they were tyrants and enemies, and were wrathful, and in their wrath did not notice that their behaviour was unseemly, and that even Korostelev, with his close-cropped head, saw it all. After dinner Ryabovsky made haste to say good-bye and get away.

"Where are you off to?" Olga Ivanovna would ask him in the hall, looking at him with hatred.

Scowling and screwing up his eyes, he mentioned some lady of their acquaintance, and it was evident that he was laughing at her jealousy and wanted to annoy her. She went to her bedroom and lay down on her bed; from jealousy, anger, a sense of humiliation and shame, she bit the pillow and began sobbing aloud. Dymov left Korostelev in the drawing-room, went into the bedroom, and with a desperate and embarrassed face said softly:

"Don't cry so loud, little mother; there's no need. You must be quiet about it. You must not let people see. . . . You know what is done is done, and can't be mended."

Not knowing how to ease the burden of her jealousy, which actually set her temples throbbing with pain, and thinking still that things might be set right, she would wash, powder her tear-stained face, and fly off to the lady mentioned.

Not finding Ryabovsky with her, she would drive off to a second, then to a third. At first she was ashamed to go about like this, but afterwards she got used to it, and it would happen that in one evening she would make the round of all her female acquaintances in search of Ryabovsky, and they all understood it.

One day she said to Ryabovsky of her husband:

"That man crushes me with his magnanimity."

This phrase pleased her so much that when she met the artists who knew of her affair with Ryabovsky she said every time of her husband, with a vigorous movement of her arm:

"That man crushes me with his magnanimity."

Their manner of life was the same as it had been the year before. On Wednesdays they were "At Home"; an actor recited, the artists sketched. The violoncellist played, a singer sang, and invariably at half-past eleven the door leading to the dining-room opened and Dymov, smiling, said:

"Come to supper, gentlemen."

As before, Olga Ivanovna hunted celebrities, found them, was not satisfied, and went in pursuit of fresh ones. As before, she came back late every night; but now Dymov was not, as last year, asleep, but sitting in his study at work of some sort. He went to bed at three o'clock and got up at eight.

One evening when she was getting ready to go to the theatre and standing before the pier glass, Dymov came into her bedroom, wearing his dresscoat and a white tie. He was smiling gently and looked into his wife's face joyfully, as in old days; his face was radiant.

"I have just been defending my thesis," he said, sitting down and smoothing his knees.

"Defending?" asked Olga Ivanovna.

"Oh, oh!" he laughed, and he craned his neck to see his wife's face in the mirror, for she was still standing with her back to him, doing up her hair. "Oh, oh," he repeated, "do you know it's very possible they may offer me the Readership in General Pathology? It seems like it."

It was evident from his beaming, blissful face that if Olga Ivanovna had shared with him his joy and triumph he would have forgiven her everything, both the present and the future, and would have forgotten everything, but she did not understand what was meant by a "readership" or by "general pathology"; besides, she was afraid of being late for the theatre, and she said nothing.

He sat there another two minutes, and with a guilty smile went away.

VII

It had been a very troubled day.

Dymov had a very bad headache; he had no breakfast, and did not go to the hospital, but spent the whole time lying on his sofa in the study. Olga Ivanovna went as usual at midday to see Ryabovsky, to show him her still-life sketch, and to ask him why he had not been to see her the evening before. The sketch seemed to her worthless, and she had painted it only in order to have an additional reason for going to the artist.

She went in to him without ringing, and as she was taking off her goloshes in the entry she heard a sound as of something running softly in the studio, with a feminine rustle of skirts; and as she hastened to peep in she caught a momentary glimpse of a bit of brown petticoat, which vanished behind a big picture draped, together with the easel, with black calico, to the floor. There could be no doubt that a woman was hiding there. How often Olga Ivanovna herself had taken refuge behind that picture!

Ryabovsky, evidently much embarrassed, held out both hands to her, as though surprised at her arrival, and said with a forced smile:

"Aha! Very glad to see you! Anything nice to tell me?"

Olga Ivanovna's eyes filled with tears. She felt ashamed and bitter, and would not for a million roubles have consented to speak in the presence of the outsider, the rival, the deceitful woman who was standing now behind the picture, and probably giggling malignantly.

"I have brought you a sketch," she said timidly in a thin voice, and her lips quivered. "*Nature morte.*"

"Ah—ah! . . . A sketch?"

The artist took the sketch in his hands, and as he examined it walked, as it were mechanically, into the other room.

Olga Ivanovna followed him humbly.

"*Nature morte* . . . first-rate sort," he muttered, falling into rhyme. "Kurort . . . sport . . . port . . ."

From the studio came the sound of hurried footsteps and the rustle of a skirt.

So she had gone.Olga Ivanovna wanted to scream aloud, to hit the artist on the head with something heavy, but she could see nothing through her tears, was crushed by her shame, and felt herself, not Olga Ivanovna, not an artist, but a little insect.

"I am tired . . ." said the artist languidly, looking at the sketch and tossing his head as though struggling with drowsiness. "It's very nice, of course, but here a sketch today, a sketch last year, another sketch in a month . . . I wonder you are not bored with them. If I were you I should give up painting and work seriously at music or something. You're not an artist, you know, but a musician. But you can't think how tired I am! I'll tell them to bring us some tea, shall I?"

He went out of the room, and Olga Ivanovna heard him give some order to his footman. To avoid farewells and explanations, and above all to avoid bursting into sobs, she ran as fast as she could, before Ryabovsky came back, to the entry, put on her goloshes, and went out into the street; then she breathed easily, and felt she was free for ever from Ryabovsky and from painting and from the burden of shame which had so crushed her in the studio. It was all over!

She drove to her dressmaker's; then to see Barnay,* who had only arrived the day before; from Barnay to a music-shop, and all the time she was thinking how she would write Ryabovsky a cold, cruel letter full of personal dignity, and how in the spring or the summer she would go with Dymov to the Crimea, free herself finally from the past there, and begin a new life.

On getting home late in the evening she sat down in the

---

*German actor.

drawing-room, without taking off her things, to begin the letter. Ryabovsky had told her she was not an artist, and to pay him out she wrote to him now that he painted the same thing every year, and said exactly the same thing every day; that he was at a standstill, and that nothing more would come of him than had come already. She wanted to write, too, that he owed a great deal to her good influence, and that if he was going wrong it was only because her influence was paralysed by various dubious persons like the one who had been hiding behind the picture that day.

"Little mother!" Dymov called from the study, without opening the door.

"What is it?"

"Don't come in to me, but only come to the door—that's right. . . . The day before yesterday I must have caught diphtheria at the hospital, and now . . . I am ill. Make haste and send for Korostelev."

Olga Ivanovna always called her husband by his surname, as she did all the men of her acquaintance; she disliked his Christian name, Osip, because it reminded her of the Osip of Gogol* and the silly pun on his name. But now she cried:

"Osip, it cannot be!"

"Send for him; I feel ill," Dymov said behind the door, and she could hear him go back to the sofa and lie down. "Send!" she heard his voice faintly.

"Good Heavens!" thought Olga Ivanovna, turning chill with horror. "Why, it's dangerous!"

For no reason she took the candle and went into the bedroom, and there, reflecting what she must do, glanced casually at herself in the pier glass. With her pale, frightened face, in a jacket with sleeves high on the shoulders, with yellow ruches on her bosom, and with stripes running in unusual directions on her skirt, she seemed to herself horrible and disgusting. She suddenly felt poignantly sorry for Dymov, for his boundless love for her, for his young life, and even for the desolate little bed in which he had not slept for so long; and she remembered his habitual, gentle, submissive smile. She

---

*Comic character in the play *The Inspector-General* (1836), by Nikolai Gogol.

wept bitterly, and wrote an imploring letter to Korostelev. It was two o'clock in the night.

VIII

When towards eight o'clock in the morning Olga Ivanovna, her head heavy from want of sleep and her hair unbrushed, came out of her bedroom, looking unattractive and with a guilty expression on her face, a gentleman with a black beard, apparently the doctor, passed by her into the entry. There was a smell of drugs. Korostelev was standing near the study door, twisting his left moustache with his right hand.

"Excuse me, I can't let you go in," he said surlily to Olga Ivanovna; "it's catching. Besides, it's no use, really; he is delirious, anyway."

"Has he really got diphtheria?" Olga Ivanovna asked in a whisper.

"People who wantonly risk infection ought to be hauled up and punished for it," muttered Korostelev, not answering Olga Ivanovna's question. "Do you know why he caught it? On Tuesday he was sucking up the mucus through a pipette from a boy with diphtheria. And what for? It was stupid. . . . Just from folly. . . ."

"Is it dangerous, very?" asked Olga Ivanovna.

"Yes; they say it is the malignant form. We ought to send for Shrek really."

A little red-haired man with a long nose and a Jewish accent arrived; then a tall, stooping, shaggy individual, who looked like a head deacon; then a stout young man with a red face and spectacles. These were doctors who came to watch by turns beside their colleague. Korostelev did not go home when his turn was over, but remained and wandered about the rooms like an uneasy spirit. The maid kept getting tea for the various doctors, and was constantly running to the chemist, and there was no one to do the rooms. There was a dismal stillness in the flat.

Olga Ivanovna sat in her bedroom and thought that God was punishing her for having deceived her husband. That silent, unrepining, uncomprehended creature, robbed by his mildness of all personality and will, weak from excessive kindness, had been suffering in obscurity somewhere on his sofa, and had not complained. And if he were to complain even in delirium, the doctors watching by his bedside would learn that diphtheria was not the only cause of his sufferings. They would ask Korostelev. He knew all about it, and it was not for nothing that he looked at his friend's wife with eyes that seemed to say that she was the real chief criminal and diphtheria was only her accomplice. She did not think now of the moonlight evening on the Volga, nor the words of love, nor their poetical life in the peasant's hut. She thought only that from an idle whim, from self-indulgence, she had sullied herself all over from head to foot in something filthy, sticky, which one could never wash off. . . .

"Oh, how fearfully false I've been!" she thought, recalling the troubled passion she had known with Ryabovsky. "Curse it all! . . ."

At four o'clock she dined with Korostelev. He did nothing but scowl and drink red wine, and did not eat a morsel. She ate nothing, either. At one minute she was praying inwardly and vowing to God that if Dymov recovered she would love him again and be a faithful wife to him. Then, forgetting herself for a minute, she would look at Korostelev, and think: "Surely it must be dull to be a humble, obscure person, not remarkable in any way, especially with such a wrinkled face and bad manners!" Then it seemed to her that God would strike her dead that minute for not having once been in her husband's study, for fear of infection. And altogether she had a dull, despondent feeling and a conviction that her life was spoilt, and that there was no setting it right anyhow. . . .

After dinner darkness came on. When Olga Ivanovna went into the drawing-room Korostelev was asleep on the sofa, with a gold-embroidered silk cushion under his head.

"Khee-poo-ah," he snored—"khee-poo-ah."

And the doctors as they came to sit up and went away again did not notice this disorder. The fact that a strange man was asleep and snoring in the drawing-room, and the sketches on the walls and the exquisite decoration of the room, and the fact that the lady of the house was dishevelled and untidy—all that aroused not the slightest interest now. One of the doctors chanced to laugh at something, and the laugh had a strange and timid sound that made one's heart ache.

When Olga Ivanovna went into the drawing-room next time, Korostelev was not asleep, but sitting up and smoking.

"He has diphtheria of the nasal cavity," he said in a low voice, "and the heart is not working properly now. Things are in a bad way, really."

"But you will send for Shrek?" said Olga Ivanovna.

"He has been already. It was he noticed that the diphtheria had passed into the nose. What's the use of Shrek! Shrek's no use at all, really. He is Shrek, I am Korostelev, and nothing more."

The time dragged on fearfully slowly. Olga Ivanovna lay down in her clothes on her bed, that had not been made all day, and sank into a doze. She dreamed that the whole flat was filled up from floor to ceiling with a huge piece of iron, and that if they could only get the iron out they would all be light-hearted and happy. Waking, she realized that it was not the iron but Dymov's illness that was weighing on her.

"Nature morte, port . . ." she thought, sinking into forgetfulness again. "Sport . . . Kurort . . . and what of Shrek? Shrek . . . trek . . . wreck. . . . And where are my friends now? Do they know that we are in trouble? Lord, save . . . spare! Shrek . . . trek . . ."

And again the iron was there. . . . The time dragged on slowly, though the clock on the lower storey struck frequently. And bells were continually ringing as the doctors arrived. . . . The housemaid came in with an empty glass on a tray, and asked, "Shall I make the bed, madam?" and getting no answer, went away.

The clock below struck the hour. She dreamed of the rain on the Volga; and again some one came into her bedroom, she thought a stranger. Olga Ivanovna jumped up, and recognized Korostelev.

"What time is it?" she asked.

"About three."

"Well, what is it?"

"What, indeed! . . . I've come to tell you he is passing. . . ."

He gave a sob, sat down on the bed beside her, and wiped away the tears with his sleeve. She could not grasp it at once, but turned cold all over and began slowly crossing herself.

"He is passing," he repeated in a shrill voice, and again he gave a sob. "He is dying because he sacrificed himself. What a loss for science!" he said bitterly. "Compare him with all of us. He was a great man, an extraordinary man! What gifts! What hopes we all had of him!" Korostelev went on, wringing his hands: "Merciful God, he was a man of science; we shall never look on his like again. Osip Dymov, what have you done—aie, aie, my God!"

Korostelev covered his face with both hands in despair, and shook his head.

"And his moral force," he went on, seeming to grow more and more exasperated against some one. "Not a man, but a pure, good, loving soul, and clean as crystal. He served science and died for science. And he worked like an ox night and day—no one spared him—and with his youth and his learning he had to take a private practice and work at translations at night to pay for these . . . vile rags!"

Korostelev looked with hatred at Olga Ivanovna, snatched at the sheet with both hands and angrily tore it, as though it were to blame.

"He did not spare himself, and others did not spare him. Oh, what's the use of talking!"

"Yes, he was a rare man," said a bass voice in the drawing-room.

Olga Ivanovna remembered her whole life with him from the beginning to the end, with all its details, and suddenly she understood that he really was an extraordinary, rare, and, compared with every one else she knew, a great man. And remembering how her father, now dead, and all the other doctors had behaved to him, she realized that they really had seen in him a future celebrity. The walls, the ceiling, the lamp, and the carpet on the floor, seemed to be winking at her sarcastically, as though they would say, "You were blind! you were blind!" With a wail she flung herself out of the bedroom, dashed by some unknown man in the drawing-room, and ran into her husband's study. He was lying motionless on the sofa, covered to the waist with a quilt. His face was fearfully thin and sunken, and was of a greyish-yellow colour such as is never seen in the living; only from the forehead, from the black eyebrows and from the familiar smile, could he be recognized as Dymov. Olga Ivanovna hurriedly felt his chest, his forehead, and his hands. The chest was still warm, but the forehead and hands were unpleasantly cold, and the half-open eyes looked, not at Olga Ivanovna, but at the quilt.

"Dymov!" she called aloud, "Dymov!" She wanted to explain to him that it had been a mistake, that all was not lost, that life might still be beautiful and happy, that he was an extraordinary, rare, great man, and that she would all her life worship him and bow down in homage and holy awe before him. . . .

"Dymov!" she called him, patting him on the shoulder, unable to believe that he would never wake again. "Dymov! Dymov!"

In the drawing-room Korostelev was saying to the housemaid:

"Why keep asking? Go to the church beadle and enquire where they live. They'll wash the body and lay it out, and do everything that is necessary."

IN EXILE

Old Semyon, nicknamed Canny, and a young Tatar, whom no one knew by name, were sitting on the river-bank by the camp-fire; the other three ferry-men were in the hut. Semyon, an old man of sixty, lean and toothless, but broad-shouldered and still healthy-looking, was drunk; he would have gone in to sleep long before, but he had a bottle in his pocket and he was afraid that the fellows in the hut would ask him for vodka. The Tatar was ill and weary, and wrapping himself up in his rags was describing how nice it was in the Simbirsk province,* and what a beautiful and clever wife he had left behind at home. He was not more than twenty-five, and now by the light of the camp-fire, with his pale and sick, mournful face, he looked like a boy.

"To be sure, it is not paradise here," said Canny. "You can see for yourself, the water, the bare banks, clay, and nothing else. . . . Easter has long passed and yet there is ice on the river, and this morning there was snow. . . ."

"It's bad! it's bad!" said the Tatar, and looked round him in terror.

The dark, cold river was flowing ten paces away; it grumbled, lapped against the hollow clay banks and raced on swiftly towards the far-away sea. Close to the bank there was the dark blur of a big barge, which the ferrymen called a "karbos." Far away on the further bank, lights, dying down and flickering up again, zigzagged like little snakes; they were burning last year's grass. And beyond the little

*On the Volga River, some 480 miles east of Moscow.

snakes there was darkness again. There little icicles could be heard knocking against the barge. It was damp and cold. . . .

The Tatar glanced at the sky. There were as many stars as at home, and the same blackness all round, but something was lacking. At home in the Simbirsk province the stars were quite different, and so was the sky.

"It's bad! it's bad!" he repeated.

"You will get used to it," said Semyon, and he laughed. "Now you are young and foolish, the milk is hardly dry on your lips, and it seems to you in your foolishness that you are more wretched than anyone; but the time will come when you will say to yourself: 'I wish no one a better life than mine.' You look at me. Within a week the floods will be over and we shall set up the ferry; you will all go wandering off about Siberia while I shall stay and shall begin going from bank to bank. I've been going like that for twenty-two years, day and night. The pike and the salmon are under the water while I am on the water. And thank God for it, I want nothing; God give everyone such a life."

The Tatar threw some dry twigs on the camp-fire, lay down closer to the blaze, and said:

"My father is a sick man. When he dies my mother and wife will come here. They have promised."

"And what do you want your wife and mother for?" asked Canny. "That's mere foolishness, my lad. It's the devil confounding you, damn his soul! Don't you listen to him, the cursed one. Don't let him have his way. He is at you about the women, but you spite him; say, 'I don't want them!' He is on at you about freedom, but you stand up to him and say: 'I don't want it!' I want nothing, neither father nor mother, nor wife, nor freedom, nor post, nor paddock; I want nothing, damn their souls!"

Semyon took a pull at the bottle and went on:

"I am not a simple peasant, not of the working class, but the son of a deacon, and when I was free I lived at Kursk;* I used to wear a frock-coat, and now I have brought myself to such a pass that I can sleep naked on the ground and eat grass. And I wish no one a bet-

*Old city about 300 miles south of Moscow.

ter life. I want nothing and I am afraid of nobody, and the way I look at it is that there is nobody richer and freer than I am. When they sent me here from Russia from the first day I stuck it out; I want nothing! The devil was at me about my wife and about my home and about freedom, but I told him: 'I want nothing.' I stuck to it, and here you see I live well, and I don't complain, and if anyone gives way to the devil and listens to him, if but once, he is lost, there is no salvation for him: he is sunk in the bog to the crown of his head and will never get out.

"It is not only a foolish peasant like you, but even gentlemen, well-educated people, are lost. Fifteen years ago they sent a gentleman here from Russia. He hadn't shared something with his brothers and had forged something in a will. They did say he was a prince or a baron, but maybe he was simply an official—who knows? Well, the gentleman arrived here, and first thing he bought himself a house and land in Muhortinskoe. 'I want to live by my own work,' says he, 'in the sweat of my brow, for I am not a gentleman now,' says he, 'but a settler.' 'Well,' says I, 'God help you, that's the right thing.' He was a young man then, busy and careful; he used to mow himself and catch fish and ride sixty miles on horseback. Only this is what happened: from the very first year he took to riding to Gyrino for the post; he used to stand on my ferry and sigh: 'Ech, Semyon, how long it is since they sent me any money from home!' 'You don't want money, Vassily Sergeyitch,' says I. 'What use is it to you? You cast away the past, and forget it as though it had never been at all, as though it had been a dream, and begin to live anew. Don't listen to the devil,' says I; 'he will bring you to no good, he'll draw you into a snare. Now you want money,' says I, 'but in a very little while you'll be wanting something else, and then more and more. If you want to be happy,' says I, 'the chief thing is not to want anything. Yes. . . . If,' says I, 'if Fate has wronged you and me cruelly, it's no good asking for her favor and bowing down to her, but you despise her and laugh at her, or else she will laugh at you.' That's what I said to him. . . .

"Two years later I ferried him across to this side, and he was rubbing his hands and laughing. 'I am going to Gyrino to meet my wife,' says he. 'She was sorry for me,' says he; 'she has come. She is good and kind.' And he was breathless with joy. So a day later he came with his wife. A beautiful young lady in a hat; in her arms was a baby girl. And lots of luggage of all sorts. And my Vassily Sergeyitch was fussing round her; he couldn't take his eyes off her and couldn't say enough in praise of her. 'Yes, brother Semyon, even in Siberia people can live!' 'Oh, all right,' thinks I, 'it will be a different tale presently.' And from that time forward he went almost every week to inquire whether money had not come from Russia. He wanted a lot of money. 'She is losing her youth and beauty here in Siberia for my sake,' says he, 'and sharing my bitter lot with me, and so I ought,' says he, 'to provide her with every comfort. . . .'

"To make it livelier for the lady he made acquaintance with the officials and all sorts of riff-raff. And of course he had to give food and drink to all that crew, and there had to be a piano and a shaggy lapdog on the sofa—plague take it! . . . Luxury, in fact, self-indulgence. The lady did not stay with him long. How could she? The clay, the water, the cold, no vegetables for you, no fruit. All around you ignorant and drunken people and no sort of manners, and she was a spoilt lady from Petersburg or Moscow. . . . To be sure she moped. Besides, her husband, say what you like, was not a gentleman now, but a settler—not the same rank.

"Three years later, I remember, on the eve of the Assumption, there was shouting from the further bank. I went over with the ferry, and what do I see but the lady, all wrapped up, and with her a young gentleman, an official. A sledge with three horses. . . . I ferried them across here, they got in and away like the wind. They were soon lost to sight. And towards morning Vassily Sergeyitch galloped down to the ferry. 'Didn't my wife come this way with a gentleman in spectacles, Semyon?' 'She did,' said I; 'you may look for the wind in the fields!' He galloped in pursuit of them. For five days and nights he was riding after them. When I ferried him over to the other side afterwards, he flung himself on the ferry and beat his head on the boards of the ferry and howled. 'So that's how it is,' says I. I laughed, and reminded him 'people can live even in Siberia!' And he beat his head harder than ever. . . .

"Then he began longing for freedom. His wife had slipped off to Russia, and of course he was drawn there to see her and to get her away from her lover. And he took, my lad, to galloping almost every day, either to the post or to town to see the commanding officer; he kept sending in petitions for them to have mercy on him and let him go back home; and he used to say that he had spent some two hundred roubles on telegrams alone. He sold his land and mortgaged his house to the Jews. He grew gray and bent, and yellow in the face, as though he was in consumption. If he talked to you he would go, khee—khee—khee, . . . and there were tears in his eyes. He kept rushing about like this with petitions for eight years, but now he has grown brighter and more cheerful again: he has found another whim to give way to. You see, his daughter has grown up. He looks at her, and she is the apple of his eye. And to tell the truth she is all right, good-looking, with black eyebrows and a lively disposition. Every Sunday he used to ride with her to church in Gyrino. They used to stand on the ferry, side by side, she would laugh and he could not take his eyes off her. 'Yes, Semyon,' says he, 'people can live even in Siberia. Even in Siberia there is happiness. Look,' says he, 'what a daughter I have got! I warrant you wouldn't find another like her for a thousand versts round.' 'Your daughter is all right,' says I, 'that's true, certainly.' But to myself I thought: 'Wait a bit, the wench is young, her blood is dancing, she wants to live, and there is no life here.' And she did begin to pine, my lad. . . . She faded and faded, and now she can hardly crawl about. Consumption.

"So you see what Siberian happiness is, damn its soul! You see how people can live in Siberia. . . . He has taken to going from one doctor to another and taking them home with him. As soon as he hears that two or three hundred miles away there is a doctor or a sorcerer, he will drive to fetch him. A terrible lot of money he spent on doctors, and to my thinking he had better have spent the money on drink. . . . She'll die just the same. She is certain to die, and then it will be all over with him. He'll hang himself from grief or run away to Russia—that's a sure thing. He'll run away and they'll catch him, then he will be tried, sent to prison, he will have a taste of the lash. . . ."

"Good! good!" said the Tatar, shivering with cold.

"What is good?" asked Canny.

"His wife, his daughter. . . . What of prison and what of sorrow!—anyway, he did see his wife and his daughter. . . . You say, want nothing. But 'nothing' is bad! His wife lived with him three years—that was a gift from God. 'Nothing' is bad, but three years is good. How not understand?"

Shivering and hesitating, with effort picking out the Russian words of which he knew but few, the Tatar said that God forbid one should fall sick and die in a strange land, and be buried in the cold and dark earth; that if his wife came to him for one day, even for one hour, that for such happiness he would be ready to bear any suffering and to thank God. Better one day of happiness than nothing.

Then he described again what a beautiful and clever wife he had left at home. Then, clutching his head in both hands, he began crying and assuring Semyon that he was not guilty, and was suffering for nothing. His two brothers and an uncle had carried off a peasant's horses, and had beaten the old man till he was half dead, and the commune had not judged fairly, but had contrived a sentence by which all the three brothers were sent to Siberia, while the uncle, a rich man, was left at home.

"You will get used to it!" said Semyon.

The Tatar was silent, and stared with tear-stained eyes at the fire; his face expressed bewilderment and fear, as though he still did not understand why he was here in the darkness and the wet, beside strangers, and not in the Simbirsk province.

Canny lay near the fire, chuckled at something, and began humming a song in an undertone.

"What joy has she with her father?" he said a little later. "He loves her and he rejoices in her, that's true; but, mate, you must mind your ps and qs with him, he is a strict old man, a harsh old man. And young wenches don't want strictness. They want petting and ha-ha-ha! and ho-ho-ho! and scent and pomade. Yes. . . . Ech! life, life," sighed Semyon, and he got up heavily. "The vodka is all gone, so it is time to sleep. Eh? I am going, my lad. . . ."

Left alone, the Tatar put on more twigs, lay down and stared at the fire; he began thinking of his own village and of his wife. If his wife could only come for a month, for a day; and then if she liked she might go back again. Better a month or even a day than nothing. But if his wife kept her promise and came, what would he have to feed her on? Where could she live here?

"If there were not something to eat, how could she live?" the Tatar asked aloud.

He was paid only ten kopecks for working all day and all night at the oar; it is true that travelers gave him tips for tea and for vodka, but the men shared all they received among themselves, and gave nothing to the Tatar, but only laughed at him. And from poverty he was hungry, cold, and frightened. . . . Now, when his whole body was aching and shivering, he ought to go into the hut and lie down to sleep; but he had nothing to cover him there, and it was colder than on the river-bank; here he had nothing to cover him either, but at least he could make up the fire. . . .

In another week, when the floods were quite over and they set the ferry going, none of the ferrymen but Semyon would be wanted, and the Tatar would begin going from village to village begging for alms and for work. His wife was only seventeen; she was beautiful, spoilt, and shy; could she possibly go from village to village begging alms with her face unveiled? No, it was terrible even to think of that. . . .

It was already getting light; the barge, the bushes of willow on the water, and the waves could be clearly discerned, and if one looked round there was the steep clay slope; at the bottom of it the hut thatched with dingy brown straw, and the huts of the village lay clustered higher up. The cocks were already crowing in the village.

The rusty red clay slope, the barge, the river, the strange, unkind people, hunger, cold, illness, perhaps all that was not real. Most likely it was all a dream, thought the Tatar. He felt that he was asleep and heard his own snoring. . . . Of course he was at home in the Simbirsk province, and he had only to call his wife by name for her to answer; and in the next room was his mother. . . . What terrible dreams there are, though! What are they for? The Tatar smiled and opened his eyes. What river was this, the Volga?

Snow was falling.

"Boat!" was shouted on the further side. "Boat!"

The Tatar woke up, and went to wake his mates and row over to the other side. The ferrymen came on to the river-bank, putting on their torn sheepskins as they walked, swearing with voices husky from sleepiness and shivering from the cold. On waking from their sleep, the river, from which came a breath of piercing cold, seemed to strike them as revolting and horrible. They jumped into the barge without hurrying themselves. . . . The Tatar and the three ferrymen took the long, broad-bladed oars, which in the darkness looked like the claws of crabs; Semyon leaned his stomach against the tiller. The shout on the other side still continued, and two shots were fired from a revolver, probably with the idea that the ferrymen were asleep or had gone to the pothouse in the village.

"All right, you have plenty of time," said Semyon in the tone of a man convinced that there was no necessity in this world to hurry—that it would lead to nothing, anyway.

The heavy, clumsy barge moved away from the bank and floated between the willow-bushes, and only the willows slowly moving back showed that the barge was not standing still but moving. The ferrymen swung the oars evenly in time; Semyon lay with his stomach on the tiller and, describing a semicircle in the air, flew from one side to the other. In the darkness it looked as though the men were sitting on some antediluvian animal with long paws, and were moving on it through a cold, desolate land, the land of which one sometimes dreams in nightmares.

They passed beyond the willows and floated out into the open. The creak and regular splash of the oars was heard on the further shore, and a shout came: "Make haste! make haste!"

Another ten minutes passed, and the barge banged heavily against the landing-stage.

"And it keeps sprinkling and sprinkling," muttered Semyon, wiping the snow from his face; "and where it all comes from God only knows."

On the bank stood a thin man of medium height, in a jacket lined with fox-fur and in a white lambskin cap. He was standing at a little distance from his horses and not moving; he had a gloomy, concentrated expression, as though he were trying to remember something and angry with his untrustworthy memory. When Semyon went up to him and took off his cap, smiling, he said:

"I am hastening to Anastasyevka. My daughter's worse again, and they say that there is a new doctor at Anastasyevka."

They dragged the carriage on to the barge and floated back. The man whom Semyon addressed as Vassily Sergeyitch stood all the time motionless, tightly compressing his thick lips and staring off into space; when his coachman asked permission to smoke in his presence he made no answer, as though he had not heard. Semyon, lying with his stomach on the tiller, looked mockingly at him and said:

"Even in Siberia people can live—can li-ive!"

There was a triumphant expression on Canny's face, as though he had proved something and was delighted that things had happened as he had foretold. The unhappy helplessness of the man in the foxskin coat evidently afforded him great pleasure.

"It's muddy driving now, Vassily Sergeyitch," he said when the horses were harnessed again on the bank. "You should have put off going for another fortnight, when it will be drier. Or else not have gone at all. . . . If any good would come of your going—but as you know yourself, people have been driving about for years and years, day and night, and it's always been no use. That's the truth."

Vassily Sergeyitch tipped him without a word, got into his carriage and drove off.

"There, he has galloped off for a doctor!" said Semyon, shrinking from the cold. "But looking for a good doctor is like chasing the wind in the fields or catching the devil by the tail, plague take your soul! What a queer chap, Lord forgive me a sinner!"

The Tatar went up to Canny, and, looking at him with hatred and repulsion, shivering, and mixing Tatar words with his broken Russian, said: "He is good . . . good; but you are bad! You are bad! The gentleman is a good soul, excellent, and you are a beast, bad! The gentleman is alive, but you are a dead carcass. . . . God created man to be alive, and to have joy and grief and sorrow; but you want nothing, so you are not alive, you are stone, clay! A stone wants nothing and you want nothing. You are a stone, and God does not love you, but He loves the gentleman!"

Everyone laughed; the Tatar frowned contemptuously, and with a wave of his hand wrapped himself in his rags and went to the camp-fire. The ferrymen and Semyon sauntered to the hut.

"It's cold," said one ferryman huskily as he stretched himself on the straw with which the damp clay floor was covered.

"Yes, it's not warm," another assented. "It's a dog's life. . . ."

They all lay down. The door was thrown open by the wind and the snow drifted into the hut; nobody felt inclined to get up and shut the door: they were cold, and it was too much trouble.

"I am all right," said Semyon as he began to doze. "I wouldn't wish anyone a better life."

"You are a tough one, we all know. Even the devils won't take you!"

Sounds like a dog's howling came from outside.

"What's that? Who's there?"

"It's the Tatar crying."

"I say. . . . He's a queer one!"

"He'll get u-used to it!" said Semyon, and at once fell asleep.

The others were soon asleep too. The door remained unclosed.

WARD NO. 6

I

In the hospital yard there stands a small lodge surrounded by a perfect forest of burdocks, nettles, and wild hemp. Its roof is rusty, the chimney is tumbling down, the steps at the front-door are rotting away and overgrown with grass, and there are only traces left of the stucco. The front of the lodge faces the hospital; at the back it looks out into the open country, from which it is separated by the grey hospital fence with nails on it. These nails, with their points upwards, and the fence, and the lodge itself, have that peculiar, desolate, God-forsaken look which is only found in our hospital and prison buildings.

If you are not afraid of being stung by the nettles, come by the narrow footpath that leads to the lodge, and let us see what is going on inside. Opening the first door, we walk into the entry. Here along the walls and by the stove every sort of hospital rubbish lies littered about. Mattresses, old tattered dressing-gowns, trousers, blue striped shirts, boots and shoes no good for anything—all these remnants are piled up in heaps, mixed up and crumpled, mouldering and giving out a sickly smell.

The porter, Nikita, an old soldier wearing rusty good-conduct stripes, is always lying on the litter with a pipe between his teeth. He has a grim, surly, battered-looking face, overhanging eyebrows which give him the expression of a sheep-dog of the steppes, and a red nose; he is short and looks thin and scraggy, but he is of imposing deportment and his fists are vigorous. He belongs to the class of simple-hearted, practical, and dull-witted people, prompt in carrying out orders, who like discipline better than anything in the world, and so are convinced that it is their duty to beat people. He showers blows on the face, on the chest, on the back, on whatever comes first, and is convinced that there would be no order in the place if he did not.

Next you come into a big, spacious room which fills up the whole lodge except for the entry. Here the walls are painted a dirty blue, the ceiling is as sooty as in a hut without a chimney—it is evident that in the winter the stove smokes and the room is full of fumes. The windows are disfigured by iron gratings on the inside. The wooden floor is grey and full of splinters. There is a stench of sour cabbage, of smouldering wicks, or bugs, and of ammonia, and for the first minute this stench gives you the impression of having walked into a menagerie. . . .

There are bedsteads screwed to the floor. Men in blue hospital dressing-gowns, and wearing night-caps in the old style, are sitting and lying on them. These are the lunatics.

There are five of them in all here. Only one is of the upper class, the rest are all artisans. The one nearest the door—a tall, lean workman with shining red whiskers and tear-stained eyes—sits with his head propped on his hand, staring at the same point. Day and night he grieves, shaking his head, sighing and smiling bitterly. He rarely takes a part in conversation and usually makes no answer to questions; he eats and drinks mechanically when food is offered him. From his agonizing, throbbing cough, his thinness, and the flush on his cheeks, one may judge that he is in the first stage of consumption. Next him is a little, alert, very lively old man, with a pointed beard and curly black hair like a negro's. By day he walks up and down the ward from window to window, or sits on his bed, cross-legged like a Turk, and, ceaselessly as a bullfinch whistles, softly sings and titters. He shows his childish gaiety and lively character at night also when he gets up to say his prayers—that is, to beat himself on the chest with his fists, and to scratch with his fingers at the door. This is the Jew Moiseika, an imbecile, who went crazy twenty years ago when his hat factory was burnt down.

And of all the inhabitants of Ward No. 6, he is the only one who is allowed to go out of the lodge, and even out of the yard into the street. He has enjoyed this privilege for years, probably because he is an old inhabitant of the hospital—a quiet, harmless imbecile, the buffoon of the town, where people are used to seeing him surrounded by boys and dogs. In his wretched gown, in his absurd night-cap, and in slippers, sometimes with bare legs and even without trousers, he walks about the streets, stopping at the gates and little shops, and begging for a copper. In one place they will give him some kvass, in another some bread, in another a copper, so that he generally goes back to the ward feeling rich and well fed. Everything that he brings back Nikita takes from him for his own benefit. The soldier does this roughly, angrily turning the Jew's pockets inside out, and calling God to witness that he will not let him go into the street again, and that breach of the regulations is worse to him than anything in the world.

Moiseika likes to make himself useful. He gives his companions water, and covers them up when they are asleep; he promises each of them to bring him back a kopeck, and to make him a new cap; he feeds with a spoon his neighbour on the left, who is paralyzed. He acts in this way, not from compassion nor from any considerations of a humane kind, but through imitation, unconsciously dominated by Gromov, his neighbour on the right hand.

Ivan Dmitritch Gromov, a man of thirty-three, who is a gentleman by birth, and has been a court usher and provincial secretary, suffers from the mania of persecution. He either lies curled up in bed, or walks from corner to corner as though for exercise; he very rarely sits down. He is always excited, agitated, and overwrought by a sort of vague, undefined expectation. The faintest rustle in the entry or shout in the yard is enough to make him raise his head and begin listening: whether they are coming for him, whether they are looking for him. And at such times his face expresses the utmost uneasiness and repulsion.

I like his broad face with its high cheek-bones, always pale and unhappy, and reflecting, as though in a mirror, a soul tormented by conflict and long-continued terror. His grimaces are strange and abnormal, but the delicate lines traced on his face by profound, genuine suffering show intelligence and sense, and there is a warm and healthy light in his eyes. I like the man himself, courteous, anxious to be of use, and extraordinarily gentle to everyone except Nikita. When anyone drops a button or a spoon, he jumps up from his bed quickly and picks it up; every day he says good-morning to his companions, and when he goes to bed he wishes them good-night.

Besides his continually overwrought condition and his grimaces, his madness shows itself in the following way also. Sometimes in the evenings he wraps himself in his dressing-gown, and, trembling all over, with his teeth chattering, begins walking rapidly from corner to corner and between the bedsteads. It seems as though he is in a violent fever. From the way he suddenly stops and glances at his companions, it can be seen that he is longing to say something very important, but, apparently reflecting that they would not listen, or would not understand him, he shakes his head impatiently and goes on pacing up and down. But soon the desire to speak gets the upper hand of every consideration, and he will let himself go and speak fervently and passionately. His talk is disordered and feverish like delirium, disconnected, and not always intelligible, but, on the other hand, something extremely fine may be felt in it, both in the words and the voice. When he talks you recognize in him the lunatic and the man. It is difficult to reproduce on paper his insane talk. He speaks of the baseness of mankind, of violence trampling on justice, of the glorious life which will one day be upon earth, of the window-gratings, which remind him every minute of the stupidity and cruelty of oppressors. It makes a disorderly, incoherent potpourri of themes old but not yet out of date.

II

Some twelve or fifteen years ago an official called Gromov, a highly respectable and prosperous person, was living in his own house in the principal street of the town. He had two sons, Sergey and Ivan. When Sergey was student in his fourth year he was taken ill with galloping consumption and died, and his death was, as it were, the first of a whole series of calamities which suddenly showered on the Gromov family. Within a week of Sergey's funeral the old father was put on his trial for fraud and misappropriation, and he died of typhoid in the prison hospital soon afterwards. The house, with all their belongings, was sold by auction, and Ivan Dmitritch and his mother were left entirely without means.

Hitherto in his father's lifetime, Ivan Dmitritch, who was studying in the University of Petersburg, had received an allowance of sixty or seventy roubles a month, and had had no conception of poverty; now he had to make an abrupt change in his life. He had to spend his time from morning to night giving lessons for next to nothing, to work at copying, and with all that to go hungry, as all his earnings were sent to keep his mother. Ivan Dmitritch could not stand such a life; he lost heart and strength, and, giving up the university, went home.

Here, through interest, he obtained the post of teacher in the district school, but could not get on with his colleagues, was not liked by the boys, and soon gave up the post. His mother died. He was for six months without work, living on nothing but bread and water; then he became a court usher. He kept this post until he was dismissed owing to his illness.

He had never even in his young student days given the impression of being perfectly healthy. He had always been pale, thin, and given to catching cold; he ate little and slept badly. A single glass of wine went to his head and made him hysterical. He always had a craving for society, but, owing to his irritable temperament and suspiciousness, he never became very intimate with anyone, and had no friends. He always spoke with contempt of his fellow-townsmen, saying that their coarse ignorance and sleepy animal existence seemed to him loathsome and horrible. He spoke in a loud tenor, with heat, and invariably either with scorn and indignation, or with wonder and enthusiasm, and always with perfect sincerity. Whatever one talked to him about he always brought it round to the same subject: that life was dull and stifling in the town; that the townspeople had no lofty interests, but lived a dingy, meaningless life, diversified by violence, coarse profligacy, and hypocrisy; that scoundrels were well fed and clothed, while honest men lived from hand to mouth; that they needed schools, a progressive local paper, a theatre, public lectures, the co-ordination of the intellectual elements; that society must see its failings and be horrified. In his criticisms of people he laid on the colours thick, using only black and white, and no fine shades; mankind was divided for him into honest men and scoundrels: there was nothing in between. He always spoke with passion and enthusiasm of women and of love, but he had never been in love.

In spite of the severity of his judgments and his nervousness, he was liked, and behind his back was spoken of affectionately as Vanya. His innate refinement and readiness to be of service, his good breeding, his moral purity, and his shabby coat, his frail appearance and family misfortunes, aroused a kind, warm, sorrowful feeling. Moreover, he was well educated and well read; according to the townspeople's notions, he knew everything, and was in their eyes something like a talking encyclopædia.

He had read a great deal. He would sit at the club, nervously pulling at his beard and looking through the magazines and books; and from his face one could see that he was not reading, but devouring the pages without giving himself time to digest what he read. It must be supposed that reading was one of his morbid habits, as he fell upon anything that came into his hands with equal avidity, even last year's newspapers and calendars. At home he always read lying down.

III

One autumn morning Ivan Dmitritch, turning up the collar of his greatcoat and splashing through the mud, made his way by side-streets and back lanes to see some artisan, and to collect some payment that was owing. He was in a gloomy mood, as he always was in the morning. In one of the side-streets he was met by two convicts in fetters and four soldiers with rifles in charge of them. Ivan Dmitritch had very often met convicts before, and they had always excited feelings of compassion and discomfort in him; but now this meeting made a peculiar, strange impression on him. It suddenly seemed to him for some reason that he, too, might be put into fetters and led through the mud to prison like that. After visiting the artisan, on the way home he met near the post office a police superintendent of his acquaintance, who greeted him and walked a few paces along the street with him, and for some reason this seemed to him suspicious. At home he could not get the convicts or the soldiers with their rifles out of his head all day, and an unaccountable inward agitation prevented him from reading or concentrating his mind. In the evening he did not light his lamp, and at night he could not sleep, but kept thinking that he might be arrested, put into fetters, and thrown into prison. He did not know of any harm he had done, and could be certain that he would never be guilty of murder, arson, or theft in the future either; but was it not easy to commit a crime by accident, unconsciously, and was not false witness always possible, and, indeed, miscarriage of justice? It was not without good reason that the agelong experience of the simple people teaches that beggary and prison are ills none can be safe from. A judicial mistake is very possible as legal proceedings are conducted nowadays, and there is nothing to be wondered at in it. People who have an official, professional relation to other men's sufferings—for instance, judges, police officers, doctors—in course of time, through habit, grow so callous that they cannot, even if they wish it, take any but a formal attitude to their clients; in this respect they are not different from the peasant who slaughters sheep and calves in the back-yard, and does not notice the blood. With this formal, soulless attitude to human personality the judge needs but one thing—time—in order to deprive an innocent man of all rights of property, and to condemn him to penal servitude. Only the time spent on performing certain formalities for which the judge is paid his salary, and then—it is all over. Then you may look in vain for justice and protection in this dirty, wretched little town a hundred and fifty miles from a railway station! And, indeed, is it not absurd even to think of justice when every kind of violence is accepted by society as a rational and consistent necessity, and every act of mercy—for instance, a verdict of acquittal—calls forth a perfect outburst of dissatisfied and revengeful feeling?

In the morning Ivan Dmitritch got up from his bed in a state of horror, with cold perspiration on his forehead, completely convinced that he might be arrested any minute. Since his gloomy thoughts of yesterday had haunted him so long, he thought, it must be that there was some truth in them. They could not, indeed, have come into his mind without any grounds whatever.

A policeman walking slowly passed by the windows: that was not for nothing. Here were two men standing still and silent near the house. Why were they silent? And agonizing days and nights followed for Ivan Dmitritch. Everyone who passed by the windows or came into the yard seemed to him a spy or a detective. At midday the chief of the police usually drove down the street with a pair of horses; he was going from his estate near the town to the police department; but Ivan Dmitritch fancied every time that he was driving especially quickly, and that he had a peculiar expression: it was evident that he was in haste to announce that there was a very important criminal in town. Ivan Dmitritch started at every ring at the bell and knock at the gate, and was agitated whenever he came upon anyone new at his landlady's; when he met police officers and gendarmes he smiled and began whistling so as to seem unconcerned. He could not sleep for whole nights in succession expecting to be arrested, but he snored loudly and sighed as though in deep sleep, that his landlady might think he was asleep; for if he could not sleep it meant that he was tormented by the stings of conscience—what a piece of evidence! Facts and common sense persuaded him that all these terrors were nonsense and morbidity, that if one looked at the matter more broadly there was nothing really terrible in arrest and imprisonment—so long as the conscience is at ease; but the more sensibly and logically he reasoned, the more acute and agonizing his mental distress became. It might be compared with the story of a hermit who tried to cut a dwelling-place for himself in a virgin forest; the more zealously he worked with his axe, the thicker the forest grew. In the end Ivan Dmitritch, seeing it was useless, gave up reasoning altogether, and abandoned himself entirely to despair and terror.

He began to avoid people and to seek solitude. His official work had been distasteful to him before: now it became unbearable to him. He was afraid they would somehow get him into trouble, would put a bribe in his pocket unnoticed and then denounce him, or that he would accidentally make a mistake in official papers that would appear to be fraudulent, or would lose other people's money. It is strange that his imagination had never at other times been so agile and inventive as now, when every day he thought of thousands of different reasons for being seriously anxious over his freedom and honour; but, on the other hand, his interest in the outer world, in books in particular, grew sensibly fainter, and his memory began to fail him.

In the spring when the snow melted there were found in the ravine near the cemetery two half-decomposed corpses—the bodies of an old woman and a boy bearing the traces of death by violence. Nothing was talked of but these bodies and their unknown murderers. That people might not think he had been guilty of the crime, Ivan Dmitritch walked about the streets, smiling, and when he met acquaintances he turned pale, flushed, and began declaring that there was no greater crime than the murder of the weak and defenceless. But this duplicity soon exhausted him, and after some reflection he decided that in his position the best thing to do was to hide in his landlady's cellar. He sat in the cellar all day and then all night, then another day, was fearfully cold, and waiting till dusk, stole secretly like a thief back to his room. He stood in the middle of the room till daybreak, listening without stirring. Very early in the morning, before sunrise, some workmen came into the house. Ivan Dmitritch knew perfectly well that they had come to mend the stove in the kitchen, but terror told him that they were police officers disguised as workmen. He slipped stealthily out of the flat, and, overcome by terror, ran along the street without his cap and coat. Dogs raced after him barking, a peasant shouted somewhere behind him, the wind whistled in his ears, and it seemed to Ivan Dmitritch that the force and violence of the whole world was massed together behind his back and was chasing after him.

He was stopped and brought home, and his landlady sent for a doctor. Doctor Andrey Yefimitch, of whom we shall have more to say hereafter, prescribed cold compresses on his head and laurel drops, shook his head, and went away, telling the landlady he should not come again, as one should not interfere with people who are going out of their minds. As he had not the means to live at home and be nursed, Ivan Dmitritch was soon sent to the hospital, and was there put into the ward for venereal patients. He could not sleep at night, was full of whims and fancies, and disturbed the patients, and was soon afterwards, by Andrey Yefimitch's orders, transferred to Ward No. 6.

Within a year Ivan Dmitritch was completely forgotten in the town, and his books, heaped up by his landlady in a sledge in the shed, were pulled to pieces by boys.

IV

Ivan Dmitritch's neighbour on the left hand is, as I have said already, the Jew Moiseika; his neighbour on the right hand is a peasant so rolling in fat that he is almost spherical, with a blankly stupid face, utterly devoid of thought. This is a motionless, gluttonous, unclean animal who has long ago lost all powers of thought or feeling. An acrid, stifling stench always comes from him.

Nikita, who has to clean up after him, beats him terribly with all his might, not sparing his fists; and what is dreadful is not his being beaten—that one can get used to—but the fact that this stupefied creature does not respond to the blows with a sound or a movement, nor by a look in the eyes, but only sways a little like a heavy barrel.

The fifth and last inhabitant of Ward No. 6 is a man of the artisan class who has once been a sorter in the post office, a thinnish, fair little man with a good-natured but rather sly face. To judge from the clear, cheerful look in his calm and intelligent eyes, he has some pleasant idea in his mind, and has some very important and agreeable secret. He has under his pillow and under his mattress something that he never shows anyone, not from fear of its being taken from him and stolen, but from modesty. Sometimes he goes to the window, and turning his back to his companions, puts something on his breast, and bending his head, looks at it; if you go up to him at such a moment, he is overcome with confusion and snatches something off his breast. But it is not difficult to guess his secret.

"Congratulate me," he often says to Ivan Dmitritch; "I have been presented with the Stanislav order of the second degree with the star.* The second degree with the star is only given to foreigners, but for some reason they want to make an exception for me," he says with a smile, shrugging his shoulders in perplexity. "That I must confess I did not expect."

"I don't understand anything about that," Ivan Dmitritch replies morosely.

"But do you know what I shall attain to sooner or later?" the former sorter persists, screwing up his eyes slily. "I shall certainly get the Swedish 'Polar Star.' That's an order it is worth working for, a white cross with a black ribbon. It's very beautiful."

Probably in no other place is life so monotonous as in this ward. In the morning the patients, except the paralytic and the fat peasant, wash in the entry at a big tub and wipe themselves with the skirts of their dressing-gowns; after that they drink tea out of tin mugs which Nikita brings them out of the main building. Everyone is allowed one mugful. At midday they have soup made out of sour

---

*Decoration for distinction introduced by Peter the Great.

cabbage and boiled grain, in the evening their supper consists of grain left from dinner. In the intervals they lie down, sleep, look out of window, and walk from one corner to the other. And so every day. Even the former sorter always talks of the same orders.

Fresh faces are rarely seen in Ward No. 6. The doctor has not taken in any new mental cases for a long time, and the people who are fond of visiting lunatic asylums are few in this world. Once every two months Semyon Lazaritch, the barber, appears in the ward. How he cuts the patients' hair, and how Nikita helps him to do it, and what a trepidation the lunatics are always thrown into by the arrival of the drunken, smiling barber, we will not describe.

No one even looks into the ward except the barber. The patients are condemned to see day after day no one but Nikita.

A rather strange rumour has, however, been circulating in the hospital of late.

It is rumoured that the doctor has begun to visit Ward No. 6.

V

A strange rumor!

Dr. Andrey Yefimitch Ragin is a strange man in his way. They say that when he was young he was very religious, and prepared himself for a clerical career, and that when he had finished his studies at the high school in 1863 he intended to enter a theological academy, but that his father, a surgeon and doctor of medicine, jeered at him and declared point-blank that he would disown him if he became a priest. How far this is true I don't know, but Andrey Yefimitch himself has more than once confessed that he has never had a natural bent for medicine or science in general.

However that may have been, when he finished his studies in the medical faculty he did not enter the priesthood. He showed no special devoutness, and was no more like a priest at the beginning of his medical career than he is now.

His exterior is heavy, coarse like a peasant's, his face, his beard, his flat hair, and his coarse, clumsy figure, suggest an overfed, intemperate, and harsh innkeeper on the highroad. His face is surly-looking and covered with blue veins, his eyes are little and his nose is red. With his height and broad shoulders he has huge hands and feet; one would think that a blow from his fist would knock the life out of anyone, but his step is soft, and his walk is cautious and insinuating; when he meets anyone in a narrow passage he is always the first to stop and make way, and to say, not in a bass, as one would expect, but in a high, soft tenor: "I beg your pardon!" He has a little swelling on his neck which prevents him from wearing stiff starched collars, and so he always goes about in soft linen or cotton shirts. Altogether he does not dress like a doctor. He wears the same suit for ten years, and the new clothes, which he usually buys at a Jewish shop, look as shabby and crumpled on him as his old ones; he sees patients and dines and pays visits all in the same coat; but this is not due to niggardliness, but to complete carelessness about his appearance.

When Andrey Yefimitch came to the town to take up his duties the "institution founded to the glory of God" was in a terrible condition. One could hardly breathe for the stench in the wards, in the passages, and in the courtyards of the hospital. The hospital servants, the nurses, and their children slept in the wards together with the patients. They complained that there was no living for beetles, bugs, and mice. The surgical wards were never free from erysipelas. There were only two scalpels and not one thermometer in the whole hospital; potatoes were kept in the baths. The superintendent, the housekeeper, and the medical assistant robbed the patients, and of the old doctor, Andrey Yefimitch's predecessor, people declared that he secretly sold the hospital alcohol, and that he kept a regular harem consisting of nurses and female patients. These disorderly proceedings were perfectly well known in the town, and were even exaggerated, but people took them calmly; some justified them on the ground that there were only peasants and working men in the hospital, who could not be dissatisfied, since they were much worse off at home than in the hospital—they couldn't be fed on woodcocks! Others said in excuse that the town alone, without help from the Zemstvo, was not equal to maintaining a good hospital; thank God for having one at all, even a poor one. And the newly formed Zemstvo did not open infirmaries either in the town or the neighbourhood, relying on the fact that the town already had its hospital.

After looking over the hospital Andrey Yefimitch came to the conclusion that it was an immoral institution and extremely prejudicial to the health of the townspeople. In his opinion the most sensible thing that could be done was to let out the patients and close the hospital. But he reflected that his will alone was not enough to do this, and that it would be useless; if physical and moral impurity were driven out of one place, they would only move to another; one must wait for it to wither away of itself. Besides, if people open a hospital and put up with having it, it must be because they need it; superstition and all the nastiness and abominations of daily life were necessary, since in process of time they worked out to something sensible, just as manure turns into black earth. There was nothing on earth so good that it had not something nasty about its first origin.

When Andrey Yefimitch undertook his duties he was apparently not greatly concerned about the irregularities at the hospital. He only asked the attendants and nurses not to sleep in the wards, and had two cupboards of instruments put up; the superintendent, the housekeeper, the medical assistant, and the erysipelas remained unchanged.

Andrey Yefimitch loved intelligence and honesty intensely, but he had no strength of will nor belief in his right to organize an intelligent and honest life about him. He was absolutely unable to give orders, to forbid things, and to insist. It seemed as though he had taken a vow never to raise his voice and never to make use of the imperative. It was difficult for him to say "Fetch" or "Bring"; when he wanted his meals he would cough hesitatingly and say to the cook: "How about tea? . . ." or "How about dinner? . . ." To dismiss the superintendent or to tell him to leave off stealing, or to abolish the unnecessary parasitic post altogether, was absolutely beyond his powers. When Andrey Yefimitch was deceived or flattered, or accounts he knew to be cooked were brought him to sign, he would turn as red as a crab and feel guilty, but yet he would sign the accounts. When the patients complained to him of being hungry or of the roughness of the nurses, he would be confused and mutter guiltily: "Very well, very well, I will go into it later. . . . Most likely there is some misunderstanding. . . ."

At first Andrey Yefimitch worked very zealously. He saw patients every day from morning till dinnertime, performed operations, and even attended confinements. The ladies said of him that he was attentive and clever at diagnosing diseases, especially those of women and children. But in process of time the work unmistakably wearied him by its monotony and obvious uselessness. To-day one sees thirty patients, and to-morrow they have increased to thirty-five, the next day forty, and so on from day to day, from year to year, while the mortality in the town did not decrease and the patients did not leave off coming. To be any real help to forty patients between morning and dinner was not physically possible, so it could but lead to deception. If twelve thousand patients were seen in a year it meant, if one looked at it simply, that twelve thousand men were deceived. To put those who were seriously ill into wards, and to treat them according to the principles of science, was impossible, too, because though there were principles there was no science; if he were to put aside philosophy and pedantically follow the rules as other doctors did, the things above all necessary were cleanliness and ventilation instead of dirt, wholesome nourishment instead of broth made of stinking, sour cabbage, and good assistants instead of thieves; and, indeed, why hinder people dying if death is the normal and legitimate end of everyone? What is gained if some shopkeeper or clerk lives an extra five or ten years? If the aim of medicine is by drugs to alleviate suffering, the question forces itself on one: why alleviate it? In the first place, they say that suffering leads man to perfection; and in the second, if mankind really learns to alleviate its sufferings with pills and drops, it will completely abandon religion and philosophy, in which it has hitherto found not merely protection from all sorts of trouble, but even happiness. Pushkin* suffered terrible agonies before his death, poor Heine† lay paralyzed for several years; why, then, should not some Andrey Yefimitch or Matryona Savishna be ill, since their lives had nothing of importance in them, and would have been entirely empty and like the life of an amœba except for suffering?

Oppressed by such reflections, Andrey Yefimitch relaxed his efforts and gave up visiting the hospital every day.

---

*The great Russian poet Aleksandr Pushkin (1799–1837).
†German poet Heinrich Heine (1797–1856).

VI

His life was passed like this. As a rule he got up at eight o'clock in the morning, dressed, and drank his tea. Then he sat down in his study to read, or went to the hospital. At the hospital the out-patients were sitting in the dark, narrow little corridor waiting to be seen by the doctor. The nurses and the attendants, tramping with their boots over the brick floors, ran by them; gaunt-looking patients in dressing-gowns passed; dead bodies and vessels full of filth were carried by; the children were crying, and there was a cold draught. Andrey Yefimitch knew that such surroundings were torture to feverish, consumptive, and impressionable patients; but what could be done? In the consulting-room he was met by his assistant, Sergey Sergeyitch—a fat little man with a plump well-washed shaven face, with soft, smooth manners, wearing a new loosely cut suit, and looking more like a senator than a medical assistant. He had an immense practice in the town, wore a white tie, and considered himself more proficient than the doctor, who had no practice. In the corner of the consulting-room there stood a huge ikon in a shrine with a heavy lamp in front of it, and near it a candle-stand with a white cover on it. On the walls hung portraits of bishops, a view of the Svyatogorsky Monastery,* and wreaths of dried cornflowers. Sergey Sergeyitch was religious, and liked solemnity and decorum. The ikon had been put up at his expense; at his instructions some one of the patients read the hymns of praise in the consulting-room on Sundays, and after the reading Sergey Sergeyich himself went through the wards with a censer and burned incense.

There were a great many patients, but the time was short, and so the work was confined to the asking of a few brief questions and the administration of some drugs, such as castor-oil or volatile ointment. Andrey Yefimitch would sit with his cheek resting in his hand, lost in thought and asking questions mechanically. Sergey Sergeyitch sat down too, rubbing his hands, and from time to time putting in his word.

---

*Founded in 1566; the site of Pushkin's tomb.

"We suffer pain and poverty," he would say, "because we do not pray to the merciful God as we should. Yes!"

Andrey Yefimitch never performed any operations when he was seeing patients; he had long ago given up doing so, and the sight of blood upset him. When he had to open a child's mouth in order to look at its throat, and the child cried and tried to defend itself with its little hands, the noise in his ears made his head go round and brought tears into his eyes. He would make haste to prescribe a drug, and motion to the woman to take the child away.

He was soon wearied by the timidity of the patients and their incoherence, by the proximity of the pious Sergey Sergeyitch, by the portraits on the walls, and by his own questions which he had asked over and over again for twenty years. And he would go away after seeing five or six patients. The rest would be seen by his assistant in his absence.

With the agreeable thought that, thank God, he had no private practice now, and that no one would interrupt him, Andrey Yefimitch sat down to the table immediately on reaching home and took up a book. He read a great deal and always with enjoyment. Half his salary went on buying books, and of the six rooms that made up his abode three were heaped up with books and old magazines. He liked best of all works on history and philosophy; the only medical publication to which he subscribed was *The Doctor*,* of which he always read the last pages first. He would always go on reading for several hours without a break and without being weary. He did not read as rapidly and impulsively as Ivan Dmitritch had done in the past, but slowly and with concentration, often pausing over a passage which he liked or did not find intelligible. Near the books there always stood a decanter of vodka, and a salted cucumber or a pickled apple lay beside it, not on a plate, but on the baize table-cloth. Every half-hour he would pour himself out a glass of vodka and drink it without taking his eyes off the book. Then without looking at it he would feel for the cucumber and bite off a bit.

At three o'clock he would go cautiously to the kitchen door, cough, and say: "Daryushka, what about dinner? . . ."

---

*Medical newspaper published in St. Petersburg.

After his dinner—a rather poor and untidily served one—Andrey Yefimitch would walk up and down his rooms with his arms folded, thinking. The clock would strike four, then five, and still he would be walking up and down thinking. Occasionally the kitchen door would creak, and the red and sleepy face of Daryushka would appear.

"Andrey Yefimitch, isn't it time for you to have your beer?" she would ask anxiously.

"No, it is not time yet . . ." he would answer. "I'll wait a little. . . . I'll wait a little. . . ."

Towards the evening the postmaster, Mihail Averyanitch, the only man in the town whose society did not bore Andrey Yefimitch, would come in. Mihail Averyanitch had once been a very rich landowner, and had served in the cavalry, but had come to ruin, and was forced by poverty to take a job in the post office late in life. He had a hale and hearty appearance, luxuriant grey whiskers, the manners of a well-bred man, and a loud, pleasant voice. He was good-natured and emotional, but hot-tempered. When anyone in the post office made a protest, expressed disagreement, or even began to argue, Mihail Averyanitch would turn crimson, shake all over, and shout in a voice of thunder, "Hold your tongue!" so that the post office had long enjoyed the reputation of an institution which it was terrible to visit. Mihail Averyanitch liked and respected Andrey Yefimitch for his culture and the loftiness of his soul; he treated the other inhabitants of the town superciliously, as though they were his subordinates.

"Here I am," he would say, going in to Andrey Yefimitch. "Good-evening, my dear fellow! I'll be bound, you are getting sick of me, aren't you?"

"On the contrary, I am delighted," said the doctor. "I am always glad to see you."

The friends would sit down on the sofa in the study and for some time would smoke in silence.

"Daryushka, what about the beer?" Andrey Yefimitch would say.

They would drink their first bottle still in silence, the doctor brooding and Mihail Averyanitch with a gay and animated face, like a man who has something very interesting to tell. The doctor was always the one to begin the conversation.

"What a pity," he would say quietly and slowly, not looking his friend in the face (he never looked anyone in the face)—"what a great pity it is that there are no people in our town who are capable of carrying on intelligent and interesting conversation, or care to do so. It is an immense privation for us. Even the educated class do not rise above vulgarity; the level of their development, I assure you, is not a bit higher than that of the lower orders."

"Perfectly true. I agree."

"You know, of course," the doctor went on quietly and deliberately, "that everything in this world is insignificant and uninteresting except the higher spiritual manifestations of the human mind. Intellect draws a sharp line between the animals and man, suggests the divinity of the latter, and to some extent even takes the place of the immortality which does not exist. Consequently the intellect is the only possible source of enjoyment. We see and hear of no trace of intellect about us, so we are deprived of enjoyment. We have books, it is true, but that is not at all the same as living talk and converse. If you will allow me to make a not quite apt comparison: books are the printed score, while talk is the singing."

"Perfectly true."

A silence would follow. Daryushka would come out of the kitchen and with an expression of blank dejection would stand in the doorway to listen, with her face propped on her fist.

"Eh!" Mihail Averyanitch would sigh. "To expect intelligence of this generation!"

And he would describe how wholesome, entertaining, and interesting life had been in the past. How intelligent the educated class in Russia used to be, and what lofty ideas it had of honour and friendship; how they used to lend money without an IOU, and it was thought a disgrace not to give a helping hand to a comrade in need; and what campaigns, what adventures, what skirmishes, what comrades, what women! And the Caucasus, what a marvelous country! The wife of a battalion commander, a queer woman, used to put on an officer's uniform and drive off into the mountains in the evening, alone, without a guide. It was said that she had a love affair with some princeling in the native village.

"Queen of Heaven, Holy Mother . . ." Daryushka would sigh.

"And how we drank! And how we ate! And what desperate liberals we were!"

Andrey Yefimitch would listen without hearing; he was musing as he sipped his beer.

"I often dream of intellectual people and conversation with them," he said suddenly, interrupting Mihail Averyanitch. "My father gave me an excellent education, but under the influence of the ideas of the sixties made me become a doctor. I believe if I had not obeyed him then, by now I should have been in the very centre of the intellectual movement. Most likely I should have become a member of some university. Of course, intellect, too, is transient and not eternal, but you know why I cherish a partiality for it. Life is a vexatious trap; when a thinking man reaches maturity and attains to full consciousness he cannot help feeling that he is in a trap from which there is no escape. Indeed, he is summoned without his choice by fortuitous circumstances from non-existence into life . . . what for? He tries to find out the meaning and object of his existence; he is told nothing, or he is told absurdities; he knocks and it is not opened to him; death comes to him—also without his choice. And so, just as in prison men held together by common misfortune feel more at ease when they are together, so one does not notice the trap in life when people with a bent for analysis and generalization meet together and pass their time in the interchange of proud and free ideas. In that sense the intellect is the source of an enjoyment nothing can replace."

"Perfectly true."

Not looking his friend in the face, Andrey Yefimitch would go on, quietly and with pauses, talking about intellectual people and conversation with them, and Mihail Averyanitch would listen attentively and agree: "Perfectly true."

"And you do not believe in the immortality of the soul?" he would ask suddenly.

"No, honoured Mihail Averyanitch; I do not believe it, and have no grounds for believing it."

"I must own I doubt it too. And yet I have a feeling as though I should never die. Oh, I think to myself: 'Old fogey, it is time you were dead!' But there is a little voice in my soul says: 'Don't believe it; you won't die.' "

Soon after nine o'clock Mihail Averyanitch would go away. As he put on his fur coat in the entry he would say with a sigh:

"What a wilderness fate has carried us to, though, really! What's most vexatious of all is to have to die here. Ech! . . ."

VII

After seeing his friend out Andrey Yefimitch would sit down at the table and begin reading again. The stillness of the evening, and afterwards of the night, was not broken by a single sound, and it seemed as though time were standing still and brooding with the doctor over the book, and as though there were nothing in existence but the books and the lamp with the green shade. The doctor's coarse peasant-like face was gradually lighted up by a smile of delight and enthusiasm over the progress of the human intellect. Oh, why is not man immortal? he thought. What is the good of the brain centres and convolutions, what is the good of sight, speech, self-consciousness, genius, if it is all destined to depart into the soil, and in the end to grow cold together with the earth's crust, and then for millions of years to fly with the earth round the sun with no meaning and no object? To do that there was no need at all to draw man with his lofty, almost godlike intellect out of non-existence, and then, as though in mockery, to turn him into clay. The transmutation of substances! But what cowardice to comfort oneself with that cheap substitute for immortality! The unconscious processes that take place in nature are lower even than the stupidity of man, since in stupidity there is, anyway, consciousness and will, while in those processes there is absolutely nothing. Only the coward who has more fear of death than dignity can comfort himself with the fact that his body will in time live again in the grass, in the stones, in the toad. To find one's immortality in the transmutation of substances is as strange as to prophesy a brilliant future for the case after a precious violin has been broken and become useless.

When the clock struck, Andrey Yefimitch would sink back into his chair and close his eyes to think a little. And under the influence of the fine ideas of which he had been reading he would, unawares, recall his past and his present. The past was hateful—better not to think of it. And it was the same in the present as in the past. He knew that at the very time when his thoughts were floating together with the cooling earth round the sun, in the main building beside his abode people were suffering in sickness and physical impurity: someone perhaps could not sleep and was making war upon the insects, someone was being infected by erysipelas, or moaning over too tight a bandage; perhaps the patients were playing cards with the nurses and drinking vodka. According to the yearly return, twelve thousand people had been deceived; the whole hospital rested as it had done twenty years ago on thievery, filth, scandals, gossip, on gross quackery, and, as before, it was an immoral institution extremely injurious to the health of the inhabitants. He knew that Nikita knocked the patients about behind the barred windows of Ward No. 6, and that Moiseika went about the town every day begging alms.

On the other hand, he knew very well that a magical change had taken place in medicine during the last twenty-five years. When he was studying at the university he had fancied that medicine would soon be overtaken by the fate of alchemy and metaphysics; but now when he was reading at night the science of medicine touched him and excited his wonder, and even enthusiasm. What unexpected brilliance, what a revolution! Thanks to the antiseptic system operations were performed such as the great Pirogov* had considered impossible even *in spe.* Ordinary Zemstvo doctors were venturing to perform the resection of the kneecap; of abdominal operations only one per cent. was fatal; while stone was considered such a trifle that they did not even write about it. A radical cure for syphilis had been discovered. And the theory of heredity, hypnotism, the discoveries of Pasteur† and of Koch,‡ hygiene based on statistics, and the work of our Zemstvo doctors!

Psychiatry with its modern classification of mental diseases, methods of diagnosis, and treatment, was a perfect Elborus in

---

*Russian surgeon and educator Nikolai Pirogov (1810–1881).

†French chemist and microbiologist Louis Pasteur (1822–1895) developed the process of pasteurization: boiling liquids (milk, beer, wine) to destroy microbes that cause disease.

‡German bacteriologist Robert Koch (1843–1910) established the bacterial cause of many infectious diseases.

comparison with what had been in the past. They no longer poured cold water on the heads of lunatics nor put strait-waistcoats upon them; they treated them with humanity, and even, so it was stated in the papers, got up balls and entertainments for them. Andrey Yefimitch knew that with modern tastes and views such an abomination as Ward No. 6 was possible only a hundred and fifty miles from a railway in a little town where the mayor and all the town council were half-illiterate tradesmen who looked upon the doctor as an oracle who must be believed without any criticism even if he had poured molten lead into their mouths; in any other place the public and the newspapers would long ago have torn this little Bastille to pieces.

"But, after all, what of it?" Andrey Yefimitch would ask himself, opening his eyes. "There is the antiseptic system, there is Koch, there is Pasteur, but the essential reality is not altered a bit; ill-health and mortality are still the same. They get up balls and entertainments for the mad, but still they don't let them go free; so it's all nonsense and vanity, and there is no difference in reality between the best Vienna clinic and my hospital." But depression and a feeling akin to envy prevented him from feeling indifferent; it must have been owing to exhaustion. His heavy head sank on to the book, he put his hands under his face to make it softer, and thought: "I serve in a pernicious institution and receive a salary from people whom I am deceiving. I am not honest, but then, I of myself am nothing, I am only part of an inevitable social evil: all local officials are pernicious and receive their salary for doing nothing. . . . And so for my dishonesty it is not I who am to blame, but the times. . . . If I had been born two hundred years later I should have been different. . . ."

When it struck three he would put out his lamp and go into his bedroom; he was not sleepy.

VIII

Two years before, the Zemstvo in a liberal mood had decided to allow three hundred roubles a year to pay for additional medical service in the town till the Zemstvo hospital should be opened, and the district doctor, Yevgeny Fyodoritch Hobotov, was invited to the town to assist Andrey Yefimitch. He was a very young man—not yet thirty—tall and dark, with broad cheek-bones and little eyes; his forefathers had probably come from one of the many alien races of Russia. He arrived in the town without a farthing, with a small portmanteau, and a plain young woman whom he called his cook. This woman had a baby at the breast. Yevgeny Fyodoritch used to go about in a cap with a peak, and in high boots, and in the winter wore a sheepskin. He made great friends with Sergey Sergeyitch, the medical assistant, and with the treasurer, but held aloof from the other officials, and for some reason called them aristocrats. He had only one book in his lodgings, "The Latest Prescriptions of the Vienna Clinic for 1881." When he went to a patient he always took this book with him. He played billiards in the evening at the club: he did not like cards. He was very fond of using in conversation such expressions as "endless bobbery," "canting soft soap," "shut up with your finicking. . . ."

He visited the hospital twice a week, made the round of the wards, and saw out-patients. The complete absence of antiseptic treatment and the cupping roused his indignation, but he did not introduce any new system, being afraid of offending Andrey Yefimitch. He regarded his colleague as a sly old rascal, suspected him of being a man of large means, and secretly envied him. He would have been very glad to have his post.

IX

On a spring evening towards the end of March, when there was no snow left on the ground and the starlings were singing in the hospital garden, the doctor went out to see his friend the postmaster as far as the gate. At that very moment the Jew Moiseika, returning with his booty, came into the yard. He had no cap on, and his bare feet were thrust into goloshes; in his hand he had a little bag of coppers.

"Give me a kopeck!" he said to the doctor, smiling, and shivering with cold. Andrey Yefimitch, who could never refuse anyone anything, gave him a ten-kopeck piece.

"How bad that is!" he thought, looking at the Jew's bare feet with their thin red ankles. "Why, it's wet."

And stirred by a feeling akin both to pity and disgust, he went into the lodge behind the Jew, looking now at his bald head, now at his ankles. As the doctor went in, Nikita jumped up from his heap of litter and stood at attention.

"Good-day, Nikita," Andrey Yefimitch said mildly. "That Jew should be provided with boots or something, he will catch cold."

"Certainly, your honour. I'll inform the superintendent."

"Please do; ask him in my name. Tell him that I asked."

The door into the ward was open. Ivan Dmitritch, lying propped on his elbow on the bed, listened in alarm to the unfamiliar voice, and suddenly recognized the doctor. He trembled all over with anger, jumped up, and with a red and wrathful face, with his eyes starting out of his head, ran out into the middle of the road.

"The doctor has come!" he shouted, and broke into a laugh. "At last! Gentlemen, I congratulate you. The doctor is honouring us with a visit! Cursed reptile!" he shrieked, and stamped in a frenzy such as had never been seen in the ward before. "Kill the reptile! No, killing's too good. Drown him in the midden-pit!"

Andrey Yefimitch, hearing this, looked into the ward from the entry and asked gently: "What for?"

"What for?" shouted Ivan Dmitritch, going up to him with a menacing air and convulsively wrapping himself in his dressing-gown. "What for? Thief!" he said with a look of repulsion, moving his lips as though he would spit at him. "Quack! hangman!"

"Calm yourself," said Andrey Yefimitch, smiling guiltily. "I assure you I have never stolen anything; and as to the rest, most likely you greatly exaggerate. I see you are angry with me. Calm yourself, I beg, if you can, and tell me coolly what are you angry for?"

"What are you keeping me here for?"

"Because you are ill."

"Yes, I am ill. But you know dozens, hundreds of madmen are walking about in freedom because your ignorance is incapable of distinguishing them from the sane. Why am I and these poor wretches to be shut up here like scapegoats for all the rest? You, your assistant, the superintendent, and all your hospital rabble, are immeasurably inferior to every one of us morally; why then are we shut up and you not? Where's the logic of it?"

"Morality and logic don't come in, it all depends on chance. If anyone is shut up he has to stay, and if anyone is not shut up he can walk about, that's all. There is neither morality nor logic in my being a doctor and your being a mental patient, there is nothing but idle chance."

"That twaddle I don't understand . . ." Ivan Dmitritch brought out in a hollow voice, and he sat down on his bed.

Moiseika, whom Nikita did not venture to search in the presence of the doctor, laid out on his bed pieces of bread, bits of paper, and little bones, and, still shivering with cold, began rapidly in a singsong voice saying something in Yiddish. He most likely imagined that he had opened a shop.

"Let me out," said Ivan Dmitritch, and his voice quivered.

"I cannot."

"But why, why?"

"Because it is not in my power. Think, what use will it be to you if I do let you out? Go. The townspeople or the police will detain you or bring you back."

"Yes, yes, that's true," said Ivan Dmitritch, and he rubbed his forehead. "It's awful! But what am I to do, what?"

Andrey Yefimitch liked Ivan Dmitritch's voice and his intelligent young face with its grimaces. He longed to be kind to the young man and soothe him; he sat down on the bed beside him, thought, and said:

"You ask me what to do. The very best thing in your position would be to run away. But, unhappily, that is useless. You would be taken up. When society protects itself from the criminal, mentally deranged, or otherwise inconvenient people, it is invincible. There is only one thing left for you: to resign yourself to the thought that your presence here is inevitable."

"It is no use to anyone."

"So long as prisons and madhouses exist someone must be shut up in them. If not you, I. If not I, some third person. Wait till in the distant future prisons and madhouses no longer exist, and there will be neither bars on the windows nor hospital gowns. Of course, that time will come sooner or later."

Ivan Dmitritch smiled ironically.

"You are jesting," he said, screwing up his eyes. "Such gentlemen as you and your assistant Nikita have nothing to do with the future, but you may be sure, sir, better days will come! I may express myself cheaply, you may laugh, but the dawn of a new life is at hand; truth and justice will triumph, and—our turn will come! I shall not live to see it, I shall perish, but some people's great-grandsons will see it. I greet them with all my heart and rejoice, rejoice with them! Onward! God be your help, friends!"

With shining eyes Ivan Dmitritch got up, and stretching his hands towards the window, went on with emotion in his voice:

"From behind these bars I bless you! Hurrah for truth and justice! I rejoice!"

"I see no particular reason to rejoice," said Andrey Yefimitch, who thought Ivan Dmitritch's movement theatrical, though he was delighted by it. "Prisons and madhouses there will not be, and truth, as you have just expressed it, will triumph; but the reality of things, you know, will not change, the laws of nature will still remain the same. People will suffer pain, grow old, and die just as they do now. However magnificent a dawn lighted up your life, you would yet in the end be nailed up in a coffin and thrown into a hole."

"And immortality?"

"Oh, come, now!"

"You don't believe in it, but I do. Somebody in Dostoevsky or Voltaire* said that if there had not been a God men would have invented him. And I firmly believe that if there is no immortality the great intellect of man will sooner or later invent it."

"Well said," observed Andrey Yefimitch, smiling with pleasure; "it's a good thing you have faith. With such a belief one may live happily even shut up within walls. You have studied somewhere, I presume?"

"Yes, I have been at the university, but did not complete my studies."

"You are a reflecting and thoughtful man. In any surroundings you can find tranquillity in yourself. Free and deep thinking which strives for the comprehension of life, and complete contempt for the foolish bustle of the world—those are two blessings beyond any that man has ever known. And you can possess them even though you lived behind threefold bars. Diogenes† lived in a tub, yet he was happier than all the kings of the earth."

---

*French novelist, poet, dramatist, historian, satirist François Marie Arouet de Voltaire once remarked, "If God did not exist, he would have to be invented."

†The Greek philosopher Diogenes (c.412–323 B.C.) taught that virtue is to be found in a simple life; he lived in a tub and discarded his last utensil, a cup, when he saw a man drink from his hands.

"Your Diogenes was a blockhead," said Ivan Dmitritch morosely. "Why do you talk to me about Diogenes and some foolish comprehension of life?" he cried, growing suddenly angry and leaping up. "I love life; I love it passionately. I have the mania of persecution, a continual agonizing terror; but I have moments when I am overwhelmed by the thirst for life, and then I am afraid of going mad. I want dreadfully to live, dreadfully!"

He walked up and down the ward in agitation, and said, dropping his voice:

"When I dream I am haunted by phantoms. People come to me, I hear voices and music, and I fancy I am walking through woods or by the seashore, and I long so passionately for movement, for interests. . . . Come, tell me, what news is there?" asked Ivan Dmitritch; "what's happening?"

"Do you wish to know about the town or in general?"

"Well, tell me first about the town, and then in general."

"Well, in the town it is appallingly dull. . . . There's no one to say a word to, no one to listen to. There are no new people. A young doctor called Hobotov has come here recently."

"He had come in my time. Well, he is a low cad, isn't he?"

"Yes, he is a man of no culture. It's strange, you know. . . . Judging by every sign, there is no intellectual stagnation in our capital cities; there is a movement—so there must be real people there too; but for some reason they always send us such men as I would rather not see. It's an unlucky town!"

"Yes, it is an unlucky town," sighed Ivan Dmitritch, and he laughed. "And how are things in general? What are they writing in the papers and reviews?"

It was by now dark in the ward. The doctor got up, and, standing, began to describe what was being written abroad and in Russia, and the tendency of thought that could be noticed now. Ivan Dmitritch listened attentively and put questions, but suddenly, as though recalling something terrible, clutched at his head and lay down on the bed with his back to the doctor.

"What's the matter?" asked Andrey Yefimitch.

"You will not hear another word from me," said Ivan Dmitritch rudely. "Leave me alone."

"Why so?"

"I tell you, leave me alone. Why the devil do you persist?"

Andrey Yefimitch shrugged his shoulders, heaved a sigh, and went out. As he crossed the entry he said: "You might clear up here, Nikita . . . there's an awfully stuffy smell."

"Certainly, your honour."

"What an agreeable young man!" thought Andrey Yefimitch, going back to his flat. "In all the years I have been living here I do believe he is the first I have met with whom one can talk. He is capable of reasoning and is interested in just the right things."

While he was reading, and afterwards, while he was going to bed, he kept thinking about Ivan Dmitritch, and when he woke next morning he remembered that he had the day before made the acquaintance of an intelligent and interesting man, and determined to visit him again as soon as possible.

X

Ivan Dmitritch was lying in the same position as on the previous day, with his head clutched in both hands and his legs drawn up. His face was not visible.

"Good-day, my friend," said Andrey Yefimitch. "You are not asleep, are you?"

"In the first place, I am not your friend," Ivan Dmitritch articulated into the pillow; "and in the second, your efforts are useless; you will not get one word out of me."

"Strange," muttered Andrey Yefimitch in confusion. "Yesterday we talked peacefully, but suddenly for some reason you took offence and broke off all at once. . . . Probably I expressed myself awkwardly, or perhaps gave utterance to some idea which did not fit in with your convictions. . . ."

"Yes, a likely idea!" said Ivan Dmitritch, sitting up and looking at the doctor with irony and uneasiness. His eyes were red. "You can go and spy and probe somewhere else, it's no use your doing it here. I knew yesterday what you had come for."

"A strange fancy," laughed the doctor. "So you suppose me to be a spy?"

"Yes, I do. . . . A spy or a doctor who has been charged to test me—it's all the same——"

"Oh, excuse me, what a queer fellow you are really!"

The doctor sat down on the stool near the bed and shook his head reproachfully.

"But let us suppose you are right," he said, "let us suppose that I am treacherously trying to trap you into saying something so as to betray you to the police. You would be arrested and then tried. But would you be any worse off being tried and in prison than you are here? If you are banished to a settlement, or even sent to penal servitude, would it be worse than being shut up in this ward? I imagine it would be no worse. . . . What, then, are you afraid of?"

These words evidently had an effect on Ivan Dmitritch. He sat down quietly.

It was between four and five in the afternoon—the time when Andrey Yefimitch usually walked up and down his rooms, and Daryushka asked whether it was not time for his beer. It was a still, bright day.

"I came out for a walk after dinner, and here I have come, as you see," said the doctor. "It is quite spring."

"What month is it? March?" asked Ivan Dmitritch.

"Yes, the end of March."

"Is it very muddy?"

"No, not very. There are already paths in the garden."

"It would be nice now to drive in an open carriage somewhere into the country," said Ivan Dmitritch, rubbing his red eyes as though he were just awake, "then to come home to a warm, snug study, and . . . and to have a decent doctor to cure one's headache. . . . It's so long since I have lived like a human being. It's disgusting here! Insufferably disgusting!"

After his excitement of the previous day he was exhausted and listless, and spoke unwillingly. His fingers twitched, and from his face it could be seen that he had a splitting headache.

"There is no real difference between a warm, snug study and this ward," said Andrey Yefimitch. "A man's peace and contentment do not lie outside a man, but in himself."

"What do you mean?"

"The ordinary man looks for good and evil in external things—that is, in carriages, in studies—but a thinking man looks for it in himself."

"You should go and preach that philosophy in Greece, where it's warm and fragrant with the scent of pomegranates, but here it is not suited to the climate. With whom was it I was talking of Diogenes? Was it with you?"

"Yes, with me yesterday."

"Diogenes did not need a study or a warm habitation; it's hot there without. You can lie in your tub and eat oranges and olives. But bring him to Russia to live: he'd be begging to be let indoors in May, let alone December. He'd be doubled up with the cold."

"No. One can be insensible to cold as to every other pain. Marcus Aurelius* says: 'A pain is a vivid idea of pain; make an effort of will to change that idea, dismiss it, cease to complain, and the pain will disappear.' That is true. The wise man, or simply the reflecting, thoughtful man, is distinguished precisely by his contempt for suffering; he is always contented and surprised at nothing."

"Then I am an idiot, since I suffer and am discontented and surprised at the baseness of mankind."

"You are wrong in that; if you will reflect more on the subject you will understand how insignificant is all that external world that agitates us. One must strive for the comprehension of life, and in that is true happiness."

"Comprehension . . ." repeated Ivan Dmitritch frowning. "External, internal. . . . Excuse me, but I don't understand it. I only know," he said, getting up and looking angrily at the doctor—"I only know that God has created me of warm blood and nerves, yes, indeed! If organic tissue is capable of life it must react to every stimulus. And I do! To pain I respond with tears and outcries, to baseness with indignation, to filth with loathing. To my mind, that is just what is called life. The lower the organism, the less sensitive it is, and the more feebly it reacts to stimulus; and the higher it is, the more responsively and vigorously it reacts to reality. How is it you don't know that? A doctor, and not know such trifles! To despise suffering, to be always contented, and to be surprised at nothing, one must reach this condition"—and Ivan Dmitritch pointed to the peasant who was a mass of fat—"or to harden oneself by suffering to such a point that one loses all sensibility to it—that is, in other

*The second-century Roman emperor and Stoic philosopher; author of *Meditations.*

words, to cease to live. You must excuse me, I am not a sage or a philosopher," Ivan Dmitritch continued with irritation, "and I don't understand anything about it. I am not capable of reasoning."

"On the contrary, your reasoning is excellent."

"The Stoics, whom you are parodying, were remarkable people, but their doctrine crystallized two thousand years ago and has not advanced, and will not advance, an inch forward, since it is not practical or living. It had a success only with the minority which spends its life in savouring all sorts of theories and ruminating over them; the majority did not understand it. A doctrine which advocates indifference to wealth and to the comforts of life, and a contempt for suffering and death, is quite unintelligible to the vast majority of men, since that majority has never known wealth or the comforts of life; and to despise suffering would mean to it despising life itself, since the whole existence of man is made up of the sensations of hunger, cold, injury, loss, and a Hamlet-like dread of death. The whole of life lies in these sensations; one may be oppressed by it, one may hate it, but one cannot despise it. Yes, so, I repeat, the doctrine of the Stoics can never have a future; from the beginning of time up to to-day you see continually increasing the struggle, the sensibility to pain, the capacity of responding to stimulus."

Ivan Dmitritch suddenly lost the thread of his thoughts, stopped, and rubbed his forehead with vexation.

"I meant to say something important, but I have lost it," he said. "What was I saying? Oh, yes! This is what I mean: one of the Stoics sold himself into slavery to redeem his neighbour, so, you see, even a Stoic did react to stimulus, since, for such a generous act as the destruction of oneself for the sake of one's neighbour, he must have had a soul capable of pity and indignation. Here in prison I have forgotten everything I have learned, or else I could have recalled something else. Take Christ, for instance: Christ responded to reality by weeping, smiling, being sorrowful and moved to wrath, even overcome by misery. He did not go to meet His sufferings with a smile, He did not despise death, but prayed in the Garden of Gethsemane* that this cup might pass Him by."

---

*Site of Christ's agonizing vision of his imminent arrest and suffering; see accounts in the Bible: Matthew 26:36–42 and Mark 14:32–36.

Ivan Dmitritch laughed and sat down.

"Granted that a man's peace and contentment lie not outside but in himself," he said, "granted that one must despise suffering and not be surprised at anything, yet on what ground do you preach the theory? Are you a sage? A philosopher?"

"No, I am not a philosopher, but everyone ought to preach it because it is reasonable."

"No, I want to know how it is that you consider yourself competent to judge of 'comprehension,' contempt for suffering, and so on. Have you ever suffered? Have you any idea of suffering? Allow me to ask you, were you ever thrashed in your childhood?"

"No, my parents had an aversion for corporal punishment."

"My father used to flog me cruelly; my father was a harsh, sickly Government clerk with a long nose and a yellow neck. But let us talk of you. No one has laid a finger on you all your life, no one has scared you nor beaten you; you are as strong as a bull. You grew up under your father's wing and studied at his expense, and then you dropped at once into a sinecure. For more than twenty years you have lived rent free with heating, lighting, and service all provided, and had the right to work how you pleased and as much as you pleased, even to do nothing. You were naturally a flabby, lazy man, and so you have tried to arrange your life so that nothing should disturb you or make you move. You have handed over your work to the assistant and the rest of the rabble while you sit in peace and warmth, save money, read, amuse yourself with reflections, with all sorts of lofty nonsense, and" (Ivan Dmitritch looked at the doctor's red nose) "with boozing; in fact, you have seen nothing of life, you know absolutely nothing of it, and are only theoretically acquainted with reality; you despise suffering and are surprised at nothing for a very simple reason: vanity of vanities, the external and the internal, contempt for life, for suffering and for death, comprehension, true happiness—that's the philosophy that suits the Russian sluggard best. You see a peasant beating his wife, for instance. Why interfere? Let him beat her, they will both die sooner or later, anyway; and, besides, he who beats injures by his blows, not the person he is beating, but himself. To get drunk is stupid and unseemly, but if you drink you die, and if you don't drink you die. A peasant woman comes with toothache . . . well, what of it? Pain is the idea of pain, and besides 'there is no living in this world without illness; we shall all die, and so, go away, woman, don't hinder me from thinking and drinking vodka.' A young man asks advice, what he is to do, how he is to live; anyone else would think before answering, but you have got the answer ready: strive for 'comprehension' or for true happiness. And what is that fantastic 'true happiness'? There's no answer, of course. We are kept here behind barred windows, tortured, left to rot; but that is very good and reasonable, because there is no difference at all between this ward and a warm, snug study. A convenient philosophy. You can do nothing, and your conscience is clear, and you feel you are wise. . . . No, sir, it is not philosophy, it's not thinking, it's not breadth of vision, but laziness, fakirism, drowsy stupefaction. Yes," cried Ivan Dmitritch, getting angry again, "you despise suffering, but I'll be bound if you pinch your finger in the door you will howl at the top of your voice."

"And perhaps I shouldn't howl," said Andrey Yefimitch, with a gentle smile.

"Oh, I dare say! Well, if you had a stroke of paralysis, or supposing some fool or bully took advantage of his position and rank to insult you in public, and if you knew he could do it with impunity, then you would understand what it means to put people off with comprehension and true happiness."

"That's original," said Andrey Yefimitch, laughing with pleasure and rubbing his hands. "I am agreeably struck by your inclination for drawing generalizations, and the sketch of my character you have just drawn is simply brilliant. I must confess that talking to you gives me great pleasure. Well, I've listened to you, and now you must graciously listen to me."

XI

The conversation went on for about an hour longer, and apparently made a deep impression on Andrey Yefimitch. He began going to the ward every day. He went there in the mornings and after dinner, and often the dusk of evening found him in conversation with Ivan Dmitritch. At first Ivan Dmitritch held aloof from him, suspected him of evil designs, and openly expressed his hostility. But afterwards he got used to him, and his abrupt manner changed to one of condescending irony.

Soon it was all over the hospital that the doctor, Andrey Yefimitch, had taken to visiting Ward No. 6. No one—neither Sergey Sergeyitch, nor Nikita, nor the nurses—could conceive why he went there, why he stayed there for hours together, what he was talking about, and why he did not write prescriptions. His actions seemed strange. Often Mihail Averyanitch did not find him at home, which had never happened in the past, and Daryushka was greatly perturbed, for the doctor drank his beer now at no definite time, and sometimes was even late for dinner.

One day—it was at the end of June—Dr. Hobotov went to see Andrey Yefimitch about something. Not finding him at home, he proceeded to look for him in the yard; there he was told that the old doctor had gone to see the mental patients. Going into the lodge and stopping in the entry, Hobotov heard the following conversation:

"We shall never agree, and you will not succeed in converting me to your faith," Ivan Dmitritch was saying irritably; "you are utterly ignorant of reality, and you have never known suffering, but have only like a leech fed beside the sufferings of others, while I have been in continual suffering from the day of my birth till to-day. For that reason, I tell you frankly, I consider myself superior to you and more competent in every respect. It's not for you to teach me."

"I have absolutely no ambition to convert you to my faith," said Andrey Yefimitch gently, and with regret that the other refused to understand him. "And that is not what matters, my friend; what matters is not that you have suffered and I have not. Joy and suffering are passing; let us leave them, never mind them. What matters is that you and I think; we see in each other people who are capable of thinking and reasoning, and that is a common bond between us however different our views. If you knew, my friend, how sick I am of the universal senselessness, ineptitude, stupidity, and with what delight I always talk with you! You are an intelligent man, and I enjoy your company."

Hobotov opened the door an inch and glanced into the ward; Ivan Dmitritch in his night-cap and the doctor Andrey Yefimitch were sitting side by side on the bed. The madman was grimacing, twitching, and convulsively wrapping himself in his gown, while the doctor sat motionless with bowed head, and his face was red and look[ed] helpless and sorrowful. Hobotov shrugged his shoulders, grinned, and glanced at Nikita. Nikita shrugged his shoulders too.

Next day Hobotov went to the lodge, accompanied by the assistant. Both stood in the entry and listened.

"I fancy our old man has gone clean off his chump!" said Hobotov as he came out of the lodge.

"Lord have mercy upon us sinners!" sighed the decorous Sergey Sergeyitch, scrupulously avoiding the puddles that he might not muddy his polished boots. "I must own, honoured Yevgeny Fyodoritch, I have been expecting it for a long time."

XII

After this Andrey Yefimitch began to notice a mysterious air in all around him. The attendants, the nurses, and the patients looked at him inquisitively when they met him, and then whispered together. The superintendent's little daughter Masha, whom he liked to meet in the hospital garden, for some reason ran away from him now when he went up with a smile to stroke her on the head. The postmaster no longer said, "Perfectly true," as he listened to him, but in unaccountable confusion muttered, "Yes, yes, yes . . ." and looked at him with a grieved and thoughtful expression; for some reason he took to advising his friend to give up vodka and beer, but as a man of delicate feeling he did not say this directly, but hinted it, telling him first about the commanding officer of his battalion, an excellent man, and then about the priest of the regiment, a capital fellow, both of whom drank and fell ill, but on giving up drinking completely regained their health. On two or three occasions Andrey Yefimitch was visited by his colleague Hobotov, who also advised him to give up spirituous liquors, and for no apparent reason recommended him to take bromide.

In August Andrey Yefimitch got a letter from the mayor of the town asking him to come on very important business. On arriving at the town hall at the time fixed, Andrey Yefimitch found there the military commander, the superintendent of the district school, a member of the town council, Hobotov, and a plump, fair gentleman who was introduced to him as a doctor. This doctor, with a Polish surname difficult to pronounce, lived at a pedigree stud-farm twenty miles away, and was now on a visit to the town.

"There's something that concerns you," said the member of the town council, addressing Andrey Yefimitch after they had all greeted one another and sat down to the table. "Here Yevgeny Fyodoritch says that there is not room for the dispensary in the main building, and that it ought to be transferred to one of the lodges. That's of no consequence—of course it can be transferred, but the point is that the lodge wants doing up."

"Yes, it would have to be done up," said Andrey Yefimitch after a moment's thought. "If the corner lodge, for instance, were fitted up as a dispensary, I imagine it would cost at least five hundred roubles. An unproductive expenditure!"

Everyone was silent for a space.

"I had the honour of submitting to you ten years ago," Andrey Yefimitch went on in a low voice, "that the hospital in its present form is a luxury for the town beyond its means. It was built in the forties, but things were different then. The town spends too much on unnecessary buildings and superfluous staff. I believe with a different system two model hospitals might be maintained for the same money."

"Well, let us have a different system, then!" the member of the town council said briskly.

"I have already had the honour of submitting to you that the medical department should be transferred to the supervision of the Zemstvo."

"Yes, transfer the money to the Zemstvo and they will steal it," laughed the fair-haired doctor.

"That's what it always comes to," the member of the council assented, and he also laughed.

Andrey Yefimitch looked with apathetic, lustreless eyes at the fair-haired doctor and said: "One should be just."

Again there was silence. Tea was brought in. The military commander, for some reason much embarrassed, touched Andrey Yefimitch's hand across the table and said: "You have quite forgotten us, doctor. But of course you are a hermit: you don't play cards and don't like women. You would be dull with fellows like us."

They all began saying how boring it was for a decent person to live in such a town. No theatre, no music, and at the last dance at the club there had been about twenty ladies and only two gentlemen. The young men did not dance, but spent all the time crowding round the refreshment bar or playing cards.

Not looking at anyone and speaking slowly in a low voice, Andrey Yefimitch began saying what a pity, what a terrible pity it was that the townspeople should waste their vital energy, their hearts, and their minds on cards and gossip, and should have neither the power nor the inclination to spend their time in interesting conversation and reading, and should refuse to take advantage of the enjoyments of the mind. The mind alone was interesting and worthy of attention, all the rest was low and petty. Hobotov listened to his colleague attentively and suddenly asked:

"Andrey Yefimitch, what day of the month is it?"

Having received an answer, the fair-haired doctor and he, in the tone of examiners conscious of their lack of skill, began asking Andrey Yefimitch what was the day of the week, how many days there were in the year, and whether it was true that there was a remarkable prophet living in Ward No. 6.

In response to the last question Andrey Yefimitch turned rather red and said: "Yes, he is mentally deranged, but he is an interesting young man."

They asked him no other questions.

When he was putting on his overcoat in the entry, the military commander laid a hand on his shoulder and said with a sigh:

"It's time for us old fellows to rest!"

As he came out of the hall, Andrey Yefimitch understood that it had been a committee appointed to enquire into his mental condition. He recalled the questions that had been asked him, flushed crimson, and for some reason, for the first time in his life, felt bitterly grieved for medical science.

"My God . . ." he thought, remembering how these doctors had just examined him; "why, they have only lately been hearing lectures on mental pathology; they had passed on examination—what's the explanation of this crass ignorance? They have not a conception of mental pathology!"

And for the first time in his life he felt insulted and moved to anger.

In the evening of the same day Mihail Averyanitch came to see him. The postmaster went up to him without waiting to greet him, took him by both hands, and said in an agitated voice:

"My dear fellow, my dear friend, show me that you believe in my genuine affection and look on me as your friend!" And preventing Andrey Yefimitch from speaking, he went on, growing excited: "I love you for your culture and nobility of soul. Listen to me, my dear fellow. The rules of their profession compel the doctors to conceal the truth from you, but I blurt out the plain truth like a soldier. You are not well! Excuse me, my dear fellow, but it is the truth; everyone about you has been noticing it for a long time. Dr. Yevgeny Fyodoritch has just told me that it is essential for you to rest and distract your mind for the sake of your health. Perfectly true! Excellent! In a day or two I am taking a holiday and am going away for a sniff of a different atmosphere. Show that you are a friend to me, let us go together! Let us go for a jaunt as in the good old days."

"I feel perfectly well," said Andrey Yefimitch after a moment's thought. "I can't go away. Allow me to show you my friendship in some other way."

To go off with no object, without his books, without his Daryushka, without his beer, to break abruptly through the routine of life, established for twenty years—the idea for the first minute struck him as wild and fantastic, but he remembered the conversation at the Zemstvo committee and the depressing feelings with which he had returned home, and the thought of a brief absence from the town in which stupid people looked on him as a madman was pleasant to him.

"And where precisely do you intend to go?" he asked.

"To Moscow, to Petersburg, to Warsaw. . . . I spent the five happiest years of my life in Warsaw. What a marvelous town! Let us go, my dear fellow!"

XIII

A week later it was suggested to Andrey Yefimitch that he should have a rest—that is, send in his resignation—a suggestion he received with indifference, and a week later still, Mihail Averyanitch and he were sitting in a posting carriage driving to the nearest railway station. The days were cool and bright, with a blue sky and a transparent distance. They were two days driving the hundred and fifty miles to the railway station, and stayed two nights on the way. When at the posting station the glasses given them for their tea had not been properly washed, or the drivers were slow in harnessing the horses, Mihail Averyanitch would turn crimson, and quivering all over would shout:

"Hold your tongue! Don't argue!"

And in the carriage he talked without ceasing for a moment, describing his campaigns in the Caucasus and in Poland. What adventures he had had, what meetings! He talked loudly and opened his eyes so wide with wonder that he might well be thought to be lying. Moreover, as he talked he breathed in Andrey Yefimitch's face and laughed into his ear. This bothered the doctor and prevented him from thinking or concentrating his mind.

In the train they travelled, from motives of economy, third-class in a non-smoking compartment. Half the passengers were decent people. Mihail Averyanitch soon made friends with everyone, and moving from one seat to another, kept saying loudly that they ought not to travel by these appalling lines. It was a regular swindle! A very different thing riding on a good horse: one could do over seventy miles a day and feel fresh and well after it. And our bad harvests were due to the draining of the Pinsk marshes;* altogether, the way things were done was dreadful. He got excited, talked loudly, and would not let others speak. This endless chatter to the accompaniment of loud laughter and expressive gestures wearied Andrey Yefimitch.

"Which of us is the madman?" he thought with vexation. "I, who

---

*Extensive marshlands on both sides of the Pripyat River, near the town of Pinsk in Byelorussia; largest such tract in Europe.

try not to disturb my fellow-passengers in any way, or this egoist who thinks that he is cleverer and more interesting than anyone here, and so will leave no one in peace?"

In Moscow Mihail Averyanitch put on a military coat without epaulettes and trousers with red braid on them. He wore a military cap and overcoat in the street, and soldiers saluted him. It seemed to Andrey Yefimitch, now, that his companion was a man who had flung away all that was good and kept only what was bad of all the characteristics of a country gentleman that he had once possessed. He liked to be waited on even when it was quite unnecessary. The matches would be lying before him on the table, and he would see them and shout to the waiter to give him the matches; he did not hesitate to appear before a maidservant in nothing but his underclothes; he used the familiar mode of address to all footmen indiscriminately, even old men, and when he was angry called them fools and blockheads. This, Andrey Yefimitch thought, was like a gentleman, but disgusting.

First of all Mihail Averyanitch led his friend to the Iversky Madonna.* He prayed fervently, shedding tears and bowing down to the earth, and when he had finished, heaved a deep sigh and said:

"Even though one does not believe it makes one somehow easier when one prays a little. Kiss the ikon, my dear fellow."

Andrey Yefimitch was embarrassed and he kissed the image, while Mihail Averyanitch pursed up his lips and prayed in a whisper, and again tears came into his eyes. Then they went to the Kremlin and looked there at the Tsar-cannon and the Tsar-bell,† and even touched them with their fingers, admired the view over the river, visited St. Saviour's and the Rumyantsev museum.

They dined at Tyestov's.‡ Mihail Averyanitch looked a long time at the menu, stroking his whiskers, and said in the tone of a gourmand accustomed to dine in restaurants:

"We shall see what you give us to eat to-day, angel!"

---

*The most revered miracle-working icon in Moscow.

†Objects of historical veneration in Moscow's Kremlin.

‡Three sites of interest in Moscow: St. Saviour's, a memorial to the Napoleonic wars of 1812–1814; the Rumyantsev museum, built in 1787 to house the collection of Count Nicholas Rumyantsev, who gave it to the nation; and Tyestov's, a well-known restaurant.

XIV

The doctor walked about, looked at things, ate and drank, but he had all the while one feeling: annoyance with Mihail Averyanitch. He longed to have a rest from his friend, to get away from him, to hide himself, while the friend thought it his duty not to let the doctor move a step away from him, and to provide him with as many distractions as possible. When there was nothing to look at he entertained him with conversation. For two days Andrey Yefimitch endured it, but on the third he announced to his friend that he was ill and wanted to stay at home for the whole day; his friend replied that in that case he would stay too—that really he needed rest, for he was run off his legs already. Andrey Yefimitch lay on the sofa, with his face to the back, and clenching his teeth, listened to his friend, who assured him with heat that sooner or later France would certainly thrash Germany, that there were a great many scoundrels in Moscow, and that it was impossible to judge of a horse's quality by its outward appearance. The doctor began to have a buzzing in his ears and palpitations of the heart, but out of delicacy could not bring himself to beg his friend to go away or hold his tongue. Fortunately Mihail Averyanitch grew weary of sitting in the hotel room, and after dinner he went out for a walk.

As soon as he was alone Andrey Yefimitch abandoned himself to a feeling of relief. How pleasant to lie motionless on the sofa and to know that one is alone in the room! Real happiness is impossible without solitude. The fallen angel betrayed God probably because he longed for solitude, of which the angels know nothing. Andrey Yefimitch wanted to think about what he had seen and heard during the last few days, but he could not get Mihail Averyanitch out of his head.

"Why, he has taken a holiday and come with me out of friendship, out of generosity," thought the doctor with vexation; "nothing could be worse than this friendly supervision. I suppose he is good-natured and generous and a lively fellow, but he is a bore. An insufferable bore. In the same way there are people who never say anything but what is clever and good, yet one feels that they are dull-witted people."

For the following days Andrey Yefimitch declared himself ill and would not leave the hotel room; he lay with his face to the back of the sofa, and suffered agonies of weariness when his friend entertained him with conversation, or rested when his friend was absent. He was vexed with himself for having come, and with his friend, who grew every day more talkative and more free-and-easy; he could not succeed in attuning his thoughts to a serious and lofty level.

"This is what I get from the real life Ivan Dmitritch talked about," he thought, angry at his own pettiness. "It's of no consequence, though. . . . I shall go home, and everything will go on as before. . . ."

It was the same thing in Petersburg too; for whole days together he did not leave the hotel room, but lay on the sofa and only got up to drink beer.

Mihail Averyanitch was all haste to get to Warsaw.

"My dear man, what should I go there for?" said Andrey Yefimitch in an imploring voice. "You go alone and let me get home! I entreat you!"

"On no account," protested Mihail Averyanitch. "It's a marvelous town."

Andrey Yefimitch had not the strength of will to insist on his own way, and much against his inclination went to Warsaw. There he did not leave the hotel room, but lay on the sofa, furious with himself, with his friend, and with the waiters, who obstinately refused to understand Russian; while Mihail Averyanitch, healthy, hearty, and full of spirits as usual, went about the town from morning to night, looking for his old acquaintances. Several times he did not return home at night. After one night spent in some unknown haunt he returned home early in the morning, in a violently excited condition, with a red face and tousled hair. For a long time he walked up and down the rooms muttering something to himself, then stopped and said:

"Honour before everything."

After walking up and down a little longer he clutched his head in both hands and pronounced in a tragic voice: "Yes, honour before everything! Accursed be the moment when the idea first entered my head to visit this Babylon! My dear friend," he added, addressing the doctor, "you may despise me, I have played and lost; lend me five hundred roubles!"

Andrey Yefimitch counted out five hundred roubles and gave them to his friend without a word. The latter, still crimson with shame and anger, incoherently articulated some useless vow, put on his cap, and went out. Returning two hours later he flopped into an easy-chair, heaved a loud sigh, and said:

"My honour is saved. Let us go, my friend; I do not care to remain another hour in this accursed town. Scoundrels! Austrian spies!"

By the time the friends were back in their own town it was November, and deep snow was lying in the streets. Dr. Hobotov had Andrey Yefimitch's post; he was still living in his old lodgings, waiting for Andrey Yefimitch to arrive and clear out of the hospital apartments. The plain woman whom he called his cook was already established in one of the lodges.

Fresh scandals about the hospital were going the round of the town. It was said that the plain woman had quarrelled with the superintendent, and that the latter had crawled on his knees before her begging forgiveness. On the very first day he arrived Andrey Yefimitch had to look out for lodgings.

"My friend," the postmaster said to him timidly, "excuse an indiscreet question: what means have you at your disposal?"

Andrey Yefimitch, without a word, counted out his money and said: "Eighty-six roubles."

"I don't mean that," Mihail Averyanitch brought out in confusion, misunderstanding him; "I mean, what have you to live on?"

"I tell you, eighty-six roubles . . . I have nothing else."

Mihail Averyanitch looked upon the doctor as an honourable man, yet he suspected that he had accumulated a fortune of at least twenty thousand. Now learning that Andrey Yefimitch was a beggar, that he had nothing to live on he was for some reason suddenly moved to tears and embraced his friend.

XV

Andrey Yefimitch now lodged in a little house with three windows. There were only three rooms besides the kitchen in the little house. The doctor lived in two of them which looked into the street, while Daryushka and the landlady with her three children lived in the third room and the kitchen. Sometimes the landlady's lover, a drunken peasant who was rowdy and reduced the children and Daryushka to terror, would come for the night. When he arrived and established himself in the kitchen and demanded vodka, they all felt very uncomfortable, and the doctor would be moved by pity to take the crying children into his room and let them lie on his floor, and this gave him great satisfaction.

He got up as before at eight o'clock, and after his morning tea sat down to read his old books and magazines: he had no money for new ones. Either because the books were old, or perhaps because of the change in his surroundings, reading exhausted him, and did not grip his attention as before. That he might not spend his time in idleness he made a detailed catalogue of his books and gummed little labels on their backs, and this mechanical, tedious work seemed to him more interesting than reading. The monotonous, tedious work lulled his thoughts to sleep in some unaccountable way, and the time passed quickly while he thought of nothing. Even sitting in the kitchen, peeling potatoes with Daryushka or picking over the buckwheat grain, seemed to him interesting. On Saturdays and Sundays he went to church. Standing near the wall and half closing his eyes, he listened to the singing and thought of his father, of his mother, of the university, of the religions of the world; he felt calm and melancholy, and as he went out of the church afterwards he regretted that the service was so soon over. He went twice to the hospital to talk to Ivan Dmitritch. But on both occasions Ivan Dmitritch was unusually excited and ill-humoured; he bade the doctor leave him in peace, as he had long been sick of empty chatter, and declared, to make up for all his sufferings, he asked from the damned scoundrels only one favour—solitary confinement. Surely they would not refuse him even that? On both occasions when Andrey Yefimitch was taking leave of him and wishing him good-night, he answered rudely and said:

"Go to hell!"

And Andrey Yefimitch did not know now whether to go to him for the third time or not. He longed to go.

In old days Andrey Yefimitch used to walk about his rooms and think in the interval after dinner, but now from dinner-time till evening tea he lay on the sofa with his face to the back and gave himself up to trivial thoughts which he could not struggle against. He was mortified that after more than twenty years of service he had been given neither a pension nor any assistance. It is true that he had not done his work honestly, but, then, all who are in the Service get a pension without distinction whether they are honest or not. Contemporary justice lies precisely in the bestowal of grades, orders, and pensions, not for moral qualities or capacities, but for service whatever it may have been like. Why was he alone to be an exception? He had no money at all. He was ashamed to pass by the shop and look at the woman who owned it. He owed thirty-two roubles for beer already. There was money owing to the landlady also. Daryushka sold old clothes and books on the sly, and told lies to the landlady, saying that the doctor was just going to receive a large sum of money.

He was angry with himself for having wasted on travelling the thousand roubles he had saved up. How useful that thousand roubles would have been now! He was vexed that people would not leave him in peace. Hobotov thought it his duty to look in on his sick colleague from time to time. Everything about him was revolting to Andrey Yefimitch—his well-fed face and vulgar, condescending tone, and his use of the word "colleague," and his high top-boots; the most revolting thing was that he thought it was his duty to treat Andrey Yefimitch, and thought that he really was treating him. On every visit he brought a bottle of bromide and rhubarb pills.

Mihail Averyanitch, too, thought it his duty to visit his friend and entertain him. Every time he went in to Andrey Yefimitch with an affectation of ease, laughed constrainedly, and began assuring him that he was looking very well to-day, and that, thank God, he was on the highroad to recovery, and from this it might be concluded that he looked on his friend's condition as hopeless. He had not yet repaid his Warsaw debt, and was overwhelmed by shame; he was constrained, and so tried to laugh louder and talk more amusingly. His anecdotes and descriptions seemed endless now, and were an agony both to Andrey Yefimitch and himself.

In his presence Andrey Yefimitch usually lay on the sofa with his face to the wall, and listened with his teeth clenched; his soul was oppressed with rankling disgust, and after every visit from his friend he felt as though this disgust had risen higher, and was mounting into his throat.

To stifle petty thoughts he made haste to reflect that he himself, and Hobotov, and Mihail Averyanitch, would all sooner or later perish without leaving any trace on the world. If one imagined some spirit flying by the earthly globe in space in a million years he would see nothing but clay and bare rocks. Everything—culture and the moral law—would pass away and not even a burdock would grow out of them. Of what consequence was shame in the presence of a shopkeeper, of what consequence was the insignificant Hobotov or the wearisome friendship of Mihail Averyanitch? It was all trivial and nonsensical.

But such reflections did not help him now. Scarcely had he imagined the earthly globe in a million years, when Hobotov in his high top-boots or Mihail Averyanitch with his forced laugh would appear from behind a bare rock, and he even heard the shamefaced whisper: "The Warsaw debt. . . . I will repay it in a day or two, my dear fellow, without fail. . . ."

XVI

One day Mihail Averyanitch came after dinner when Andrey Yefimitch was lying on the sofa. It so happened that Hobotov arrived at the same time with his bromide. Andrey Yefimitch got up heavily and sat down, leaning both arms on the sofa.

"You have a much better colour to-day than you had yesterday, my dear man," began Mihail Averyanitch. "Yes, you look jolly. Upon my soul, you do!"

"It's high time you were well, colleague," said Hobotov, yawning. "I'll be bound, you are sick of this bobbery."

"And we shall recover," said Mihail Averyanitch cheerfully. "We shall live another hundred years! To be sure!"

"Not a hundred years, but another twenty," Hobotov said reassuringly. "It's all right, all right, colleague; don't lose heart. . . . Don't go piling it on!"

"We'll show what we can do," laughed Mihail Averyanitch, and he slapped his friend on the knee. "We'll show them yet! Next summer, please God, we shall be off to the Caucasus, and we will ride all over it on horseback—trot, trot, trot! And when we are back from the Caucasus I shouldn't wonder if we will all dance at the wedding." Mihail Averyanitch gave a sly wink. "We'll marry you, my dear boy, we'll marry you. . . ."

Andrey Yefimitch felt suddenly that the rising disgust had mounted to his throat, his heart began beating violently.

"That's vulgar," he said, getting up quickly and walking away to the window. "Don't you understand that you are talking vulgar nonsense?"

He meant to go on softly and politely, but against his will he suddenly clenched his fists and raised them above his head.

"Leave me alone," he shouted in a voice unlike his own, flushing crimson and shaking all over. "Go away, both of you!"

Mihail Averyanitch and Hobotov got up and stared at him first with amazement and then with alarm.

"Go away, both!" Andrey Yefimitch went on shouting. "Stupid people! Foolish people! I don't want either your friendship or your medicines, stupid man! Vulgar! Nasty!"

Hobotov and Mihail Averyanitch, looking at each other in bewilderment, staggered to the door and went out. Andrey Yefimitch snatched up the bottle of bromide and flung it after them; the bottle broke with a crash on the door-frame.

"Go to the devil!" he shouted in a tearful voice, running out into the passage. "To the devil!"

When his guests were gone Andrey Yefimitch lay down on the sofa, trembling as though in a fever, and went on for a long while repeating: "Stupid people! Foolish people!"

When he was calmer, what occurred to him first of all was the thought that poor Mihail Averyanitch must be feeling fearfully ashamed and depressed now, and that it was all dreadful. Nothing like this had ever happened to him before. Where was his intelligence and his tact? Where was his comprehension of things and his philosophical indifference?

The doctor could not sleep all night for shame and vexation with himself, and at ten o'clock next morning he went to the post office and apologized to the postmaster.

"We won't think again of what has happened," Mihail Averyanitch, greatly touched, said with a sigh, warmly pressing his hand. "Let bygones be bygones. Lyubavkin," he suddenly shouted so loud that all the postmen and other persons present started, "hand a chair; and you wait," he shouted to a peasant woman who was stretching out a registered letter to him through the grating. "Don't you see that I am busy? We will not remember the past," he went on, affectionately addressing Andrey Yefimitch; "sit down, I beg you, my dear fellow."

For a minute he stroked his knees in silence, and then said:

"I have never had a thought of taking offence. Illness is no joke, I understand. Your attack frightened the doctor and me yesterday, and we had a long talk about you afterwards. My dear friend, why won't you treat your illness seriously? You can't go on like this. . . . Excuse me speaking openly as a friend," whispered Mihail Averyanitch. "You live in the most unfavourable surroundings, in a crowd, in uncleanliness, no one to look after you, no money for proper treatment. . . . My dear friend, the doctor and I implore you with all our hearts, listen to our advice: go into the hospital! There you will have wholesome food and attendance and treatment. Though, between ourselves, Yevgeny Fyodoritch is *mauvais ton,* yet he does understand his work, you can fully rely upon him. He has promised me he will look after you."

Andrey Yefimitch was touched by the postmaster's genuine sympathy and the tears which suddenly glittered on his cheeks.

"My honoured friend, don't believe it!" he whispered, laying his hand on his heart; "don't believe them. It's all a sham. My illness is only that in twenty years I have only found one intelligent man in the whole town, and he is mad. I am not ill at all, it's simply that I have got into an enchanted circle which there is no getting out of. I don't care; I am ready for anything."

"Go into the hospital, my dear fellow."

"I don't care if it were into the pit."

"Give me your word, my dear man, that you will obey Yevgeny Fyodoritch in everything."

"Certainly I will give you my word. But I repeat, my honoured friend, I have got into an enchanted circle. Now everything, even the genuine sympathy of my friends, leads to the same thing—to my ruin. I am going to my ruin, and I have the manliness to recognize it."

"My dear fellow, you will recover."

"What's the use of saying that?" said Andrey Yefimitch, with irritation. "There are few men who at the end of their lives do not experience what I am experiencing now. When you are told that you have something such as diseased kidneys or enlarged heart, and you begin being treated for it, or are told you are mad or a criminal—that is, in fact, when people suddenly turn their attention to you—you may be sure you have got into an enchanted circle from which you will not escape. You will try to escape and make things worse. You had better give in, for no human efforts can save you. So it seems to me."

Meanwhile the public was crowding at the grating. That he might not be in their way, Andrey Yefimitch got up and began to take leave. Mihail Averyanitch made him promise on his honour once more, and escorted him to the outer door.

Towards evening on the same day Hobotov, in his sheepskin and his high top-boots, suddenly made his appearance, and said to Andrey Yefimitch in a tone as though nothing had happened the day before:

"I have come on business, colleague. I have come to ask you whether you would not join me in a consultation. Eh?"

Thinking that Hobotov wanted to distract his mind with an outing, or perhaps really to enable him to earn something, Andrey Yefimitch put on his coat and hat, and went out with him into the street. He was glad of the opportunity to smooth over his fault of the previous day and to be reconciled, and in his heart thanked Hobotov, who did not even allude to yesterday's scene and was evidently sparing him. One would never have expected such delicacy from this uncultured man.

"Where is your invalid?" asked Andrey Yefimitch.

"In the hospital. . . . I have long waited to show him to you. A very interesting case."

They went into the hospital yard, and going round the main building, turned towards the lodge where the mental cases were kept, and all this, for some reason, in silence. When they went into the lodge Nikita as usual jumped up and stood at attention.

"One of the patients here has a lung complication," Hobotov said in an undertone, going into the ward with Andrey Yefimitch. "You wait here, I'll be back directly. I am going for a stethoscope."

And he went away.

XVII

It was getting dusk. Ivan Dmitritch was lying on his bed with his face thrust into his pillow; the paralytic was sitting motionless, crying quietly and moving his lips. The fat peasant and the former sorter were asleep. It was quiet.

Andrey Yefimitch sat down on Ivan Dmitritch's bed and waited. But half an hour passed, and instead of Hobotov, Nikita came into the ward with a dressing-gown, some underlinen, and a pair of slippers in a heap on his arm.

"Please change your things, your honour," he said softly. "Here is your bed; come this way," he added, pointing to an empty bedstead which had obviously been recently brought into the ward. "It's all right; please God, you will recover."

Andrey Yefimitch understood it all. Without saying a word he crossed to the bed to which Nikita pointed and sat down; seeing that Nikita was standing waiting, he undressed entirely and he felt ashamed. Then he put on the hospital clothes; the drawers were very short, the shirt was long, and the dressing-gown smelt of smoked fish.

"Please God, you will recover," repeated Nikita, and he gathered up Andrey Yefimitch's clothes into his arms, went out, and shut the door after him.

"No matter . . ." thought Andrey Yefimitch, wrapping himself in his dressing-gown in a shamefaced way and feeling that he looked like a convict in his new costume. "It's no matter. . . . It does not matter whether it's a dress-coat or a uniform or this dressing-gown. . . ."

But how about his watch? And the notebook that was in the side-pocket? And his cigarettes? Where had Nikita taken his clothes? Now perhaps to the day of his death he would not put on trousers, a waistcoat, and high boots. It was all somehow strange and even incomprehensible at first. Andrey Yefimitch was even now convinced that there was no difference between his landlady's house and Ward No. 6, that everything in this world was nonsense and vanity of vanities. And yet his hands were trembling, his feet were cold, and he was filled with dread at the thought that soon Ivan Dmitritch would get up and see that he was in a dressing-gown. He got up and walked across the room and sat down again.

Here he had been sitting already half an hour, an hour, and he was miserably sick of it: was it really possible to live here a day, a week, and even years like these people? Why, he had been sitting here, had walked about and sat down again; he could get up and look out of window and walk from corner to corner again, and then what? Sit so all the time, like a post, and think? No, that was scarcely possible.

Andrey Yefimitch lay down, but at once got up, wiped the cold sweat from his brow with his sleeve, and felt that his whole face smelt of smoked fish. He walked about again.

"It's some misunderstanding . . ." he said, turning out the palms of his hands in perplexity. "It must be cleared up. There is a misunderstanding. . . ."

Meanwhile Ivan Dmitritch woke up; he sat up and propped his cheeks on his fists. He spat. Then he glanced lazily at the doctor, and apparently for the first minute did not understand; but soon his sleepy face grew malicious and mocking.

"Aha! so they have put you in here, too, old fellow?" he said in a voice husky from sleepiness, screwing up one eye. "Very glad to see you. You sucked the blood of others, and now they will suck yours. Excellent!"

"It's a misunderstanding . . ." Andrey Yefimitch brought out, frightened by Ivan Dmitritch's words; he shrugged his shoulders and repeated: "It's some misunderstanding. . . ."

Ivan Dmitritch spat again and lay down.

"Cursed life," he grumbled, "and what's bitter and insulting, this life will not end in compensation for our sufferings, it will not end with apotheosis as it would in an opera, but with death; peasants will come and drag one's dead body by the arms and the legs to the cellar. Ugh! Well, it does not matter. . . . We shall have our good time in the other world. . . . I shall come here as a ghost from the other world and frighten these reptiles. I'll turn their hair grey."

Moiseika returned, and, seeing the doctor, held out his hand.

"Give me one little kopeck," he said.

XVIII

Andrey Yefimitch walked away to the window and looked out into the open country. It was getting dark, and on the horizon to the right a cold crimson moon was mounting upwards. Not far from the hospital fence, not much more than two hundred yards away, stood a tall white house shut in by a stone wall. This was the prison.

"So this is real life," thought Andrey Yefimitch, and he felt frightened.

The moon and the prison, and the nails on the fence, and the far-away flames at the bone-charring factory were all terrible. Behind him there was the sound of a sigh. Andrey Yefimitch looked round and saw a man with glittering stars and orders on his breast, who was smiling and slily winking. And this, too, seemed terrible.

Andrey Yefimitch assured himself that there was nothing special about the moon or the prison, that even sane persons wear orders, and that everything in time will decay and turn to earth, but he was suddenly overcome with despair; he clutched at the grating with both hands and shook it with all his might. The strong grating did not yield.

Then that it might not be so dreadful he went to Ivan Dmitritch's bed and sat down.

"I have lost heart, my dear fellow," he muttered, trembling and wiping away the cold sweat, "I have lost heart."

"You should be philosophical," said Ivan Dmitritch ironically.

"My God, my God. . . . Yes, yes. . . . You were pleased to say once that there was no philosophy in Russia, but that all people, even the paltriest, talk philosophy. But you know the philosophizing of the paltriest does not harm anyone," said Andrey Yefimitch in a tone as if he wanted to cry and complain. "Why, then, that malignant laugh, my friend, and how can these paltry creatures help philosophizing if they are not satisfied? For an intelligent, educated man, made in God's image, proud and loving freedom, to have no alternative but to be a doctor in a filthy, stupid, wretched little town, and to spend his whole life among bottles, leeches, mustard plasters! Quackery, narrowness, vulgarity! Oh, my God!"

"You are talking nonsense. If you don't like being a doctor you should have gone in for being a statesman."

"I could not, I could not do anything. We are weak, my dear friend. . . . I used to be indifferent. I reasoned boldly and soundly, but at the first coarse touch of life upon me I have lost heart. . . . Prostration. . . . We are weak, we are poor creatures . . . and you, too, my dear friend, you are intelligent, generous, you drew in good impulses with your mother's milk, but you had hardly entered upon life when you were exhausted and fell ill. . . . Weak, weak!"

Andrey Yefimitch was all the while at the approach of evening tormented by another persistent sensation besides terror and the feeling of resentment. At last he realized that he was longing for a smoke and for beer.

"I am going out, my friend," he said. "I will tell them to bring a light; I can't put up with this. . . . I am not equal to it. . . ."

Andrey Yefimitch went to the door and opened it, but at once Nikita jumped up and barred his way.

"Where are you going? You can't, you can't!" he said. "It's bedtime."

"But I'm only going out for a minute to walk about the yard," said Andrey Yefimitch.

"You can't, you can't; it's forbidden. You know that yourself."

"But what difference will it make to anyone if I do go out?" asked Andrey Yefimitch, shrugging his shoulders. "I don't understand. Nikita, I must go out!" he said in a trembling voice. "I must."

"Don't be disorderly, it's not right," Nikita said peremptorily.

"This is beyond everything," Ivan Dmitritch cried suddenly, and he jumped up. "What right has he not to let you out? How dare they keep us here? I believe it is clearly laid down in the law that no one can be deprived of freedom without trial! It's an outrage! It's tyranny!"

"Of course it's tyranny," said Andrey Yefimitch, encouraged by Ivan Dmitritch's outburst. "I must go out, I want to. He has no right! Open, I tell you."

"Do you hear, you dull-witted brute?" cried Ivan Dmitritch, and he banged on the door with his fist. "Open the door, or I will break it open! Torturer!"

"Open the door," cried Andrey Yefimitch, trembling all over; "I insist!"

"Talk away!" Nikita answered through the door, "talk away. . . ."

"Anyhow, go and call Yevgeny Fyodoritch! Say that I beg him to come for a minute!"

"His honour will come of himself to-morrow."

"They will never let us out," Ivan Dmitritch was going on meanwhile. "They will leave us to rot here! Oh, Lord, can there really be no hell in the next world, and will these wretches be forgiven? Where is justice? Open the door, you wretch! I am choking!" he cried in a hoarse voice, and flung himself upon the door. "I'll dash out my brains, murderers!"

Nikita opened the door quickly, and roughly with both his hands and his knee shoved Andrey Yefimitch back, then swung his arm and punched him in the face with his fist. It seemed to Andrey Yefimitch as though a huge salt wave enveloped him from his head downwards and dragged him to the bed; there really was a salt taste in his mouth: most likely the blood was running from his teeth. He waved his arms as though he were trying to swim out and clutched at the bedstead, and at the same moment felt Nikita hit him twice on the back.

Ivan Dmitritch gave a loud scream. He must have been beaten too.

Then all was still, the faint moonlight came through the grating, and a shadow like a net lay on the floor. It was terrible. Andrey Yefimitch lay and held his breath: he was expecting with horror to be struck again. He felt as though someone had taken a sickle, thrust it into him, and turned it round several times in his breast and bowels. He bit the pillow from pain and clenched his teeth, and all at once through the chaos in his brain there flashed the terrible unbearable thought that these people, who seemed now like black shadows in the moonlight, had to endure such pain day by day for years. How could it have happened that for more than twenty years he had not known it and had refused to know it? He knew nothing of pain, had no conception of it, so he was not to blame, but his conscience, as inexorable and as rough as Nikita, made him turn cold from the crown of his head to his heels. He leaped up, tried to cry out with all his might, and to run in haste to kill Nikita, and then Hobotov, the superintendent and the assistant, and then himself; but no sound came from his chest, and his legs would not obey him. Gasping for breath, he tore at the dressing-gown and the shirt on his breast, rent them, and fell senseless on the bed.

XIX

Next morning his head ached, there was a droning in his ears and a feeling of utter weakness all over. He was not ashamed at recalling his weakness the day before. He had been cowardly, had even been afraid of the moon, had openly expressed thoughts and feelings such as he had not expected in himself before; for instance, the thought that the paltry people who philosophized were really dissatisfied. But now nothing mattered to him.

He ate nothing, he drank nothing. He lay motionless and silent.

"It is all the same to me," he thought when they asked him questions. "I am not going to answer. . . . It's all the same to me."

After dinner Mihail Averyanitch brought him a quarter of a pound of tea and a pound of fruit pastilles. Daryushka came too and stood for a whole hour by the bed with an expression of dull grief on her face. Dr. Hobotov visited him. He brought a bottle of bromide and told Nikita to fumigate the ward with something.

Towards evening Andrey Yefimitch died of an apoplectic stroke. At first he had a violent shivering fit and a feeling of sickness; something revolting as it seemed, penetrating through his whole body, even to his finger-tips, strained from his stomach to his head and flooded his eyes and ears. There was a greenness before his eyes. Andrey Yefimitch understood that his end had come, and remembered that Ivan Dmitritch, Mihail Averyanitch, and millions of people believed in immortality. And what if it really existed? But he did not want immortality, and he thought of it only for one instant. A herd of deer, extraordinarily beautiful and graceful, of which he had been reading the day before, ran by him; then a peasant woman stretched out her hand to him with a registered letter. . . . Mihail Averyanitch said something, then it all vanished, and Andrey Yefimitch sank into oblivion for ever.

The hospital porters came, took him by his arms and his legs, and carried him away to the chapel.

There he lay on the table, with open eyes, and the moon shed its light upon him at night. In the morning Sergey Sergeyitch came, prayed piously before the crucifix, and closed his former chief's eyes.

Next day Andrey Yefimitch was buried. Mihail Averyanitch and Daryushka were the only people at the funeral.

ROTHSCHILD'S FIDDLE

The town was a little one, worse than a village, and it was inhabited by scarcely any but old people who died with an infrequency that was really annoying. In the hospital and in the prison fortress very few coffins were needed. In fact business was bad. If Yakov Ivanov had been an undertaker in the chief town of the province he would certainly have had a house of his own, and people would have addressed him as Yakov Matveyitch; here in this wretched little town people called him simply Yakov; his nickname in the street was for some reason Bronze, and he lived in a poor way like a humble peasant, in a little old hut in which there was only one room, and in this room he and Marfa, the stove, a double bed, the coffins, his bench, and all their belongings were crowded together.

Yakov made good, solid coffins. For peasants and working people he made them to fit himself, and this was never unsuccessful, for there were none taller and stronger than he, even in the prison, though he was seventy. For gentry and for women he made them to measure, and used an iron foot-rule for the purpose. He was very unwilling to take orders for children's coffins, and made them straight off without measurements, contemptuously, and when he was paid for the work he always said:

"I must confess I don't like *trumpery* jobs."

Apart from his trade, playing the fiddle brought him in a small income.

The Jews' orchestra conducted by Moisey Ilyitch Shahkes, the tinsmith, who took more than half their receipts for himself, played as a rule at weddings in the town. As Yakov played very well on the fiddle, especially Russian songs, Shahkes sometimes invited him to join the orchestra at a fee of half a rouble a day, in addition to tips from the visitors. When Bronze sat in the orchestra first of all his face became crimson and perspiring; it was hot, there was a suffocating smell of garlic, the fiddle squeaked, the double bass wheezed close to his right ear, while the flute wailed at his left, played by a gaunt, red-haired Jew who had a perfect network of red and blue veins all over his face, and who bore the name of the famous millionaire Rothschild. And this accursed Jew contrived to play even the liveliest things plaintively. For no apparent reason Yakov little by little became possessed by hatred and contempt for the Jews, and especially for Rothschild; he began to pick quarrels with him, rail at him in unseemly language and once even tried to strike him, and Rothschild was offended and said, looking at him ferociously:

"If it were not that I respect you for your talent, I would have sent you flying out of the window."

Then he began to weep. And because of this Yakov was not often asked to play in the orchestra; he was only sent for in case of extreme necessity in the absence of one of the Jews.

Yakov was never in a good temper, as he was continually having to put up with terrible losses. For instance, it was a sin to work on Sundays or Saints' days, and Monday was an unlucky day, so that in the course of the year there were some two hundred days on which, whether he liked it or not, he had to sit with his hands folded. And only think, what a loss that meant. If anyone in the town had a wedding without music, or if Shahkes did not send for Yakov, that was a loss, too. The superintendent of the prison was ill for two years and was wasting away, and Yakov was impatiently waiting for him to die, but the superintendent went away to the chief town of the province to be doctored, and there took and died. There's a loss for you, ten roubles at least, as there would have been an expensive coffin to make, lined with brocade. The thought of his losses haunted Yakov, especially at night; he laid his fiddle on the bed beside him, and when all sorts of nonsensical ideas came into his mind he touched a string; the fiddle gave out a sound in the darkness, and he felt better.

On the sixth of May of the previous year Marfa had suddenly been taken ill. The old woman's breathing was laboured, she drank a great deal of water, and she staggered as she walked, yet she lighted the stove in the morning and even went herself to get water. Towards evening she lay down. Yakov played his fiddle all day; when it was quite dark he took the book in which he used every day to put down his losses, and, feeling dull, he began adding up the total for the year. It came to more than a thousand roubles. This so agitated him that he flung the reckoning beads down, and trampled them under his feet. Then he picked up the reckoning beads, and again spent a long time clicking with them and heaving deep, strained sighs. His face was crimson and wet with perspiration. He thought that if he had put that lost thousand roubles in the bank, the interest for a year would have been at least forty roubles, so that forty roubles was a loss too. In fact, wherever one turned there were losses and nothing else.

"Yakov!" Marfa called unexpectedly. "I am dying."

He looked round at his wife. Her face was rosy with fever, unusually bright and joyful-looking. Bronze, accustomed to seeing her face always pale, timid, and unhappy-looking, was bewildered. It looked as if she really were dying and were glad that she was going away for ever from that hut, from the coffins, and from Yakov. . . . And she gazed at the ceiling and moved her lips, and her expression was one of happiness, as though she saw death as her deliverer and were whispering with him.

It was daybreak; from the windows one could see the flush of dawn. Looking at the old woman, Yakov for some reason reflected that he had not once in his life been affectionate to her, had had no feeling for her, had never once thought to buy her a kerchief, or to bring her home some dainty from a wedding, but had done nothing but shout at her, scold her for his losses, shake his fists at her; it is true he had never actually beaten her, but he had frightened her, and at such times she had always been numb with terror. Why, he had forbidden her to drink tea because they spent too much without that, and she drank only hot water. And he understood why she had such a strange, joyful face now, and he was overcome with dread.

As soon as it was morning he borrowed a horse from a neighbour and took Marfa to the hospital. There were not many patients there, and so he had not long to wait, only three hours. To his great satisfaction the patients were not being received by the doctor, who was himself ill, but by the assistant, Maxim Nikolaitch, an old man of whom everyone in the town used to say that, though he drank and was quarrelsome, he knew more than the doctor.

"I wish you good-day," said Yakov, leading his old woman into the consulting room. "You must excuse us, Maxim Nikolaitch, we are always troubling you with our trumpery affairs. Here you see my better half is ailing, the partner of my life, as they say, excuse the expression. . . ."

Knitting his grizzled brows and stroking his whiskers the assistant began to examine the old woman, and she sat on a stool, a wasted, bent figure with a sharp nose and open mouth, looking like a bird that wants to drink.

"H——m . . . Ah! . . ." the assistant said slowly, and he heaved a sigh. "Influenza and possibly fever. There's typhus in the town now. Well, the old woman has lived her life, thank God. . . . How old is she?"

"She'll be seventy in another year, Maxim Nikolaitch."

"Well, the old woman has lived her life, it's time to say good-bye."

"You are quite right in what you say, of course, Maxim Nikolaitch," said Yakov, smiling from politeness, "and we thank you feelingly for your kindness, but allow me to say every insect wants to live."

"To be sure," said the assistant, in a tone which suggested that it depended upon him whether the woman lived or died. "Well, then, my good fellow, put a cold compress on her head, and give her these powders twice a day, and so good-bye. Bonjour."

From the expression of his face Yakov saw that it was a bad case, and that no sort of powders would be any help; it was clear to him that Marfa would die very soon, if not to-day, to-morrow. He nudged the assistant's elbow, winked at him, and said in a low voice:

"If you would just cup her, Maxim Nikolaitch."

"I have no time, I have no time, my good fellow. Take your old woman and go in God's name. Good-bye."

"Be so gracious," Yakov besought him. "You know yourself that if, let us say, it were her stomach or her inside that were bad, then powders or drops, but you see she had got a chill! In a chill the first thing is to let blood, Maxim Nikolaitch."

But the assistant had already sent for the next patient, and a peasant woman came into the consulting room with a boy.

"Go along, go along," he said to Yakov, frowning. "It's no use to——"

"In that case put on leeches, anyway! Make us pray for you for ever."

The assistant flew into a rage and shouted:

"You speak to me again! You blockhead. . . ."

Yakov flew into a rage too, and he turned crimson all over, but he did not utter a word. He took Marfa on his arm and led her out of the room. Only when they were sitting in the cart he looked morosely and ironically at the hospital, and said:

"A nice set of artists they have settled here! No fear, but he would have cupped a rich man, but even a leech he grudges to the poor. The Herods!"

When they got home and went into the hut, Marfa stood for ten minutes holding on to the stove. It seemed to her that if she were to lie down Yakov would talk to her about his losses, and scold her for lying down and not wanting to work. Yakov looked at her drearily and thought that to-morrow was St. John the Divine's, and next day St. Nikolay the Wonder-worker's, and the day after that was Sunday, and then Monday, an unlucky day. For four days he would not be able to work, and most likely Marfa would die on one of those days; so he would have to make the coffin to-day. He picked up his iron rule, went up to the old woman and took her measure. Then she lay down, and he crossed himself and began making the coffin.

When the coffin was finished Bronze put on his spectacles and wrote in his book: "Marfa Ivanov's coffin, two roubles, forty kopecks."

And he heaved a sigh. The old woman lay all the time silent with her eyes closed. But in the evening, when it got dark, she suddenly called the old man.

"Do you remember, Yakov," she asked, looking at him joyfully. "Do you remember fifty years ago God gave us a little baby with flaxen hair? We used always to be sitting by the river then, singing songs . . . under the willows," and laughing bitterly, she added: "The baby girl died."

Yakov racked his memory, but could not remember the baby or the willows.

"It's your fancy," he said.

The priest arrived; he administered the sacrament and extreme unction. Then Marfa began muttering something unintelligible, and towards morning she died. Old women, neighbours, washed her, dressed her and laid her in the coffin. To avoid paying the sacristan, Yakov read the psalms over the body himself, and they got nothing out of him for the grave, as the grave-digger was a crony of his. Four peasants carried the coffin to the graveyard, not for money, but from respect. The coffin was followed by old women, beggars, and a couple of crazy saints, and the people who met it crossed themselves piously. . . . And Yakov was very much pleased that it was so creditable, so decorous, and so cheap, and no offence to anyone. As he took his last leave of Marfa he touched the coffin and thought: "A good piece of work!"

But as he was going back from the cemetery he was overcome by acute depression. He didn't feel quite well: his breathing was laboured and feverish, his legs felt weak, and he had a craving for drink. And thoughts of all sorts forced themselves on his mind. He remembered again that all his life he had never felt for Marfa, had never been affectionate to her. The fifty-two years they had lived in the same hut had dragged on a long, long time, but it had somehow happened that in all that time he had never once thought of her, had paid no attention to her, as though she had been a cat or a dog. And yet, every day, she had lighted the stove, had cooked and baked, had gone for the water, had chopped the wood, had slept with him in the same bed, and when he came home drunk from the weddings always reverently hung his fiddle on the wall and put him to bed, and all this in silence, with a timid, anxious expression.

Rothschild, smiling and bowing, came to meet Yakov.

"I was looking for you, uncle," he said. "Moisey Ilyitch sends you his greetings and bids you come to him at once."

Yakov felt in no mood for this. He wanted to cry.

"Leave me alone," he said, and walked on.

"How can you," Rothschild said, fluttered, running on in front. "Moisey Ilyitch will be offended! He bade you come at once!"

Yakov was revolted at the Jew's gasping for breath and blinking, and having so many red freckles on his face. And it was disgusting to look at his green coat with black patches on it, and all his fragile, refined figure.

"Why are you pestering me, garlic?" shouted Yakov. "Don't persist!"

The Jew got angry and shouted too:

"Not so noisy, please, or I'll send you flying over the fence!"

"Get out of my sight!" roared Yakov, and rushed at him with his fists. "One can't live for you scabby Jews!"

Rothschild, half dead with terror, crouched down and waved his hands over his head, as though to ward off a blow; then he leapt up and ran away as fast as his legs could carry him: as he ran he gave little skips and kept clasping his hands, and Yakov could see how his long thin spine wriggled. Some boys, delighted at the incident, ran after him shouting "Jew! Jew!" Some dogs joined in the chase barking. Someone burst into a roar of laughter, then gave a whistle; the dogs barked with even more noise and unanimity. Then a dog must have bitten Rothschild, as a desperate, sickly scream was heard.

Yakov went for a walk on the grazing ground, then wandered on at random in the outskirts of the town, while the street boys shouted:

"Here's Bronze! Here's Bronze!"

He came to the river, where the curlews floated in the air uttering shrill cries and the ducks quacked. The sun was blazing hot, and there was a glitter from the water, so that it hurt the eyes to look at it. Yakov walked by a path along the bank and saw a plump, rosy-cheeked lady come out of the bathing-shed, and thought about her: "Ugh! you otter!"

Not far from the bathing-shed boys were catching crayfish with bits of meat; seeing him, they began shouting spitefully, "Bronze! Bronze!" And then he saw an old spreading willow-tree with a big hollow in it, and a crow's nest on it. . . . And suddenly there rose up vividly in Yakov's memory a baby with flaxen hair, and the willow-tree Marfa had spoken of. Why, that is it, the same willow-tree—green, still, and sorrowful. . . . How old it has grown, poor thing!

He sat down under it and began to recall the past. On the other bank, where now there was the water meadow, in those days there stood a big birchwood, and yonder on the bare hillside that could be seen on the horizon an old, old pine forest used to be a bluish patch in the distance. Big boats used to sail on the river. But now it was all smooth and unruffled, and on the other bank there stood now only one birch-tree, youthful and slender like a young lady, and there was nothing on the river but ducks and geese, and it didn't look as though there had ever been boats on it. It seemed as though even the geese were fewer than of old. Yakov shut his eyes, and in his imagination huge flocks of white geese soared, meeting one another.

He wondered how it had happened that for the last forty or fifty years of his life he had never once been to the river, or if he had been by it he had not paid attention to it. Why, it was a decent sized river, not a trumpery one; he might have gone in for fishing and sold the fish to merchants, officials, and the bar-keeper at the station, and then have put money in the bank; he might have sailed in a boat from one house to another, playing the fiddle, and people of all classes would have paid to hear him; he might have tried getting big boats afloat again—that would be better than making coffins; he might have bred geese, killed them and sent them in the winter to Moscow. Why, the feathers alone would very likely mount up to ten roubles in the year. But he had wasted his time, he had done nothing of this. What losses! Ah! What losses! And if he had gone in for all those things at once—catching fish and playing the fiddle, and running boats and killing geese—what a fortune he would have made! But nothing of this had happened, even in his dreams; life had passed uselessly without any pleasure, had been wasted for nothing, not even a pinch of snuff; there was nothing left in front, and if one looked back—there was nothing there but losses, and such terrible ones, it made one cold all over. And why was it a man could not live so as to avoid these losses and misfortunes? One wondered why they had cut down the birch copse and the pine forest. Why was he walking with no reason on the grazing ground? Why do people always do what isn't needful? Why had Yakov all his life scolded, bellowed, shaken his fists, ill-treated his wife, and, one might ask, what necessity was there for him to frighten and insult the Jew that day? Why did people in general hinder each other from living? What losses were due to it! What terrible losses! If it were not for hatred and malice people would get immense benefit from one another.

In the evening and the night he had visions of the baby, of the willow, of fish, of slaughtered geese, and Marfa looking in profile like a bird that wants to drink, and the pale, pitiful face of Rothschild, and faces moved down from all sides and muttered of losses. He tossed from side to side, and got out of bed five times to play the fiddle.

In the morning he got up with an effort and went to the hospital. The same Maxim Nikolaitch told him to put a cold compress on his head, and gave him some powders, and from his tone and expression of face Yakov realized that it was a bad case and that no powders would be any use. As he went home afterwards, he reflected that death would be nothing but a benefit; he would not have to eat or drink, or pay taxes or offend people, and, as a man lies in his grave not for one year but for hundreds and thousands, if one reckoned it up the gain would be enormous. A man's life meant loss: death meant gain. This reflection was, of course, a just one, but yet it was bitter and mortifying; why was the order of the world so strange, that life, which is given to man only once, passes away without benefit?

He was not sorry to die, but at home, as soon as he saw his fiddle, it sent a pang to his heart and he felt sorry. He could not take the fiddle with him to the grave, and now it would be left forlorn, and the same thing would happen to it as to the birch copse and the pine forest. Everything in this world was wasted and would be wasted! Yakov went out of the hut and sat in the doorway, pressing the fiddle to his bosom. Thinking of his wasted, profitless life, he began to play, he did not know what, but it was plaintive and touching, and tears trickled down his cheeks. And the harder he thought, the more mournfully the fiddle wailed.

The latch clicked once and again, and Rothschild appeared at the gate. He walked across half the yard boldly, but seeing Yakov he stopped short, and seemed to shrink together, and probably from terror, began making signs with his hands as though he wanted to show on his fingers what o'clock it was.

"Come along, it's all right," said Yakov in a friendly tone, and he beckoned him to come up. "Come along!"

Looking at him mistrustfully and apprehensively, Rothschild began to advance, and stopped seven feet off.

"Be so good as not to beat me," he said, ducking. "Moisey Ilyitch has sent me again. 'Don't be afraid,' he said; 'go to Yakov again and tell him,' he said, 'we can't get on without him.' There is a wedding on Wednesday. . . . Ye—es! Mr. Shapovalov is marrying his daughter to a good man. . . . And it will be a grand wedding, oo-oo!" added the Jew, screwing up one eye.

"I can't come," said Yakov, breathing hard. "I'm ill, brother."

And he began playing again, and the tears gushed from his eyes on to the fiddle. Rothschild listened attentively, standing sideways to him and folding his arms on his chest. The scared and perplexed expression on his face, little by little, changed to a look of woe and suffering; he rolled his eyes as though he were experiencing an agonizing ecstasy, and articulated, "Vachhh!" and tears slowly ran down his cheeks and trickled on his greenish coat.

And Yakov lay in bed all the rest of the day grieving. In the evening, when the priest confessing him asked, Did he remember any special sin he had committed? straining his failing memory he thought again of Marfa's unhappy face, and the despairing shriek of the Jew when the dog bit him, and said, hardly audibly, "Give the fiddle to Rothschild."

"Very well," answered the priest.

And now everyone in the town asks where Rothschild got such a fine fiddle. Did he buy it or steal it? Or perhaps it had come to him as a pledge. He gave up the flute long ago, and now plays nothing but the fiddle. As plaintive sounds flow now from his bow, as came once from his flute, but when he tries to repeat what Yakov played, sitting in the doorway, the effect is something so sad and sorrowful that his audience weeps, and he himself rolls his eyes and articulates "Vachhh! . . ." And this new air was so much liked in the town that the merchants and officials used to be continually sending for Rothschild and making him play it over and over again a dozen times.

THE STUDENT

At first the weather was fine and still. The thrushes were calling, and in the swamps close by something alive droned pitifully with a sound like blowing into an empty bottle. A snipe flew by, and the shot aimed at it rang out with a gay, resounding note in the spring air. But when it began to get dark in the forest a cold, penetrating wind blew inappropriately from the east, and everything sank into silence. Needles of ice stretched across the pools, and it felt cheerless, remote, and lonely in the forest. There was a whiff of winter.

Ivan Velikopolsky, the son of a sacristan, and a student of the clerical academy, returning home from shooting, walked all the time by the path in the water-side meadow. His fingers were numb and his face was burning with the wind. It seemed to him that the cold that had suddenly come on had destroyed the order and harmony of things, that nature itself felt ill at ease, and that was why the evening darkness was falling more rapidly than usual. All around it was deserted and peculiarly gloomy. The only light was one gleaming in the widows' gardens near the river; the village, over three miles away, and everything in the distance all round was plunged in the cold evening mist. The student remembered that, as he went out from the house, his mother was sitting barefoot on the floor in the entry, cleaning the samovar, while his father lay on the stove coughing; as it was Good Friday nothing had been cooked, and the student was terribly hungry. And now, shrinking from the cold, he thought that just such a wind had blown in the days of Rurik and in the time of Ivan the Terrible* and Peter,† and in their time there had been just the same desperate poverty and hunger, the same thatched roofs with holes in them, ignorance, misery, the same desolation around, the same darkness, the same feeling of oppression—all these had existed, did exist, and would exist, and the lapse of a thousand years would make life no better. And he did not want to go home.

The gardens were called the widows' because they were kept by two widows, mother and daughter. A camp fire was burning brightly with a crackling sound, throwing out light far around on the ploughed earth. The widow Vasilisa, a tall, fat old woman in a man's coat, was standing by and looking thoughtfully into the fire; her daughter Lukerya, a little pock-marked woman with a stupid-looking face, was sitting on the ground, washing a caldron and spoons. Apparently they had just had supper. There was a sound of men's voices; it was the labourers watering their horses at the river.

"Here you have winter back again," said the student, going up to the camp fire. "Good evening."

Vasilisa started, but at once recognized him and smiled cordially.

"I did not know you; God bless you," she said. "You'll be rich."

They talked. Vasilisa, a woman of experience, who had been in service with the gentry, first as a wet-nurse, afterwards as a children's nurse, expressed herself with refinement, and a soft, sedate smile never left her face; her daughter Lukerya, a village peasant woman, who had been crushed by her husband, simply screwed up her eyes at the student and said nothing, and she had a strange expression like that of a deaf mute.

"At just such a fire the Apostle Peter warmed himself," said the student, stretching out his hands to the fire, "so it must have been cold then, too. Ah, what a terrible night it must have been, granny! An utterly dismal long night!"

He looked round at the darkness, shook his head abruptly and asked:

"No doubt you have been at the reading of the Twelve Gospels?"

---

*Ivan IV (1530–1584), the first Russian czar.

†Peter I, also known as Peter the Great (1672–1725), had a major role building the Russian empire.

"Yes, I have," answered Vasilisa.

"If you remember at the Last Supper Peter said to Jesus, 'I am ready to go with Thee into darkness and unto death.' And our Lord answered him thus: 'I say unto thee, Peter, before the cock croweth thou wilt have denied Me thrice.' After the supper Jesus went through the agony of death in the garden and prayed, and poor Peter was weary in spirit and faint, his eyelids were heavy and he could not struggle against sleep. He fell asleep. Then you heard how Judas the same night kissed Jesus and betrayed Him to His tormentors. They took Him bound to the high priest and beat Him, while Peter, exhausted, worn out with misery and alarm, hardly awake, you know, feeling that something awful was just going to happen on earth, followed behind. . . . He loved Jesus passionately, intensely, and now he saw from far off how He was beaten. . . ."

Lukerya left the spoons and fixed an immovable stare upon the student.

"They came to the high priest's," he went on; "they began to question Jesus, and meantime the labourers made a fire in the yard as it was cold, and warmed themselves. Peter, too, stood with them near the fire and warmed himself as I am doing. A woman, seeing him, said: 'He was with Jesus, too'—that is as much as to say that he, too, should be taken to be questioned. And all the labourers that were standing near the fire must have looked sourly and suspiciously at him, because he was confused and said: 'I don't know Him.' A little while after again someone recognized him as one of Jesus' disciples and said: 'Thou, too, art one of them,' but again he denied it. And for the third time someone turned to him: 'Why, did I not see thee with Him in the garden to-day?' For the third time he denied it. And immediately after that time the cock crowed, and Peter, looking from afar off at Jesus, remembered the words He had said to him in the evening. . . . He remembered, he came to himself, went out of the yard and wept bitterly—bitterly. In the Gospel it is written: 'He went out and wept bitterly.' I imagine it: the still, still, dark, dark garden, and in the stillness, faintly audible, smothered sobbing. . . ."

The student sighed and sank into thought. Still smiling, Vasilisa suddenly gave a gulp, big tears flowed freely down her cheeks, and she screened her face from the fire with her sleeve as though ashamed of her tears, and Lukerya, staring immovably at the student, flushed crimson, and her expression became strained and heavy like that of someone enduring intense pain.

The labourers came back from the river, and one of them riding a horse was quite near, and the light from the fire quivered upon him. The student said good-night to the widows and went on. And again the darkness was about him and his fingers began to be numb. A cruel wind was blowing, winter really had come back and it did not feel as though Easter would be the day after to-morrow.

Now the student was thinking about Vasilisa: since she had shed tears all that had happened to Peter the night before the Crucifixion must have some relation to her. . . .

He looked round. The solitary light was still gleaming in the darkness and no figures could be seen near it now. The student thought again that if Vasilisa had shed tears, and her daughter had been troubled, it was evident that what he had just been telling them about, which had happened nineteen centuries ago, had a relation to the present—to both women, to the desolate village, to himself, to all people. The old woman had wept, not because he could tell the story touchingly, but because Peter was near to her, because her whole being was interested in what was passing in Peter's soul.

And joy suddenly stirred in his soul, and he even stopped for a minute to take breath. "The past," he thought, "is linked with the present by an unbroken chain of events flowing one out of another." And it seemed to him that he had just seen both ends of that chain; that when he touched one end the other quivered.

When he crossed the river by the ferry boat and afterwards, mounting the hill, looked at his village and towards the west where the cold purple sunset lay a narrow streak of light, he thought that truth and beauty which had guided human life there in the garden and in the yard of the high priest had continued without interruption to this day, and had evidently always been the chief thing in human life and in all earthly life, indeed; and the feeling of youth, health, vigour—he was only twenty-two—and the inexpressible sweet expectation of happiness, of unknown mysterious happiness, took possession of him little by little, and life seemed to him enchanting, marvelous, and full of lofty meaning.

THE DARLING

Olenka, the daughter of the retired collegiate assessor, Plemyanniakov, was sitting in her back porch, lost in thought. It was hot, the flies were persistent and teasing, and it was pleasant to reflect that it would soon be evening. Dark rainclouds were gathering from the east, and bringing from time to time a breath of moisture in the air.

Kukin, who was the manager of an open-air theatre called the Tivoli, and who lived in the lodge, was standing in the middle of the garden looking at the sky.

"Again!" he observed despairingly. "It's going to rain again! Rain every day, as though to spite me! I might as well hang myself! It's ruin! Fearful losses every day."

He flung up his hands, and went on, addressing Olenka:

"There! that's the life we lead, Olga Semyonovna. It's enough to make one cry. One works and does one's utmost; one wears oneself out, getting no sleep at night, and racks one's brain what to do for the best. And then what happens? To begin with, one's public is ignorant, boorish. I give them the very best operetta, a dainty masque, first-rate music-hall artists. But do you suppose that's what they want! They don't understand anything of that sort. They want a clown; what they ask for is vulgarity. And then look at the weather! Almost every evening it rains. It started on the tenth of May, and it's kept it up all May and June. It's simply awful! The public doesn't come, but I've to pay the rent just the same, and pay the artists."

The next evening the clouds would gather again, and Kukin would say with an hysterical laugh:

"Well, rain away, then! Flood the garden, drown me! Damn my

luck in this world and the next! Let the artists have me up! Send me to prison!—to Siberia!—the scaffold! Ha, ha, ha!"

And next day the same thing.

Olenka listened to Kukin with silent gravity, and sometimes tears came into her eyes. In the end his misfortunes touched her; she grew to love him. He was a small thin man, with a yellow face, and curls combed forward on his forehead. He spoke in a thin tenor; as he talked his mouth worked on one side, and there was always an expression of despair on his face; yet he aroused a deep and genuine affection in her. She was always fond of someone, and could not exist without loving. In earlier days she had loved her papa, who now sat in a darkened room, breathing with difficulty; she had loved her aunt who used to come every other year from Bryansk;* and before that, when she was at school, she had loved her French master. She was a gentle, soft-hearted, compassionate girl, with mild, tender eyes and very good health. At the sight of her full rosy cheeks, her soft white neck with a little dark mole on it, and the kind, naïve smile, which came into her face when she listened to anything pleasant, men thought, "Yes, not half bad," and smiled too, while lady visitors could not refrain from seizing her hand in the middle of a conversation, exclaiming in a gush of delight, "You darling!"

The house in which she had lived from her birth upwards, and which was left her in her father's will, was at the extreme end of the town, not far from the Tivoli. In the evenings and at night she could hear the band playing, and the crackling and banging of fireworks, and it seemed to her that it was Kukin struggling with his destiny, storming the entrenchments of his chief foe, the indifferent public; there was a sweet thrill at her heart, she had no desire to sleep, and when he returned home at daybreak, she tapped softly at her bedroom window, and showing him only her face and one shoulder through the curtain, she gave him a friendly smile. . . .

He proposed to her, and they were married. And when he had a closer view of her neck and her plump, fine shoulders, he threw up his hands, and said:

"You darling!"

---

*Twelfth-century town 215 miles southwest of Moscow.

He was happy, but as it rained on the day and night of his wedding, his face still retained an expression of despair.

They got on very well together. She used to sit in his office, to look after things in the Tivoli, to put down the accounts and pay the wages. And her rosy cheeks, her sweet, naïve, radiant smile, were to be seen now at the office window, now in the refreshment bar or behind the scenes at the theatre. And already she used to say to her acquaintances that the theatre was the chief and most important thing in life, and that it was only through the drama that one could derive true enjoyment and become cultivated and humane.

"But do you suppose the public understands that?" she used to say. "What they want is a clown. Yesterday we gave 'Faust Inside Out,' and almost all the boxes were empty; but if Vanitchka and I had been producing some vulgar thing, I assure you the theatre would have been packed. To-morrow Vanitchka and I are doing 'Orpheus in Hell.'* Do come."

And what Kukin said about the theatre and the actors she repeated. Like him she despised the public for their ignorance and their indifference to art; she took part in the rehearsals, she corrected the actors, she kept an eye on the behaviour of the musicians, and when there was an unfavourable notice in the local paper, she shed tears, and then went to the editor's office to set things right.

The actors were fond of her and used to call her "Vanitchka and I," and "the darling"; she was sorry for them and used to lend them small sums of money, and if they deceived her, she used to shed a few tears in private, but did not complain to her husband.

They got on well in the winter too. They took the theatre in the town for the whole winter, and let it for short terms to a Little Russian company or to a conjurer, or to a local dramatic society. Olenka grew stouter, and was always beaming with satisfaction, while Kukin grew thinner and yellower, and continually complained of their terrible losses, although he had not done badly all the winter. He used to cough at night, and she used to give him hot raspberry tea or lime-flower water, to rub him with eau-de-cologne and to wrap him in her warm shawls.

**Orphée aux enfers* (1858), an operetta by Jacques Offenbach.

"You're such a sweet pet!" she used to say with perfect sincerity, stroking his hair. "You're such a pretty dear!"

Towards Lent he went to Moscow to collect a new troupe, and without him she could not sleep, but sat all night at her window, looking at the stars, and she compared herself with the hens, who are awake all night and uneasy when the cock is not in the hen-house. Kukin was detained in Moscow, and wrote that he would be back at Easter, adding some instructions about the Tivoli. But on the Sunday before Easter, late in the evening, came a sudden ominous knock at the gate; someone was hammering on the gate as though on a barrel—boom, boom, boom! The drowsy cook went flopping with her bare feet through the puddles, as she ran to open the gate.

"Please open," said someone outside in a thick bass. "There is a telegram for you."

Olenka had received telegrams from her husband before, but this time for some reason she felt numb with terror. With shaking hands she opened the telegram and read as follows:

"Ivan Petrovitch died suddenly to-day. Awaiting immate instructions fufuneral Tuesday."

That was how it was written in the telegram—"fufuneral," and the utterly incomprehensible word "immate." It was signed by the stage manager of the operatic company.

"My darling!" sobbed Olenka. "Vanitchka, my precious, my darling! Why did I ever meet you! Why did I know you and love you! Your poor heart-broken Olenka is all alone without you!"

Kukin's funeral took place on Tuesday in Moscow, Olenka returned home on Wednesday, and as soon as she got indoors she threw herself on her bed and sobbed so loudly that it could be heard next door, and in the street.

"Poor darling!" the neighbours said, as they crossed themselves. "Olga Semyonovna, poor darling! How she does take on!"

Three months later Olenka was coming home from mass, melancholy and in deep mourning. It happened that one of her neighbours, Vassily Andreitch Pustovalov, returning home from church, walked back beside her. He was the manager at Babakayev's, the timber merchant's. He wore a straw hat, a white waistcoat, and a gold watch-chain, and looked more like a country gentleman than a man in trade.

"Everything happens as it is ordained, Olga Semyonovna," he said gravely, with a sympathetic note in his voice; "and if any of our dear ones die, it must be because it is the will of God, so we ought to have fortitude and bear it submissively."

After seeing Olenka to her gate, he said good-bye and went on. All day afterwards she heard his sedately dignified voice, and whenever she shut her eyes she saw his dark beard. She liked him very much. And apparently she had made an impression on him too, for not long afterwards an elderly lady, with whom she was only slightly acquainted, came to drink coffee with her, and as soon as she was seated at table began to talk about Pustovalov, saying that he was an excellent man whom one could thoroughly depend upon, and that any girl would be glad to marry him. Three days later Pustovalov came himself. He did not stay long, only about ten minutes, and he did not say much, but when he left, Olenka loved him—loved him so much that she lay awake all night in a perfect fever, and in the morning she sent for the elderly lady. The match was quickly arranged, and then came the wedding.

Pustovalov and Olenka got on very well together when they were married.

Usually he sat in the office till dinner-time, then he went out on business, while Olenka took his place, and sat in the office till evening, making up accounts and booking orders.

"Timber gets dearer every year; the price rises twenty per cent.," she would say to her customers and friends. "Only fancy we used to sell local timber, and now Vassitchka always has to go for wood to the Mogilev* district. And the freight!" she would add, covering her cheeks with her hands in horror. "The freight!"

It seemed to her that she had been in the timber trade for ages and ages, and that the most important and necessary thing in life was timber; and there was something intimate and touching to her

---

*Mogilev is a thirteenth-century town in Byelorussia, some 110 miles east of Minsk; long variously ruled by Russia, Poland, and Sweden, it was annexed by Russia in 1772.

in the very sound of words such as "baulk," "post," "beam," "pole," "scantling," "batten," "lath," "plank," etc.

At night when she was asleep she dreamed of perfect mountains of planks and boards, and long strings of waggons, carting timber somewhere far away. She dreamed that a whole regiment of six-inch beams forty feet high, standing on end, was marching upon the timber-yard; that logs, beams, and boards knocked together with the resounding crash of dry wood, kept falling and getting up again, piling themselves on each other. Olenka cried out in her sleep, and Pustovalov said to her tenderly: "Olenka, what's the matter, darling? Cross yourself!"

Her husband's ideas were hers. If he thought the room was too hot, or that business was slack, she thought the same. Her husband did not care for entertainments, and on holidays he stayed at home. She did likewise.

"You are always at home or in the office," her friends said to her. "You should go to the theatre, darling, or to the circus."

"Vassitchka and I have no time to go to theatres," she would answer sedately. "We have no time for nonsense. What's the use of these theatres?"

On Saturdays Pustovalov and she used to go to the evening service; on holidays to early mass, and they walked side by side with softened faces as they came home from church. There was a pleasant fragrance about them both, and her silk dress rustled agreeably. At home they drank tea, with fancy bread and jams of various kinds, and afterwards they ate pie. Every day at twelve o'clock there was a savoury smell of beetroot soup and of mutton or duck in their yard, and on fast-days of fish, and no one could pass the gate without feeling hungry. In the office the samovar was always boiling, and customers were regaled with tea and cracknels. Once a week the couple went to the baths and returned side by side, both red in the face.

"Yes, we have nothing to complain of, thank God," Olenka used to say to her acquaintances. "I wish everyone were as well off as Vassitchka and I."

When Pustovalov went away to buy wood in the Mogilev district, she missed him dreadfully, lay awake and cried. A young veterinary surgeon in the army, called Smirnin, to whom they had let their lodge, used sometimes to come in in the evening. He used to talk to her and play cards with her, and this entertained her in her husband's absence. She was particularly interested in what he told her of his home life. He was married and had a little boy, but was separated from his wife because she had been unfaithful to him, and now he hated her and used to send her forty roubles a month for the maintenance of their son. And hearing of all this, Olenka sighed and shook her head. She was sorry for him.

"Well, God keep you," she used to say to him at parting, as she lighted him down the stairs with a candle. "Thank you for coming to cheer me up, and may the Mother of God give you health."

And she always expressed herself with the same sedateness and dignity, the same reasonableness, in imitation of her husband. As the veterinary surgeon was disappearing behind the door below, she would say:

"You know, Vladimir Platonitch, you'd better make it up with your wife. You should forgive her for the sake of your son. You may be sure the little fellow understands."

And when Pustovalov came back, she told him in a low voice about the veterinary surgeon and his unhappy home life, and both sighed and shook their heads and talked about the boy, who, no doubt, missed his father, and by some strange connection of ideas, they went up to the holy ikons, bowed to the ground before them and prayed that God would give them children.

And so the Pustovalovs lived for six years quietly and peaceably in love and complete harmony.

But behold! one winter day after drinking hot tea in the office, Vassily Andreitch went out into the yard without his cap on to see about sending off some timber, caught cold and was taken ill. He had the best doctors, but he grew worse and died after four months' illness. And Olenka was a widow once more.

"I've nobody, now you've left me, my darling," she sobbed, after her husband's funeral. "How can I live without you, in wretchedness and misery! Pity me, good people, all alone in the world!"

She went about dressed in black with long "weepers," and gave up wearing hat and gloves for good. She hardly ever went out, except to church, or to her husband's grave, and led the life of a nun. It was not till six months later that she took off the weepers and opened the shutters of the windows. She was sometimes seen in the mornings, going with her cook to market for provisions, but what went on in her house and how she lived now could only be surmised. People guessed, from seeing her drinking tea in her garden with the veterinary surgeon, who read the newspaper aloud to her, and from the fact that, meeting a lady she knew at the post-office, she said to her:

"There is no proper veterinary inspection in our town, and that's the cause of all sorts of epidemics. One is always hearing of people's getting infection from the milk supply, or catching diseases from horses and cows. The health of domestic animals ought to be as well cared for as the health of human beings."

She repeated the veterinary surgeon's words, and was of the same opinion as he about everything. It was evident that she could not live a year without some attachment, and had found new happiness in the lodge. In anyone else this would have been censured, but no one could think ill of Olenka; everything she did was so natural. Neither she nor the veterinary surgeon said anything to other people of the change in their relations, and tried, indeed, to conceal it, but without success, for Olenka could not keep a secret. When he had visitors, men serving in his regiment, and she poured out tea or served the supper, she would begin talking of the cattle plague, of the foot and mouth disease, and of the municipal slaughter-houses. He was dreadfully embarrassed, and when the guests had gone, he would seize her by the hand and hiss angrily:

"I've asked you before not to talk about what you don't understand. When we veterinary surgeons are talking among ourselves, please don't put your word in. It's really annoying."

And she would look at him with astonishment and dismay, and ask him in alarm: "But, Voloditchka, what *am* I to talk about?"

And with tears in her eyes she would embrace him, begging him not to be angry, and they were both happy.

But this happiness did not last long. The veterinary surgeon departed, departed for ever with his regiment, when it was transferred to a distant place—to Siberia, it may be. And Olenka was left alone.

Now she was absolutely alone. Her father had long been dead, and his arm-chair lay in the attic, covered with dust and lame of one leg. She got thinner and plainer, and when people met her in the street they did not look at her as they used to, and did not smile to her; evidently her best years were over and left behind, and now a new sort of life had begun for her, which did not bear thinking about. In the evening Olenka sat in the porch, and heard the band playing and the fireworks popping in the Tivoli, but now the sound stirred no response. She looked into her yard without interest, thought of nothing, wished for nothing, and afterwards when night came on she went to bed and dreamed of her empty yard. She ate and drank as it were unwillingly.

And what was worst of all, she had no opinions of any sort. She saw the objects about her and understood what she saw, but could not form any opinion about them, and did not know what to talk about. And how awful it is not to have any opinions! One sees a bottle, for instance, or the rain, or a peasant driving in his cart, but what the bottle is for, or the rain, or the peasant, and what is the meaning of it, one can't say, and could not even for a thousand roubles. When she had Kukin, or Pustovalov, or the veterinary surgeon, Olenka could explain everything, and give her opinion about anything you like, but now there was the same emptiness in her brain and in her heart as there was in her yard outside. And it was as harsh and as bitter as wormwood in the mouth.

Little by little the town grew in all directions. The road became a street, and where the Tivoli and the timber-yard had been, there were new turnings and houses. How rapidly time passes! Olenka's house grew dingy, the roof got rusty, the shed sank on one side, and the whole yard was overgrown with docks and stinging-nettles. Olenka herself had grown plain and elderly; in summer she sat in the porch, and her soul, as before, was empty and dreary and full of bitterness. In winter she sat at her window and looked at the snow. When she caught the scent of spring, or heard the chime of the church bells, a sudden rush of memories from the past came over her, there was a tender ache in her heart, and her eyes brimmed over with tears; but this was only for a minute, and then came emptiness again and the sense of the futility of life. The black kitten, Briska, rubbed against her and purred softly, but Olenka was not touched by these feline caresses. That was not what she needed. She wanted a love that would absorb her whole being, her whole soul and reason—that would give her ideas and an object in life, and would warm her old blood. And she would shake the kitten off her skirt and say with vexation:

"Get along; I don't want you!"

And so it was, day after day and year after year, and no joy, and no opinions. Whatever Mavra, the cook, said she accepted.

One hot July day, towards evening, just as the cattle were being driven by, and the whole yard was full of dust, someone suddenly knocked at the gate. Olenka went to open it herself and was dumbfounded when she looked out: she saw Smirnin, the veterinary surgeon, grey-headed, and dressed as a civilian. She suddenly remembered everything. She could not help crying and letting her head fall on his breast without uttering a word, and in the violence of her feeling she did not notice how they both walked into the house and sat down to tea.

"My dear Vladimir Platonitch! What fate has brought you?" she muttered, trembling with joy.

"I want to settle here for good, Olga Semyonovna," he told her. "I have resigned my post, and have come to settle down and try my luck on my own account. Besides, it's time for my boy to go to school. He's a big boy. I am reconciled with my wife, you know."

"Where is she?" asked Olenka.

"She's at the hotel with the boy, and I'm looking for lodgings."

"Good gracious, my dear soul! Lodgings! Why not have my house? Why shouldn't that suit you? Why, my goodness, I wouldn't take any rent!" cried Olenka in a flutter, beginning to cry again. "You live here, and the lodge will do nicely for me. Oh dear! how glad I am!"

Next day the roof was painted and the walls were whitewashed, and Olenka, with her arms akimbo, walked about the yard giving directions. Her face was beaming with her old smile, and she was brisk and alert as though she had waked from a long sleep. The veterinary's wife arrived—a thin, plain lady, with short hair and a peevish expression. With her was her little Sasha, a boy of ten, small for his age, blue-eyed, chubby, with dimples in his cheeks. And scarcely had the boy walked into the yard when he ran after the cat, and at once there was the sound of his gay, joyous laugh.

"Is that your puss, auntie?" he asked Olenka. "When she has little ones, do give us a kitten. Mamma is awfully afraid of mice."

Olenka talked to him, and gave him tea. Her heart warmed and there was a sweet ache in her bosom, as though the boy had been her own child. And when he sat at the table in the evening, going over his lessons, she looked at him with deep tenderness and pity as she murmured to herself:

"You pretty pet! . . . my precious! . . . Such a fair little thing, and so clever."

"An island is a piece of land which is entirely surrounded by water," he read aloud.

"An island is a piece of land," she repeated, and this was the first opinion to which she gave utterance with positive conviction after so many years of silence and dearth of ideas.

Now she had opinions of her own, and at supper she talked to Sasha's parents, saying how difficult the lessons were at the high schools, but that yet the high school was better than a commercial one, since with a high school education all careers were open to one, such as being a doctor or an engineer.

Sasha began going to the high school. His mother departed to Harkov* to her sister's and did not return; his father used to go off every day to inspect cattle, and would often be away from home for three days together, and it seemed to Olenka as though Sasha was entirely abandoned, that he was not wanted at home, that he was being starved, and she carried him off to her lodge and gave him a little room there.

And for six months Sasha had lived in the lodge with her. Every morning Olenka came into his bedroom and found him fast asleep, sleeping noiselessly with his hand under his cheek. She was sorry to wake him.

"Sashenka," she would say mournfully, "get up, darling. It's time for school."

He would get up, dress and say his prayers, and then sit down to breakfast, drink three glasses of tea, and eat two large cracknels and half a buttered roll. All this time he was hardly awake and a little ill-humoured in consequence.

---

*Mid-seventeenth century city, 400 miles south of Moscow; in mid-eighteenth century, capital of the Ukraine; later superseded by Kiev.

"You don't quite know your fable, Sashenka," Olenka would say, looking at him as though he were about to set off on a long journey. "What a lot of trouble I have with you! You must work and do your best, darling, and obey your teachers."

"Oh, do leave me alone!" Sasha would say.

Then he would go down the street to school, a little figure, wearing a big cap and carrying a satchel on his shoulder. Olenka would follow him noiselessly.

"Sashenka!" she would call after him, and she would pop into his hand a date or a caramel. When he reached the street where the school was, he would feel ashamed of being followed by a tall, stout woman; he would turn round and say:

"You'd better go home, auntie. I can go the rest of the way alone."

She would stand still and look after him fixedly till he had disappeared at the school-gate.

Ah, how she loved him! Of her former attachments not one had been so deep; never had her soul surrendered to any feeling so spontaneously, so disinterestedly, and so joyously as now that her maternal instincts were aroused. For this little boy with the dimple in his cheek and the big school cap, she would have given her whole life, she would have given it with joy and tears of tenderness. Why? Who can tell why?

When she had seen the last of Sasha, she returned home, contented and serene, brimming over with love; her face, which had grown younger during the last six months, smiled and beamed; people meeting her looked at her with pleasure.

"Good morning,Olga Semyonovna, darling. How are you, darling?"

"The lessons at the high school are very difficult now," she would relate at the market. "It's too much; in the first class yesterday they gave him a fable to learn by heart, and a Latin translation and a problem. You know it's too much for a little chap."

And she would begin talking about the teachers, the lessons, and the school books, saying just what Sasha said.

At three o'clock they had dinner together: in the evening they learned their lessons together and cried. When she put him to bed, she would stay a long time making the cross over him and murmuring a prayer; then she would go to bed and dream of that far-away misty future when Sasha would finish his studies and become a doctor or an engineer, would have a big house of his own with horses and a carriage, would get married and have children. . . . She would fall asleep still thinking of the same thing, and tears would run down her cheeks from her closed eyes, while the black cat lay purring beside her: "Mrr, mrr, mrr."

Suddenly there would come a loud knock at the gate.

Olenka would wake up breathless with alarm, her heart throbbing. Half a minute later would come another knock.

"It must be a telegram from Harkov," she would think, beginning to tremble from head to foot. "Sasha's mother is sending for him from Harkov. . . . Oh, mercy on us!"

She was in despair. Her head, her hands, and her feet would turn chill, and she would feel that she was the most unhappy woman in the world. But another minute would pass, voices would be heard: it would turn out to be the veterinary surgeon coming home from the club.

"Well, thank God!" she would think.

And gradually the load in her heart would pass off, and she would feel at ease. She would go back to bed thinking of Sasha, who lay sound asleep in the next room, sometimes crying out in his sleep:

"I'll give it to you! Get away! Shut up!"

A DOCTOR'S VISIT

The Professor received a telegram from the Lyalikovs' factory; he was asked to come as quickly as possible. The daughter of some Madame Lyalikov, apparently the owner of the factory, was ill, and that was all that one could make out of the long, incoherent telegram. And the Professor did not go himself, but sent instead his assistant, Korolyov.

It was two stations from Moscow, and there was a drive of three miles from the station. A carriage with three horses had been sent to the station to meet Korolyov; the coachman wore a hat with a peacock's feather on it, and answered every question in a loud voice like a soldier: "No, sir!" "Certainly, sir!"

It was Saturday evening; the sun was setting, the workpeople were coming in crowds from the factory to the station, and they bowed to the carriage in which Korolyov was driving. And he was charmed with the evening, the farmhouses and villas on the road, and the birch-trees, and the quiet atmosphere all around, when the fields and woods and the sun seemed preparing, like the workpeople now on the eve of the holiday, to rest, and perhaps to pray. . . .

He was born and had grown up in Moscow; he did not know the country, and he had never taken any interest in factories, or been inside one, but he had happened to read about factories, and had been in the houses of manufacturers and had talked to them; and whenever he saw a factory far or near, he always thought how quiet and peaceable it was outside, but within there was always sure to be impenetrable ignorance and dull egoism on the side of the owners, wearisome, unhealthy toil on the side of the workpeople, squabbling, vermin, vodka. And now when the workpeople timidly and respectfully made way for the carriage, in their faces, their caps, their walk, he read physical impurity, drunkenness, nervous exhaustion, bewilderment.

They drove in at the factory gates. On each side he caught glimpses of the little houses of workpeople, of the faces of women, of quilts and linens on the railings. "Look out!" shouted the coachman, not pulling up the horses. It was a wide courtyard without grass, with five immense blocks of buildings with tall chimneys a little distance one from another, warehouses and barracks, and over everything a sort of grey powder as though from dust. Here and there, like oases in the desert, there were pitiful gardens, and the green and red roofs of the houses in which the managers and clerks lived. The coachman suddenly pulled up the horses, and the carriage stopped at the house, which had been newly painted grey; here was a flower garden, with a lilac bush covered with dust, and on the yellow steps at the front door there was a strong smell of paint.

"Please come in, doctor," said women's voices in the passage and the entry, and at the same time he heard sighs and whisperings. "Pray walk in. . . . We've been expecting you so long . . . we're in real trouble. Here, this way."

Madame Lyalikov—a stout elderly lady wearing a black silk dress with fashionable sleeves, but, judging from her face, a simple uneducated woman—looked at the doctor in a flutter, and could not bring herself to hold out her hand to him; she did not dare. Beside her stood a personage with short hair and a pince-nez; she was wearing a blouse of many colours, and was very thin and no longer young. The servants called her Christina Dmitryevna, and Korolyov guessed that this was the governess. Probably, as the person of most education in the house, she had been charged to meet and receive the doctor, for she began immediately, in great haste, stating the causes of the illness, giving trivial and tiresome details, but without saying who was ill or what was the matter.

The doctor and the governess were sitting talking while the lady of the house stood motionless at the door, waiting. From the conversation Korolyov learned that the patient was Madame Lyalikov's only daughter and heiress, a girl of twenty, called Liza; she had been ill for a long time, and had consulted various doctors, and the previous night she had suffered till morning from such violent palpitations of the heart, that no one in the house had slept, and they had been afraid she might die.

"She has been, one may say, ailing from a child," said Christina Dmitryevna in a sing-song voice, continually wiping her lips with her hand. "The doctors say it is nerves; when she was a little girl she was scrofulous, and the doctors drove it inwards, so I think it may be due to that."

They went to see the invalid. Fully grown up, big and tall, but ugly like her mother, with the same little eyes and disproportionate breadth of the lower part of the face, lying with her hair in disorder, muffled up to the chin, she made upon Korolyov at the first minute the impression of a poor, destitute creature, sheltered and cared for here out of charity, and he could hardly believe that this was the heiress of the five huge buildings.

"I am the doctor come to see you," said Korolyov. "Good evening."

He mentioned his name and pressed her hand, a large, cold, ugly hand; she sat up, and, evidently accustomed to doctors, let herself be sounded, without showing the least concern that her shoulders and chest were uncovered.

"I have palpitations of the heart," she said, "It was so awful all night. . . . I almost died of fright! Do give me something."

"I will, I will; don't worry yourself."

Korolyov examined her and shrugged his shoulders.

"The heart is all right," he said; "it's all going on satisfactorily; everything is in good order. Your nerves must have been playing pranks a little, but that's so common. The attack is over by now, one must suppose; lie down and go to sleep."

At that moment a lamp was brought into the bedroom. The patient screwed up her eyes at the light, then suddenly put her hands to her head and broke into sobs. And the impression of a destitute, ugly creature vanished, and Korolyov no longer noticed the little eyes or the heavy development of the lower part of the face. He saw a soft, suffering expression which was intelligent and touching: she seemed to him altogether graceful, feminine, and simple; and he longed to soothe her, not with drugs, not with advice, but with simple, kindly words. Her mother put her arms round her head and hugged her. What despair, what grief was in the old woman's face! She, her mother, had reared her and brought her up, spared nothing, and devoted her whole life to having her daughter taught French, dancing, music: had engaged a dozen teachers for her; had consulted the best doctors, kept a governess. And now she could not make out the reason of these tears, why there was all this misery, she could not understand, and was bewildered; and she had a guilty, agitated, despairing expression, as though she had omitted something very important, had left something undone, had neglected to call in somebody—and whom, she did not know.

"Lizanka, you are crying again . . . again," she said, hugging her daughter to her. "My own, my darling, my child, tell me what it is! Have pity on me! Tell me."

Both wept bitterly. Korolyov sat down on the side of the bed and took Liza's hand.

"Come, give over; it's no use crying," he said kindly. "Why, there is nothing in the world that is worth those tears. Come, we won't cry; that's no good. . . ."

And inwardly he thought:

"It's high time she was married. . . ."

"Our doctor at the factory gave her kalibromati," said the governess, "but I notice it only makes her worse. I should have thought that if she is given anything for the heart it ought to be drops. . . . I forget the name. . . . Convallaria, isn't it?"

And there followed all sorts of details. She interrupted the doctor, preventing his speaking, and there was a look of effort on her face, as though she supposed that, as the woman of most education in the house, she was duty bound to keep up a conversation with the doctor, and on no other subject but medicine.

Korolyov felt bored.

"I find nothing special the matter," he said, addressing the mother as he went out of the bedroom. "If your daughter is being attended by the factory doctor, let him go on attending her. The treatment so far has been perfectly correct, and I see no reason for changing your doctor. Why change? It's such an ordinary trouble; there's nothing seriously wrong."

He spoke deliberately as he put on his gloves, while Madame Lyalikov stood without moving, and looked at him with her tearful eyes.

"I have half an hour to catch the ten o'clock train," he said. "I hope I am not too late."

"And can't you stay?" she asked, and tears trickled down her cheeks again. "I am ashamed to trouble you, but if you would be so good. . . . For God's sake," she went on in an undertone, glancing towards the door, "do stay to-night with us! She is all I have . . . my only daughter. . . . She frightened me last night; I can't get over it. . . . Don't go away, for goodness' sake! . . ."

He wanted to tell her that he had a great deal of work in Moscow, that his family were expecting him home; it was disagreeable to him to spend the evening and the whole night in a strange house quite needlessly; but he looked at her face, heaved a sigh, and began taking off his gloves without a word.

All the lamps and candles were lighted in his honour in the drawing-room and the dining-room. He sat down at the piano and began turning over the music. Then he looked at the pictures on the walls, at the portraits. The pictures, oil-paintings in gold frames, were views of the Crimea—a stormy sea with a ship, a Catholic monk with a wineglass; they were all dull, smooth daubs, with no trace of talent in them. There was not a single good-looking face among the portraits, nothing but broad cheekbones and astonished-looking eyes. Lyalikov, Liza's father, had a low forehead and a self-satisfied expression; his uniform sat like a sack on his bulky plebeian figure; on his breast was a medal and a Red Cross Badge. There was little sign of culture, and the luxury was senseless and haphazard, and was as ill fitting as that uniform. The floors irritated him with their brilliant polish, the lustres on the chandelier irritated him, and he was reminded for some reason of the story of the merchant who used to go to the baths with a medal on his neck. . . .

He heard a whispering in the entry; some one was softly snoring. And suddenly from outside came harsh, abrupt, metallic sounds, such as Korolyov had never heard before, and which he did not understand now; they roused strange, unpleasant echoes in his soul.

"I believe nothing would induce me to remain here to live . . ." he thought, and went back to the music-books again.

"Doctor, please come to supper!" the governess called him in a low voice.

He went into supper. The table was large and laid with a vast number of dishes and wines, but there were only two to supper: himself and Christina Dmitryevna. She drank Madeira,* ate rapidly, and talked, looking at him through her pince-nez:

"Our workpeople are very contented. We have performances at the factory every winter; the workpeople act themselves. They have lectures with a magic lantern, a splendid tea-room, and everything they want. They are very much attached to us, and when they heard that Lizanka was worse they had a service sung for her. Though they have no education, they have their feelings, too."

"It looks as though you have no man in the house at all," said Korolyov.

"Not one. Pyotr Nikantoritch died a year and a half ago, and left us alone. And so there are the three of us. In the summer we live here, and in winter we live in Moscow, in Polianka. I have been living with them for eleven years—as one of the family."

At supper they served sterlet, chicken rissoles, and stewed fruit; the wines were expensive French wines.

"Please don't stand on ceremony, doctor," said Christina Dmitryevna, eating and wiping her mouth with her fist, and it was evident she found her life here exceedingly pleasant. "Please have some more."

After supper the doctor was shown to his room, where a bed had been made up for him, but he did not feel sleepy. The room was stuffy and it smelt of paint; he put on his coat and went out.

It was cool in the open air; there was already a glimmer of dawn, and all the five blocks of buildings, with their tall chimneys, barracks, and warehouses, were distinctly outlined against the damp air. As it was a holiday, they were not working, and the windows were dark, and in only one of the buildings was there a furnace burning; two windows were crimson, and fire mixed with smoke came from time to time from the chimney. Far away beyond the yard the frogs were croaking and the nightingales singing.

Looking at the factory buildings and the barracks, where the workpeople were asleep, he thought again what he always thought when he saw a factory. They may have performances for the

---

*Wine from the Portuguese island of Madeira.

workpeople, magic lanterns, factory doctors, and improvements of all sorts, but, all the same, the workpeople he had met that day on his way from the station did not look in any way different from those he had known long ago in his childhood, before there were factory performances and improvements. As a doctor accustomed to judging correctly of chronic complaints, the radical cause of which was incomprehensible and incurable, he looked upon factories as something baffling, the cause of which also was obscure and not removable, and all the improvements in the life of the factory hands he looked upon not as superfluous, but as comparable with the treatment of incurable illnesses.

"There is something baffling in it, of course . . ." he thought, looking at the crimson windows. "Fifteen hundred or two thousand workpeople are working without rest in unhealthy surroundings, making bad cotton goods, living on the verge of starvation, and only waking from this nightmare at rare intervals in the tavern; a hundred people act as overseers, and the whole life of that hundred is spent in imposing fines, in abuse, in injustice, and only two or three so-called owners enjoy the profits, though they don't work at all, and despise the wretched cotton. But what are the profits, and how do they enjoy them? Madame Lyalikov and her daughter are unhappy—it makes one wretched to look at them; the only one who enjoys her life is Christina Dmitryevna, a stupid, middle-aged maiden lady in pince-nez. And so it appears that all these five blocks of buildings are at work, and inferior cotton is sold in the Eastern markets, simply that Christina Dmitryevna may eat sterlet and drink Madeira."

Suddenly there came a strange noise, the same sound Korolyov had heard before supper. Some one was striking a sheet of metal near one of the buildings; he struck a note, and then at once checked the vibrations, so that short, abrupt, discordant sounds were produced, rather like "Dair . . . dair . . . dair. . . ." Then there was half a minute of stillness, and from another building there came sounds equally abrupt and unpleasant, lower bass notes: "Drin . . . drin . . . drin. . . ." Eleven times. Evidently it was the watchman striking the hour.

Near the third building he heard: "Zhuk . . . zhuk . . . zhuk. . . ." And so near all the buildings, and then behind the barracks and beyond the gates. And in the stillness of the night it seemed as though these sounds were uttered by a monster with crimson eyes—the devil himself, who controlled the owners and the work-people alike, and was deceiving both.

Korolyov went out of the yard into the open country.

"Who goes there?" some one called to him at the gates in an abrupt voice.

"It's just like being in prison," he thought, and made no answer.

Here the nightingales and the frogs could be heard more distinctly, and one could feel it was a night in May. From the station came the noise of a train; somewhere in the distance drowsy cocks were crowing; but, all the same, the night was still, the world was sleeping tranquilly. In a field not far from the factory there could be seen the framework of a house and heaps of building materials: Korolyov sat down on the planks and went on thinking.

"The only person who feels happy here is the governess, and the factory hands are working for her gratification. But that's only apparent: she is only the figurehead. The real person, for whom everything is being done, is the devil."

And he thought about the devil, in whom he did not believe, and he looked round at the two windows where the fires were gleaming. It seemed to him that out of those crimson eyes the devil himself was looking at him—that unknown force that had created the mutual relation of the strong and the weak, that coarse blunder which one could never correct. The strong must hinder the weak from living—such was the law of Nature; but only in a newspaper article or in a school book was that intelligible and easily accepted. In the hotchpotch which was everyday life, in the tangle of trivialities out of which human relations were woven, it was no longer a law, but a logical absurdity, when the strong and the weak were both equally victims of their mutual relations, unwillingly submitting to some directing force, unknown, standing outside life, apart from man.

So thought Korolyov, sitting on the planks, and little by little he was possessed by a feeling that this unknown and mysterious force was really close by and looking at him. Meanwhile the east was growing paler, time passed rapidly; when there was not a soul anywhere near, as though everything were dead, the five buildings and their chimneys against the grey background of the dawn had a peculiar look—not the same as by day; one forgot altogether that inside there were steam motors, electricity, telephones, and kept thinking of lake-dwellings, of the Stone Age, feeling the presence of a crude, unconscious force. . . .

And again there came the sound: "Dair . . . dair . . . dair . . . dair . . ." twelve times. Then there was stillness, stillness for half a minute, and at the other end of the yard there rang out.

"Drin . . . drin . . . drin. . . ."

"Horribly disagreeable," thought Korolyov.

"Zhuk . . . zhuk . . ." there resounded from a third place, abruptly, sharply, as though with annoyance—"Zhuk . . . zhuk. . . ."

And it took four minutes to strike twelve. Then there was a hush; and again it seemed as though everything were dead.

Korolyov sat a little longer, then went to the house, but sat up for a good while longer. In the adjoining rooms there was whispering, there was a sound of shuffling slippers and bare feet.

"Is she having another attack?" thought Korolyov.

He went out to have a look at the patient. By now it was quite light in the rooms, and a faint glimmer of sunlight, piercing through the morning mist, quivered on the floor and on the wall of the drawing-room. The door of Liza's room was open, and she was sitting in a low chair beside her bed, with her hair down, wearing a dressing-gown and wrapped in a shawl. The blinds were down on the windows.

"How do you feel?" asked Korolyov.

"Thank you."

He touched her pulse, then straightened her hair, that had fallen over her forehead.

"You are not asleep," he said. "It's beautiful weather outside. It's spring. The nightingales are singing, and you sit in the dark and think of something."

She listened and looked into his face; her eyes were sorrowful and intelligent, and it was evident she wanted to say something to him.

"Does this happen to you often?" he said.

She moved her lips, and answered:

"Often, I feel wretched almost every night."

At that moment the watchman in the yard began striking two o'clock. They heard: "Dair . . . dair . . ." and she shuddered.

"Do those knockings worry you?" he asked.

"I don't know. Everything here worries me," she answered, and pondered. "Everything worries me. I hear sympathy in your voice; it seemed to me as soon as I saw you that I could tell you all about it."

"Tell me, I beg you."

"I want to tell you of my opinion. It seems to me that I have no illness, but that I am weary and frightened, because it is bound to be so and cannot be otherwise. Even the healthiest person can't help being uneasy if, for instance, a robber is moving about under his window. I am constantly being doctored," she went on, looking at her knees, and she gave a shy smile. "I am very grateful, of course, and I do not deny that the treatment is a benefit; but I should like to talk, not with a doctor, but with some intimate friend who would understand me and would convince me that I was right or wrong."

"Have you no friends?" asked Korolyov.

"I am lonely. I have a mother; I love her, but, all the same, I am lonely. That's how it happens to be. . . . Lonely people read a great deal, but say little and hear little. Life for them is mysterious; they are mystics and often see the devil where he is not. Lermontov's Tamara was lonely and she saw the devil."

"Do you read a great deal?"

"Yes. You see, my whole time is free from morning till night. I read by day, and by night my head is empty; instead of thoughts there are shadows in it."

"Do you see anything at night?" asked Korolyov.

"No, but I feel. . . ."

She smiled again, raised her eyes to the doctor, and looked at him so sorrowfully, so intelligently; and it seemed to him that she trusted him, and that she wanted to speak frankly to him, and that she thought the same as he did. But she was silent, perhaps waiting for him to speak.

And he knew what to say to her. It was clear to him that she needed as quickly as possible to give up the five buildings and the million if she had it—to leave the devil that looked out at night; it was clear to him, too, that she thought so herself, and was only waiting for some one she trusted to confirm her.

But he did not know how to say it. How? One is shy of asking men under sentence what they have been sentenced for; and in the same way it is awkward to ask very rich people what they want so much money for, why they make such a poor use of their wealth, why they don't give it up, even when they see in it their unhappiness; and if they begin a conversation about it themselves, it is usually embarrassing, awkward, and long.

"How is one to say it?" Korolyov wondered. "And is it necessary to speak?"

And he said what he meant in a roundabout way:

"You in the position of a factory owner and a wealthy heiress are dissatisfied; you don't believe in your right to it; and here now you can't sleep. That, of course, is better than if you were satisfied, slept soundly, and thought everything was satisfactory. Your sleeplessness does you credit; in any case, it is a good sign. In reality, such a conversation as this between us now would have been unthinkable for our parents. At night they did not talk, but slept sound; we, our generation, sleep badly, are restless, but talk a great deal, and are always trying to settle whether we are right or not. For our children or grandchildren that question—whether they are right or not—will have been settled. Things will be clearer for them than for us. Life will be good in fifty years' time; it's only a pity we shall not last out till then. It would be interesting to have a peep at it."

"What will our children and grandchildren do?" asked Liza.

"I don't know. . . . I suppose they will throw it all up and go away."

"Go where?"

"Where? . . . Why, where they like," said Korolyov; and he laughed. "There are lots of places a good, intelligent person can go to."

He glanced at his watch.

"The sun has risen, though," he said. "It is time you were asleep. Undress and sleep soundly. Very glad to have made your acquaintance," he went on, pressing her hand. "You are a good, interesting woman. Good-night!"

He went to his room and went to bed.

In the morning when the carriage was brought round they all came out on to the steps to see him off. Liza, pale and exhausted, was in a white dress as though for a holiday, with a flower in her hair; she looked at him, as yesterday, sorrowfully and intelligently, smiled and talked, and all with an expression as though she wanted to tell him something special, important—him alone. They could hear the larks trilling and the church bells pealing. The windows in the factory buildings were sparkling gaily, and, driving across the yard and afterwards along the road to the station, Korolyov thought neither of the workpeople nor of lake dwellings, nor of the devil, but thought of the time, perhaps close at hand, when life would be as bright and joyous as that still Sunday morning; and he thought how pleasant it was on such a morning in the spring to drive with three horses in a good carriage, and to bask in the sunshine.

GOOSEBERRIES

The whole sky had been overcast with rain-clouds from early morning; it was a still day, not hot, but heavy, as it is in grey dull weather when the clouds have been hanging over the country for a long while, when one expects rain and it does not come. Ivan Ivanovitch, the veterinary surgeon, and Burkin, the high-school teacher, were already tired from walking, and the fields seemed to them endless. Far ahead of them they could just see the windmills of the village of Mironositskoe; on the right stretched a row of hillocks which disappeared in the distance behind the village, and they both knew that this was the bank of the river, that there were meadows, green willows, homesteads there, and that if one stood on one of the hillocks one could see from it the same vast plain, telegraph-wires, and a train which in the distance looked like a crawling caterpillar, and that in clear weather one could even see the town. Now, in still weather, when all nature seemed mild and dreamy, Ivan Ivanovitch and Burkin were filled with love of that countryside, and both thought how great, how beautiful a land it was.

"Last time we were in Prokofy's barn," said Burkin, "you were about to tell me a story."

"Yes; I meant to tell you about my brother."

Ivan Ivanovitch heaved a deep sigh and lighted a pipe to begin to tell his story, but just at that moment the rain began. And five minutes later heavy rain came down, covering the sky, and it was hard to tell when it would be over. Ivan Ivanovitch and Burkin stopped in hesitation; the dogs, already drenched, stood with their tails between their legs gazing at them feelingly.

"We must take shelter somewhere," said Burkin. "Let us go to Alehin's; it's close by."

"Come along."

They turned aside and walked through mown fields, sometimes going straight forward, sometimes turning to the right, till they came out on the road. Soon they saw poplars, a garden, then the red roofs of barns; there was a gleam of the river, and the view opened on to a broad expanse of water with a windmill and a white bath-house: this was Sofino, where Alehin lived.

The watermill was at work, drowning the sound of the rain; the dam was shaking. Here wet horses with drooping heads were standing near their carts, and men were walking about covered with sacks. It was damp, muddy, and desolate; the water looked cold and malignant. Ivan Ivanovitch and Burkin were already conscious of a feeling of wetness, messiness, and discomfort all over, their feet were heavy with mud, and when, crossing the dam, they went up to the barns, they were silent, as though they were angry with one another.

In one of the barns there was the sound of a winnowing machine, the door was open, and clouds of dust were coming from it. In the doorway was standing Alehin himself, a man of forty, tall and stout, with long hair, more like a professor or an artist than a landowner. He had on a white shirt that badly needed washing, a rope for a belt, drawers instead of trousers, and his boots, too, were plastered up with mud and straw. His eyes and nose were black with dust. He recognized Ivan Ivanovitch and Burkin, and was apparently much delighted to see them.

"Go into the house, gentlemen," he said, smiling; "I'll come directly, this minute."

It was a big two-storeyed house. Alehin lived in the lower storey, with arched ceilings and little windows, where the bailiffs had once lived; here everything was plain, and there was a smell of rye bread, cheap vodka, and harness. He went upstairs into the best rooms only on rare occasions, when visitors came. Ivan Ivanovitch and Burkin were met in the house by a maid-servant, a young woman so beautiful that they both stood still and looked at one another.

"You can't imagine how delighted I am to see you, my friends," said Alehin, going into the hall with them. "It is a surprise! Pelagea," he said, addressing the girl, "give our visitors something to change into. And, by the way, I will change too. Only I must first go and wash, for I almost think I have not washed since spring. Wouldn't you like to come into the bath-house? and meanwhile they will get things ready here."

Beautiful Pelagea, looking so refined and soft, brought them towels and soap, and Alehin went to the bath-house with his guests.

"It's a long time since I had a wash," he said, undressing. "I have got a nice bath-house, as you see—my father built it—but I somehow never have time to wash."

He sat down on the steps and soaped his long hair and his neck, and the water round him turned brown.

"Yes, I must say," said Ivan Ivanovitch meaningly, looking at his head.

"It's a long time since I washed . . ." said Alehin with embarrassment, giving himself a second soaping, and the water near him turned dark blue, like ink.

Ivan Ivanovitch went outside, plunged into the water with a loud splash, and swam in the rain, flinging his arms out wide. He stirred the water into waves which set the white lilies bobbing up and down; he swam to the very middle of the millpond and dived, and came up a minute later in another place, and swam on, and kept on diving, trying to touch the bottom.

"Oh, my goodness!" he repeated continually, enjoying himself thoroughly. "Oh, my goodness!" He swam to the mill, talked to the peasants there, then returned and lay on his back in the middle of the pond, turning his face to the rain. Burkin and Alehin were dressed and ready to go, but he still went on swimming and diving. "Oh, my goodness! . . ." he said. "Oh, Lord, have mercy on me! . . ."

"That's enough!" Burkin shouted to him.

They went back to the house. And only when the lamp was lighted in the big drawing-room upstairs, and Burkin and Ivan Ivanovitch, attired in silk dressing-gowns and warm slippers, were sitting in arm-chairs; and Alehin, washed and combed, in a new coat, was walking about the drawing-room, evidently enjoying the feeling of warmth, cleanliness, dry clothes, and light shoes; and when lovely Pelagea, stepping noiselessly on the carpet and smiling softly, handed tea and jam on a tray—only then Ivan Ivanovitch began on his story, and it seemed as though not only Burkin and

Alehin were listening, but also the ladies, young and old, and the officers who looked down upon them sternly and calmly from their gold frames.

"There are two of us brothers," he began—"I, Ivan Ivanovitch, and my brother, Nikolay Ivanovitch, two years younger. I went in for a learned profession and became a veterinary surgeon, while Nikolay sat in a government office from the time he was nineteen. Our father, Tchimsha-Himalaisky, was a kantonist, but he rose to be an officer and left us a little estate and the rank of nobility. After his death the little estate went in debts and legal expenses; but, anyway, we had spent our childhood running wild in the country. Like peasant children, we passed our days and nights in the fields and the woods, looked after horses, stripped the bark off the trees, fished, and so on. . . . And, you know, whoever has once in his life caught perch or has seen the migrating of the thrushes in autumn, watched how they float in flocks over the village on bright, cool days, he will never be a real townsman, and will have a yearning for freedom to the day of his death. My brother was miserable in the government office. Years passed by, and he went on sitting in the same place, went on writing the same papers and thinking of one and the same thing—how to get into the country. And this yearning by degrees passed into a definite desire, into a dream of buying himself a little farm somewhere on the banks of a river or a lake.

"He was a gentle, good-natured fellow, and I was fond of him, but I never sympathized with this desire to shut himself up for the rest of his life in a little farm of his own. It's the correct thing to say that a man needs no more than six feet of earth. But six feet is what a corpse needs, not a man. And they say, too, now, that if our intellectual classes are attracted to the land and yearn for a farm, it's a good thing. But these farms are just the same as six feet of earth. To retreat from town, from the struggle, from the bustle of life, to retreat and bury oneself in one's farm—it's not life, it's egoism, laziness, it's monasticism of a sort, but monasticism without good works. A man does not need six feet of earth or a farm, but the whole globe, all nature, where he can have room to display all the qualities and peculiarities of his free spirit.

"My brother Nikolay, sitting in his government office, dreamed of how he would eat his own cabbages, which would fill the whole yard with such a savoury smell, take his meals on the green grass, sleep in the sun, sit for whole hours on the seat by the gate gazing at the fields and the forest. Gardening books and the agricultural hints in calendars were his delight, his favourite spiritual sustenance; he enjoyed reading newspapers, too, but the only things he read in them were the advertisements of so many acres of arable land and a grass meadow with farm-houses and buildings, a river, a garden, a mill and millponds, for sale. And his imagination pictured the garden-paths, flowers and fruit, starling cotes, the carp in the pond, and all that sort of thing, you know. These imaginary pictures were of different kinds according to the advertisements which he came across, but for some reason in every one of them he had always to have gooseberries. He could not imagine a homestead, he could not picture an idyllic nook, without gooseberries.

"'Country life has its conveniences,' he would sometimes say. 'You sit on the verandah and you drink tea, while your ducks swim on the pond, there is a delicious smell everywhere, and . . . and the gooseberries are growing.'

"He used to draw a map of his property, and in every map there were the same things—*(a)* house for the family, *(b)* servants' quarters, *(c)* kitchen-garden, *(d)* gooseberry-bushes. He lived parsimoniously, was frugal in food and drink, his clothes were beyond description; he looked like a beggar, but kept on saving and putting money in the bank. He grew fearfully avaricious. I did not like to look at him, and I used to give him something and send him presents for Christmas and Easter, but he used to save that too. Once a man is absorbed by an idea there is no doing anything with him.

"Years passed: he was transferred to another province. He was over forty, and he was still reading the advertisements in the papers and saving up. Then I heard he was married. Still with the same object of buying a farm and having gooseberries, he married an elderly and ugly widow without a trace of feeling for her, simply because she had filthy lucre. He went on living frugally after marrying her, and kept her short of food, while he put her money in the bank in his name.

"Her first husband had been a postmaster, and with him she was accustomed to pies and home-made wines, while with her second husband she did not get enough black bread; she began to pine away with this sort of life, and three years later she gave up her soul to God. And I need hardly say that my brother never for one moment imagined that he was responsible for her death. Money, like vodka, makes a man queer. In our town there was a merchant who, before he died, ordered a plateful of honey and ate up all his money and lottery tickets with the honey, so that no one might get the benefit of it. While I was inspecting cattle at a railway-station, a cattle-dealer fell under an engine and had his leg cut off. We carried him into the waiting-room, the blood was flowing—it was a horrible thing—and he kept asking them to look for his leg and was very much worried about it; there were twenty roubles in the boot on the leg that had been cut off, and he was afraid they would be lost."

"That's a story from a different opera," said Burkin.

"After his wife's death," Ivan Ivanovitch went on, after thinking for half a minute, "my brother began looking out for an estate for himself. Of course, you may look about for five years and yet end by making a mistake, and buying something quite different from what you have dreamed of. My brother Nikolay bought through an agent a mortgaged estate of three hundred and thirty acres, with a house for the family, with servants' quarters, with a park, but with no orchard, no gooseberry-bushes, and no duck-pond; there was a river, but the water in it was the colour of coffee, because on one side of the estate there was a brickyard and on the other a factory for burning bones. But Nikolay Ivanovitch did not grieve much; he ordered twenty gooseberry-bushes, planted them, and began living as a country gentleman.

"Last year I went to pay him a visit. I thought I would go and see what it was like. In his letters my brother called his estate 'Tchumbaroklov Waste, alias Himalaiskoe.' I reached 'alias Himalaiskoe' in the afternoon. It was hot. Everywhere there were ditches, fences, hedges, fir-trees planted in rows, and there was no knowing how to get to the yard, where to put one's horse. I went up to the house, and was met by a fat red dog that looked like a pig. It wanted to bark, but it was too lazy. The cook, a fat, barefooted woman, came out of the kitchen, and she, too, looked like a pig, and said that her master was resting after dinner. I went in to see my brother. He was sitting up in bed with a quilt over his legs; he had grown older, fatter, wrinkled; his cheeks, his nose, and his mouth all stuck out—he looked as though he might begin grunting into the quilt at any moment.

"We embraced each other, and shed tears of joy and of sadness at the thought that we had once been young and now were both grey-headed and near the grave. He dressed, and led me out to show me the estate.

"'Well, how are you getting on here?' I asked.

"'Oh, all right, thank God; I am getting on very well.'

"He was no more a poor timid clerk, but a real landowner, a gentleman. He was already accustomed to it, had grown used to it, and liked it. He ate a great deal, went to the bath-house, was growing stout, was already at law with the village commune and both factories, and was very much offended when the peasants did not call him 'Your Honour.' And he concerned himself with the salvation of his soul in a substantial, gentlemanly manner, and performed deeds of charity, not simply, but with an air of consequence. And what deeds of charity! He treated the peasants for every sort of disease with soda and castor oil, and on his name-day had a thanksgiving service in the middle of the village, and then treated the peasants to a gallon of vodka—he thought that was the thing to do. Oh, those horrible gallons of vodka! One day the fat landowner hauls the peasants up before the district captain for trespass, and next day, in honour of a holiday, treats them to a gallon of vodka, and they drink and shout 'Hurrah!' and when they are drunk bow down to his feet. A change of life for the better, and being well-fed and idle develop in a Russian the most insolent self-conceit. Nikolay Ivanovitch, who at one time in the government office was afraid to have any views of his own, now could say nothing that was not gospel truth, and uttered such truths in the tone of a prime minister. 'Education is essential, but for the peasants it is premature.' 'Corporal punishment is harmful as a rule, but in some cases it is necessary and there is nothing to take its place.'

"'I know the peasants and understand how to treat them,' he would say. 'The peasants like me. I need only to hold up my little finger and the peasants will do anything I like.'

"And all this, observe, was uttered with a wise, benevolent smile. He repeated twenty times over 'We noblemen,' 'I as a noble'; obviously he did not remember that our grandfather was a peasant, and our father a soldier. Even our surname Tchimsha-Himalaisky, in reality is incongruous, seemed to him now melodious, distinguished, and very agreeable.

"But the point just now is not he, but myself. I want to tell you about the change that took place in me during the brief hours I spent at his country place. In the evening, when we were drinking tea, the cook put on the table a plateful of gooseberries. They were not bought, but his own gooseberries, gathered for the first time since the bushes were planted. Nikolay Ivanovitch laughed and looked for a minute in silence at the gooseberries, with tears in his eyes; he could not speak for excitement. Then he put one gooseberry in his mouth, looked at me with the triumph of a child who has at last received his favourite toy, and said:

" 'How delicious!'

"And he ate them greedily, continually repeating, 'Ah, how delicious! Do taste them!'

"They were sour and unripe, but, as Pushkin says:

> " 'Dearer to us the falsehood that exalts
> Than hosts of baser truths.' *

"I saw a happy man whose cherished dream was so obviously fulfilled, who had attained his object in life, who had gained what he wanted, who was satisfied with his fate and himself. There is always, for some reason, an element of sadness mingled with my thoughts of human happiness, and, on this occasion, at the sight of a happy man I was overcome by an oppressive feeling that was close upon despair. It was particularly oppressive at night. A bed was made up for me in the room next to my brother's bedroom, and I could hear that he was awake, and that he kept getting up and going to the plate of gooseberries and taking one. I reflected how many satisfied, happy people there really are! What a suffocating force it is! You look at life: the insolence and idleness of the strong, the ignorance and brutishness of the weak, incredible poverty all about us, overcrowding, degeneration, drunkenness, hypocrisy, lying. . . . Yet all is

*From the poem "A hero," by the great Russian poet Aleksandr Pushkin.

calm and stillness in the houses and in the streets; of the fifty thousand living in a town, there is not one who would cry out, who would give vent to his indignation aloud. We see the people going to market for provisions, eating by day, sleeping by night, talking their silly nonsense, getting married, growing old, serenely escorting their dead to the cemetery; but we do not see and we do not hear those who suffer, and what is terrible in life goes on somewhere behind the scenes. . . . Everything is quiet and peaceful, and nothing protests but mute statistics: so many people gone out of their minds, so many gallons of vodka drunk, so many children dead from malnutrition. . . . And this order of things is evidently necessary; evidently the happy man only feels at ease because the unhappy bear their burdens in silence, and without that silence happiness would be impossible. It's a case of general hypnotism. There ought to be behind the door of every happy, contented man some one standing with a hammer continually reminding him with a tap that there are unhappy people; that however happy he may be, life will show him her laws sooner or later, trouble will come for him—disease, poverty, losses, and no one will see or hear, just as now he neither sees nor hears others. But there is no man with a hammer; the happy man lives at his ease, and trivial daily cares faintly agitate him like the wind in the aspen-tree—and all goes well.

"That night I realized that I, too, was happy and contented," Ivan Ivanovitch went on, getting up. "I, too, at dinner and at the hunt liked to lay down the law on life and religion, and the way to manage the peasantry. I, too, used to say that science was light, that culture was essential, but for the simple people reading and writing was enough for the time. Freedom is a blessing, I used to say; we can no more do without it than without air, but we must wait a little. Yes, I used to talk like that, and now I ask, 'For what reason are we to wait?'" asked Ivan Ivanovitch, looking angrily at Burkin. "Why wait, I ask you? What grounds have we for waiting? I shall be told, it can't be done all at once; every idea takes shape in life gradually, in its due time. But who is it says that? Where is the proof that it's right? You will fall back upon the natural order of things, the uniformity of phenomena; but is there order and uniformity in the fact that I, a living, thinking man, stand over a chasm and wait for it to close of itself, or to fill up with mud at the very time when perhaps

I might leap over it or build a bridge across it? And again, wait for the sake of what? Wait till there's no strength to live? And meanwhile one must live, and one wants to live!

"I went away from my brother's early in the morning, and ever since then it has been unbearable for me to be in town. I am oppressed by its peace and quiet; I am afraid to look at the windows, for there is no spectacle more painful to me now than the sight of a happy family sitting round the table drinking tea. I am old and am not fit for the struggle; I am not even capable of hatred; I can only grieve inwardly, feel irritated and vexed; but at night my head is hot from the rush of ideas, and I cannot sleep. . . . Ah, if I were young!"

Ivan Ivanovitch walked backwards and forwards in excitement, and repeated: "If I were young!"

He suddenly went up to Alehin and began pressing first one of his hands and then the other.

"Pavel Konstantinovitch," he said in an imploring voice, "don't be calm and contented, don't let yourself be put to sleep! While you are young, strong, confident, be not weary in well-doing! There is no happiness, and there ought not to be; but if there is a meaning and an object in life, that meaning and object is not our happiness, but something greater and more rational. Do good!"

And all this Ivan Ivanovitch said with a pitiful, imploring smile, as though he were asking him a personal favour.

Then all three sat in arm-chairs at different ends of the drawing-room and were silent. Ivan Ivanovitch's story had not satisfied either Burkin or Alehin. When the generals and ladies gazed down from their gilt frames, looking in the dusk as though they were alive, it was dreary to listen to the story of the poor clerk who ate gooseberries. They felt inclined, for some reason, to talk about elegant people, about women. And their sitting in the drawing-room where everything—the chandeliers in their covers, the arm-chairs, and the carpet under their feet—reminded them that those very people who were now looking down from their frames had once moved about, sat, drunk tea in this room, and the fact that lovely Pelagea was moving noiselessly about was better than any story.

Alehin was fearfully sleepy; he had got up early, before three o'clock in the morning, to look after his work, and now his eyes were closing; but he was afraid his visitors might tell some interesting story after he had gone, and he lingered on. He did not go into the question whether what Ivan Ivanovitch had just said was right and true. His visitors did not talk of groats, nor of hay, nor of tar, but of something that had no direct bearing on his life, and he was glad and wanted them to go on.

"It's bed-time, though," said Burkin, getting up. "Allow me to wish you good-night."

Alehin said good-night and went downstairs to his own domain, while the visitors remained upstairs. They were both taken for the night to a big room where there stood two old wooden beds decorated with carvings, and in the corner was an ivory crucifix. The big cool beds, which had been made by the lovely Pelagea, smelt agreeably of clean linen.

Ivan Ivanovitch undressed in silence and got into bed.

"Lord forgive us sinners!" he said, and put his head under the quilt.

His pipe lying on the table smelt strongly of stale tobacco, and Burkin could not sleep for a long while, and kept wondering where the oppressive smell came from.

The rain was pattering on the window-panes all night.

THE LADY WITH THE DOG

I

It was said that a new person had appeared on the sea-front: a lady with a little dog. Dmitri Dmitritch Gurov, who had by then been a fortnight at Yalta,* and so was fairly at home there, had begun to take an interest in new arrivals. Sitting in Verney's pavilion, he saw, walking on the sea-front, a fair-haired young lady of medium height, wearing a *béret;* a white Pomeranian dog was running behind her.

And afterwards he met her in the public gardens and in the square several times a day. She was walking alone, always wearing the same *béret,* and always with the same white dog; no one knew who she was, and everyone called her simply "the lady with the dog."

"If she is here alone without a husband or friends, it wouldn't be amiss to make her acquaintance," Gurov reflected.

He was under forty, but he had a daughter already twelve years old, and two sons at school. He had been married young, when he was a student in his second year, and by now his wife seemed half as old again as he. She was a tall, erect woman with dark eyebrows, staid and dignified, and, as she said of herself, intellectual. She read a great deal, used phonetic spelling, called her husband, not Dmitri, but Dimitri, and he secretly considered her unintelligent, narrow, inelegant, was afraid of her, and did not like to be at home. He had begun being unfaithful to her long ago—had been unfaithful to her often, and, probably on that account, almost always spoke ill of women, and when they were talked about in his presence, used to call them "the lower race."

It seemed to him that he had been so schooled by bitter experience that he might call them what he liked, and yet he could not get

*Resort town in Crimea, set amid orchards and vineyards.

on for two days together without "the lower race." In the society of men he was bored and not himself, with them he was cold and uncommunicative; but when he was in the company of women he felt free, and knew what to say to them and how to behave; and he was at ease with them even when he was silent. In his appearance, in his character, in his whole nature, there was something attractive and elusive which allured women and disposed them in his favour; he knew that, and some force seemed to draw him, too, to them.

Experience often repeated, truly bitter experience, had taught him long ago that with decent people, especially Moscow people—always slow to move and irresolute—every intimacy, which at first so agreeably diversifies life and appears a light and charming adventure, inevitably grows into a regular problem of extreme intricacy, and in the long run the situation becomes unbearable. But at every fresh meeting with an interesting woman this experience seemed to slip out of his memory, and he was eager for life, and everything seemed simple and amusing.

One evening he was dining in the gardens, and the lady in the *béret* came up slowly to take the next table. Her expression, her gait, her dress, and the way she did her hair told him that she was a lady, that she was married, that she was in Yalta for the first time and alone, and that she was dull there. . . . The stories told of the immorality in such places as Yalta are to a great extent untrue; he despised them, and knew that such stories were for the most part made up by persons who would themselves have been glad to sin if they had been able; but when the lady sat down at the next table three paces from him, he remembered these tales of easy conquests, of trips to the mountains, and the tempting thought of a swift, fleeting love affair, a romance with an unknown woman, whose name he did not know, suddenly took possession of him.

He beckoned coaxingly to the Pomeranian, and when the dog came up to him he shook his finger at it. The Pomeranian growled, Gurov shook his finger at it again.

The lady looked at him and at once dropped her eyes.

"He doesn't bite," she said, and blushed.

"May I give him a bone?" he asked; and when she nodded he asked courteously, "Have you been long in Yalta?"

"Five days."

"And I have already dragged out a fortnight here."

There was a brief silence.

"Time goes fast, and yet it is so dull here!" she said, not looking at him.

"That's only the fashion to say it is dull here. A provincial will live in Belyov* or Zhidra† and not be dull, and when he comes here it's 'Oh, the dulness! Oh, the dust!' One would think he came from Grenada."

She laughed. Then both continued eating in silence, like strangers, but after dinner they walked side by side; and there sprang up between them the light jesting conversation of people who are free and satisfied, to whom it does not matter where they go or what they talk about. They walked and talked of the strange light on the sea: the water was of a soft warm lilac hue, and there was a golden streak from the moon upon it. They talked of how sultry it was after a hot day. Gurov told her that he came from Moscow, that he had taken his degree in Arts, but had a post in a bank; that he had trained as an opera-singer, but had given it up, that he owned two houses in Moscow. . . . And from her he learnt that she had grown up in Petersburg, but had lived in S—— since her marriage two years before, that she was staying another month in Yalta, and that her husband, who needed a holiday too, might perhaps come and fetch her. She was not sure whether her husband had a post in a Crown Department or under the Provincial Council—and was amused by her own ignorance. And Gurov learnt, too, that she was called Anna Sergeyevna.

Afterwards he thought about her in his room at the hotel—thought she would certainly meet him next day; it would be sure to happen. As he got into bed he thought how lately she had been a girl at school, doing lessons like his own daughter; he recalled the diffidence, the angularity, that was still manifest in her laugh and her manner of talking with a stranger. This must have been the first time in her life she had been alone in surroundings in which she was followed, looked at, and spoken to merely from a secret motive

---

*Town some 150 miles from Moscow.

†Town some 200 miles from Moscow.

which she could hardly fail to guess. He recalled her slender, delicate neck, her lovely grey eyes.

"There's something pathetic about her, anyway," he thought, and fell asleep.

II

A week had passed since they had made acquaintance. It was a holiday. It was sultry indoors, while in the street the wind whirled the dust round and round, and blew people's hats off. It was a thirsty day, and Gurov often went into the pavilion, and pressed Anna Sergeyevna to have syrup and water or an ice. One did not know what to do with oneself.

In the evening when the wind had dropped a little, they went out on to the groyne to see the steamer come in. There were a great many people walking about the harbour; they had gathered to welcome someone, bringing bouquets. And two peculiarities of a well-dressed Yalta crowd were very conspicuous: the elderly ladies were dressed like young ones, and there were great numbers of generals.

Owing to the roughness of the sea, the steamer arrived late, after the sun had set, and it was a long time turning about before it reached the groyne. Anna Sergeyevna looked through her lorgnette at the steamer and the passengers as though looking for acquaintances, and when she turned to Gurov her eyes were shining. She talked a great deal and asked disconnected questions, forgetting next moment what she had asked; then she dropped her lorgnette in the crush.

The festive crowd began to disperse; it was too dark to see people's faces. The wind had completely dropped, but Gurov and Anna Sergeyevna still stood as though waiting to see someone else come from the steamer. Anna Sergeyevna was silent now, and sniffed the flowers without looking at Gurov.

"The weather is better this evening," he said. "Where shall we go now? Shall we drive somewhere?"

She made no answer.

Then he looked at her intently, and all at once put his arm round her and kissed her on the lips, and breathed in the moisture and the fragrance of the flowers; and he immediately looked round him, anxiously wondering whether anyone had seen them.

"Let us go to your hotel," he said softly. And both walked quickly.

The room was close and smelt of the scent she had bought at the Japanese shop. Gurov looked at her and thought: "What different people one meets in the world!" From the past he preserved memories of careless, good-natured women, who loved cheerfully and were grateful to him for the happiness he gave them, however brief it might be; and of women like his wife who loved without any genuine feeling, with superfluous phrases, affectedly, hysterically, with an expression that suggested that it was not love nor passion, but something more significant; and of two or three others, very beautiful, cold women, on whose faces he had caught a glimpse of a rapacious expression—an obstinate desire to snatch from life more than it could give, and these were capricious, unreflecting, domineering, unintelligent women not in their first youth, and when Gurov grew cold to them their beauty excited his hatred, and the lace on their linen seemed to him like scales.

But in this case there was still the diffidence, the angularity of inexperienced youth, an awkward feeling; and there was a sense of consternation as though someone had suddenly knocked at the door. The attitude of Anna Sergeyevna—"the lady with the dog"—to what had happened was somehow peculiar, very grave, as though it were her fall—so it seemed, and it was strange and inappropriate. Her face drooped and faded, and on both sides of it her long hair hung down mournfully; she mused in a dejected attitude like "the woman who was a sinner" in an old-fashioned picture.

"It's wrong," she said. "You will be the first to despise me now."

There was a water-melon on the table. Gurov cut himself a slice and began eating it without haste. There followed at least half an hour of silence.

Anna Sergeyevna was touching; there was about her the purity of a good, simple woman who had seen little of life. The solitary candle burning on the table threw a faint light on her face, yet it was clear that she was very unhappy.

"How could I despise you?" asked Gurov. "You don't know what you are saying."

"God forgive me," she said, and her eyes filled with tears. "It's awful."

"You seem to feel you need to be forgiven."

"Forgiven? No. I am a bad, low woman; I despise myself and don't attempt to justify myself. It's not my husband but myself I have deceived. And not only just now; I have been deceiving myself for a long time. My husband may be a good, honest man, but he is a flunkey! I don't know what he does there, what his work is, but I know he is a flunkey! I was twenty when I was married to him. I have been tormented by curiosity; I wanted something better. 'There must be a different sort of life,' I said to myself. I wanted to live! To live, to live! . . . I was fired by curiosity . . . you don't understand it, but, I swear to God, I could not control myself; something happened to me: I could not be restrained. I told my husband I was ill, and came here. . . . And here I have been walking about as though I were dazed, like a mad creature; . . . and now I have become a vulgar, contemptible woman whom anyone may despise."

Gurov felt bored already, listening to her. He was irritated by the naïve tone, by this remorse, so unexpected and inopportune; but for the tears in her eyes, he might have thought she was jesting or playing a part.

"I don't understand," he said softly. "What is it you want?"

She hid her face on his breast and pressed close to him.

"Believe me, believe me, I beseech you . . ." she said. "I love a pure, honest life, and sin is loathsome to me. I don't know what I am doing. Simple people say: 'The Evil One has beguiled me.' And I may say of myself now that the Evil One has beguiled me."

"Hush, hush! . . ." he muttered.

He looked at her fixed, scared eyes, kissed her, talked softly and affectionately, and by degrees she was comforted, and her gaiety returned; they both began laughing.

Afterwards when they went out there was not a soul on the seafront. The town with its cypresses had quite a deathlike air, but the sea still broke noisily on the shore; a single barge was rocking on the waves, and the lantern was blinking sleepily on it.

They found a cab and drove to Oreanda.*

"I found out your surname in the hall just now: it was written on

---

*Beautiful spot on the Crimean coast near Yalta.

the board—Von Diderits," said Gurov. "Is your husband a German?"

"No; I believe his grandfather was a German, but he is an Orthodox Russian himself."

At Oreanda they sat on a seat not far from the church, looked down at the sea, and were silent. Yalta was hardly visible through the morning mist; white clouds stood motionless on the mountain-tops. The leaves did not stir on the trees, grasshoppers chirruped, and the monotonous hollow sound of the sea, rising up from below, spoke of the peace, of the eternal sleep awaiting us. So it must have sounded when there was no Yalta, no Oreanda here; so it sounds now, and it will sound as indifferently and monotonously when we are all no more. And in this constancy, in this complete indifference to the life and death of each of us, there lies hid, perhaps, a pledge of our eternal salvation, of the unceasing movement of life upon earth, of unceasing progress towards perfection. Sitting beside a young woman who in the dawn seemed so lovely, soothed and spellbound in these magical surroundings—the sea, mountains, clouds, the open sky—Gurov thought how in reality everything is beautiful in this world when one reflects: everything except what we think or do ourselves when we forget our human dignity and the higher aims of our existence.

A man walked up to them—probably a keeper—looked at them and walked away. And this detail seemed mysterious and beautiful, too. They saw a steamer come from Theodosia,* with its lights out in the glow of dawn.

"There is dew on the grass," said Anna Sergeyevna, after a silence.

"Yes. It's time to go home."

They went back to the town.

Then they met every day at twelve o'clock on the sea-front, lunched and dined together, went for walks, admired the sea. She complained that she slept badly, that her heart throbbed violently; asked the same questions, troubled now by jealousy and now by the fear that he did not respect her sufficiently. And often in the square

---

*Resort on the Crimean coast.

or gardens, when there was no one near them, he suddenly drew her to him and kissed her passionately. Complete idleness, these kisses in broad daylight while he looked round in dread of someone's seeing them, the heat, the smell of the sea, and the continual passing to and fro before him of idle, well-dressed, well-fed people, made a new man of him; he told Anna Sergeyevna how beautiful she was, how fascinating. He was impatiently passionate, he would not move a step away from her, while she was often pensive and continually urged him to confess that he did not respect her, did not love her in the least, and thought of her as nothing but a common woman. Rather late almost every evening they drove somewhere out of town, to Oreanda or to the waterfall; and the expedition was always a success, the scenery invariably impressed them as grand and beautiful.

They were expecting her husband to come, but a letter came from him, saying that there was something wrong with his eyes, and he entreated his wife to come home as quickly as possible. Anna Sergeyevna made haste to go.

"It's a good thing I am going away," she said to Gurov. "It's the finger of destiny!"

She went by coach and he went with her. They were driving the whole day. When she had got into a compartment of the express, and when the second bell had rung, she said:

"Let me look at you once more . . . look at you once again. That's right."

She did not shed tears, but was so sad that she seemed ill, and her face was quivering.

"I shall remember you . . . think of you," she said. "God be with you; be happy. Don't remember evil against me. We are parting for ever—it must be so, for we ought never to have met. Well, God be with you."

The train moved off rapidly, its lights soon vanished from sight, and a minute later there was no sound of it, as though everything had conspired together to end as quickly as possible that sweet delirium, that madness. Left alone on the platform, and gazing into the dark distance, Gurov listened to the chirrup of the grasshoppers and the hum of the telegraph wires, feeling as though he had only just waked up. And he thought, musing, that there had been another episode or adventure in his life, and it, too, was at an end, and nothing was left of it but a memory. . . . He was moved, sad, and conscious of a slight remorse. This young woman whom he would never meet again had not been happy with him; he was genuinely warm and affectionate with her, but yet in his manner, his tone, and his caresses there had been a shade of light irony, the coarse condescension of a happy man who was, besides, almost twice her age. All the time she had called him kind, exceptional, lofty; obviously he had seemed to her different from what he really was, so he had unintentionally deceived her. . . .

Here at the station was already a scent of autumn; it was a cold evening.

"It's time for me to go north," thought Gurov as he left the platform. "High time!"

III

At home in Moscow everything was in its winter routine; the stoves were heated, and in the morning it was still dark when the children were having breakfast and getting ready for school, and the nurse would light the lamp for a short time. The frosts had begun already. When the first snow has fallen, on the first day of sledge-driving it is pleasant to see the white earth, the white roofs, to draw soft, delicious breath, and the season brings back the days of one's youth. The old limes and birches, white with hoar-frost, have a good-natured expression; they are nearer to one's heart than cypresses and palms, and near them one doesn't want to be thinking of the sea and the mountains.

Gurov was Moscow born; he arrived in Moscow on a fine frosty day, and when he put on his fur coat and warm gloves, and walked along Petrovka, and when on Saturday evening he heard the ringing of the bells, his recent trip and the places he had seen lost all charm for him. Little by little he became absorbed in Moscow life, greedily read three newspapers a day, and declared he did not read the Moscow papers on principle! He already felt a longing to go to restaurants, clubs, dinner-parties, anniversary celebrations, and he felt flattered at entertaining distinguished lawyers and artists, and at playing cards with a professor at the doctors' club. He could already eat a whole plateful of salt fish and cabbage. . . .

In another month, he fancied, the image of Anna Sergeyevna would be shrouded in a mist in his memory, and only from time to time would visit him in his dreams with a touching smile as others did. But more than a month passed, real winter had come, and everything was still clear in his memory as though he had parted with Anna Sergeyevna only the day before. And his memories glowed more and more vividly. When in the evening stillness he heard from his study the voices of his children, preparing their lessons, or when he listened to a song or the organ at the restaurant, or the storm howled in the chimney, suddenly everything would rise up in his memory: what had happened on the groyne, and the early morning with the mist on the mountains, and the steamer coming from Theodosia, and the kisses. He would pace a long time about his room, remembering it all and smiling; then his memories passed into dreams, and in his fancy the past was mingled with what was to come. Anna Sergeyevna did not visit him in dreams, but followed him about everywhere like a shadow and haunted him. When he shut his eyes he saw her as though she were living before him, and she seemed to him lovelier, younger, tenderer than she was; and he imagined himself finer than he had been in Yalta. In the evenings she peeped out at him from the bookcase, from the fireplace, from the corner—he heard her breathing, the caressing rustle of her dress. In the street he watched the women, looking for someone like her.

He was tormented by an intense desire to confide his memories to someone. But in his home it was impossible to talk of his love, and he had no one outside; he could not talk to his tenants nor to anyone at the bank. And what had he to talk of? Had he been in love, then? Had there been anything beautiful, poetical, or edifying or simply interesting in his relations with Anna Sergeyevna? And there was nothing for him but to talk vaguely of love, of woman, and no one guessed what it meant; only his wife twitched her black eyebrows, and said: "The part of a ladykiller does not suit you at all, Dimitri."

One evening, coming out of the doctors' club with an official with whom he had been playing cards, he could not resist saying:

"If only you knew what a fascinating woman I made the acquaintance of in Yalta!"

The official got into his sledge and was driving away, but turned suddenly and shouted:

"Dmitri Dmitritch!"

"What?"

"You were right this evening: the sturgeon was a bit too strong!"

These words, so ordinary, for some reason moved Gurov to indignation, and struck him as degrading and unclean. What savage manners, what people! What senseless nights, what uninteresting, uneventful days! The rage for card-playing, the gluttony, the drunkenness, the continual talk always about the same thing. Useless pursuits and conversations always about the same things absorb the better part of one's time, the better part of one's strength, and in the end there is left a life grovelling and curtailed, worthless and trivial, and there is no escaping or getting away from it—just as though one were in a madhouse or a prison.

Gurov did not sleep all night, and was filled with indignation. And he had a headache all next day. And the next night he slept badly; he sat up in bed, thinking, or paced up and down his room. He was sick of his children, sick of the bank; he had no desire to go anywhere or to talk of anything.

In the holidays in December he prepared for a journey, and told his wife he was going to Petersburg to do something in the interests of a young friend—and he set off for S——. What for? He did not very well know himself. He wanted to see Anna Sergeyevna and to talk with her—to arrange a meeting, if possible.

He reached S—— in the morning, and took the best room at the hotel, in which the floor was covered with grey army cloth, and on the table was an inkstand, grey with dust and adorned with a figure on horseback, with its hat in its hand and its head broken off. The hotel porter gave him the necessary information; Von Diderits lived in a house of his own in Old Gontcharny Street—it was not far from the hotel: he was rich and lived in good style, and had his own horses; everyone in the town knew him. The porter pronounced the name "Dridirits."

Gurov went without haste to Old Gontcharny Street and found

the house. Just opposite the house stretched a long grey fence adorned with nails.

"One would run away from a fence like that," thought Gurov, looking from the fence to the windows of the house and back again.

He considered: to-day was a holiday, and the husband would probably be at home. And in any case it would be tactless to go into the house and upset her. If he were to send her a note it might fall into her husband's hands, and then it might ruin everything. The best thing was to trust to chance. And he kept walking up and down the street by the fence, waiting for the chance. He saw a beggar go in at the gate and dogs fly at him; then an hour later he heard a piano, and the sounds were faint and indistinct. Probably it was Anna Sergeyevna playing. The front door suddenly opened, and an old woman came out, followed by the familiar white Pomeranian. Gurov was on the point of calling to the dog, but his heart began beating violently, and in his excitement he could not remember the dog's name.

He walked up and down, and loathed the grey fence more and more, and by now he thought irritably that Anna Sergeyevna had forgotten him, and was perhaps already amusing herself with some-one else, and that that was very natural in a young woman who had nothing to look at from morning till night but that confounded fence. He went back to his hotel room and sat for a long while on the sofa, not knowing what to do, then he had dinner and a long nap.

"How stupid and worrying it is!" he thought when he woke and looked at the dark windows: it was already evening. "Here I've had a good sleep for some reason. What shall I do in the night?"

He sat on the bed, which was covered by a cheap grey blanket, such as one sees in hospitals, and he taunted himself in his vexation:

"So much for the lady with the dog . . . so much for the adven-ture. . . . You're in a nice fix. . . ."

That morning at the station a poster in large letters had caught his eyes. "The Geisha"* was to be performed for the first time. He thought of this and went to the theatre.

---

*Operetta from London by Sidney Jones.

"It's quite possible she may go to the first performance," he thought.

The theatre was full. As in all provincial theatres, there was a fog above the chandelier, the gallery was noisy and restless; in the front row the local dandies were standing up before the beginning of the performance, with their hands behind them; in the Governor's box the Governor's daughter, wearing a boa, was sitting in the front seat, while the Governor himself lurked modestly behind the curtain with only his hands visible; the orchestra was a long time tuning up; the stage curtain swayed. All the time the audience were coming in and taking their seats Gurov looked at them eagerly.

Anna Sergeyevna, too, came in. She sat down in the third row, and when Gurov looked at her his heart contracted, and he understood clearly that for him there was in the whole world no creature so near, so precious, and so important to him; she, this little woman, in no way remarkable, lost in a provincial crowd, with a vulgar lorgnette in her hand, filled his whole life now, was his sorrow and his joy, the one happiness that he now desired for himself, and to the sounds of the inferior orchestra, of the wretched provincial violins, he thought how lovely she was. He thought and dreamed.

A young man with small side-whiskers, tall and stooping, came in with Anna Sergeyevna and sat down beside her; he bent his head at every step and seemed to be continually bowing. Most likely this was the husband whom at Yalta, in a rush of bitter feeling, she had called a flunkey. And there really was in his long figure, his side-whiskers, and the small bald patch on his head, something of the flunkey's obsequiousness; his smile was sugary, and in his buttonhole there was some badge of distinction like the number on a waiter.

During the first interval the husband went away to smoke; she remained alone in her stall. Gurov, who was sitting in the stalls, too, went up to her and said in a trembling voice, with a forced smile:

"Good evening."

She glanced at him and turned pale, then glanced again with horror, unable to believe her eyes, and tightly gripped the fan and the lorgnette in her hands, evidently struggling with herself not to faint. Both were silent. She was sitting, he was standing, frightened by her confusion and not venturing to sit down beside her. The violins and the flute began tuning up. He felt suddenly frightened; it seemed as though all the people in the boxes were looking at them. She got up and went quickly to the door; he followed her, and both walked senselessly along passages, and up and down stairs, and figures in legal, scholastic, and civil service uniforms, all wearing badges, flitted before their eyes. They caught glimpses of ladies, of fur coats hanging on pegs; the draughts blew on them, bringing a smell of stale tobacco. And Gurov, whose heart was beating violently, thought:

"Oh, heavens! Why are these people here and this orchestra! . . ."

And at that instant he recalled how when he had seen Anna Sergeyevna off at the station he had thought that everything was over and they would never meet again. But how far they were still from the end!

On the narrow, gloomy staircase over which was written "To the Amphitheatre," she stopped.

"How you have frightened me!" she said, breathing hard, still pale and overwhelmed. "Oh, how you have frightened me! I am half dead. Why have you come? Why?"

"But do understand, Anna, do understand . . ." he said hastily in a low voice. "I entreat you to understand. . . ."

She looked at him with dread, with entreaty, with love; she looked at him intently, to keep his features more distinctly in her memory.

"I am so unhappy," she went on, not heeding him. "I have thought of nothing but you all the time; I live only in the thought of you. And I wanted to forget, to forget you; but why, oh why, have you come?"

On the landing above them two schoolboys were smoking and looking down, but that was nothing to Gurov; he drew Anna Sergeyevna to him, and began kissing her face, her cheeks, and her hands.

"What are you doing, what are you doing!" she cried in horror, pushing him away. "We are mad. Go away to-day; go away at once. . . . I beseech you by all that is sacred, I implore you. . . . There are people coming this way!"

Someone was coming up the stairs.

"You must go away," Anna Sergeyevna went on in a whisper. "Do you hear, Dmitri Dmitritch? I will come and see you in Moscow. I have never been happy; I am miserable now, and I never, never shall be happy, never! Don't make me suffer still more! I swear I'll come to Moscow. But now let us part. My precious, good, dear one, we must part!"

She pressed his hand and began rapidly going downstairs, looking round at him, and from her eyes he could see that she really was unhappy. Gurov stood for a little while, listened, then, when all sound had died away, he found his coat and left the theatre.

IV

And Anna Sergeyevna began coming to see him in Moscow. Once in two or three months she left S——, telling her husband that she was going to consult a doctor about an internal complaint—and her husband believed her, and did not believe her. In Moscow she stayed at the Slaviansky Bazaar hotel,* and at once sent a man in a red cap to Gurov. Gurov went to see her, and no one in Moscow knew of it.

Once he was going to see her in this way on a winter morning (the messenger had come the evening before when he was out). With him walked his daughter, whom he wanted to take to school: it was on the way. Snow was falling in big wet flakes.

"It's three degrees above freezing-point, and yet it is snowing," said Gurov to his daughter. "The thaw is only on the surface of the earth; there is quite a different temperature at a greater height in the atmosphere."

"And why are there no thunderstorms in the winter, father?"

He explained that, too. He talked, thinking all the while that he was going to see *her,* and no living soul knew of it, and probably never would know. He had two lives: one, open, seen and known by all who cared to know, full of relative truth and of relative falsehood, exactly like the lives of his friends and acquaintances; and another life running its course in secret. And through some strange, perhaps accidental, conjunction of circumstances, everything that was essen-

*Large hotel in Moscow where Chekhov himself sometimes stayed.

tial, of interest and of value to him, everything in which he was sincere and did not deceive himself, everything that made the kernel of his life, was hidden from other people; and all that was false in him, the sheath in which he hid himself to conceal the truth—such, for instance, as his work in the bank, his discussions at the club, his "lower race," his presence with his wife at anniversary festivities—all that was open. And he judged of others by himself, not believing in what he saw, and always believing that every man had his real, most interesting life under the cover of secrecy and under the cover of night. All personal life rested on secrecy, and possibly it was partly on that account that civilized man was so nervously anxious that personal privacy should be respected.

After leaving his daughter at school, Gurov went on to the Saviansky Bazaar. He took off his fur coat below, went upstairs, and softly knocked at the door. Anna Sergeyevna, wearing his favourite grey dress, exhausted by the journey and the suspense, had been expecting him since the evening before. She was pale; she looked at him, and did not smile, and he had hardly come in when she fell on his breast. Their kiss was slow and prolonged, as though they had not met for two years.

"Well, how are you getting on there?" he asked. "What news?"

"Wait; I'll tell you directly. . . . I can't talk."

She could not speak; she was crying. She turned away from him, and pressed her handkerchief to her eyes.

"Let her have her cry out. I'll sit down and wait," he thought, and he sat down in an arm-chair.

Then he rang and asked for tea to be brought him, and while he drank his tea she remained standing at the window with her back to him. She was crying from emotion, from the miserable consciousness that their life was so hard for them; they could only meet in secret, hiding themselves from people, like thieves! Was not their life shattered?

"Come, do stop!" he said.

It was evident to him that this love of theirs would not soon be over, that he could not see the end of it. Anna Sergeyevna grew more and more attached to him. She adored him, and it was unthinkable to say to her that it was bound to have an end some day; besides, she would not have believed it!

He went up to her and took her by the shoulders to say something affectionate and cheering, and at that moment he saw himself in the looking-glass.

His hair was already beginning to turn grey. And it seemed strange to him that he had grown so much older, so much plainer during the last few years. The shoulders on which his hands rested were warm and quivering. He felt compassion for this life, still so warm and lovely, but probably already not far from beginning to fade and wither like his own. Why did she love him so much? He always seemed to women different from what he was, and they loved in him not himself, but the man created by their imagination, whom they had been eagerly seeking all their lives; and afterwards, when they noticed their mistake, they loved him all the same. And not one of them had been happy with him. Time passed, he had made their acquaintance, got on with them, parted, but he had never once loved; it was anything you like, but not love.

And only now when his head was grey he had fallen properly, really in love—for the first time in his life.

Anna Sergeyevna and he loved each other like people very close and akin, like husband and wife, like tender friends; it seemed to them that fate itself had meant them for one another, and they could not understand why he had a wife and she a husband; and it was as though they were a pair of birds of passage, caught and forced to live in different cages. They forgave each other for what they were ashamed of in their past, they forgave everything in the present, and felt that this love of theirs had changed them both.

In moments of depression in the past he had comforted himself with any arguments that came into his mind, but now he no longer cared for arguments; he felt profound compassion, he wanted to be sincere and tender. . . .

"Don't cry, my darling," he said. "You've had your cry; that's enough. . . . Let us talk now, let us think of some plan."

Then they spent a long while taking counsel together, talked of how to avoid the necessity for secrecy, for deception, for living in different towns and not seeing each other for long at a time. How could they be free from this intolerable bondage?

"How? How?" he asked, clutching his head. "How?"

And it seemed as though in a little while the solution would be found, and then a new and splendid life would begin; and it was clear to both of them that they had still a long, long way to go, and that the most complicated and difficult part of it was only just beginning.

IN THE RAVINE

I

The village of Ukleevo lay in a ravine so that only the belfry and the chimneys of the printed cotton factories could be seen from the high-road and the railway-station. When visitors asked what village this was, they were told:

"That's the village where the deacon ate all the caviare at the funeral."

It had happened at the dinner at the funeral of Kostukov that the old deacon saw among the savouries some large-grained caviare and began eating it greedily; people nudged him, tugged at his arm, but he seemed petrified with enjoyment: felt nothing, and only went on eating. He ate up all the caviare, and there were four pounds in the jar. And years had passed since then, the deacon had long been dead, but the caviare was still remembered. Whether life was so poor here or people had not been clever enough to notice anything but that unimportant incident that had occurred ten years before, anyway the people had nothing else to tell about the village Ukleevo.

The village was never free from fever, and there was boggy mud there even in the summer, especially under the fences over which hung old willow-trees that gave deep shade. Here there was always a smell from the factory refuse and the acetic acid which was used in the finishing of the cotton print.

The three cotton factories and the tanyard were not in the village itself but a little way off. They were small factories, and not more than four hundred workmen were employed in all of them. The tanyard often made the water in the little river stink; the refuse contaminated the meadows, the peasants' cattle suffered from Siberian plague, and orders were given that the factory should be closed. It was considered to be closed, but went on working in secret with the connivance of the local police officer and the district doctor, who was paid ten roubles a month by the owner. In the whole village there were only two decent houses built of brick with iron roofs; one of them was the local court, in the other, a two-storeyed house just opposite the church, there lived a shopkeeper from Epifan* called Grigory Petrovitch Tsybukin.

Grigory kept a grocer's shop, but that was only for appearance sake: in reality he sold vodka, cattle, hides, grain, and pigs; he traded in anything that came to hand, and when, for instance, magpies were wanted abroad for ladies' hats, he made some thirty kopecks on every pair of birds; he bought timber for felling, lent money at interest, and altogether was a sharp old man, full of resources.

He had two sons. The elder, Anisim, was in the police in the detective department and was rarely at home. The younger, Stepan, had gone in for trade and helped his father: but no great help was expected from him as he was weak in health and deaf; his wife Aksinya, a handsome woman with a good figure, who wore a hat and carried a parasol on holidays, got up early and went to bed late, and ran about all day long, picking up her skirts and jingling her keys, going from the granary to the cellar and from there to the shop, and old Tsybukin looked at her good-humouredly while his eyes glowed, and at such moments he regretted she had not been married to his elder son instead of to the younger one, who was deaf, and who evidently knew very little about female beauty.

The old man had always an inclination for family life, and he loved his family more than anything on earth, especially his elder son, the detective, and his daughter-in-law. Aksinya had no sooner married the deaf son than she began to display an extraordinary gift for business, and knew who could be allowed to run up a bill and who could not: she kept the keys and would not trust them even to her husband; she kept the accounts by means of the reckoning beads, looked at the horses' teeth like a peasant, and was always laughing or shouting; and whatever she did or said the old man was simply delighted and muttered:

"Well done, daughter-in-law! You are a smart wench!"

He was a widower, but a year after his son's marriage he could not resist getting married himself. A girl was found for him, living

---

*Village some 150 miles from Moscow.

twenty miles from Ukleevo, called Varvara Nikolaevna, no longer quite young, but good-looking, comely, and belonging to a decent family. As soon as she was installed into the upper-storey room everything in the house seemed to brighten up as though new glass had been put into all the windows. The lamps gleamed before the ikons, the tables were covered with snow-white cloths, flowers with red buds made their appearance in the windows and in the front garden, and at dinner, instead of eating from a single bowl, each person had a separate plate set for him. Varvara Nikolaevna had a pleasant, friendly smile, and it seemed as though the whole house were smiling, too. Beggars and pilgrims, male and female, began to come into the yard, a thing which had never happened in the past; the plaintive sing-song voices of the Ukleevo peasant women and the apologetic coughs of weak, seedy-looking men, who had been dismissed from the factory for drunkenness, were heard under the windows. Varvara helped them with money, with bread, with old clothes, and afterwards, when she felt more at home, began taking things out of the shop. One day the deaf man saw her take four ounces of tea and that disturbed him.

"Here, mother's taken four ounces of tea," he informed his father afterwards; "where is that to be entered?"

The old man made no reply but stood still and thought a moment, moving his eyebrows, and then went upstairs to his wife.

"Varvarushka, if you want anything out of the shop," he said affectionately, "take it, my dear. Take it and welcome; don't hesitate."

And the next day the deaf man, running across the yard, called to her:

"If there is anything you want, mother, take it."

There was something new, something gay and light-hearted in her giving of alms, just as there was in the lamps before the ikons and in the red flowers. When at Carnival or at the church festival, which lasted for three days, they sold the peasants tainted salt meat, smelling so strong it was hard to stand near the tub of it, and took scythes, caps, and their wives' kerchiefs in pledge from the drunken men; when the factory hands stupefied with bad vodka lay rolling in the mud, and sin seemed to hover thick like a fog in the air, then it was a relief to think that up there in the house there was a gentle, neatly dressed woman who had nothing to do with salt meat or vodka; her charity had in those burdensome, murky days the effect of a safety-valve in a machine.

The days in Tsybukin's house were spent in business cares. Before the sun had risen in the morning Aksinya was panting and puffing as she washed in the outer room, and the samovar was boiling in the kitchen with a hum that boded no good. Old Grigory Petrovitch, dressed in a long black coat, cotton breeches and shiny top-boots, looking a dapper little figure, walked about the rooms, tapping with his little heels like the father-in-law in a well-known song. The shop was opened. When it was daylight a racing droshky was brought up to the front door and the old man got jauntily on to it, pulling his big cap down to his ears; and, looking at him, no one would have said he was fifty-six. His wife and daughter-in-law saw him off, and at such times when he had on a good, clean coat, and had in the droshky a huge black horse that had cost three hundred roubles, the old man did not like the peasants to come up to him with their complaints and petitions; he hated the peasants and disdained them, and if he saw some peasants waiting at the gate, he would shout angrily:

"Why are you standing there? Go further off."

Or if it were a beggar, he would say:

"God will provide!"

He used to drive off on business; his wife, in a dark dress and a black apron, tidied the rooms or helped in the kitchen. Aksinya attended to the shop, and from the yard could be heard the clink of bottles and of money, her laughter and loud talk, and the anger of customers whom she had offended; and at the same time it could be seen that the secret sale of vodka was already going on in the shop. The deaf man sat in the shop, too, or walked about the street bareheaded, with his hands in his pockets looking absent-mindedly now at the huts, now at the sky overhead. Six times a day they had tea; four times a day they sat down to meals; and in the evening they counted over their takings, put them down, went to bed, and slept soundly.

All the three cotton factories in Ukleevo and the houses of the factory owners—Hrymin Seniors, Hrymin Juniors, and Kostukov—were on a telephone. The telephone was laid on in the local court, too, but it soon ceased to work as bugs and beetles bred there.

The elder of the rural district had had little education and wrote every word in the official documents in capitals. But when the telephone was spoiled he said:

"Yes, now we shall be badly off without a telephone."

The Hrymin Seniors were continually at law with the Juniors, and sometimes the Juniors quarrelled among themselves and began going to law, and their factory did not work for a month or two till they were reconciled again, and this was an entertainment for the people of Ukleevo, as there was a great deal of talk and gossip on the occasion of each quarrel. On holidays Kostukov and the Juniors used to get up races, used to dash about Ukleevo and run over calves. Aksinya, rustling her starched petticoats, used to promenade in a low-necked dress up and down the street near her shop; the Juniors used to snatch her up and carry her off as though by force. Then old Tsybukin would drive out to show his new horse and take Varvara with him.

In the evening, after the races, when people were going to bed, an expensive concertina was played in the Juniors' yard and, if it were a moonlight night, those sounds sent a thrill of delight to the heart, and Ukleevo no longer seemed a wretched hole.

II

The elder son Anisim came home very rarely, only on great holidays, but he often sent by a returning villager presents and letters written in very good writing by some other hand, always on a sheet of foolscap in the form of a petition. The letters were full of expressions that Anisim never made use of in conversation: "Dear papa and mamma, I send you a pound of flower tea for the satisfaction of your physical needs."

At the bottom of every letter was scratched, as though with a broken pen: "Anisim Tsybukin," and again in the same excellent hand: "Agent."

The letters were read aloud several times, and the old father, touched, red with emotion, would say:

"Here he did not care to stay at home, he has gone in for an intellectual line. Well, let him! Every man to his own job!"

It happened just before Carnival there was a heavy storm of rain mixed with hail; the old man and Varvara went to the window to look at it, and lo and behold! Anisim drove up in a sledge from the station. He was quite unexpected. He came indoors, looking anxious and troubled about something, and he remained the same all the time; there was something free and easy in his manner. He was in no haste to go away, it seemed as though he had been dismissed from the service. Varvara was pleased at his arrival; she looked at him with a sly expression, sighed, and shook her head.

"How is this, my friends?" she said. "Tut, tut, the lad's in his twenty-eighth year, and he is still leading a gay bachelor life; tut, tut, tut. . . ."

From the other room her soft, even speech sounded like tut, tut, tut. She began whispering with her husband and Aksinya, and their faces wore the same sly and mysterious expression as though they were conspirators.

It was decided to marry Anisim.

"Oh, tut, tut . . . the younger brother has been married long ago," said Varvara, "and you are still without a helpmate like a cock at a fair. What is the meaning of it? Tut, tut, you will be married, please God, then as you choose—you will go into the service and your wife will remain here at home to help us. There is no order in your life, young man, and I see you have forgotten how to live properly. Tut, tut, it's the same trouble with all you townspeople."

When the Tsybukins married, the most handsome girls were chosen as brides for them as rich men. For Anisim, too, they found a handsome one. He was himself of an uninteresting and inconspicuous appearance; of a feeble, sickly build and short stature; he had full, puffy cheeks which looked as though he were blowing them out; his eyes looked with a keen, unblinking stare; his beard was red and scanty, and when he was thinking he always put it into his mouth and bit it; moreover he often drank too much, and that was noticeable from his face and his walk. But when he was informed that they had found a very beautiful bride for him, he said:

"Oh well, I am not a fright myself. All of us Tsybukins are handsome, I may say."

The village of Torguevo was near the town. Half of it had lately been incorporated into the town, the other half remained a village. In the first—the town half—there was a widow living in her own little house; she had a sister living with her who was quite poor and went out to work by the day, and this sister had a daughter called Lipa, a girl who went out to work, too. People in Torguevo were already talking about Lipa's good looks, but her terrible poverty put everyone off; people opined that some widower or elderly man would marry her regardless of her poverty, or would perhaps take her to himself without marriage, and that her mother would get enough to eat living with her. Varvara heard about Lipa from the matchmakers, and she drove over to Torguevo.

Then a visit of inspection was arranged at the aunt's, with lunch and wine all in due order, and Lipa wore a new pink dress made on purpose for this occasion, and a crimson ribbon like a flame gleamed in her hair. She was pale-faced, thin, and frail, with soft, delicate features sunburnt from working in the open air; a shy, mournful smile always hovered about her face, and there was a child-like look in her eyes, trustful and curious.

She was young, quite a little girl, her bosom still scarcely perceptible, but she could be married because she had reached the legal age. She really was beautiful, and the only thing that might be thought unattractive was her big masculine hands which hung idle now like two big claws.

"There is no dowry—and we don't think much of that," said Tsybukin to the aunt. "We took a wife from a poor family for our son Stepan, too, and now we can't say too much for her. In house and in business alike she has hands of gold."

Lipa stood in the doorway and looked as though she would say: "Do with me as you will, I trust you," while her mother Praskovya the work-woman hid herself in the kitchen numb with shyness. At one time in her youth a merchant whose floors she was scrubbing stamped at her in a rage; she went chill with terror and there always was a feeling of fear at the bottom of her heart. When she was frightened her arms and legs trembled and her cheeks twitched. Sitting in the kitchen she tried to hear what the visitors were saying, and she kept crossing herself, pressing her fingers to her forehead, and gazing at the ikons. Anisim, slightly drunk, opened the door into the kitchen and said in a free-and-easy way:

"Why are you sitting in here, precious mamma? We are dull without you."

And Praskovya, overcome with timidity, pressing her hands to her lean, wasted bosom, said:

"Oh, not at all. . . . It's very kind of you."

After the visit of inspection the wedding-day was fixed. Then Anisim walked about the rooms at home whistling, or suddenly thinking of something, would fall to brooding and would look at the floor fixedly, silently, as though he would probe to the depths of the earth. He expressed neither pleasure that he was to be married, married so soon, on Low Sunday, nor a desire to see his bride, but simply went on whistling. And it was evident he was only getting married because his father and stepmother wished him to, and because it was the custom in the village to marry the son in order to have a woman to help in the house. When he went away he seemed in no haste, and behaved altogether not as he had done on previous visits—was particularly free and easy, and talked inappropriately.

III

In the village Shikalovo lived two dressmakers, sisters, belonging to the Flagellant sect.* The new clothes for the wedding were ordered from them, and they often came to try them on, and stayed a long while drinking tea. They were making Varvara a brown dress with black lace and bugles on it, and Aksinya a light green dress with a yellow front, with a train. When the dressmakers had finished their work Tsybukin paid them not in money but in goods from the shop, and they went away depressed carrying parcels of tallow candles and tins of sardines which they did not in the least need, and when they got out of the village into the open country they sat down on a hillock and cried.

Anisim arrived three days before the wedding, rigged out in new clothes from top to toe. He had dazzling india-rubber goloshes, and instead of a cravat wore a red cord with little balls on it, and over his shoulder he had hung an overcoat, also new, without putting his arms into the sleeves.

After crossing himself sedately before the ikon, he greeted his fa-

*Religious sect whose members whip themselves as part of their devotions.

ther and gave him ten silver roubles and ten half-roubles; to Varvara he gave as much, and to Aksinya twenty quarter-roubles. The chief charm of the present lay in the fact that all the coins, as though carefully matched, were new and glittered in the sun. Trying to seem grave and sedate he pursed up his face and puffed out his cheeks, and he smelt of spirits. Probably he had visited the refreshment bar at every station. And again there was a free-and-easiness about the man—something superfluous and out of place. Then Anisim had lunch and drank tea with the old man, and Varvara turned the new coins over in her hands and enquired about villagers who had gone to live in the town.

"They are all right, thank God, they get on quite well," said Anisim. "Only something has happened to Ivan Yegorov: his old wife Sofya Nikiforovna is dead. From consumption. They ordered the memorial dinner for the peace of her soul at the confectioner's at two and a half roubles a head. And there was real wine. Those who were peasants from our village—they paid two and a half roubles for them, too. They ate nothing, as though a peasant would understand sauce!"

"Two and a half," said his father, shaking his head.

"Well, it's not like the country there, you go into a restaurant to have a snack of something, you ask for one thing and another, others join till there is a party of us, one has a drink—and before you know where you are it is daylight and you've three or four roubles each to pay. And when one is with Samorodov he likes to have coffee with brandy in it after everything, and brandy is sixty kopecks for a little glass."

"And he is making it all up," said the old man enthusiastically; "he is making it all up, lying!"

"I am always with Samorodov now. It is Samorodov who writes my letters to you. He writes splendidly. And if I were to tell you, mamma," Anisim went on gaily, addressing Varvara, "the sort of fellow that Samorodov is, you would not believe me. We call him Muhtar because he is black like an Armenian. I can see through him, I know all his affairs like the five fingers of my hand, and he feels that, and he always follows me about, we are regular inseparables. He seems not to like it in a way, but he can't get on without me. Where I go he goes. I have a correct, trustworthy eye, mamma.

One sees a peasant selling a shirt in the market-place. 'Stay, that shirt's stolen.' And really it turns out it is so: the shirt was a stolen one."

"What do you tell from?" asked Varvara.

"Not from anything, I have just an eye for it. I know nothing about the shirt, only for some reason I seem drawn to it: it's stolen, and that's all I can say. Among us detectives it's come to their saying, 'Oh, Anisim has gone to shoot snipe!' That means looking for stolen goods. Yes. . . . Anybody can steal, but it is another thing to keep! The earth is wide, but there is nowhere to hide stolen goods."

"In our village a ram and two ewes were carried off last week," said Varvara, and she heaved a sigh, "and there is no one to try and find them. . . . Oh, tut, tut. . . ."

"Well, I might have a try. I don't mind."

The day of the wedding arrived. It was a cool but bright, cheerful April day. People were driving about Ukleevo from early morning with pairs or teams of three horses decked with many-coloured ribbons on their yokes and manes, with a jingle of bells. The rooks, disturbed by this activity, were cawing noisily in the willows, and the starlings sang their loudest unceasingly as though rejoicing that there was a wedding at the Tsybukins'.

Indoors the tables were already covered with long fish, smoked hams, stuffed fowls, boxes of sprats, pickled savouries of various sorts, and a number of bottles of vodka and wine; there was a smell of smoked sausage and of sour tinned lobster. Old Tsybukin walked about near the tables, tapping with his heels and sharpening the knives against each other. They kept calling Varvara and asking for things, and she was constantly with a distracted face running breathlessly into the kitchen, where the man cook from Kostukov's and the woman cook from Hrymin Juniors' had been at work since early morning. Aksinya, with her hair curled, in her stays without her dress on, in new creaky boots, flew about the yard like a whirlwind showing glimpses of her bare knees and bosom.

It was noisy, there was a sound of scolding and oaths; passersby stopped at the wide-open gates, and in everything there was a feeling that something extraordinary was happening.

"They have gone for the bride!"

The bells began jingling and died away far beyond the village. . . .

Between two and three o'clock people ran up: again there was a jingling of bells: they were bringing the bride! The church was full, the candelabra were lighted, the choir were singing from music books as old Tsybukin had wished it. The glare of the lights and the bright coloured dresses dazzled Lipa; she felt as though the singers with their loud voices were hitting her on the head with a hammer. Her boots and the stays, which she had put on for the first time in her life, pinched her, and her face looked as though she had only just come to herself after fainting; she gazed about without understanding. Anisim, in his black coat with a red cord instead of a tie, stared at the same spot lost in thought, and when the singers shouted loudly he hurriedly crossed himself. He felt touched and disposed to weep. This church was familiar to him from earliest childhood; at one time his dead mother used to bring him here to take the sacrament; at one time he used to sing in the choir; every ikon he remembered so well, every corner. Here he was being married, he had to take a wife for the sake of doing the proper thing, but he was not thinking of that now, he had forgotten his wedding completely. Tears dimmed his eyes so that he could not see the ikons, he felt heavy at heart; he prayed and besought God that the misfortunes that threatened him, that were ready to burst upon him to-morrow, if not to-day, might somehow pass him by as storm-clouds in time of drought pass over the village without yielding one drop of rain. And so many sins were heaped up in the past, so many sins, all getting away from them or setting them right was so beyond hope that it seemed incongruous even to ask forgiveness. But he did ask forgiveness, and even gave a loud sob, but no one took any notice of that, since they all supposed he had had a drop too much.

There was a sound of a fretful childish wail:

"Take me away, mamma darling!"

"Quiet there!" cried the priest.

When they returned from the church people ran after them; there were crowds, too, round the shop, round the gates, and in the yard under the windows. The peasant women came in to sing songs of congratulation to them. The young couple had scarcely crossed the threshold when the singers, who were already standing in the outer room with their music books, broke into a loud chant at the top of their voices; a band ordered expressly from the town began playing. Foaming Don wine was brought in tall wineglasses, and Elizarov, a carpenter who did jobs by contract, a tall, gaunt old man with eyebrows so bushy that his eyes could scarcely be seen, said, addressing the happy pair:

"Anisim and you, my child, love one another, live in God's way, little children, and the Heavenly Mother will not abandon you."

He leaned his face on the old father's shoulder and gave a sob.

"Grigory Petrovitch, let us weep, let us weep with joy!" he said in a thin voice, and then at once burst out laughing in a loud bass guffaw. "Ho-ho-ho! This is a fine daughter-in-law for you too! Everything is in its place in her; all runs smoothly, no creaking, the mechanism works well, lots of screws in it."

He was a native of the Yegoryevsky* district, but had worked in the factories in Ukleevo and the neighbourhood from his youth up, and had made it his home. He had been a familiar figure for years as old and gaunt and lanky as now, and for years he had been nicknamed "Crutch." Perhaps because he had been for forty years occupied in repairing the factory machinery he judged everybody and everything by its soundness or its need of repair. And before sitting down to the table he tried several chairs to see whether they were solid, and he touched the smoked fish also.

After the Don wine, they all sat down to the table. The visitors talked, moving their chairs. The singers were singing in the outer room. The band was playing, and at the same time the peasant women in the yard were singing their songs all in chorus—and there was an awful, wild medley of sounds which made one giddy.

Crutch turned round in his chair and prodded his neighbours with his elbows, prevented people from talking, and laughed and cried alternately.

"Little children, little children, little children," he muttered rapidly. "Aksinya, my dear, Varvara darling, we will live all in peace and harmony, my dear little axes. . . ."

He drank little and was now only drunk from one glass of English bitters. The revolting bitters, made from nobody knows what,

---

*Town about 80 miles from Moscow.

intoxicated everyone who drank it as though it had stunned them. Their tongues began to falter.

The local clergy, the clerks from the factories with their wives, the tradesmen and tavern-keepers from the other villages were present. The clerk and the elder of the rural district who had served together for fourteen years, and who had during all that time never signed a single document for anybody nor let a single person out of the local court without deceiving or insulting him, were sitting now side by side, both fat and well-fed, and it seemed as though they were so saturated in injustice and falsehood that even the skin of their faces were somehow peculiar, fraudulent. The clerk's wife, a thin woman with a squint, had brought all her children with her, and like a bird of prey looked aslant at the plates and snatched anything she could get hold of to put in her own or her children's pockets.

Lipa sat as though turned to stone, still with the same expression as in church. Anisim had not said a single word to her since he had made her acquaintance, so that he did not yet know the sound of her voice; and now, sitting beside her, he remained mute and went on drinking bitters, and when he got drunk he began talking to the aunt who was sitting opposite:

"I have a friend called Samorodov. A peculiar man. He is by rank an honorary citizen, and he can talk. But I know him through and through, auntie, and he feels it. Pray join me in drinking to the health of Samorodov, auntie!"

Varvara, worn out and distracted, walked round the table pressing the guests to eat, and was evidently pleased that there were so many dishes and that everything was so lavish—no one could disparage them now. The sun set, but the dinner went on: the guests were beyond knowing what they were eating or drinking, it was impossible to distinguish what was said, and only from time to time when the band subsided some peasant woman could be heard shouting:

"They have sucked the blood out of us, the Herods; a pest on them!"

In the evening they danced to the band. The Hrymin Juniors came, bringing their wine, and one of them, when dancing a quadrille, held a bottle in each hand and a wineglass in his mouth, and that made everyone laugh. In the middle of the quadrille they suddenly crooked their knees and danced in a squatting position; Aksinya in green flew by like a flash, stirring up a wind with her train. Someone trod on her flounce and Crutch shouted:

"Aie, they have torn off the panel! Children!"

Aksinya had naïve grey eyes which rarely blinked, and a naïve smile played continually on her face. And in those unblinking eyes, and in that little head on the long neck, and in her slenderness there was something snake-like; all in green but for the yellow on her bosom, she looked with a smile on her face as a viper looks out of the young rye in the spring at the passersby, stretching itself and lifting its head. The Hrymins were free in their behaviour to her, and it was very noticeable that she was on intimate terms with the elder of them. But her deaf husband saw nothing, he did not look at her; he sat with his legs crossed and ate nuts, cracking them so loudly that it sounded like pistol shots.

But, behold, old Tsybukin himself walked into the middle of the room and waved his handkerchief as a sign that he, too, wanted to dance the Russian dance, and all over the house and from the crowd in the yard rose a roar of approbation:

"*He's* going to dance! *He* himself!"

Varvara danced, but the old man only waved his handkerchief and kicked up his heels, but the people in the yard, propped against one another, peeping in at the windows, were in raptures, and for the moment forgave him everything—his wealth and the wrongs he had done them.

"Well done, Grigory Petrovitch!" was heard in the crowd. "That's right, do your best! You can still play your part! Ha-ha!"

It was kept up till late, till two o'clock in the morning. Anisim, staggering, went to take leave of the singers and bandsmen, and gave each of them a new half-rouble. His father, who was not staggering but still seemed to be standing on one leg, saw his guests off, and said to each of them:

"The wedding has cost two thousand."

As the party was breaking up, someone took the Shikalovo innkeeper's good coat instead of his own old one, and Anisim suddenly flew into a rage and began shouting:

"Stop, I'll find it at once; I know who stole it, stop."

He ran out into the street and pursued someone. He was caught, brought back home and shoved, drunken, red with anger, and wet, into the room where the aunt was undressing Lipa, and was locked in.

IV

Five days had passed. Anisim, who was preparing to go, went upstairs to say good-bye to Varvara. All the lamps were burning before the ikons, there was a smell of incense, while she sat at the window knitting a stocking of red wool.

"You have not stayed with us long," she said. "You've been dull, I dare say. Oh, tut, tut. . . . We live comfortably; we have plenty of everything. We celebrated your wedding properly, in good style; your father says it came to two thousand. In fact we live like merchants, only it's dreary. We treat the people very badly. My heart aches, my dear; how we treat them, my goodness! Whether we exchange a horse or buy something or hire a labourer—it's cheating in everything. Cheating and cheating. The Lenten oil in the shop is bitter, rancid, the people have pitch that is better. But surely, tell me, pray, couldn't we sell good oil?"

"Every man to his job, mamma."

"But you know we all have to die? Oy, oy, really you ought to talk to your father . . . !"

"Why, you should talk to him yourself."

"Well, well, I did put in my word, but he said just what you do: 'Every man to his own job.' Do you suppose in the next world they'll consider what job you have been put to? God's judgment is just."

"Of course no one will consider," said Anisim, and he heaved a sigh. "There is no God, anyway, you know, mamma, so what considering can there be?"

Varvara looked at him with surprise, burst out laughing, and clasped her hands. Perhaps because she was so genuinely surprised at his words and looked at him as though he were a queer person, he was confused.

"Perhaps there is a God, only there is no faith. When I was being married I was not myself. Just as you may take an egg from under a hen and there is a chicken chirping in it, so my conscience was beginning to chirp in me, and while I was being married I thought all the time there was a God! But when I left the church it was nothing. And indeed, how can I tell whether there is a God or not? We are not taught right from childhood, and while the babe is still at his mother's breast he is only taught 'every man to his own job.' Father does not believe in God, either. You were saying that Guntorev had some sheep stolen. . . . I have found them; it was a peasant at Shikalovo stole them; he stole them, but father's got the fleeces . . . so that's all his faith amounts to."

Anisim winked and wagged his head.

"The elder does not believe in God, either," he went on. "And the clerk and the deacon, too. And as for their going to church and keeping the fasts, that is simply to prevent people talking ill of them, and in case it really may be true that there will be a Day of Judgment. Nowadays people say that the end of the world has come because people have grown weaker, do not honour their parents, and so on. All that is nonsense. My idea, mamma, is that all our trouble is because there is so little conscience in people. I see through things, mamma, and I understand. If a man has a stolen shirt I see it. A man sits in a tavern and you fancy he is drinking tea and no more, but to me the tea is neither here nor there; I see further, he has no conscience. You can go about the whole day and not meet one man with a conscience. And the whole reason is that they don't know whether there is a God or not. . . . Well, good-bye, mamma, keep alive and well, don't remember evil against me."

Anisim bowed down at Varvara's feet.

"I thank you for everything, mamma," he said. "You are a great gain to our family. You are a very lady-like woman, and I am very pleased with you."

Much moved, Anisim went out, but returned again and said:

"Samorodov has got me mixed up in something: I shall either make my fortune or come to grief. If anything happens, then you must comfort my father, mamma."

"Oh nonsense, don't you worry, tut, tut, tut . . . God is merciful. And Anisim, you should be affectionate to your wife, instead of giving each other sulky looks as you do; you might smile at least."

"Yes, she is rather a queer one," said Anisim, and he gave a sigh.

"She does not understand anything, she never speaks. She is very young, let her grow up."

A tall, sleek white stallion was already standing at the front door, harnessed to the chaise.

Old Tsybukin jumped in jauntily with a run and took the reins. Anisim kissed Varvara, Aksinya, and his brother. On the steps Lipa, too, was standing; she was standing motionless, looking away, and it seemed as though she had not come to see him off but just by chance for some unknown reason. Anisim went up to her and just touched her cheek with his lips.

"Good-bye," he said.

And without looking at him she gave a strange smile; her face began to quiver, and everyone for some reason felt sorry for her. Anisim, too, leaped into the chaise with a bound and put his arms jauntily akimbo, for he considered himself a good-looking fellow.

When they drove up out of the ravine Anisim kept looking back towards the village. It was a warm, bright day. The cattle were being driven out for the first time, and the peasant girls and women were walking by the herd in their holiday dresses. The dun-coloured bull bellowed, glad to be free, and pawed the ground with his forefeet. On all sides, above and below, the larks were singing. Anisim looked round at the elegant white church—it had only lately been white-washed—and he thought how he had been praying in it five days before; he looked round at the school with its green roof, at the little river in which he used once to bathe and catch fish, and there was a stir of joy in his heart, and he wished that walls might rise up from the ground and prevent him from going further, and that he might be left with nothing but the past.

At the station they went to the refreshment-room and drank a glass of sherry each. His father felt in his pocket for his purse to pay.

"I will stand treat," said Anisim. The old man, touched and delighted, slapped him on the shoulder, and winked to the waiter as much as to say, "See what a fine son I have got."

"You ought to stay at home in the business, Anisim," he said; "you would be worth any price to me! I would shower gold on you from head to foot, my son."

"It can't be done, papa."

The sherry was sour and smelt of sealing-wax, but they had another glass.

When old Tsybukin returned home from the station, for the first moment he did not recognize his younger daughter-in-law. As soon as her husband had driven out of the yard, Lipa was transformed and suddenly brightened up. Wearing a threadbare old petticoat, with her feet bare and her sleeves tucked up to the shoulders, she was scrubbing the stairs in the entry and singing in a silvery little voice, and when she brought out a big tub of dirty water and looked up at the sun with her child-like smile it seemed as though she, too, were a lark.

An old labourer who was passing by the door shook his head and cleared his throat.

"Yes, indeed, your daughters-in-law, Grigory Petrovitch, are a blessing from God," he said. "Not women, but treasures!"

V

On Friday, the 8th of July, Elizarov, nicknamed Crutch, and Lipa were returning from the village of Kazanskoe, where they had been to a service on the occasion of a church holiday in honour of the Holy Mother of Kazan. A good distance after them walked Lipa's mother Praskovya, who always fell behind, as she was ill and short of breath. It was drawing towards evening.

"A-a-a . . ." said Crutch, wondering as he listened to Lipa. "A-a! . . . We-ell!"

"I am very fond of jam, Ilya Makaritch," said Lipa. "I sit down in my little corner and drink tea and eat jam. Or I drink it with Varvara Nikolaevna, and she tells some story full of feeling. We have a lot of jam—four jars. 'Have some, Lipa; eat as much as you like.' "

"A-a-a, four jars!"

"They live very well. We have white bread with our tea; and meat, too, as much as one wants. They live very well, only I am frightened with them, Ilya Makaritch. Oh, oh, how frightened I am!"

"Why are you frightened, child?" asked Crutch, and he looked back to see how far Praskovya was behind.

"To begin with, when the wedding had been celebrated I was

afraid of Anisim Grigoritch. Anisim Grigoritch did nothing, he didn't ill-treat me, only when he comes near me a cold shiver runs all over me, through all my bones. And I did not sleep one night, I trembled all over and kept praying to God. And now I am afraid of Aksinya, Ilya Makaritch. It's not that she does anything, she is always laughing, but sometimes she glances at the window, and her eyes are so fierce and there is a gleam of green in them—like the eyes of the sheep in the shed. The Hrymin Juniors are leading her astray: 'Your old man,' they tell her, 'has a bit of land at Butyokino, a hundred and twenty acres,' they say, 'and there is sand and water there, so you, Aksinya,' they say, 'build a brickyard there and we will go shares in it.' Bricks now are twenty roubles the thousand, it's a profitable business. Yesterday at dinner Aksinya said to my father-in-law: 'I want to build a brickyard at Butyokino; I'm going into business on my own account.' She laughed as she said it. And Grigory Petrovitch's face darkened, one could see he did not like it. 'As long as I live,' he said, 'the family must not break up, we must go on altogether.' She gave a look and gritted her teeth. . . . Fritters were served, she would not eat them."

"A-a-a! . . ." Crutch was surprised.

"And tell me, if you please, when does she sleep?" said Lipa. "She sleeps for half an hour, then jumps up and keeps walking and walking about to see whether the peasants have not set fire to something, have not stolen something. . . . I am frightened with her, Ilya Makaritch. And the Hrymin Juniors did not go to bed after the wedding, but drove to the town to go to law with each other; and folks do say it is all on account of Aksinya. Two of the brothers have promised to build her a brickyard, but the third is offended, and the factory has been at a standstill for a month, and my uncle Prohor is without work and goes about from house to house getting crusts. 'Hadn't you better go working on the land or sawing up wood, meanwhile, uncle?' I tell him; 'why disgrace yourself?' 'I've got out of the way of it,' he says; 'I don't know how to do any sort of peasant's work now, Lipinka. . . .' "

They stopped to rest and wait for Praskovya near a copse of young aspen-trees. Elizarov had long been a contractor in a small way, but he kept no horses, going on foot all over the district with nothing but a little bag in which there was bread and onions, and stalking along with big strides, swinging his arms. And it was difficult to walk with him.

At the entrance to the copse stood a milestone. Elizarov touched it; read it. Praskovya reached them out of breath. Her wrinkled and always scared-looking face was beaming with happiness; she had been at church to-day like anyone else, then she had been to the fair and there had drunk pear cider. For her this was unusual, and it even seemed to her now that she had lived for her own pleasure that day for the first time in her life. After resting they all three walked on side by side. The sun had already set, and its beams filtered through the copse, casting a light on the trunks of the trees. There was a faint sound of voices ahead. The Ukleevo girls had long before pushed on ahead but had lingered in the copse, probably gathering mushrooms.

"Hey, wenches!" cried Elizarov. "Hey, my beauties!"

There was a sound of laughter in response.

"Crutch is coming! Crutch! The old horse-radish."

And the echo laughed, too. And then the copse was left behind. The tops of the factory chimneys came into view. The cross on the belfry glittered: this was the village: "the one at which the deacon ate all the caviare at the funeral." Now they were almost home; they only had to go down into the big ravine. Lipa and Praskovya, who had been walking barefooted, sat down on the grass to put on their boots; Elizarov sat down with them. If they looked down from above Ukleevo looked beautiful and peaceful with its willow-trees, its white church, and its little river, and the only blot on the picture was the roof of the factories, painted for the sake of cheapness a gloomy ashen grey. On the slope on the further side they could see the rye—some in stacks and sheaves here and there as though strewn about by the storm, and some freshly cut lying in swathes; the oats, too, were ripe and glistened now in the sun like mother-of-pearl. It was harvest-time. To-day was a holiday, to-morrow they would harvest the rye and carry the hay, and then Sunday a holiday again; every day there were mutterings of distant thunder. It was misty and looked like rain, and, gazing now at the fields, everyone thought, God grant we get the harvest in in time; and everyone felt gay and joyful and anxious at heart.

"Mowers ask a high price nowadays," said Praskovya. "One rouble and forty kopecks a day."

People kept coming and coming from the fair at Kazanskoe: peasant women, factory workers in new caps, beggars, children. . . . Here a cart would drive by stirring up the dust and behind it would run an unsold horse, and it seemed glad it had not been sold; then a cow was led along by the horns, resisting stubbornly; then a cart again, and in it drunken peasants swinging their legs. An old woman led a little boy in a big cap and big boots; the boy was tired out with the heat and the heavy boots which prevented his bending his legs at the knees, but yet blew unceasingly with all his might at a tin trumpet. They had gone down the slope and turned into the street, but the trumpet could still be heard.

"Our factory owners don't seem quite themselves . . ." said Elizarov. "There's trouble. Kostukov is angry with me. 'Too many boards have gone on the cornices.' 'Too many? As many have gone on it as were needed, Vassily Danilitch; I don't eat them with my porridge.' 'How can you speak to me like that?' said he, 'you good-for-nothing blockhead! Don't forget yourself! It was I made you a contractor.' 'That's nothing so wonderful,' said I. 'Even before I was a contractor I used to have tea every day.' 'You are a rascal . . .' he said. I said nothing. 'We are rascals in this world,' thought I, 'and you will be rascals in the next. . . .' Ha-ha-ha! The next day he was softer. 'Don't you bear malice against me for my words, Makaritch,' he said. 'If I said too much,' says he, 'what of it? I am a merchant of the first guild, your superior—you ought to hold your tongue.' 'You,' said I, 'are a merchant of the first guild and I am a carpenter, that's correct. And Saint Joseph was a carpenter, too. Ours is a righteous calling and pleasing to God, and if you are pleased to be my superior you are very welcome to it, Vassily Danilitch.' And later on, after that conversation I mean, I thought: 'Which was the superior? A merchant of the first guild or a carpenter?' The carpenter must be, my child!"

Crutch thought a minute and added:

"Yes, that's how it is, child. He who works, he who is patient is the superior."

By now the sun had set and a thick mist as white as milk was rising over the river, in the church enclosure, and in the open spaces round the factories. Now when the darkness was coming on rapidly, when lights were twinkling below, and when it seemed as though the mist were hiding a fathomless abyss, Lipa and her mother, who were born in poverty and prepared to live so till the end, giving up to others everything except their frightened, gentle souls, may have fancied for a minute perhaps that in the vast mysterious world, among the endless series of lives, they, too, counted for something, and they, too, were superior to someone; they liked sitting here at the top, they smiled happily and forgot that they must go down below again all the same.

At last they went home again. The mowers were sitting on the ground at the gates near the shop. As a rule the Ukleevo peasants did not go to Tsybukin's to work, and they had to hire strangers, and now in the darkness it seemed as though there were men sitting there with long black beards. The shop was open, and through the doorway they could see the deaf man playing draughts with a boy. The mowers were singing softly, scarcely audibly, or loudly demanding their wages for the previous day, but they were not paid for fear they should go away before to-morrow. Old Tsybukin, with his coat off, was sitting in his waistcoat with Aksinya under the birch-tree, drinking tea; a lamp was burning on the table.

"I say, grandfather," a mower called from outside the gates, as though taunting him, "pay us half anyway! Hey, grandfather."

And at once there was a sound of laughter, and then again they sang hardly audibly. . . . Crutch, too, sat down to have some tea.

"We have been at the fair, you know," he began telling them. "We have had a walk, a very nice walk, my children, praise the Lord. But an unfortunate thing happened: Sashka the blacksmith bought some tobacco and gave the shopman half a rouble, to be sure. And the half-rouble was a false one"—Crutch went on, and he meant to speak in a whisper, but he spoke in a smothered, husky voice which was audible to everyone. "The half-rouble turned out to be a bad one. He was asked where he got it. 'Anisim Tsybukin gave it me,' he said. 'When I went to his wedding,' he said. They called the police inspector, took the man away. . . . Look out, Grigory Petrovitch, that nothing comes of it, no talk. . . ."

"Gra-ndfather!" the same voice called tauntingly outside the gates. "Gra-andfather!"

A silence followed.

"Ah, little children, little children, little children . . ." Crutch muttered rapidly, and he got up. He was overcome with drowsiness. "Well, thank you for the tea, for the sugar, little children. It is time to sleep. I am like a bit of rotten timber nowadays, my beams are crumbling under me. Ho-ho-ho! I suppose it's time I was dead."

And he gave a gulp. Old Tsybukin did not finish his tea but sat on a little, pondering; and his face looked as though he were listening to the footsteps of Crutch, who was far away down the street.

"Sashka the blacksmith told a lie, I expect," said Aksinya, guessing his thoughts.

He went into the house and came back a little later with a parcel; he opened it, and there was the gleam of roubles—perfectly new coins. He took one, tried it with his teeth, flung it on the tray; then flung down another.

"The roubles really are false . . ." he said, looking at Aksinya and seeming perplexed. "These are those Anisim brought, his present. Take them, daughter," he whispered, and thrust the parcel into her hands. "Take them and throw them into the well . . . confound them! And mind there is no talk about it. Harm might come of it. . . . Take away the samovar, put out the light."

Lipa and her mother sitting in the barn saw the lights go out one after the other; only overhead in Varvara's room there were blue and red lamps gleaming, and a feeling of peace, content, and happy ignorance seemed to float down from there. Praskovya could never get used to her daughter's being married to a rich man, and when she came she huddled timidly in the outer room with a deprecating smile on her face, and tea and sugar were sent out to her. And Lipa, too, could not get used to it either, and after her husband had gone away she did not sleep in her bed, but lay down anywhere to sleep, in the kitchen or the barn, and every day she scrubbed the floor or washed the clothes, and felt as though she were hired by the day. And now, on coming back from the service, they drank tea in the kitchen with the cook, then they went into the barn and lay down on the ground between the sledge and the wall. It was dark here and smelt of harness. The lights went out about the house, then they could hear the deaf man shutting up the shop, the mowers settling themselves about the yard to sleep. In the distance at the Hrymin

Juniors' they were playing on the expensive concertina. . . . Praskovya and Lipa began to go to sleep.

And when they were awakened by somebody's steps it was bright moonlight; at the entrance of the barn stood Aksinya with her bedding in her arms.

"Maybe it's a bit cooler here," she said; then she came in and lay down almost in the doorway so that the moonlight fell full upon her.

She did not sleep, but breathed heavily, tossing from side to side with the heat, throwing off almost all the bedclothes. And in the magic moonlight what a beautiful, what a proud animal she was! A little time passed, and then steps were heard again: the old father, white all over, appeared in the doorway.

"Aksinya," he called, "are you here?"

"Well?" she responded angrily.

"I told you just now to throw the money into the well, have you done so?"

"What next, throwing property into the water! I gave them to the mowers. . . ."

"Oh my God!" cried the old man, dumbfounded and alarmed. "Oh my God! you wicked woman. . . ."

He flung up his hands and went out, and he kept saying something as he went away. And a little later Aksinya sat up and sighed heavily with annoyance, then got up and, gathering up her bedclothes in her arms, went out.

"Why did you marry me into this family, mother?" said Lipa.

"One has to be married, daughter. It was not us who ordained it."

And a feeling of inconsolable woe was ready to take possession of them. But it seemed to them that someone was looking down from the height of the heavens, out of the blue from where the stars were seeing everything that was going on in Ukleevo, watching over them. And however great was wickedness, still the night was calm and beautiful, and still in God's world there is and will be truth and justice as calm and beautiful, and everything on earth is only waiting to be made one with truth and justice, even as the moonlight is blended with the night.

And both, huddling close to one another, fell asleep comforted.

VI

News had come long before that Anisim had been put in prison for coining and passing bad money. Months passed, more than half a year passed, the long winter was over, spring had begun, and everyone in the house and the village had grown used to the fact that Anisim was in prison. And when anyone passed by the house or the shop at night he would remember that Anisim was in prison; and when they rang at the churchyard for some reason, that, too, reminded them that he was in prison awaiting trial.

It seemed as though a shadow had fallen upon the house. The house looked darker, the roof was rustier, the heavy iron-bound door into the shop, which was painted green, was covered with cracks, or, as the deaf man expressed it, "blisters"; and old Tsybukin seemed to have grown dingy, too. He had given up cutting his hair and beard, and looked shaggy. He no longer sprang jauntily into his chaise, nor shouted to beggars: "God will provide!" His strength was on the wane, and that was evident in everything. People were less afraid of him now, and the police officer drew up a formal charge against him in the shop though he received his regular bribe as before; and three times the old man was called up to the town to be tried for illicit dealing in spirits, and the case was continually adjourned owing to the non-appearance of witnesses, and old Tsybukin was worn out with worry.

He often went to see his son, hired somebody, handed in a petition to somebody else, presented a holy banner to some church. He presented the governor of the prison in which Anisim was confined with a silver glass stand with a long spoon and the inscription: "The soul knows its right measure."

"There is no one to look after things for us," said Varvara. "Tut, tut. . . . You ought to ask someone of the gentlefolks, they would write to the head officials. . . . At least they might let him out on bail! Why wear the poor fellow out?"

She, too, was grieved, but had grown stouter and whiter; she lighted the lamps before the ikons as before, and saw that everything in the house was clean, and regaled the guests with jam and apple cheese. The deaf man and Aksinya looked after the shop. A new project was in progress—a brickyard in Butyokino—and Aksinya went there almost every day in the chaise. She drove herself, and when she met acquaintances she stretched out her neck like a snake out of the young rye, and smiled naïvely and enigmatically. Lipa spent her time playing with the baby which had been born to her before Lent. It was a tiny, thin, pitiful little baby, and it was strange that it should cry and gaze about and be considered a human being, and even be called Nikifor. He lay in his swinging cradle, and Lipa would walk away towards the door and say, bowing to him:

"Good day, Nikifor Anisimitch!"

And she would rush at him and kiss him. Then she would walk away to the door, bow again, and say:

"Good day, Nikifor Anisimitch!"

And he kicked up his little red legs, and his crying was mixed with laughter like the carpenter Elizarov's.

At last the day of the trial was fixed. Tsybukin went away five days before. Then they heard that the peasants called as witnesses had been fetched; their old workman who had received a notice to appear went too.

The trial was on a Thursday. But Sunday had passed, and Tsybukin was still not back, and there was no news. Towards the evening on Tuesday Varvara was sitting at the open window, listening for her husband to come. In the next room Lipa was playing with her baby. She was tossing him up in her arms and saying enthusiastically:

"You will grow up ever so big, ever so big. You will be a peasant, we shall go out to work together! We shall go out to work together!"

"Come, come," said Varvara, offended. "Go out to work, what an idea, you silly girl! He will be a merchant . . . !"

Lipa sang softly, but a minute later she forgot, and again:

"You will grow ever so big, ever so big. You will be a peasant, we'll go out to work together."

"There she is at it again!"

Lipa, with Nikifor in her arms, stood still in the doorway and asked:

"Why do I love him so much, mamma? Why do I feel so sorry for him?" she went on in a quivering voice, and her eyes glistened with tears. "Who is he? What is he like? As light as a little feather, as a little crumb; but I love him; I love him like a real person. Here he can do nothing, he can't talk, and yet I know what he wants with his little eyes."

Varvara was listening; the sound of the evening train coming in to the station reached her. Had her husband come? She did not hear and she did not heed what Lipa was saying, she had no idea how the time passed, but only trembled all over—not from dread, but intense curiosity. She saw a cart full of peasants roll quickly by with a rattle. It was the witnesses coming back from the station. When the cart passed the shop the old workman jumped out and walked into the yard. She could hear him being greeted in the yard and being asked some questions. . . .

"Deprivation of rights and all his property," he said loudly, "and six years' penal servitude in Siberia."

She could see Aksinya come out of the shop by the back way; she had just been selling kerosene, and in one hand held a bottle and in the other a can, and in her mouth she had some silver coins.

"Where is father?" she asked, lisping.

"At the station," answered the labourer. "'When it gets a little darker,' he said, 'then I shall come.'"

And when it became known all through the household that Anisim was sentenced to penal servitude, the cook in the kitchen suddenly broke into a wail as though at a funeral, imagining that this was demanded by the proprieties:

"There is no one to care for us now you have gone, Anisim Grigoritch, our bright falcon. . . ."

The dogs began barking in alarm. Varvara ran to the window, and rushing about in distress, shouted to the cook with all her might, straining her voice:

"Sto-op, Stepanida, sto-op! Don't harrow us, for Christ's sake!"

They forgot to set the samovar, they could think of nothing. Only Lipa could not make out what it was all about and went on playing with her baby.

When the old father arrived from the station they asked him no questions. He greeted them and walked through all the rooms in silence; he had no supper.

"There was no one to see about things . . ." Varvara began when they were alone. "I said you should have asked some of the gentry, you would not heed me at the time. . . . A petition would . . ."

"I saw to things," said her husband with a wave of his hand. "When Anisim was condemned I went to the gentleman who was defending him. 'It's no use now,' he said, 'it's too late'; and Anisim said the same; it's too late. But all the same as I came out of the court I made an agreement with a lawyer, I paid him something in advance. I'll wait a week and then I will go again. It is as God wills."

Again the old man walked through all the rooms, and when he went back to Varvara he said:

"I must be ill. My head's in a sort of . . . fog. My thoughts are in a maze."

He closed the door that Lipa might not hear, and went on softly:

"I am unhappy about my money. Do you remember on Low Sunday before his wedding Anisim's bringing me some new roubles and half-roubles? One parcel I put away at the time, but the others I mixed with my own money. When my uncle Dmitri Filatitch—the kingdom of heaven be his—was alive, he used constantly to go journeys to Moscow and to the Crimea to buy goods. He had a wife, and this same wife, when he was away buying goods, used to take up with other men. She had half a dozen children. And when uncle was in his cups he would laugh and say: 'I never can make out,' he used to say, 'which are my children and which are other people's.' An easy-going disposition, to be sure; and so I now can't distinguish which are genuine roubles and which are false ones. And it seems to me that they are all false."

"Nonsense, God bless you."

"I take a ticket at the station, I give the man three roubles, and I keep fancying they are false. And I am frightened. I must be ill."

"There's no denying it, we are all in God's hands. . . . Oh dear, dear . . ." said Varvara, and she shook her head. "You ought to think about this, Grigory Petrovitch: you never know, anything may happen, you are not a young man. See they don't wrong your grandchild when you are dead and gone. Oy, I am afraid they will be unfair to Nikifor! He has as good as no father, his mother's young and foolish . . . you ought to secure something for him, poor little boy, least the land, Butyokino, Grigory Petrovitch, really! Think it over!"

Varvara went on persuading him. "The pretty boy, one is sorry for him! You go to-morrow and make out a deed; why put it off?"

"I'd forgotten about my grandson," said Tsybukin. "I must go and have a look at him. So you say the boy is all right? Well, let him grow up, please God."

He opened the door and, crooking his finger, beckoned to Lipa. She went up to him with the baby in her arms.

"If there is anything you want, Lipinka, you ask for it," he said. "And eat anything you like, we don't grudge it, so long as it does you good. . . ." He made the sign of the cross over the baby. "And take care of my grandchild. My son is gone, but my grandson is left."

Tears rolled down his cheeks; he gave a sob and went away. Soon afterwards he went to bed and slept soundly after seven sleepless nights.

VII

Old Tsybukin went to the town for a short time. Someone told Aksinya that he had gone to the notary to make his will and that he was leaving Butyokino, the very place where she had set up a brick-yard, to Nikifor, his grandson. She was informed of this in the morning when old Tsybukin and Varvara were sitting near the steps under the birch-tree, drinking their tea. She closed the shop in the front and at the back, gathered together all the keys she had, and flung them at her father-in-law's feet.

"I am not going on working for you," she began in a loud voice, and suddenly broke into sobs. "It seems I am not your daughter-in-law, but a servant! Everybody's jeering and saying, 'See what a servant the Tsybukins have got hold of!' I did not come to you for wages! I am not a beggar, I am not a slave, I have a father and a mother."

She did not wipe away her tears, she fixed upon her father-in-law eyes full of tears, vindictive, squinting with wrath; her face and neck were red and tense, and she was shouting at the top of her voice.

"I don't mean to go on being a slave!" she went on. "I am worn out. When it is work, when it is sitting in the shop day in and day out, scurrying out at night for vodka—then it is my share, but when it is giving away the land then it is for that convict's wife and her imp. She is mistress here, and I am her servant. Give her everything, the convict's wife, and may it choke her; I am going home! Find yourselves some other fool, you damned Herods!"

Tsybukin had never in his life scolded or punished his children, and had never dreamed that one of his family could speak to him rudely or behave disrespectfully; and now he was very much frightened; he ran into the house and there hid behind the cupboard. And Varvara was so much flustered that she could not get up from her seat, and only waved her hands before her as though she were warding off a bee.

"Oh Holy Saints! what's the meaning of it?" she muttered in horror. "What is she shouting? Oh dear, dear! . . . People will hear! Hush. Oh, hush!"

"He has given Butyokino to the convict's wife," Aksinya went on bawling. "Give her everything now, I don't want anything from you! Let me alone! You are all a gang of thieves here! I have seen my fill of it, I have had enough! You have robbed folks coming in and going out; you have robbed old and young alike, you brigands! And who has been selling vodka without a licence? And false money? You've filled boxes full of false coins, and now I am no more use!"

A crowd had by now collected at the open gate and was staring into the yard.

"Let the people look," bawled Aksinya. "I will shame you all! You shall burn with shame! You shall grovel at my feet. Hey! Stepan," she called to the deaf man, "let us go home this minute! Let us go to my father and mother; I don't want to live with convicts. Get ready!"

Clothes were hanging on lines stretched across the yard; she snatched off her petticoats and blouses still wet and flung them into the deaf man's arms. Then in her fury she dashed about the yard by the linen, tore down all of it, and what was not hers she threw on the ground and trampled upon.

"Holy Saints, take her away," moaned Varvara. "What a woman! Give her Butyokino! Give it her, for the Lord's sake!"

"Well! Wha-at a woman!" people were saying at the gate. "She's a wo-oman! She's going it—something like!"

Aksinya ran into the kitchen where washing was going on. Lipa was washing alone, the cook had gone to the river to rinse the clothes. Steam was rising from the trough and from the cauldron on the side of the stove, and the kitchen was thick and stifling from the steam. On the floor was a heap of unwashed clothes, and Nikifor, kicking up his little red legs, had been put down on a bench near them so that if he fell he should not hurt himself. Just as Aksinya went in Lipa took the former's chemise out of the heap and put it in the trough, and was just stretching out her hand to a big ladle of boiling water which was standing on the table.

"Give it here," said Aksinya, looking at her with hatred, and snatching the chemise out of the trough; "it is not your business to touch my linen! You are a convict's wife, and ought to know your place and who you are."

Lipa gazed at her, taken aback, and did not understand, but suddenly she caught the look Aksinya turned upon the child, and at once she understood and went numb all over.

"You've taken my land, so here you are!" Saying this Aksinya snatched up the ladle with the boiling water and flung it over Nikifor.

After this there was heard a scream such as had never been heard before in Ukleevo, and no one would have believed that a little weak creature like Lipa could scream like that. And it was suddenly silent in the yard.

Aksinya walked into the house with her old naïve smile. . . . The deaf man kept moving about the yard with his arms full of linens, then he began hanging it up again, in silence, without haste. And until the cook came back from the river no one ventured to go into the kitchen and see what was there.

VIII

Nikifor was taken to the district hospital, and towards evening he died there. Lipa did not wait for them to come for her, but wrapped the dead baby in its little quilt and carried it home.

The hospital, a new one recently built, with big windows, stood high upon a hill; it was glittering from the setting sun and looked as though it were on fire from inside. There was a little village below. Lipa went down along the road, and before reaching the village sat down by a pond. A woman brought a horse down to drink and the horse did not drink.

"What more do you want?" said the woman to it softly. "What do you want?"

A boy in a red shirt, sitting at the water's edge, was washing his father's boots. And not another soul was in sight either in the village or on the hill.

"It's not drinking," said Lipa, looking at the horse.

Then the woman with the horse and the boy with the boots walked away, and there was no one left at all. The sun went to bed wrapped in cloth of gold and purple, and long clouds, red and lilac, stretched across the sky, guarded its slumbers. Somewhere far away a bittern cried, a hollow, melancholy sound like a cow shut up in a barn. The cry of that mysterious bird was heard every spring, but no one knew what it was like or where it lived. At the top of the hill by the hospital, in the bushes close to the pond, and in the fields the nightingales were trilling. The cuckoo kept reckoning someone's years and losing count and beginning again. In the pond the frogs called angrily to one another, straining themselves to bursting, and one could even make out the words: "That's what you are! That's what you are!" What a noise there was! It seemed as though all these creatures were singing and shouting so that no one might sleep on that spring night, so that all, even the angry frogs, might appreciate and enjoy every minute: life is given only once.

A silver half-moon was shining in the sky; there were many stars. Lipa had no idea how long she sat by the pond, but when she got up and walked on everybody was asleep in the little village, and there was not a single light. It was probably about nine miles' walk home, but she had not the strength, she had not the power to think how to go: the moon gleamed now in front, now on the right, and the same cuckoo kept calling in a voice grown husky, with a chuckle as though gibing at her: "Oy, look out, you'll lose your way!" Lipa walked rapidly; she lost the kerchief from her head . . . she looked at the sky and wondered where her baby's soul was now: was it following her, or floating aloft yonder among the stars and thinking nothing now of his mother? Oh, how lonely it was in the open country at night, in the midst of that singing when one cannot sing oneself; in the midst of the incessant cries of joy when one cannot oneself be joyful, when the moon, which cares not whether it is spring or winter, whether men are alive or dead, looks down as lonely, too. . . . When there is grief in the heart it is hard to be without people. If only her mother, Praskovya, had been with her, or Crutch, or the cook, or some peasant!

"Boo-oo!" cried the bittern. "Boo-oo!"

And suddenly she heard clearly the sound of human speech:

"Put the horses in, Vavila!"

By the wayside a camp fire was burning ahead of her: the flames had died down, there were only red embers. She could hear the horses munching. In the darkness she could see the outlines of two carts, one with a barrel, the other, a lower one with sacks in it, and the figures of two men; one was leading a horse to put it into the shafts, the other was standing motionless by the fire with his hands behind his back. A dog growled by the carts. The one who was leading the horse stopped and said:

"It seems as though someone were coming along the road."

"Sharik, be quiet!" the other called to the dog.

And from the voice one could tell that the second was an old man. Lipa stopped and said:

"God help you."

The old man went up to her and answered not immediately:

"Good evening!"

"Your dog does not bite, grandfather?"

"No, come along, he won't touch you."

"I have been at the hospital," said Lipa after a pause. "My little son died there. Here I am carrying him home."

It must have been unpleasant for the old man to hear this, for he moved away and said hurriedly:

"Never mind, my dear. It's God's will. You are very slow, lad," he added, addressing his companion; "look alive!"

"Your yoke's nowhere," said the young man; "it is not to be seen."

"You are a regular Vavila."

The old man picked up an ember, blew on it—only his eyes and nose were lighted up—then, when they had found the yoke, he went with the light to Lipa and looked at her, and his look expressed compassion and tenderness.

"You are a mother," he said; "every mother grieves for her child."

And he sighed and shook his head as he said it. Vavila threw something on the fire, stamped on it—and at once it was very dark; the vision vanished, and as before there were only the fields, the sky with the stars, and the noise of the birds hindering each other from sleep. And the landrail called, it seemed, in the very place where the fire had been.

But a minute passed, and again she could see the two carts and the old man and lanky Vavila. The carts creaked as they went out on the road.

"Are you holy men?" Lipa asked the old man.

"No. We are from Firsanovo."

"You looked at me just now and my heart was softened. And the young man is so gentle. I thought you must be holy men."

"Are you going far?"

"To Ukleevo."

"Get in, we will give you a lift, as far as Kuzmenki, then you go straight on and we turn off to the left."

Vavila got into the cart with the barrel and the old man and Lipa got into the other. They moved at a walking pace, Vavila in front.

"My baby was in torment all day," said Lipa. "He looked at me with his little eyes and said nothing; he wanted to speak and could not. Holy Father, Queen of Heaven! In my grief I kept falling down on the floor. I stood up and fell down by the bedside. And tell me, grandfather, why a little thing should be tormented before his death? When a grown-up person, a man or woman, are in torment their sins are forgiven, but why a little thing, when he has no sins? Why?"

"Who can tell?" answered the old man.

They drove on for half an hour in silence.

"We can't know everything, how and wherefore," said the old man. "It is ordained for the bird to have not four wings but two because it is able to fly with two; and so it is ordained for man not to know everything but only a half or a quarter. As much as he needs to know so as to live, so much he knows."

"It is better for me to go on foot, grandfather. Now my heart is all of a tremble."

"Never mind, sit still."

The old man yawned and made the sign of the cross over his mouth.

"Never mind," he repeated. "Yours is not the worst of sorrows. Life is long, there will be good and bad to come, there will be everything. Great is mother Russia," he said, and looked round on each side of him. "I have been all over Russia, and I have seen everything in her, and you may believe my words, my dear. There will be good and there will be bad. I went as a delegate from my village to Siberia, and I have been to the Amur River* and the Altai Mountains† and I settled in Siberia; I worked the land there, then I was homesick for mother Russia and I came back to my native village. We came back to Russia on foot; and I remember we went on a steamer, and I was thin as thin, all in rags, barefoot, freezing with cold, and gnawing a crust, and a gentleman who was on the steamer—the kingdom of heaven be his if he is dead—looked at me pitifully, and the tears came into his eyes. 'Ah,' he said, 'your bread is black, your days are black. . . .' And when I got home, as the saying is, there was neither stick nor stall; I had a wife, but I left her behind in Siberia, she was buried there. So I am living as a day labourer. And yet I tell you: since then I have had good as well as bad. Here I do not want to die, my dear, I would be glad to live another twenty years; so there has been more of the good. And great is our mother Russia!" and again he gazed to each side and looked round.

"Grandfather," Lipa asked, "when anyone dies, how many days does his soul walk the earth?"

"Who can tell! Ask Vavila here, he has been to school. Now they teach them everything. Vavila!" the old man called to him.

"Yes!"

"Vavila, when anyone dies, how long does his soul walk the earth?"

Vavila stopped the horse and only then answered:

"Nine days. My uncle Kirilla died and his soul lived in our hut thirteen days after."

"How do you know?"

"For thirteen days there was a knocking in the stove."

"Well, that's all right. Go on," said the old man, and it could be seen that he did not believe a word of all that.

---

*River in far-eastern Siberia and China.

†Mountain range extending from Siberia into Mongolia.

Near Kuzmenki the cart turned into the high-road while Lipa went straight on. It was by now getting light. As she went down into the ravine the Ukleevo huts and the church were hidden in fog. It was cold, and it seemed to her that the same cuckoo was calling still.

When Lipa reached home the cattle had not yet been driven out; everyone was asleep. She set down on the steps and waited. The old man was the first to come out; he understood all that had happened from the first glance at her, and for a long time he could not articulate a word, but only moved his lips without a sound.

"Ech, Lipa," he said, "you did not take care of my grandchild. . . ."

Varvara was awakened. She clasped her hands and broke into sobs, and immediately began laying out the baby.

"And he was a pretty child . . ." she said. "Oh dear, dear. . . . You only had the one child, and you did not take care enough of him, you silly girl. . . ."

There was a requiem service in the morning and the evening. The funeral took place the next day, and after it the guests and the priests ate a great deal, and with such greed that one might have thought that they had not tasted food for a long time. Lipa waited at table, and the priest, lifting his fork on which there was a salted mushroom, said to her:

"Don't grieve for the babe. For of such is the kingdom of heaven."

And only when they had all separated Lipa realized fully that there was no Nikifor and never would be, she realized it and broke into sobs. And she did not know what room to go into to sob, for she felt that now that her child was dead there was no place for her in the house, that she had no reason to be here, that she was in the way; and the others felt it, too.

"Now what are you bellowing for?" Aksinya shouted, suddenly appearing in the doorway; in honour of the funeral she was dressed all in new clothes and had powdered her face. "Shut up!"

Lipa tried to stop but could not, and sobbed louder than ever.

"Do you hear?" shouted Aksinya, and she stamped her foot in violent anger. "Who is it I am speaking to? Go out of the yard and don't set foot here again, you convict's wife. Get away."

"There, there, there," the old man put in fussily. "Aksinya, don't make such an outcry, my girl. . . . She is crying, it is only natural . . . her child is dead. . . ."

"'It's only natural,'" Aksinya mimicked him. "Let her stay the night here, and don't let me see a trace of her here to-morrow! 'It's only natural!' . . ." she mimicked him again, and, laughing, she went into the shop.

Early next morning Lipa went off to her mother at Torguevo.

IX

At the present time the steps and the front door of the shop have been repainted and are as bright as though they were new, there are gay geraniums in the windows as of old, and what happened in Tsybukin's house and yard three years ago is almost forgotten.

Grigory Petrovitch is looked upon as the master as he was in old days, but in reality everything has passed into Aksinya's hands; she buys and sells, and nothing can be done without her consent. The brickyard is working well; and as bricks are wanted for the railway the price has gone up to twenty-four roubles a thousand; peasant women and girls cart the bricks to the station and load them up in the trucks and earn a quarter-rouble a day for the work.

Aksinya has gone into partnership with the Hrymin Juniors, and their factory is now called Hrymin Juniors and Co. They have opened a tavern near the station, and now the expensive concertina is played not at the factory but at the tavern, and the head of the post office often goes there, and he, too, is engaged in some sort of traffic, and the stationmaster, too. Hrymin Juniors have presented the deaf man Stepan with a gold watch, and he is constantly taking it out of his pocket and putting it to his ear.

People say of Aksinya that she has become a person of power; and it is true that when she drives in the morning to her brickyard, handsome and happy, with the naïve smile on her face, and afterwards when she is giving orders there, one is aware of great power in her. Everyone is afraid of her in the house and in the village and in the brickyard. When she goes to the post the head of the postal department jumps up and says to her:

"I humbly beg you to be seated, Aksinya Abramovna!"

A certain landowner, middle-aged but foppish, in a tunic of fine cloth and patent leather high boots, sold her a horse, and was so carried away by talking to her that he knocked down the price to meet her wishes. He held her hand a long time and, looking into her merry, sly, naïve eyes, said:

"For a woman like you, Aksinya Ambramovna, I should be ready to do anything you please. Only say when we can meet where no one will interfere with us?"

"Why, when you please."

And since then the elderly fop drives up to the shop almost every day to drink beer. And the beer is horrid, bitter as wormwood. The landowner shakes his head, but he drinks it.

Old Tsybukin does not have anything to do with the business now at all. He does not keep any money because he cannot distinguish between the good and the false, but he is silent, he says nothing of this weakness. He has become forgetful, and if they don't give him food he does not ask for it. They have grown used to having dinner without him, and Varvara often says:

"He went to bed again yesterday without any supper."

And she says it unconcernedly because she is used to it. For some reason, summer and winter alike, he wears a fur coat, and only in very hot weather he does not go out but sits at home. As a rule putting on his fur coat, wrapping it round him and turning up his collar, he walks about the village, along the road to the station, or sits from morning till night on the seat near the church gates. He sits there without stirring. Passersby bow to him, but he does not respond, for as of old he dislikes the peasants. If he is asked a question he answers quite rationally and politely, but briefly.

There is a rumour going about in the village that his daughter-in-law turns him out of the house and gives him nothing to eat, and that he is fed by charity; some are glad, others are sorry for him.

Varvara has grown even fatter and whiter, and as before she is active in good works, and Aksinya does not interfere with her.

There is so much jam now that they have not time to eat it before the fresh fruit comes in; it goes sugary, and Varvara almost sheds tears, not knowing what to do with it.

They have begun to forget about Anisim. A letter has come from him written in verse on a big sheet of paper as though it were a petition, all in the same splendid handwriting. Evidently his friend Samorodov was sharing his punishment. Under the verses in an ugly, scarcely legible handwriting there was a single line: "I am ill here all the time; I am wretched, for Christ's sake help me!"

Towards evening—it was a fine autumn day—old Tsybukin was sitting near the church gates, with the collar of his fur coat turned up and nothing of him could be seen but his nose and the peak of his cap. At the other end of the long seat was sitting Elizarov the contractor, and beside him Yakov the school watchman, a toothless old man of seventy. Crutch and the watchman were talking.

"Children ought to give food and drink to the old. . . . Honour thy father and mother . . ." Yakov was saying with irritation, "while she, this daughter-in-law, has turned her father-in-law out of his own house; the old man has neither food nor drink, where is he to go? He has not had a morsel for these three days."

"Three days!" said Crutch, amazed.

"Here he sits and does not say a word. He has grown feeble. And why be silent? He ought to prosecute her, they wouldn't flatter her in the police court."

"Wouldn't flatter whom?" asked Crutch, not hearing.

"What?"

"The woman's all right, she does her best. In their line of business they can't get on without that . . . without sin, I mean. . . ."

"From his own house," Yakov went on with irritation. "Save up and buy your own house, then turn people out of it! She is a nice one, to be sure! A pla-ague!"

Tsybukin listened and did not stir.

"Whether it is your own house or others' it makes no difference so long as it is warm and the women don't scold . . ." said Crutch, and he laughed. "When I was young I was very fond of my Nastasya. She was a quiet woman. And she used to be always at it: 'Buy a house, Makaritch! Buy a house, Makaritch! Buy a house, Makaritch!' She was dying and yet she kept on saying, 'Buy yourself a racing droshky, Makaritch, that you may not have to walk.' And I bought her nothing but gingerbread."

"Her husband's deaf and stupid," Yakov went on, not hearing Crutch; "a regular fool, just like a goose. He can't understand anything. Hit a goose on the head with a stick and even then it does not understand."

Crutch got up to go home to the factory. Yakov also got up, and both of them went off together, still talking. When they had gone fifty paces old Tsybukin got up too, and walked after them, stepping uncertainly as though on slippery ice.

The village was already plunged in the dusk of evening and the sun only gleamed on the upper part of the road which ran wriggling like a snake up the slope. Old women were coming back from the woods and children with them; they were bringing baskets of mushrooms. Peasant women and girls came in a crowd from the station where they had been loading the trucks with bricks, and their noses and their cheeks under their eyes were covered with red brick-dust. They were singing. Ahead of them all was Lipa singing in a high voice, with her eyes turned upwards to the sky, breaking into trills as though triumphant and ecstatic that at last the day was over and she could rest. In the crowd was her mother Praskovya, who was walking with a bundle in her arms and breathless as usual.

"Good evening, Makaritch!" cried Lipa, seeing Crutch. "Good evening, darling!"

"Good evening, Lipinka," cried Crutch, delighted. "Dear girls and women, love the rich carpenter! Ho-ho! My little children, my little children. (Crutch gave a gulp.) My dear little axes!"

Crutch and Yakov went on further and could still be heard talking. Then after them the crowd was met by old Tsybukin and there was a sudden hush. Lipa and Praskovya had dropped a little behind, and when the old man was on a level with them Lipa bowed down low and said:

"Good evening, Grigory Petrovitch."

Her mother, too, bowed down. The old man stopped and, saying nothing, looked at the two in silence; his lips were quivering and his eyes full of tears. Lipa took out of her mother's bundle a piece of savoury turnover and gave it him. He took it and began eating.

The sun had by now set; its glow died away on the road above. It grew dark and cool. Lipa and Praskovya walked on and for some time they kept crossing themselves.

THE BISHOP

I

The evening service was being celebrated on the eve of Palm Sunday in the Old Petrovksy Convent. When they began distributing the palm it was close upon ten o'clock, the candles were burning dimly, the wicks wanted snuffing; it was all in a sort of mist. In the twilight of the church the crowd seemed heaving like the sea, and to Bishop Pyotr, who had been unwell for the last three days, it seemed that all the faces—old and young, men's and women's—were alike, that everyone who came up for the palm had the same expression in his eyes. In the mist he could not see the doors; the crowd kept moving and looked as though there were no end to it. The female choir was singing, a nun was reading the prayers for the day.

How stifling, how hot it was! How long the service went on! Bishop Pyotr was tired. His breathing was laboured and rapid, his throat was parched, his shoulders ached with weariness, his legs were trembling. And it disturbed him unpleasantly when a religious maniac uttered occasional shrieks in the gallery. And then all of a sudden, as though in a dream or delirium, it seemed to the bishop as though his own mother Marya Timofyevna, whom he had not seen for nine years, or some old woman just like his mother, came up to him out of the crowd, and, after taking a palm branch from him, walked away looking at him all the while good-humouredly with a kind, joyful smile until she was lost in the crowd. And for some reason tears flowed down his face. There was peace in his heart, everything was well, yet he kept gazing fixedly towards the left choir, where the prayers were being read, where in the dusk of evening you could not recognize anyone, and—wept. Tears glistened on his face and on his beard. Here someone close at hand was weeping, then someone else further away, then others and still others, and little by little the church was filled with soft weeping. And a little later, within five minutes, the nuns' choir was singing; no one was weeping and everything was as before.

Soon the service was over. When the bishop got into his carriage to drive home, the gay, melodious chime of the heavy, costly bells was filling the whole garden in the moonlight. The white walls, the white crosses on the tombs, the white birch-trees and black shadows, and the faraway moon in the sky exactly over the convent, seemed now living their own life, apart and incomprehensible, yet very near to man. It was the beginning of April, and after the warm spring day it turned cool; there was a faint touch of frost, and the breath of spring could be felt in the soft, chilly air. The road from the convent to the town was sandy, the horses had to go at a walking pace, and on both sides of the carriage in the brilliant, peaceful moonlight there were people trudging along home from church through the sand. And all was silent, sunk in thought; everything around seemed kindly, youthful, akin, everything—trees and sky and even the moon, and one longed to think that so it would be always.

At last the carriage drove into the town and rumbled along the principal street. The shops were already shut, but at Erakin's, the millionaire shopkeeper's, they were trying the new electric lights, which flickered brightly, and a crowd of people were gathered round. Then came wide, dark, deserted streets, one after another; then the high-road, the open country, the fragrance of pines. And suddenly there rose up before the bishop's eyes a white turreted wall, and behind it a tall belfry in the full moonlight, and beside it five shining, golden cupolas: this was the Pankratievsky Monastery,* in which Bishop Pyotr lived. And here, too, high above the monastery, was the silent, dreamy moon. The carriage drove in at the gate, crunching over the sand; here and there in the moonlight there were glimpses of dark monastic figures, and there was the sound of footsteps on the flag-stones. . . .

"You know, your holiness, your mamma arrived while you were away," the lay brother informed the bishop as he went into his cell.

"My mother? When did she come?"

---

*Monastery of the All Powerful.

"Before the evening service. She asked first where you were and then she went to the convent."

"Then it was her I saw in the church, just now! Oh, Lord!"

And the bishop laughed with joy.

"She bade me tell your holiness," the lay brother went on, "that she would come to-morrow. She had a little girl with her—her grandchild, I suppose. They are staying at Ovsyannikov's inn."

"What time is it now?"

"A little after eleven."

"Oh, how vexing!"

The bishop sat for a little while in the parlour, hesitating, and as it were refusing to believe it was so late. His arms and legs were stiff, his head ached. He was hot and uncomfortable. After resting a little he went into his bedroom, and there, too, he sat a little, still thinking of his mother; he could hear the lay brother going away, and Father Sisoy coughing the other side of the wall. The monastery clock struck a quarter.

The bishop changed his clothes and began reading the prayers before sleep. He read attentively those old, long familiar prayers, and at the same time thought about his mother. She had nine children and about forty grandchildren. At one time, she had lived with her husband, the deacon, in a poor village; she had lived there a very long time from the age of seventeen to sixty. The bishop remembered her from early childhood, almost from the age of three, and—how he had loved her! Sweet, precious childhood, always fondly remembered! Why did it, that long-past time that could never return, why did it seem brighter, fuller, and more festive that it had really been? When in his childhood or youth he had been ill, how tender and sympathetic his mother had been! And now his prayers mingled with the memories, which gleamed more and more brightly like a flame, and the prayers did not hinder his thinking of his mother.

When he had finished his prayers he undressed and lay down, and at once, as soon as it was dark, there rose before his mind his dead father, his mother, his native village Lesopolye . . . the creak of wheels, the bleat of sheep, the church bells on bright summer mornings, the gypsies under the window—oh, how sweet to think of it! He remembered the priest of Lesopolye, Father Simeon—mild, gentle, kindly; he was a lean little man, while his son, a divinity student, was a huge fellow and talked in a roaring bass voice. The priest's son had flown into a rage with the cook and abused her: "Ah, you Jehud's ass!" and Father Simeon overhearing it, said not a word, and was only ashamed because he could not remember where such an ass was mentioned in the Bible. After him the priest at Lesopolye had been Father Demyan, who used to drink heavily, and at times drank till he saw green snakes, and was even nicknamed Demyan Snakeseer. The schoolmaster at Lesopolye was Matvey Nikolaitch, who had been a divinity student, a kind and intelligent man, but he, too, was a drunkard; he never beat the schoolchildren, but for some reason he always had hanging on his wall a bunch of birch-twigs, and below it an utterly meaningless inscription in Latin: "Betula kinderbalsamica secuta." He had a shaggy black dog whom he called Syntax.

And his holiness laughed. Six miles from Lesopolye was the village Obnino with a wonder-working ikon. In the summer they used to carry the ikon in procession about the neighbouring villages and ring the bells the whole day long, first in one village and then in another, and it used to seem to the bishop then that joy was quivering in the air, and he (in those days his name was Pavlusha) used to follow the ikon, bareheaded and barefoot, with naïve faith, with a naïve smile, infinitely happy. In Obnino, he remembered now, there were always a lot of people, and the priest there, Father Alexey, to save time during mass, used to make his deaf nephew Ilarion read the names of those for whose health or whose souls' peace prayers were asked. Ilarion used to read them, now and then getting a five or ten kopeck piece for the service, and only when he was grey and bald, when life was nearly over, he suddenly saw written on one of the pieces of paper: "What a fool you are, Ilarion." Up to fifteen at least Pavlusha was undeveloped and idle at his lessons, so much so that they thought to taking him away from the clerical school and putting him into a shop; one day, going to the post at Obnino for letters, he had stared a long time at the post-office clerks and asked: "Allow me to ask, how do you get your salary, every month or every day?"

His holiness crossed himself and turned over on the other side, trying to stop thinking and go to sleep.

"My mother has come," he remembered and laughed.

The moon peeped in at the window, the floor was lighted up, and there were shadows on it. A cricket was chirping. Through the wall Father Sisoy was snoring in the next room, and his aged snore had a sound that suggested loneliness, forlornness, even vagrancy. Sisoy had once been housekeeper to the bishop of the diocese, and was called now "the former Father Housekeeper"; he was seventy years old, he lived in a monastery twelve miles from the town and stayed sometimes in the town, too. He had come to the Pankratievsky Monastery three days before, and the bishop had kept him that he might talk to him at his leisure about matters of business, about the arrangements here. . . .

At half-past one they began ringing for matins. Father Sisoy could be heard coughing, muttering something in a discontented voice, then he got up and walked barefoot about the rooms.

"Father Sisoy," the bishop called.

Sisoy went back to his room and a little later made his appearance in his boots, with a candle; he had on his cassock over his underclothes and on his head was an old faded skull-cap.

"I can't sleep," said the bishop, sitting up. "I must be unwell. And what it is I don't know. Fever!"

"You must have caught cold, your holiness. You must be rubbed with tallow." Sisoy stood a little and yawned. "O Lord, forgive me, a sinner."

"They had the electric lights on at Erakin's to-day," he said, "I don't like it!"

Father Sisoy was old, lean, bent, always dissatisfied with something, and his eyes were angry-looking and prominent as a crab's.

"I don't like it," he said, going away. "I don't like it. Bother it!"

II

Next day, Palm Sunday, the bishop took the service in the cathedral in the town, then he visited the bishop of the diocese, then visited a very sick old lady, the widow of a general, and at last drove home. Between one and two o'clock he had welcome visitors dining with him—his mother and his niece Katya, a child of eight years old. All dinner-time the spring sunshine was streaming in at the windows, throwing bright light on the white tablecloth and on Katya's red hair. Through the double windows they could hear the noise of the rooks and the notes of the starlings in the garden.

"It is nine years since we have met," said the old lady. "And when I looked at you in the monastery yesterday, good Lord! you've not changed a bit, except maybe you are thinner and your beard is a little longer. Holy Mother, Queen of Heaven! Yesterday at the evening service no one could help crying. I, too, as I looked at you, suddenly began crying, though I couldn't say why. His Holy Will!"

And in spite of the affectionate tone in which she said this, he could see she was constrained as though she were uncertain whether to address him formally or familiarly, to laugh or not, and that she felt herself more a deacon's widow than his mother. And Katya gazed without blinking at her uncle, his holiness, as though trying to discover what sort of a person he was. Her hair sprang up from under the comb and the velvet ribbon and stood out like a halo; she had a turned-up nose and sly eyes. The child had broken a glass before sitting down to dinner, and now her grandmother, as she talked, moved away from Katya first a wineglass and then a tumbler. The bishop listened to his mother and remembered how many, many years ago she used to take him and his brothers and sisters to relations whom she considered rich; in those days she was taken up with the care of her children, now with her grandchildren, and she had brought Katya. . . .

"Your sister, Varenka, has four children," she told him; "Katya, here, is the eldest. And your brother-in-law Father Ivan fell sick, God knows of what, and died three days before the Assumption; and my poor Varenka is left a beggar."

"And how is Nikanor getting on?" the bishop asked about his eldest brother.

"He is all right, thank God. Though he has nothing much, yet he can live. Only there is one thing: his son, my grandson Nikolasha, did not want to go into the Church; he has gone to the university to be a doctor. He thinks it is better; but who knows! His Holy Will!"

"Nikolasha cuts up dead people," said Katya, spilling water over her knees.

"Sit still, child," her grandmother observed calmly, and took the glass out of her hand. "Say a prayer, and go on eating."

"How long it is since we have seen each other!" said the bishop, and he tenderly stroked his mother's hand and shoulder; "and I missed you abroad, mother, I missed you dreadfully."

"Thank you."

"I used to sit in the evenings at the open window, lonely and alone; often there was music playing, and all at once I used to be overcome with homesickness and felt as though I would give everything only to be at home and see you."

His mother smiled, beamed, but at once she made a grave face and said:

"Thank you."

His mood suddenly changed. He looked at his mother and could not understand how she had come by that respectfulness, that timid expression of face: what was it for? And he did not recognize her. He felt sad and vexed. And then his head ached just as it had the day before; his legs felt fearfully tired, and the fish seemed to him stale and tasteless; he felt thirsty all the time. . . .

After dinner two rich ladies, landowners, arrived and sat for an hour and a half in silence with rigid countenances; the archimandrite, a silent, rather deaf man, came to see him about business. Then they began ringing for vespers; the sun was setting behind the wood and the day was over. When he returned from church, he hurriedly said his prayers, got into bed, and wrapped himself up as warm as possible.

It was disagreeable to remember the fish he had eaten at dinner. The moonlight worried him, and then he heard talking. In an adjoining room, probably in the parlour, Father Sisoy was talking politics:

"There's war among the Japanese now. They are fighting. The Japanese, my good soul, are the same as the Montenegrins; they are the same race. They were under the Turkish yoke together."

And then he heard the voice of Marya Timofyevna:

"So, having said our prayers and drunk tea, we went, you know, to Father Yegor at Novokatnoye, so . . ."

And she kept on saying, "having had tea" or "having drunk tea," and it seemed as though the only thing she had done in her life was to drink tea.

The bishop slowly, languidly, recalled the seminary, the academy.

For three years he had been Greek teacher in the seminary: by that time he could not read without spectacles. Then he had become a monk; he had been made a school inspector. Then he had defended his thesis for his degree. When he was thirty-two he had been made rector of the seminary, and consecrated archimandrite: and then his life had been so easy, so pleasant; it seemed so long, so long, no end was in sight. Then he had begun to be ill, had grown very thin and almost blind, and by the advice of the doctors had to give up everything and go abroad.

"And what then?" asked Sisoy in the next room.

"Then we drank tea . . ." answered Marya Timofyevna.

"Good gracious, you've got a green beard," said Katya suddenly in surprise, and she laughed.

The bishop remembered that the gray-headed Father Sisoy's beard really had a shade of green in it, and he laughed.

"God have mercy upon us, what we have to put up with with this girl!" said Sisoy, aloud, getting angry. "Spoilt child! Sit quiet!"

The bishop remembered the perfectly new white church in which he had conducted the services while living abroad, he remembered the sound of the warm sea. In his flat he had five lofty light rooms; in his study he had a new writing-table, lots of books. He had read a great deal and often written. And he remembered how he had pined for his native land, how a blind beggar woman had played the guitar under his window every day and sung of love, and how, as he listened, he had always for some reason thought of the past. But eight years had passed and he had been called back to Russia, and now he was a suffragan bishop, and all the past had retreated far away into the mist as though it were a dream. . . .

Father Sisoy came into the bedroom with a candle.

"I say!" he said, wondering, "are you asleep already, your holiness?"

"What is it?"

"Why, it's still early, ten o'clock or less. I bought a candle to-day; I wanted to rub you with tallow."

"I am in a fever . . ." said the bishop, and he sat up. "I really ought to have something. My head is bad. . . ."

Sisoy took off the bishop's shirt and began rubbing his chest and back with tallow.

"That's the way . . . that's the way . . ." he said. "Lord Jesus Christ . . . that's the way. I walked to the town to-day; I was at what's-his-name's—the chief priest Sidonsky's. . . . I had tea with him. I don't like him. Lord Jesus Christ. . . . That's the way. I don't like him."

III

The bishop of the diocese, a very fat old man, was ill with rheumatism or gout, and had been in bed for over a month. Bishop Pyotr went to see him almost every day, and saw all who came to ask his help. And now that he was unwell he was struck by the emptiness, the triviality of everything which they asked and for which they wept; he was vexed at their ignorance, their timidity; and all this useless, petty business oppressed him by the mass of it, and it seemed to him that now he understood the diocesan bishop, who had once in his young days written on "The Doctrines of the Freedom of the Will," and now seemed to be all lost in trivialities, to have forgotten everything, and to have no thoughts of religion. The bishop must have lost touch with Russian life while he was abroad; he did not find it easy; the peasants seemed to him coarse, the women who sought his help dull and stupid, the seminarists and their teachers uncultivated and at times savage. And the documents coming in and going out were reckoned by tens of thousands; and what documents they were! The higher clergy in the whole diocese gave the priests, young and old, and even their wives and children, marks for their behaviour—a five, a four, and sometimes even a three; and about this he had to talk and to read and write serious reports. And there was positively not one minute to spare; his soul was troubled all day long, and the bishop was only at peace when he was in church.

He could not get used, either, to the awe which, through no wish of his own, he inspired in people in spite of his quiet, modest disposition. All the people in the province seemed to him little, scared, and guilty when he looked at them. Everyone was timid in his presence, even the old chief priests; everyone "flopped" at his feet, and not long previously an old lady, a village priest's wife who had come to consult him, was so overcome by awe that she could not utter a single word, and went empty away. And he, who could never in his sermons bring himself to speak ill of people, never reproached anyone because he was so sorry for them, was moved to fury with the people who came to consult him, lost his temper and flung their petitions on the floor. The whole time he had been here, not one person had spoken to him genuinely, simply, as to a human being; even his old mother seemed now not the same! And why, he wondered, did she chatter away to Sisoy and laugh so much; while with him, her son, she was grave and usually silent and constrained, which did not suit her at all. The only person who behaved freely with him and said what he meant was old Sisoy, who had spent his whole life in the presence of bishops and had outlived eleven of them. And so the bishop was at ease with him, although, of course, he was a tedious and nonsensical man.

After the service on Tuesday, his holiness Pyotr was in the diocesan bishop's house receiving petitions there; he got excited and angry, and then drove home. He was as unwell as before; he longed to be in bed, but he had hardly reached home when he was informed that a young merchant called Erakin, who subscribed liberally to charities, had come to see him about a very important matter. The bishop had to see him. Erakin stayed about an hour, talked very loud, almost shouted, and it was difficult to understand what he said.

"God grant it may," he said as he went away. "Most essential! According to circumstances, your holiness! I trust it may!"

After him came the Mother Superior from a distant convent. And when she had gone they began ringing for vespers. He had to go to church.

In the evening the monks sang harmoniously, with inspiration. A young priest with a black beard conducted the service; and the bishop, hearing of the Bridegroom* who comes at midnight and of the Heavenly Mansion adorned for the festival, felt no repentance for his sins, no tribulation, but peace at heart and tranquillity. And he was carried back in thought to the distant past, to his childhood and youth, when, too, they used to sing of the Bridegroom and of

---

*See the parable of the ten virgins in the Bible, Matthew 25.

the Heavenly Mansion; and now that past rose up before him—living, fair, and joyful as in all likelihood it never had been. And perhaps in the other world, in the life to come, we shall think of the distant past, of our life here, with the same feeling. Who knows? The bishop was sitting near the altar. It was dark; tears flowed down his face. He thought that here he had attained everything a man in his position could attain; he had faith and yet everything was not clear, something was lacking still. He did not want to die; and he still felt that he had missed what was most important, something of which he had dimly dreamed in the past; and he was troubled by the same hopes for the future as he had felt in childhood, at the academy and abroad.

"How well they sing to-day!" he thought, listening to the singing. "How nice it is!"

IV

On Thursday he celebrated mass in the cathedral; it was the Washing of Feet. When the service was over and the people were going home, it was sunny, warm, the water gurgled in the gutters, and the unceasing trilling of the larks, tender, telling of peace, rose from the fields outside the town. The trees were already awakening and smiling a welcome, while above them the infinite, fathomless blue sky stretched into the distance, God knows whither.

On reaching home his holiness drank some tea, then changed his clothes, lay down on his bed, and told the lay brother to close the shutters on the windows. The bedroom was darkened. But what weariness, what pain in his legs and his back, a chill heavy pain, what a noise in his ears! He had not slept for a long time—for a very long time, as it seemed to him now, and some trifling detail which haunted his brain as soon as his eyes were closed prevented him from sleeping. As on the day before, sounds reached him from the adjoining rooms through the walls, voices, the jingle of glasses and teaspoons. . . . Marya Timofyevna was gaily telling Father Sisoy some story with quaint turns of speech, while the latter answered in a grumpy, ill-humoured voice: "Bother them! Not likely! What next!" And the bishop again felt vexed and then hurt that with other people his old mother behaved in a simple, ordinary way, while with him, her son, she was shy, spoke little, and did not say what she meant, and even, as he fancied, had during all those three days kept trying in his presence to find an excuse for standing up, because she was embarrassed at sitting before him. And his father? He, too, probably, if he had been living, would not have been able to utter a word in the bishop's presence. . . .

Something fell down on the floor in the adjoining room and was broken; Katya must have dropped a cup or a saucer, for Father Sisoy suddenly spat and said angrily:

"What a regular nuisance the child is! Lord forgive my transgressions! One can't provide enough for her."

Then all was quiet, the only sounds came from outside. And when the bishop opened his eyes he saw Katya in his room, standing motionless, staring at him. Her red hair, as usual, stood up from under the comb like a halo.

"Is that you, Katya?" he asked. "Who is it downstairs who keeps opening and shutting a door?"

"I don't hear it," answered Katya; and she listened.

"There, someone has just passed by."

"But that was a noise in your stomach, uncle."

He laughed and stroked her on the head.

"So you say Cousin Nikolasha cuts up dead people?" he asked after a pause.

"Yes, he is studying."

"And is he kind?"

"Oh yes, he's kind. But he drinks vodka awfully."

"And what was it your father died of?"

"Papa was weak and very, very thin, and all at once his throat was bad. I was ill then, too, and brother Fedya; we all had bad throats. Papa died, uncle, and we got well."

Her chin began quivering, and tears gleamed in her eyes and trickled down her cheeks.

"Your holiness," she said in a shrill voice, by now weeping bitterly, "uncle, mother and all of us are left very wretched. . . . Give us a little money . . . do be kind . . . uncle darling. . . ."

He, too, was moved to tears, and for a long time was too much touched to speak. Then he stroked her on the head, patted her on the shoulder and said:

"Very good, very good, my child. When the holy Easter comes, we will talk it over. . . . I will help you. . . . I will help you. . . ."

His mother came in quietly, timidly, and prayed before the ikon. Noticing that he was not sleeping, she said:

"Won't you have a drop of soup?"

"No, thank you," he answered, "I am not hungry."

"You seem to be unwell, now I look at you. I should think so; you may well be ill! The whole day on your legs, the whole day. . . . And, my goodness, it makes one's heart ache even to look at you! Well, Easter is not far off; you will rest then, please God. Then we will have a talk, too, but now I'm not going to disturb you with my chatter. Come along, Katya; let his holiness sleep a little."

And he remembered how once very long ago, when he was a boy, she had spoken exactly like that, in the same jestingly respectful tone, with a Church dignitary. . . . Only from her extraordinarily kind eyes and the timid, anxious glance she stole at him as she went out of the room could one have guessed that this was his mother. He shut his eyes and seemed to sleep, but twice heard the clock strike and Father Sisoy coughing the other side of the wall. And once more his mother came in and looked timidly at him for a minute. Someone drove up to the steps, as he could hear, in a coach or in a chaise. Suddenly a knock, the door slammed, the lay brother came into the bedroom.

"Your holiness," he called.

"Well?"

"The horses are here; it's time for the evening service."

"What o'clock is it?"

"A quarter past seven."

He dressed and drove to the cathedral. During all the "Twelve Gospels" he had to stand in the middle of the church without moving, and the first gospel, the longest and the most beautiful, he read himself. A mood of confidence and courage came over him. That first gospel, "Now is the Son of Man glorified,"* he knew by heart; and as he read he raised his eyes from time to time, and saw on both sides a perfect sea of lights and heard the splutter of candles, but, as

*See the Bible, John 13:31.

in past years, he could not see the people, and it seemed as though these were all the same people as had been round him on those days, in his childhood and his youth; that they would always be the same every year and till such time as God only knew.

His father had been a deacon, his grandfather a priest, his great-grandfather a deacon, and his whole family, perhaps from the days when Christianity had been accepted in Russia, had belonged to the priesthood; and his love for the Church services, for the priesthood, for the peal of the bells, was deep in him, ineradicable, innate. In church, particularly when he took part in the service, he felt vigorous, of good cheer, happy. So it was now. Only when the eighth gospel had been read, he felt that his voice had grown weak, even his cough was inaudible. His head had begun to ache intensely, and he was troubled by a fear that he might fall down. And his legs were indeed quite numb, so that by degrees he ceased to feel them and could not understand how or on what he was standing, and why he did not fall. . . .

It was a quarter to twelve when the service was over. When he reached home, the bishop undressed and went to bed at once without even saying his prayers. He could not speak and felt that he could not have stood up. When he had covered his head with the quilt he felt a sudden longing to be abroad, an insufferable longing! He felt that he would give his life not to see those pitiful cheap shutters, those low ceilings, not to smell that heavy monastery smell. If only there were one person to whom he could have talked, have opened his heart!

For a long while he heard footsteps in the next room and could not tell whose they were. At last the door opened, and Sisoy came in with a candle and a tea-cup in his hand.

"You are in bed already, your holiness?" he asked. "Here I have come to rub you with spirit and vinegar. A thorough rubbing does a great deal of good. Lord Jesus Christ! . . . That's the way . . . that's the way. . . . I've just been in our monastery. . . . I don't like it. I'm going away from here to-morrow, your holiness; I don't want to stay longer. Lord Jesus Christ. . . . That's the way. . . ."

Sisoy could never stay long in the same place, and he felt as though he had been a whole year in the Pankratievsky Monastery. Above all, listening to him it was difficult to understand where his home was, whether he cared for anyone or anything, whether he believed in God. . . . He did not know himself why he was a monk, and, indeed, he did not think about it, and the time when he had become a monk had long passed out of his memory; it seemed as though he had been born a monk.

"I'm going away to-morrow; God be with them all."

"I should like to talk to you. . . . I can't find the time," said the bishop softly with an effort. "I don't know anything or anybody here. . . ."

"I'll stay till Sunday if you like; so be it, but I don't want to stay longer. I am sick of them!"

"I ought not to be a bishop," said the bishop softly. "I ought to have been a village priest, a deacon . . . or simply a monk. . . . All this oppresses me . . . oppresses me."

"What? Lord Jesus Christ. . . . That's the way. Come, sleep well, your holiness! . . . What's the good of talking? It's no use. Good-night!"

The bishop did not sleep all night. And at eight o'clock in the morning he began to have hæmorrhage from the bowels. The lay brother was alarmed, and ran first to the archimandrite, then for the monastery doctor, Ivan Andreyitch, who lived in the town. The doctor, a stout old man with a long grey beard, made a prolonged examination of the bishop, and kept shaking his head and frowning, and said:

"Do you know, your holiness, you have got typhoid?"

After an hour or so of hæmorrhage the bishop looked much thinner, paler, and wasted; his face looked wrinkled, his eyes looked bigger, and he seemed older, shorter, and it seemed to him that he was thinner, weaker, more insignificant than anyone, that everything that had been had retreated far, far away and would never go on again or be repeated.

"How good," he thought, "how good!"

His old mother came. Seeing his wrinkled face and his big eyes, she was frightened, she fell on her knees by the bed and began kissing his face, his shoulders, his hands. And to her, too, it seemed that he was thinner, weaker, and more insignificant than anyone, and now she forgot that he was a bishop, and kissed him as though he were a child very near and very dear to her.

"Pavlusha, darling," she said; "my own, my darling son! . . . Why are you like this? Pavlusha, answer me!"

Katya, pale and severe, stood beside her, unable to understand what was the matter with her uncle, why there was such a look of suffering on her grandmother's face, why she was saying such sad and touching things. By now he could not utter a word, he could understand nothing, and he imagined he was a simple ordinary man, that he was walking quickly, cheerfully through the fields, tapping with his stick, while above him was the open sky bathed in sunshine, and that he was free now as a bird and could go where he liked!

"Pavlusha, my darling son, answer me," the old woman was saying. "What is it? My own!"

"Don't disturb his holiness," Sisoy said angrily, walking about the room. "Let him sleep . . . what's the use . . . it's no good. . . ."

Three doctors arrived, consulted together, and went away again. The day was long, incredibly long, then the night came on and passed slowly, slowly, and towards morning on Saturday the lay brother went in to the old mother who was lying on the sofa in the parlour, and asked her to go into the bedroom: the bishop had just breathed his last.

Next day was Easter Sunday. There were forty-two churches and six monasteries in the town; the sonorous, joyful clang of the bells hung over the town from morning till night unceasingly, setting the spring air aquiver; the birds were singing, the sun was shining brightly. The big market-square was noisy, swings were going, barrel organs were playing, accordions were squeaking, drunken voices were shouting. After midday people began driving up and down the principal street.

In short, all was merriment, everything was satisfactory, just as it had been the year before, and as it will be in all likelihood next year.

A month later a new suffragan bishop was appointed, and no one thought anything more of Bishop Pyotr, and afterwards he was completely forgotten. And only the dead man's old mother, who is living to-day with her son-in-law the deacon in a remote little district town, when she goes out at night to bring her cow in and meets other women at the pasture, begins talking of her children and her grandchildren, and says that she had a son a bishop, and this she says timidly, afraid that she may not be believed. . . .

And, indeed, there are some who do not believe her.

INSPIRED BY CHEKHOV'S STORIES

> The younger generation owe you more than we ourselves are able to realise. These books have changed our lives, no less.
>
> —Katherine Mansfield, from a letter to translator Constance Garnett

The influence of Anton Chekhov is so great in literature and drama that it is nearly impossible to chart its true extent. Chekhov, who has been called the most important short story writer of all time, believed that "brevity is the sister of talent," and many subsequent writers of the form adopted that view, including Elizabeth Bowen, Albert Camus, E. M. Forster, Franz Kafka, W. Somerset Maugham, and Virginia Woolf. Today the short story is more popular than ever, and the influence of Chekhov on the evolution of the form is indisputable.

In the English language, the model he provided is reflected particularly strongly in the work of Katherine Mansfield. So strong was Mansfield's affinity for Chekhov that she was notorious for dressing in Russian clothes, introducing herself as Katerina, Katya, or other Russian variations of her name, and often trying to act "Russian." But Mansfield's admiration for Chekhov most clearly manifests itself in the several collections of short stories she published during her brief life. From 1903, when Constance Garnett began publishing the first English translations of Chekhov's stories, Mansfield's literary style mirrored the Russian's approach to fiction. Rather than focus on plot, Mansfield allowed dialogue and imagery to carry a story's meaning. Employing her skills as an observer, she drew characters with clarity and precision. Chekhov's deft combination of comedy and pathos similarly pervades Mansfield's work, infusing the distinctive atmospheres she created.

In the early 1920s, Mansfield began translating Chekhov's letters with her friend S. S. Koteliansky. As she learned more about Chekhov's decency as a human being, she strove to improve her selfish and often cynical attitudes toward life, a change that was reflected in her fiction. Her work, which had previously criticized the upper class, began to show an affectionate view of humanity, her characters eliciting sympathy simply through her accurate and realistic renderings. In her personal life, Mansfield suffered through complicated relationships with members of her literary circle, including T. S. Eliot, Aldous Huxley, D. H. Lawrence, Bertrand Russell, and her rival, Virginia Woolf. Her husband, John Middleton Murry, was also her posthumous editor and defender of her reputation.

The literary career of Katherine Mansfield, who died of tuberculosis at age thirty-three, spanned only a few years. Nevertheless, as with Chekhov, her innovations to the short story had a tremendous impact on the development of the form.

COMMENTS & QUESTIONS

In this section, we aim to provide the reader with an array of perspectives on the text, as well as questions that challenge those perspectives. The commentary has been culled from sources as diverse as reviews contemporaneous with the work, letters written by the author, literary criticism of later generations, and appreciations written throughout history. Following the commentary, a series of questions seeks to filter Anton Chekhov's short stories through a variety of points of view and bring about a richer understanding of these enduring works.

Comments

Henry Seidel Canby

As for variety,—the Russian does not handle numerous themes. He is obsessed with the dreariness of life, and his obsession is only occasionally lifted; he has no room to wander widely through human nature. And yet his work gives an impression of variety that the American magazine never attains. He is free to be various. When the mood of gloom is off him, he experiments at will, and often with consummate success. He seems to be sublimely unconscious that readers are supposed to like only a few kinds of stories; and as unaware of the taboo upon religious or reflective narrative as of the prohibition upon the ugly in fiction. As life in any manifestation becomes interesting in his eyes, his pen moves freely. And so he makes life interesting in many varieties, even when his Russian prepossessions lead him far away from our Western moods.

Freedom. That is the word here, and also in his method of telling these stories. No one seems to have said to Tchekoff, 'Your stories must move, move, move.' Sometimes, indeed, he pauses outright, as life pauses; sometimes he seems to turn aside, as life turns aside before its progress is resumed. No one has ever made clear to him that every word from the first of the story must point unerringly toward the solution and the effect of the plot. His paragraphs spring from the characters and the situation. They are led on to the climax by the story itself. They do not drag the panting reader down a rapid action, to fling him breathless upon the 'I told you so' of a conclusion prepared in advance.

—from *The Atlantic Monthly* (July 1915)

Edward Garnett

Chekhov's range of subject, scene, and situation is so varied that it will be convenient here to classify his Tale as follows:

(a) The short humorous sketches, of which the author wrote many hundreds, chiefly in early life.
(b) Stories of the life of the town "Intelligentsia"; family and domestic pieces, of which "The Duel" and "Three Years"—a study of Moscow atmosphere and environment—are the longest.
(c) Stories of provincial life, in which a great variety of types—landowners, officials, doctors, clergy, school-teachers, merchants, innkeepers, etc.—appear.
(d) Stories of peasant life—settled types.
(e) Stories of unconventional and lawless types—roving characters.
(f) Psychological studies, such as "The Black Monk," "Ward No. 6."

One must recall here, also, Chekhov's plays, his short farces, and his descriptive account of Sahalin life.

By his supremacy as a writer of short stories, Chekhov has been termed the Russian Maupassant, and there are, indeed, several vital resemblances between the outlook of the French and of the Russian master. The art of both these unflinching realists, in its exploration of human motives, is imbued with a searching passion for truth and a poet's sensitiveness to beauty. But whereas Maupassant's mental atmosphere is clear, keen, and strong, with a touch of a hard, cold wind, Chekhov's is born of a softer, warmer, kindlier earth. Had Maupassant written "The Darling," he would have been less patient with Olenka's lack of brains, more cynical over her forgetfulness of her first and second husband. And a French Olenka would, in fact, have been less naïve than the Russian woman, and in that respe[illegible] more open to criticism.

Chekhov, though often melancholy, is rarely cynical; he looks at human nature with the charitable eye of the wise doctor who has learnt from experience that people cannot be other than what they are. It is his profundity of acceptation that blends with quiet humour and tenderness to make his mental atmosphere one of subtle emotional receptivity. In his art there is always this tinge of cool, scientific passivity blending with the sensitiveness of a sweet, responsive nature. Remark that Chekhov, unlike Dostoevsky, rarely identifies himself with his sinners and sufferers, but he stands close to all his characters, watching them quietly and registering their circumstances and feelings with such finality that to pass judgment on them appears supererogatory.

—from "A Note on Chekhov's Art" (1916)

Leonard Woolf

The short stories of Tchehov which Mrs. Garnett is translating and the third volume of which has just been published will rouse some of the oldest critical questions in the mind of any reader who has the ruminating habit. Much has been written lately in praise of Tchehov's art, and it is easy to find ecstasy over the subtlety and range of "his incomparable gift," the humour, the beauty, the delicate irony, the amazing firmness and economy in every stroke of the pen. And yet he more than any other writer challenges one to ask those ultimate questions about Art and his art. For nine out of ten of his stories end for the reader upon several notes of interrogation. You cannot put down the book after reading, say, the story of *The Lady with the Dog* or *A Doctor's Visit* without asking a great many questions about the author, about art, and about life. And the answers, I think, should be somewhat different from those offered to us by the professional and appreciative critics.

His stories raise over and over again that oldest of questions about realism. For Tchehov, as Mrs. Garnett and many others have remarked, belongs most obviously to the Maupassant school of "unflinching realists." But that after all does not take us very far, and we may and do legitimately ask about the realist what he is attempting to do with this unflinching realism. The answer is easy in the case of the old photographic and cinematographic realist. Carefully and accurately to convey a piece of bleak and naked life into the covers of a book was to him enough: that *was* the object of his art and of Art. The more accurately the writer carved and hewed facts out of words, the greater his success: and it mattered nothing whether the facts were a sunset over the blue sea or the anatomy of washerwomen, although in the process of time washerwomen came to be regarded as more real than sunsets. But if Tchehov is an unflinching realist, his object is most certainly not unflinching realism. It is true that many of his shortest short stories seem at first sight to be the work of a man who has delicately, fastidiously, and ironically picked up with the extreme tips of his fingers a little piece of real life, and then with minute care and skill pinned it by means of words into a book. . . . The precision of Tchehov's realism masks the mental stammer which afflicted him when he contemplated life. . . . Tchehov's "finality" is the finality of irony, of the man who stands a little aside from life and almost caresses its absurdities. And that is where his mental stammer comes in. His one keen and persistent emotion towards life is bewilderment. He seems to be literally stammering with unanswered questions as to the meaning of these grotesque comedies and tragedies of the human mind, these absurdities and cruelties, passions and pains and exaltations and boredoms of human relationship. And the perpetual and delicious irony, the amazing and refreshing aloofness, the cool precision and the cold realism are the methods by which Tchehov controls his bewilderment and prevents himself overwhelming his reader with a torrent of "Why's" and "What's."

—from *The New Statesman* (August 11, 1917)

G. R. Noyes

All the great realists, various in their work as Miss Austen and Tolstoy, have at least this much in common, that they give a reasonably fair presentation of one particular section of life, showing the noble chivalry of human nature, even if it may be displayed in small ways, along with its petty meanness. There remain a few writers who seem deliberately to use their literary gifts, sometimes of a high order, to invest with interest only the baffling, disheartening daily happenings that in our more discouraged moments seem the whole of existence. Such a writer is preëminently Anton Chekhov, the greatest Russian writer of short stories and the man who has described Russian futility with more unsparing skill than any other man of letters. One theme runs through all his work, that of the impotence, the powerlessness of human nature.

Russian critics explain that Chekhov portrays a certain stage in the development of Russian society. He was born in 1860 and died in 1904. His work thus falls in the reign of Alexander III (1881–94) and in the early years of that of Nicholas II, a period of general stagnation in Russian political thought and discussion, during which there was silently developing in the country the industrial movement that made possible the overthrow of the old régime in 1917. Of these nascent factors in Russian life Chekhov had no perception; he dealt with the decay of the old society, showing men and women occupied with purely personal interests—and those of the pettiest sort. His men of intellect have really no higher type of character than his idle sybarites; his reformers are of no more account than his corrupt officials; his women are guided by no finer impulses than his men. . . . Among all his characters I can find no woman who is a "positive type," and only two or three men. The best of these occurs only in the background of a tale. In "The Grasshopper" a young woman of dilettantish artistic gifts marries a doctor, older than herself, whose force of character has momentarily attracted her. She speedily becomes bored by her husband, and finds her affinity in a man of her own shallow artistic sort, who as speedily tires of her. Characteristically enough, Chekhov spends his time in drawing the shallow woman, and lets us catch mere glimpses of her admirable husband.

Nor are Chekhov's men and women even interesting in their abnormality. He has no figures like Turgenev's Rudin and Lavretsky, Dostoyevsky's Raskolnikov and Dmitry Karamazov, our affection for whom, despite their weakness or sinfulness, outlasts our memory of what happens to them. Chekhov's power is in the presentation of a ludicrous situation, whether comic or tragic, not in the individuality of the people involved in it. . . . And yet what varied futility he has portrayed! Reading him, one feels that Russia is without will or energy; that its peasants are crude, brutal, dirty; its officials lazy, untrained, dishonest; its intellectual leaders men of words, incoherent at that, not of deeds. He shows a decaying society and points out no sources of regeneration, though he may long for such. His picture helps us to understand the collapse of Russia at the present time, and offers no hope of a speedy recovery. His rival, Gorky, has described the birth of new conditions, the rise of an industrial system that, before it had itself become firm and healthy, dealt a mortal blow to the old society. Chekhov, with his eyes to the past, could see no prospect for the future except through the growth of individual patience and kindliness.

—from *The Nation* (October 12, 1918)

Questions

1. In contrasting American and Russian short fiction, does Canby imply that the former is formulaic? Is formulaic fiction incomparable with realism?

2. Garnett distinguishes Chekhov from Dostoevsky by characterizing the former as an observer. Does this comparison imply that Chekhov's fiction lacks psychological depth? Is this what leads Noyes to conclude that it is Chekhov's situations, and not his characters, that are of interest?

3. Is Chekhov's aloofness as a writer, as described by Leonard Woolf, a product of his inability to tackle the larger questions of human experience in the way that Tolstoy does?

4. "The precision of Tchehov's realism masks the mental stammer which afflicted him when he contemplated life. . . . Tchehov's 'finality' is the finality of irony, of the man who stands a little aside from life and almost caresses its absurdities. And that is where his mental stammer comes in. His one keen and persistent emotion towards life is bewilderment." So said Leonard Woolf, Virginia's husband. Look closely at one of these "stammers." Can they be read as something other than an affliction? As a tactful refusal to squeeze a multiplicity of meanings into a formula or to grab the reader by the lapels? As a desire to let us hear the echo coming out of the Void?

5. Dickens and Balzac, for instance, bring a scene before us with an abundance of detail. Chekhov is more selective: He gives us a strik-

ing image or two. Which do you prefer? Why? Do these different methods imply different attitudes toward material reality? A different theory of the nature of knowledge? Is Chekhov's refusal to idealize or to give us a happy ending finally an assault on the reader? Is he saying "get rid of your self-delusions. Here's the way it really is?"

FOR FURTHER READING

Biographies

Callow, Philip. *Chekhov: The Hidden Ground.* Chicago: Ivan R. Dee, 1998.

Hingley, Ronald. *A New Life of Anton Chekhov.* New York: Alfred A. Knopf, 1976.

Laffitte, Sophie. *Chekhov.* New York: Scribner, 1973.

Nemirovsky, Irene. *A Life of Chekhov.* Translated by Erik de Mauny. London: Grey Walls Press, 1950.

Pitcher, Harvey J. *Chekhov's Leading Lady: A Portrait of the Actress Olga Knipper.* London: John Murray, 1979.

Simmons, Ernest J. *Chekhov: A Biography.* Boston: Little, Brown, 1962.

Reminiscences

Avilov, L. A. (Lidiia Alekseevna). *Chekhov in My Life: A Love Story.* Translated and with an introduction by David Magarshack. London: John Lehmann, 1950.

Gorky, Maxim, Alexander Kuprin, and I. A. Bunin. *Reminiscences of Anton Chekhov.* Translated by S. S. Koteliansky and Leonard Woolf. New York: B. H. Huebsch, 1921.

Teleshov, N. *A Writer Remembers.* Translated by Lionel Britton. London and New York: Hutchinson, 1946.

Critical Books

Bloom, Harold, ed. *Anton Chekhov.* With an introduction by the editor. Philadelphia, PA: Chelsea House Publishers, 1999.

Bruford, W. H. *Anton Chekhov.* New Haven: Yale University Press, 1957.

Coope, John. *Doctor Chekhov.* Isle of Wight, UK: Cross Publishing, 1997.

Gerhardi, William. *Anton Chekhov: A Critical Study.* London: R. Cobden-Sanderson, 1923.

Gilman, Richard. *Chekhov's Plays: An Opening into Eternity.* New Haven: Yale University Press, 1995.

Gottlieb, Vera, and Paul Allain, eds. *The Cambridge Companion to Chekhov.* Cambridge and New York: Cambridge University Press, 2000.

Hare, Richard. *Russian Literature: From Pushkin to the Present Day.* London: Methuen, 1947.

Hingley, Ronald. *Chekhov: A Biographical and Critical Study.* 1950. Revised edition: London: Allen and Unwin, 1966.

Magarshack, David. *Chekhov the Dramatist.* 1952. Reprint: London: Eyre Methuen, 1980.

Malcolm, Janet. *Reading Chekhov: A Critical Journey.* New York: Random House, 2001.

Pritchett, V. S. *Chekhov: A Spirit Set Free.* New York: Random House, 1988.

Rayfield, Donald. *Understanding Chekhov: A Critical Study of Chekhov's Prose and Drama.* Madison: University of Wisconsin Press, 1999.

Tulloch, John. *Chekhov: A Structuralist Study.* London: Macmillan, 1980.

Wigzell, Faith, ed. *Russian Writers on Russian Writers.* Oxford and Providence, RI: Berg, 1994.

Winner, Thomas. *Chekhov and His Prose.* New York: Holt, Rinehart and Winston, 1966.

Yermilov, Vladimir. *A. P. Chekhov.* Translated by Ivy Litvinov. Moscow: Foreign Languages Publishing House.

Additional Works Cited in the Introduction

Chekhov, Anton. *Stories.* Vol. 9: 1898–1904. Translated and edited by Ronald Hingley. London: Oxford University Press, 1975.

———. *The Tales of Chekhov.* 13 vols. Translated by Constance Garnett. London: Chatto and Windus, 1916–1922. Quotations from many stories that do not appear in this edition are from Vol. 1, *The Darling and Other Stories* (1916); Vol. 2, *The Duel and Other Stories* (1916); Vol. 4, *The Party and Other Stories* (1917);

Vol. 6, *The Witch and Other Stories* (1918); and Vol. 10, *The Horse-Stealer and Other Stories* (1921).

———. *Ward Six and Other Stories.* Translated by Ann Dunnigan; afterword by Rufus W. Mathewson. New York: New American Library (Signet Classic), 1965.

Friedland, Louis S., ed. *Letters on the Short Story, the Drama and Other Literary Topics by Anton Chekhov.* London: Geoffrey Bles, 1924.

Koteliansky, S. S., and Philip Tomlinson, eds. *The Life and Letters of Anton Chekhov.* Translated by the editors; biographical note by E. Zamyatin. London: Cassell and Company, 1925.

Rayfield, Donald. *Anton Chekhov: A Life.* London: HarperCollins, 1997.

TIMELESS WORKS. NEW SCHOLARSHIP. EXTRAORDINARY VALUE.

Barnes & Noble Classics

Barnes & Noble Classics editions aim to enhance the reader's understanding and appreciation of the world's greatest books.

Comprising works judged by generations of readers to be the most profound, inspiring, and superbly written of all time, this publishing program offers affordable editions with new, accessible scholarship to students, educators, and lovers of a good story.

Visit your local bookstore or log on to **www.bn.com/classics** to discover the broad range of titles available now and forthcoming from Barnes & Noble Classics.

The Barnes & Noble Classics series celebrates the genius of the human heart.

BARNES & NOBLE CLASSICS

If you are an educator and would like to receive an Examination or Desk Copy of a Barnes & Noble Classic edition, please refer to Academic Resources on our website at WWW.BN.COM/CLASSICS or contact us at B&NCLASSICS@BN.COM.